What Comes Between Cousins

by

Jann Rowland

One Good Sonnet Publishing

By Jann Rowland
Published by One Good Sonnet Publishing:

PRIDE AND PREJUDICE VARIATIONS

Acting on Faith
A Life from the Ashes (Sequel to *Acting on Faith*)
Open Your Eyes
Implacable Resentment
An Unlikely Friendship
Bound by Love
Cassandra
Obsession
Shadows Over Longbourn
The Mistress of Longbourn
My Brother's Keeper
Coincidence
The Angel of Longbourn
Chaos Comes to Kent
In the Wilds of Derbyshire
The Companion
What Comes Between Cousins

Co-Authored with Lelia Eye

WAITING FOR AN ECHO

Waiting for an Echo Volume One: Words in the Darkness
Waiting for an Echo Volume Two: Echoes at Dawn
Waiting for an Echo Two Volume Set

A Summer in Brighton
A Bevy of Suitors
Love and Laughter: A Pride and Prejudice Short Stories Anthology

THE EARTH AND SKY TRILOGY
Co-Authored with Lelia Eye

On Wings of Air
On Lonely Paths
*On Tides of Fate**

*Forthcoming

This is a work of fiction based on the works of Jane Austen. All the characters and events portrayed in this novel are products of Jane Austen's original novel or the authors' imaginations.

WHAT COMES BETWEEN COUSINS

Cover Design by Marina Willis

Edited by Betty Madden

Published by One Good Sonnet Publishing

ISBN: 1987929772
ISBN-13: 9781987929775

To my family who have, as always, shown
their unconditional love and encouragement.

CHAPTER I

*T*here is nothing so agreeable to *most* ladies of a certain age as the prospect of an assembly. To some, however, a dance seemed much more like a chore than the amusement it is intended to be.

"I would much prefer conversation were the order of the day at an assembly," complained Mary Bennet one morning to her elder sister, Elizabeth. "I do not much care for dancing."

Elizabeth, the second eldest of the Bennet sisters and generally considered to be the cleverest, only shook her head and favored Mary with a smile. Mary's aversion to dancing was not unknown. Elizabeth thought her disinclination would be much less pronounced if she was asked to stand up more often. To that end, Elizabeth had gathered Mary and her elder sister, Jane, in her room to attempt to make Mary more appealing to the young gentlemen of the neighborhood.

"I dare say you would, Mary," replied Elizabeth. "And in some ways, I must agree with your assessment. But if you would only allow us to adjust your hair and dress a little, I think we can provoke the gentlemen of the neighborhood to swoon at the sight of you."

"A general softening of your usual disapproving glare would also be beneficial," added Jane.

Mary turned a fierce scowl on her eldest sibling. "But I *do* disapprove, Jane. There is often little decorum at assemblies. I will not behave as Lydia and Kitty do."

"Actually, Mary," replied Elizabeth, gently, to avoid offending her sister, "while the behavior at assemblies is lively, it is not objectionable for the most part.

"I will grant you that Lydia and Kitty often push the boundaries of what is acceptable," continued Elizabeth when Mary appeared likely to dispute her words. "But you do not need to behave as they, or anyone else. Simply being pleasant with the gentlemen who ask you to dance will be enough."

"*If* I am asked to dance," muttered Mary.

"If you allow us to assist you, I guarantee you will be asked to dance," replied Elizabeth, favoring her sister with a wink. Mary was not one to indulge in overt playfulness, but she smiled shyly at Elizabeth, seeming convinced, and allowed her to take charge.

The rest of the afternoon was spent in laughter and companionship between the three eldest Bennet daughters. They soon settled on a hairstyle for Mary which became her very well, indeed, and a few subtle alterations to the ball gown chosen for the night of the assembly made it more flattering without offending Mary's sensibilities. After the fact, Elizabeth was happy with their efforts, and it was easy to see that Mary was more hopeful that she would be recognized for being a pretty young woman, something which had eluded her most of her life.

As they were working on her sister's appearance, Elizabeth's thoughts kept slipping to subjects which had haunted her in recent weeks. It was interesting, she decided, that the absence of Charlotte Lucas, her friend for many years, should result in a closer relationship with Mary, for the two women were not similar at all. Charlotte was pragmatic and sensible, while Mary was too often moralizing and judgmental. But those objectionable traits in Mary's character had been softened by the new closeness of the three eldest Bennets, making her a pleasanter companion.

Charlotte! How Elizabeth railed against the unfairness of the world. Charlotte was not beautiful in the classical sense of the word—in fact, in the privacy of her own thoughts, Elizabeth considered Mary to be prettier than Charlotte, who had always struck Elizabeth as plain. But a lack of dowry and limited connections meant that Charlotte's intelligence and sensible nature was not enough to attract a suitor. As a consequence of not wishing to become a burden on her family,

Charlotte had accepted a position as a governess some months earlier and had left Meryton for her new position, leaving a disheartened Elizabeth behind, wishing her friend had not been forced to make such a desperate decision.

By all accounts, Charlotte had found satisfaction and fulfillment in her new life, and for that, Elizabeth was relieved. And her newfound closeness with Mary had come about because her closest friend was now living in another house far from the neighborhood of her birth, making her own way in the world. This new closeness had forced Elizabeth to reevaluate her life, for she knew that it should not have taken the absence of a dear friend to induce her to pay more attention to her oft-ignored younger sister. That reflection had induced her to vow that she would do better in the future. But Charlotte's absence was still felt keenly. It would continue to be so for some time, Elizabeth was certain.

They had been ensconced in her room for most of the afternoon when the door burst open and the youngest Bennet sister waltzed into the room, followed by the next eldest.

"Jane! Elizabeth!" exclaimed she, the excitement in her tone evident in its volume, which approached the proportions of a screech.

Lydia was a pretty young woman who, though she was the youngest, was also the tallest of stature other than Jane and possessed of a womanly figure, despite her tender age of only fifteen years. She was also already out in society, having been brought out on her fifteenth birthday at their mother's insistence the previous May. Lydia was neither mature enough to be out in society, in Elizabeth's opinion, nor was she interested in improving herself. In fact, Lydia was interested in little other than dancing, flirting with anything wearing pants, and behaving in the most brazen and inappropriate manner possible.

"You have missed the news we brought!" continued Lydia when her two eldest sisters did not respond to her initial address. "We have news of the new residents of Netherfield Park. Mama was so excited by it that she was forced to her room to rest her nerves."

The three eldest sisters shared glances and shaken heads; Mrs. Bennet's nerves were legendary in the neighborhood. It was a wonder that her paroxysms had not been audible all the way up to Elizabeth's room from the front sitting-room.

"What have you been doing up here all this time, anyway?" asked Kitty with a frown. "Mama said you had not come down all afternoon."

"We have been trying new styles for Mary's hair," answered Jane. "And modifying one of her dresses."

Lydia sucked in a breath, no doubt to deliver a stinging retort. She had never held back from stating her opinion of Mary's charms, and in many ways, she could be quite cruel. Before she could speak, however, Elizabeth directed such a fierce look at her, that whatever statement she was about to make was left unsaid.

"That style is quite becoming," said Kitty, speaking into the silence which Lydia's unspoken words created. "May we see your dress?"

Though she was two years Lydia's senior, Kitty was very much a follower. It was unfortunate that she endeavored to follow her younger sister's lead. Elizabeth had made attempts to divert her attention from Lydia to Jane or Elizabeth herself, but her opinion that Lydia was "more fun" than her elder sisters had thus far kept Kitty's focus on Lydia. Elizabeth hoped that might be changed by persistence, showing her younger sister she could enjoy herself without dispensing with decorum.

"Oh, hang Mary's dress!" exclaimed Lydia. "We have news of the gentlemen who are staying at Netherfield! How could dowdy Mary's dress be more important than that?"

There was little which could be done to forever suppress Lydia's unkindness, but Elizabeth still glared at her sister for her unfeeling words, and Lydia soon realized she had stepped over a line which Elizabeth—and to a lesser extent Jane—had increasingly been unwilling to allow. It was to Lydia's credit that she colored at the sight of Elizabeth's displeasure and muttered an apology. Mary, proving that she was still the same as *she* had ever been, responded with nothing more than a contemptuous sniff.

Hoping to avoid any further unpleasantness, Elizabeth quickly stepped into the breach, showing Kitty what they had done with Mary's dress. Kitty, the sister who possessed the best eye for fashion, looked it over with approval, though she did make a suggestion or two as to how it could be improved even further. Though Mary was often as disposed to disapprove of Kitty as much as she did Lydia, she was appreciative, thanking her sister and arranging to allow Kitty access to the dress later that evening to make the adjustments. All the while, Lydia sat impatiently, eager to relay whatever gossip she had managed to acquire, but knowing that she had already angered her siblings with her hasty words.

"Now, Lydia," said Elizabeth, after Kitty had examined the ball gown, "you have news of the Netherfield party?"

"I do!" exclaimed Lydia, her excitement finally released from its fetters. "Aunt Phillips has had it from Mrs. Parker that Mrs. Nichols received a large party at Netherfield only last Tuesday."

"One of whom, I suppose, is the elusive Mr. Bingley," said Elizabeth.

"Of course," said Lydia. "But that is not all, for Mr. Bingley, in addition to his closest family, has also come with a party of several gentlemen friends. Mama was beside herself at the very mention of so many eligible gentlemen."

"That is quite interesting, Lydia," said Elizabeth, "for by my account, you have made no mention of the actual number. 'Several' might mean as few as three, by my account."

"Oh, I do not think it is that few," replied Lydia with a vigorous shake of her head. "Mrs. Parker made it sound as if Netherfield is teeming with gentlemen. I should not be surprised if every bedroom is occupied!"

"If it is," said Mary, "one must wonder what has brought them all to this corner of the kingdom. It is not as if Meryton is the center of England."

"No, I dare say it is not," replied Elizabeth. "But if there are more potential partners at the upcoming assembly, I shall not complain."

Lydia nodded vigorously. "And perhaps one of them shall fall in love with me, and I shall be married first out of all my sisters."

Though Elizabeth knew that Lydia was in no way mature enough to be married, she refrained from provoking an argument by stating her opinion openly.

"Have you heard anything of the gentlemen in particular?" asked Jane with her typical diffidence.

"It is said that Mr. Bingley rides a white horse and is ever so tall and handsome," said Lydia, as if imparting a great secret.

"And his companions?" asked Elizabeth.

"I have heard nothing of them," replied Lydia. "But I am certain a man who is handsome and wealthy must have similar men as friends."

It was all Elizabeth could do not to laugh at such a silly statement, and a glance at Mary informed her that her sister was in similar straits. But Jane was not afflicted by the same feelings, for her expression had grown introspective.

"It is, of course, desirable for a man to be handsome. But I believe I would be well-pleased to be the recipient of the attentions of a kind man. Fairness of countenance does not last forever, after all."

"I agree," replied Elizabeth. "Beauty fades with age, but

intelligence, kindness, charity, and an agreeable temper—all these last throughout a man's life. I would not wish for a handsome man to fix his eyes on me if he did not also possess these other traits in abundance."

"Oh, Lord!" cried Lydia. "We were speaking of the gentlemen of Netherfield, and you have turned it into a conversation of morality! Come, Kitty—let us go and talk ourselves, for our elder sisters are all determined to become old maids."

The sight of Kitty's hesitation gave Elizabeth a little hope for the girl, though she ultimately followed her younger sister from the room. In truth, Elizabeth did not repine Lydia's desire to be elsewhere, and she did not think her two sisters felt any different.

"I wonder if that girl will ever mature," said Mary, her eyes on the door through which the two youngest had just exited.

"She is still naught but fifteen," said Elizabeth. She felt obliged to say it, though she possessed little conviction. It would be difficult to effect a change in Lydia's behavior as long as their father remained indifferent and their mother indulged her.

"Be that as it may," added Elizabeth, hoping to head off further complaints regarding their youngest siblings, "I believe Lydia is destined to be disappointed. I doubt there are so many as five eligible gentlemen staying at Netherfield. I suspect there are fewer."

"Do you know of anything of them?" asked Jane.

"Nothing official," replied Elizabeth. "But while I was walking yesterday, I chanced to walk the path that leads to the border with Netherfield, and I saw riders in the distance. One was riding a white stallion—I will grant you that. But he did not have a horde of other gentlemen at his back. In all, they were no more than three."

"Were you close enough to see any details?" asked Mary, proving her usual disinterest in such matters was feigned.

"No," replied Elizabeth with a shake of her head. "I can say they were all fine riders, but I have no other intelligence to relay. We will simply need to wait until tomorrow to have our curiosity assuaged."

By common, though unspoken, assent, the three sisters returned to their previous topic of conversation. At length, they were summoned for dinner, but their afternoon had been spent agreeably, indeed.

What Elizabeth did not mention to her sisters, and what they never suspected, was that she was more affected by Charlotte's fate than she allowed to show. While she endeavored to remain as happy as she possibly could, the sight of those three riders thundering across the fields had profoundly affected her. To be so free as those men must be a fine thing, indeed, and Elizabeth found herself wishing that she—and of course, Charlotte—could be in such circumstances themselves. Beyond that, however, Elizabeth could not quite determine how she felt.

The needs of the present must necessarily push such ponderings to the background, and as the next day was the assembly, her mother's effusions, in particular, rendered such reflections impossible.

As the five daughters assembled for the short carriage ride into Meryton, their mother moved among them, adjusting hair and dresses, settling wraps in what she thought was a more appealing fashion, pinching cheeks to provoke a rosiness Elizabeth did not feel warranted. And as she fussed over them, the sisters were subjected to her comments on the subject of her expectations and instructions for the evening.

"You must all put yourselves forward," clucked she as she adjusted Elizabeth's hair for seemingly the hundredth time. "Even you, Mary," added she, turning a stern look on what she considered to be the most problematic of her children.

"Do you not think the style of Mary's hair becomes her, Mother?" asked Elizabeth, attempting to turn her mother's attention to the changes in Mary's demeanor.

"It does, indeed," replied Mrs. Bennet. Elizabeth stifled a smile—she knew her mother could never resist the opportunity to praise the appearance of one of her daughters. Even the daughter she considered to be the plainest was not exempt.

"Mama!" exclaimed Jane. "Please assist me with my dress, for it is tight in the bodice."

In fact, Elizabeth suspected there was nothing wrong with Jane's dress. But Jane had made it a habit of deflecting her mother's attention from her younger sisters, as she was the most patient of them. Elizabeth appreciated her sister's sacrifice. Heaven knew that too much of Mrs. Bennet's flutterings was enough to send her to Bedlam!

When they stepped into the hall a little later in the evening, Elizabeth noted that her mother had ensured they arrived in advance of the beginning of the ball, no doubt eager to show her daughters to the best advantage while dancing. She would wish to show the hordes of gentlemen that they were popular and pretty, able to hold their own in a ballroom, and eager to receive them. For Elizabeth, the sight of the assembly hall without Charlotte present was a reminder of her friend's situation and how it was little likely she would be much in company with her again.

"I wish my daughter was here," said Lady Lucas when Elizabeth approached her to commiserate together. "I know Charlotte felt the need to be useful and to avoid being a burden, but I wish she had not felt it necessary to take a position. She would have been very welcome living the rest of her life at Lucas Lodge."

Elizabeth smiled sadly. "I miss her too, Lady Lucas. Have you had any news since the last time we spoke?"

The subject of her eldest daughter was one which the Lucas matron set to with a will, and they spent some pleasant moments in which Lady Lucas regaled Elizabeth with tales from Charlotte's latest letter. In fact, Elizabeth was not at all certain that Charlotte would have been welcome to remain at the estate all her life. Her younger brother and Sir William's heir—a young man by the name of Samuel, who was now five and twenty—was arrogant and unpleasant at times. Elizabeth had heard more than one snide comment from his lips about how Charlotte had seemed unable to find herself a husband. It was that, as much as Charlotte's desire to be useful, which had prompted her to seek out a position.

But Elizabeth could not say that to Lady Lucas. The woman was, in essentials, much like her friend and neighbor, Mrs. Bennet—mean of understanding, a lover of any juicy piece of gossip which reached her ears. She was possessed of a little more sense than Mrs. Bennet and a stronger grasp of propriety. But she would not hear anything against her eldest son. Elizabeth did not wish to say anything unkind, regardless.

The assembly started as they usually did, with the gentlemen of the area asking those in attendance for dances, the conversations banal and uninteresting. Elizabeth was at least heartened that of the first three dances, Mary stood up for two. For Elizabeth herself, she was rarely required to sit out, even when there was a dearth of gentlemen present, as there was that night.

And then the newcomers arrived.

Unlike the ladies of Meryton, Fitzwilliam Darcy's only desire for the evening was to escape it unscathed. Within moments of entering the assembly hall—a building which Miss Bingley had referred to as quaint several times already—Darcy heard rumors of his income being bandied about the room, rendering his already fragile temper frayed. That his companions were largely enjoying the attention did not escape his notice. One of them seemed to soak it up even more when the revelation of his identity rendered him even more of a catch, leaving Darcy as nothing more than a rich gentleman.

"Were we truly required to attend tonight?" asked Miss Bingley for the fourth time since they had exited the carriage. "The society tonight is certainly not what we would find in London, even at this time of the year."

"We must make a good impression on local society," replied Bingley. His cheerfulness in the face of his sister's incivility was one of his greatest strengths, in Darcy's opinion. That Darcy agreed with Miss Bingley's disinclination for the company in no way changed the truth of his friend's words.

"They seem to be pleasant people," said Darcy's cousin. "The dance is lively enough. I am quite pleased to be here tonight."

His commentary silenced Miss Bingley quite effectively, though Darcy could readily see that she meant to change his mind. But Hurst made some comment at that moment, and though he was a bit of a boor, Darcy was happy to give his attention to Hurst, rather than the man's sister by marriage. His wife, Louisa, was tolerable, but Miss Caroline Bingley was enough to drive a man to drink. Darcy had high hopes that on this visit, at least, *his* desirability as a prospective husband would pale beside that of his cousin.

Within moments of their arrival, one of the local gentlemen—an amiable and slightly silly man, by the name of Sir William Lucas—approached them and began to lead them around the assembly hall, introducing them to the principal families of the neighborhood. He introduced them to the members of his own family first and then directed them to where a veritable gaggle of women stood, five younger with one elder, whom Darcy was certain were all related. There, he stopped to speak to the six ladies.

"Mrs. Bennet," said he, addressing the elder woman, "Mr. Bingley has requested an introduction to your family."

"That is very good of you, sir!" exclaimed the woman. The look she directed at them all spoke to calculation—she was no doubt already scheming to arrange it so that each of the three men were paired up with her offspring. It was a scene Darcy had seen repeatedly during his time in society, and he liked it no more now than he had the first time it had happened.

"Gentlemen," said Sir William, "may I present my nearest neighbors, the Bennets. They are, by seniority, Mrs. Margaret Bennet, Miss Jane Bennet, Miss Elizabeth, Miss Mary, Miss Catherine, and Miss Lydia."

As one, the ladies curtseyed to the gentlemen, and Darcy was forced to concede they were some of the handsomest young ladies he had ever seen. The eldest, Miss Bennet, was particularly lovely, though her younger sister, Elizabeth, was possessed of dark eyes and even darker hair and was very agreeable too. Miss Mary did not possess the beauty of her elder sisters, though she was attractive and quiet. Misses Catherine and Lydia would have been far comelier had they not burst into giggles at that moment.

"Mrs. Bennet," said Sir William, turning to the ladies, "please allow me to introduce the residents of Netherfield Park. First is Mr. Charles Bingley, who has taken the lease of the estate as its master. Next to him is Mr. Fitzwilliam Darcy, who I understand is a long-time friend."

"That is correct, Sir William," said Bingley, his usual eagerness evident in his voice. "Darcy and I have been friends since university, and as Netherfield is the first estate I have leased, he has kindly agreed to assist me in learning what I need to know."

"That *is* very kind of you, sir," said the second eldest Bennet, her eyes flashing with amusement. "And does Mr. Bingley require a great deal of guidance?"

"He does, indeed," said Bingley with a laugh. "Darcy has been managing his own estate for some years now. I know no one better to be of assistance to me."

"Then you are to be commended, sir," said the girl, turning her attention back to Darcy. "I hope you will enjoy your time in our neighborhood."

"The company of good friends is all I require, Miss Elizabeth," Darcy found himself saying. "When Bingley and my cousin are present, I am assured of having that."

"Ah, yes, of course," said Sir William, taking hold of the conversation again. "May I present the final member of our triumvirate? It is a singular honor, Mrs. Bennet, to present the honorable Colonel Anthony Fitzwilliam, the Viscount Chesterfield, and heir to the Earl of Matlock."

CHAPTER II

The next day all Meryton was afire with talk of the previous night and the attendance of an actual viscount to their assembly. No one had ever heard of such a thing happening in their sleepy little community, though some of the elderly members of society claimed that a baron had once attended. But what was a baron to a viscount? A man who would one day be an earl must surely be superior in every way!

At the Bennet estate, the talk did not differ much from what the rest of the community was saying. The scheming, which had already begun, was also nothing out of the ordinary, though Longbourn was home to one who was, perhaps, far more prone to plotting openly.

As Mr. Bennet had eschewed the previous evening's festivities, he had not met the viscount there. That was not to say that he had not made the acquaintance of the man in advance.

"I cannot imagine what you mean by behaving in this way, Mrs. Bennet," said he after his wife had carried on for several minutes as the family gathered in the sitting-room. "He is *only* a viscount, after all."

"*Only a viscount?*" screeched his wife. Mr. Bennet's wince was quite noticeable to his second eldest daughter—it quite mirrored Elizabeth's own. "How can you speak such nonsense? Have you ever met a viscount yourself?"

"Indeed, I have," replied Mr. Bennet. "There were several of them at Cambridge when I attended, and some of them were even decent enough chaps." He winked at Elizabeth at this last statement. "And only last Wednesday, when I visited Netherfield to call on Mr. Bingley—at your insistence, I might add—I made the acquaintance of both Mr. Bingley's guests."

Mrs. Bennet was appalled. "You met the viscount, and you did not even inform us?"

"Your stated interest was in Mr. Bingley, my dear," replied Mr. Bennet. "I had not thought you would be interested in a mere viscount."

It was clear that Mrs. Bennet did not quite know what to make of her husband's insouciance. That anyone would consider meeting a peer inconsequential was unfathomable to her limited understanding. The thought that he might be teasing her never entered her mind—a matter which perplexed Elizabeth, considering how often he had done exactly that in the past.

The paper he had raised at his wife's sudden silence was soon dropped as he surveyed the room filled with his progeny. "Can I assume some of you might actually have danced with our visiting viscount? Or was he too high and mighty to dance with the daughters of a country gentleman?"

"No, Papa," replied Elizabeth, even as her mother sucked in a breath for another diatribe. Thankfully, Elizabeth's words distracted her verbose parent. "In fact, I found Lord Chesterfield to be pleasant and engaging. And Mary and Jane both danced with him as well."

"Only with my three eldest?" asked Mr. Bennet, turning an eye on his youngest daughters. "Pity."

Elizabeth stifled a laugh by feigning a cough. Neither Lydia nor Kitty understood the thrust of their father's statement.

"Kitty and I were not injured, Papa," said Lydia. "We were engaged for all the sets anyway. And I did not think him very handsome, though Mr. Bingley and Mr. Darcy were both frightfully handsome, indeed."

"And did either of these two gentlemen dance with my youngest and . . . liveliest daughters?"

"I dare say Mr. Bingley would have danced with everyone in the room, had there only been enough sets," replied Lydia. "But as it was, he danced with all of us. As for Mr. Darcy . . ." Lydia's nose rose into the air, a striking resemblance to the younger Bingley sister's behavior the night before, in Elizabeth's estimation. "It seemed to me he could not be satisfied with any of the young ladies, for he danced only with Mr. Bingley's sisters."

"Oh, Mr. Darcy was quite proud and disagreeable," said Mrs. Bennet, finally finding her voice.

"Indeed?" asked Mr. Bennet. "When I met him, he struck me as an intelligent man and more than willing to converse with me. He is rather reticent, I thought, but he was an agreeable fellow."

"I suspect you have the right of it, Father," said Elizabeth. "He is simply not at his best in company. I happened to be standing near him during the course of the evening, and he spoke with me in a friendly manner, though we did not speak long.

"Lord Chesterfield, however, is a very different kind of man, though they are cousins. While we were dancing, we both chanced to overhear one of the Miss Longs saying something impertinent about his position in society. Rather than being angry with her, he only laughed and informed me that he has become accustomed to it. He also confided in me that his cousin, Mr. Darcy, does not enjoy that same attention."

"And does he receive the same attention as a viscount?" demanded Mrs. Bennet. "How can such a thing be imagined?"

"It can be when you consider that Mr. Darcy's estate has an income of over ten thousand a year," replied Elizabeth.

Mrs. Bennet's eyes widened, and Elizabeth thought she might faint at the thought of such riches. Elizabeth caught her father's eye, and they shared a chuckle.

"Yes, that is what I heard too," replied Mr. Bennet. "When I visited, there was some mention of how Mr. Darcy has been the master of his estate for some years already. It appears he has been considered quite the catch in the marriage market, and it has attracted attention he would prefer not to receive."

"I had not heard such gossip," managed Mrs. Bennet.

"I cannot imagine how," said Elizabeth. "Rumors of his wealth were spoken from one end of the assembly hall to the other."

Though she professed confusion, Elizabeth knew exactly how the information had eluded her mother. Mrs. Bennet had decided that Mr. Darcy was proud and above his company early in the evening and had ignored him thereafter.

"He *is* very handsome," allowed Mrs. Bennet, speaking of Mr. Darcy. Elizabeth was forced to cover her mouth again—Mrs. Bennet's concession was tantamount to a declaration of his suitability to become the husband of one of her daughters. Mrs. Bennet's next words were a confirmation of Elizabeth's supposition.

"I believe he would do very well for one of my daughters—very well, indeed." She stopped and surveyed the room, her eyes lingering on Jane and Lydia both. "The viscount must, of course, expect the best. He will certainly favor either Jane, for her beauty, or Lydia, for her liveliness. Since Mr. Darcy is so reticent, perhaps Lydia would do well for a wife for him. She might draw him out."

"I am amused to hear you say so, Mrs. Bennet," said Mr. Bennet, the light of mischief shining in his eyes. "By my account, neither of the gentlemen in question so much as danced with Lydia."

"No, they did not," conceded Mrs. Bennet. "But if we only bring her to their attention, I am certain she will be agreeable to one of them. Jane may have the other."

Elizabeth doubted either man would consider such a silly flirt as Lydia to be agreeable, but she kept her opinion to herself. She did not wish to begin an argument.

"As for Lizzy," continued Mrs. Bennet, "if she can refrain from impertinent comments, perhaps she may attract the attention of Mr. Bingley.

"Yes," continued Mrs. Bennet, sitting in her chair with an air of self-satisfaction about her, "I believe that will do very well, indeed. I am quite set upon it."

"You may be set upon it, Mrs. Bennet," replied Mr. Bennet as he rose to his feet. "But I would remind you that these young men possess the freedom to choose their own paths in life. They might defy you and refuse to act as you have decreed. For all you know, this viscount might decide that it is Mary he cannot live without." Mr. Bennet paused and smiled at Mary. "I understand you did quite well last night, my dear. I hope you enjoyed yourself."

"Mary?" cried Lydia. "Why would Lord Chesterfield possibly choose *Mary*?"

"Perhaps because Mary is not silly and ignorant like her youngest sister," said Mary.

"Yes, perhaps that is it," said Mr. Bennet. He watched Lydia in an unfriendly manner, and it was this which prevented the girl from further stating her opinion.

"Regardless, I would ask you to refrain from putting your daughters in situations with which they will be uncomfortable, Mrs. Bennet," continued Mr. Bennet, turning his attention back to his wife.

"And remember that these men are our new neighbors. I cannot state with any degree of confidence that they will *not* eventually marry your daughters, but I believe they receive enough of such attention in London. Let us simply be their friends while they are in the neighborhood, hmm?"

With that, Mr. Bennet took his paper, rolled it up and placed it under his arm, and quit the room. Elizabeth watched him go, knowing his speech was as much as he was usually willing to make to reprimand his wife. Elizabeth had often wished he would take her firmly in hand, for she could not count the number of times Mrs. Bennet had embarrassed her in company.

"Your father might not possess much faith in you," said Mrs. Bennet. "But *I* certainly do. I am certain if you work at it, you will catch the eyes of these gentlemen. What a fine thing that would be!"

"I thank you for my share, Mama," said Lydia, "but I think I must decline. When the militia company comes, I will much prefer their company. None of the three gentlemen wear a red coat, and I would prefer an officer for a husband."

Mrs. Bennet looked at her youngest with consternation, and then a sly look came over her. "But the viscount *was* a colonel, you know. Perhaps he does not wear a red coat *now*, but I am certain he lent it much distinction when he did."

"That is true," said Lydia, tapping her lips with one finger.

"Let us not be too hasty, shall we? Perhaps this viscount will be to your liking after all. If, in the end, you do not like him, we can marry Jane to him. I am certain he could assist any man of the militia who catches your fancy. He *would*, after all, be the man's brother-in-law."

With a giggle, Lydia agreed, and she moved closer to her mother to allow them to begin planning. Kitty, though she was clearly upset that her mother had not included her in her scheming, joined them, and soon they were speaking quietly and laughing amongst themselves. Elizabeth, though she was certain they were conjuring up inanities aplenty, was relieved to be free of her mother's attention.

"I am afraid we are about to be embarrassed," said Mary, as she watched the three ladies whispering. Then she turned a wry smile to Jane and Elizabeth. "But I suppose that is truly nothing out of the ordinary. And it should not be a surprise."

Elizabeth knew there was nothing to say to Mary's words, and she refrained from stoking the fire. Instead, she turned and fixed her elder sister with a playful grin.

"Though Mama appears to be on the verge of ordering your

wedding clothes for Mr. Darcy *or* Lord Chesterfield, I suspect the other gentleman caught your eye."

Jane blushed. "Mr. Bingley *was* agreeable. I find him to be quite the handsomest man of them all, and very attentive too."

"And I suspect you are correct, Jane," replied Elizabeth, thinking back to what she had witnessed the previous evening. "Not only was he attentive to you all evening, but you were also the *only* lady with whom he danced twice."

Her blush becoming rosier, Jane attempted to change the subject. "What of you, Mary? You danced with both Mr. Bingley and Lord Chesterfield. Who did you prefer?"

"Mr. Bingley is, indeed, a good man," replied Mary. "But Lord Chesterfield is much like him in essentials. They were both at ease, spoke intelligently, and are both handsome, whatever Lydia may say. I like both men very well, indeed."

"As do I," said Elizabeth. "And I am certain Mr. Darcy will also improve upon acquaintance, particularly once he becomes accustomed to our society. For myself, I have nothing to say against any of the gentlemen we met last night, though I cannot say as much for the sisters."

"Oh?" asked Jane with a frown.

"Jane," said Elizabeth gently and with patience, "Miss Bingley showed far more evidence of thinking herself above her company than Mama accused of Mr. Darcy. Did you not see the disapproving looks she gave to us all?"

"I saw nothing of the sort," replied Jane. "She was affable to me. She is to keep house for her brother. I am sure we shall be the best of friends."

Elizabeth caught Mary's eye, and though they did not say anything, she knew they were both of one mind about the younger Bingley sister. But Jane found great difficulty in finding any new acquaintance anything other than lovely and amiable, so Elizabeth held her tongue.

"Mrs. Hurst seemed tolerable," said Mary. "I only spoke with her for a few moments, but she impressed me as a kind woman."

"I did not speak with Mrs. Hurst," said Elizabeth. Jane also stated she had not had any contact with the elder sister. "But I have great hope for them all. If nothing else, new faces are welcome to liven our gatherings."

The sisters agreed to Elizabeth's statement, and they moved on to other topics.

* * *

At Netherfield, a similar conversation was taking place, but the particulars were different from what was being discussed at Longbourn.

"In short," Miss Bingley was saying, "the society here is quite without any redeeming qualities. There is no fashion, a want of propriety, and little beauty to be found among them." Miss Bingley turned her considerable displeasure upon her brother. "I am quite put out that you signed a lease in such a backward part of the kingdom without even consulting with me or ensuring the society was at least tolerable."

"I have no notion of what you speak, Caroline," replied Bingley. "In fact, as our visits from the neighborhood gentlemen informed me, the people here are obliging and friendly. It almost seems we attended different functions last night, for I found the assembly to be a pleasant diversion.

"In fact," said he, when his sister glared at him, "I had thought you were coming to know some of the local ladies. Did you not say that you found the eldest Bennet agreeable?"

"I believe I said tolerable, Charles," replied Miss Bingley. Her superior sniff was one which seemed to convey a wealth of meaning, all of it bad. Darcy would not have been surprised to learn that she practiced it in front of the mirror constantly to get it just right.

"Jane Bennet seemed, indeed, to be a sweet girl," said Mrs. Hurst. "Though I did not have the chance of speaking with her. The third girl, Mary, was also quite agreeable."

"I am certain there is no one worth knowing among *them*. Miss Elizabeth is impertinent, Miss Mary is dull, and the two youngest are the most outrageous flirts I have ever seen."

"They are only young, Miss Bingley," said Fitzwilliam. His complacent smile informed Darcy that he was quite diverted by Miss Bingley's displeasure and was not at all above tweaking her nose. "We were all young once, were we not?"

Miss Bingley colored at the reminder of her own years—three and twenty—without a hint of a proposal of marriage. Darcy knew that the woman could have had at least one, perhaps more, had she not focused her attention on Darcy to the exclusion of all others.

"I believe, Lord Chesterfield, there must be some effort made to correct the high spirits of youth. A woman of Mrs. Bennet's ilk seems more likely to encourage such behavior than provide a check."

Though Fitzwilliam's amusement never dimmed, he nodded to indicate his agreement. Unfortunately for Miss Bingley, her victory was short-lived.

"While you *may* be correct about the youngest Bennets, I cannot agree with you regarding the elder. Miss Bennet is, as your brother has claimed, an angel. But while Misses Elizabeth and Mary may not be quite so angelic, Miss Elizabeth's wit is so disarming, I found myself captivated by it. And Miss Mary, though not so witty or pretty, is an agreeable girl too. She is sensible and engaging. What man could not find such a woman pleasant?"

Miss Bingley did not seem to know what to say. But she soon rallied, more was the pity. "You found the society acceptable?"

"It is much like any other society of its kind, Miss Bingley. There are estimable people, and there are those with whom one would prefer not to associate. No one can like everyone he meets, after all—the disparate nature of characters renders that impossible. Do you not agree?"

"When you put it in such a fashion, I suppose you must be correct. I had never considered it so."

"I understand," replied Fitzwilliam. "I have, as you know, experience with the lower levels of society and have learned to look for the good in everyone. There are undoubtedly some who consider those of the first circles to be less than estimable. I know among many of higher society there are men who are despicable in character and women who are selfish and vain, all of whom I would shun forever, given the choice. And yet, nobility can be found in the lowliest foot-soldiers, men who have never known the inside of a drawing room. Nobility, Miss Bingley, is largely a function of character, rather than birth."

Miss Bingley nodded slowly, clearly mystified. "That is an . . . interesting viewpoint for a viscount to hold."

"Ah, but I have not always been a viscount," replied Fitzwilliam. "I have had much more opportunity to learn of the true nature of the world than many a noble, born to his station and unwilling to look beyond the narrow confines of his own opinions."

"Your father must not espouse the same ideals," said Miss Bingley.

It was a direct challenge, one which Fitzwilliam met with relish. "I care little what my father believes. But, Miss Bingley, my father does not disagree with my opinions as much as you might think."

"Is there any sport today?"

"I am certain we could come up with something, Hurst," said Bingley. Darcy shook his head—Hurst could always be counted on to interject with comments concerning his shooting; it was one of his only pleasures in life. Of course, since his other pleasures included food and drink in copious amounts, and he almost always indulged in those loves, Darcy thought Hurst was largely content.

"Then we shall leave you to your sport," said Miss Bingley, seemingly eager to be out of their company.

The gentlemen were soon on the grounds of Netherfield with their rifles, the dogs, and a number of Netherfield's footmen. They shot successfully, soon bagging a brace of pheasants for that night's dinner. But whereas Hurst was usually the most accurate shooter of them all, that day, Fitzwilliam shot more birds.

"It appears you used the time in the army wisely," grunted Hurst after Fitzwilliam had made a particularly fine shot. "Were you as deadly when facing the French?"

"More so," said Fitzwilliam with a ▮▮▮▮▮ grin. "Pheasants are small and quick and can be difficult to shoot, with their weaving to and fro. Your average French soldier does not wish to move from his croissants if he does not have to, which makes him a much easier target."

Hurst barked with laughter. "So, the tyrant has managed to conquer large parts of the continent with nothing more than a rabble of croissant eaters?"

"I may have exaggerated, though only slightly. But in answer to your question, yes, I have had some success against the French." Fitzwilliam sobered. "Though I may make jests of it at times, it is only so that the horror of war does not overwhelm me. It has always seemed to me that making war is a poor way of settling grievances."

"I expect it is, Lord Chesterfield. I expect it is."

Hurst went on ahead, walking with Bingley back toward the manner, while Darcy walked with his cousin, allowing his friends to move some distance ahead of them. When he judged it unlikely they would be heard, he turned to Fitzwilliam.

"Well, Lord Chesterfield, it seems you have made a true friend or two, and you have only been at Netherfield for a few days!"

Fitzwilliam shot him a pained look. "It seems to me, Darcy, that you only use my title when you have something witty to say or you are angry with me. Whichever it is, I would prefer a return to informality. I have been naught but 'Fitzwilliam' to you for years. I would prefer it remained that way."

"I suppose I do mean to be witty," replied Darcy, scratching his chin. "But not overly so. Hurst is a simple specimen. If you can talk about guns or hunting, or you can sit by him and become soused with pleasure, you have made a lifelong friend. Miss Bingley, however, is a little more demanding."

Fitzwilliam snorted. "Great wealth and connections?"

"The very same. I dare say this sojourn in Hertfordshire might be the most tolerable *I* have ever spent with the woman, for she has a much bigger fish to catch. *I* am only a gentleman, after all."

"You sell yourself short, old man," replied Fitzwilliam. "I am quite sure she does not mean to put all her eggs in one basket. I would not be surprised if she maintained her interest in *you* while attempting to ply her trade with *me.*"

Though Fitzwilliam's words were a jest, Darcy found he could not laugh. They were no more than the truth. He would need to be as much on his guard as he ever was when in the company of Miss Caroline Bingley.

"I *am* curious," continued Fitzwilliam. "You said little concerning society this morning. I know your tastes do not mirror my own, but might I assume that you have found it at the very least tolerable?"

"As you so eloquently stated," replied Darcy, "it is much like society in any other part of the kingdom. The estates in this neighborhood are small and the people are at times a little unpolished, but I know of no true harm of them."

"But?" asked Fitzwilliam, successfully catching the hesitation in Darcy's response.

"It is nothing. You know I do not always make a good impression when I meet people."

A snort was Fitzwilliam's response. "That, my dear Darcy, is something of an understatement." Fitzwilliam paused and laughed. "In fact, had I not stepped in last night, I think you might have made a faux pas which would have set your character as disagreeable for all the neighborhood."

Darcy could not help but grimace. "Bingley knows better than to importune me to dance. He is well aware that I am not a great dancer and that I am out of sorts the first night in any new society."

"That he does," replied Fitzwilliam. "But all is well. I distracted Miss Elizabeth and danced with her before you could insert your foot into your mouth. I dare say she was a pleasant and pretty girl, indeed." Fitzwilliam regarded Darcy for a moment, before saying: "I seem to recall *you* speaking to her later in the evening as well."

"We did speak for a few moments. She is quite witty, though I wonder if she possesses more impertinence than she ought."

Fitzwilliam laughed. "Perhaps she does at that. But it is not out of the common way, and her observations are so humorously done that one cannot take offense. I gained the impression that she is quite popular in the neighborhood. You should be thankful you did not insult her."

"I am," replied Darcy. "I would not wish to insult anyone on so little acquaintance."

"Or provocation."

Darcy agreed with his cousin and allowed the subject to drop. They continued to the house, and after the chill of the day, Darcy was happy to warm himself by a cozy fire in Bingley's study. Soon—too soon—both he and Fitzwilliam would be required to brave Bingley's dragon of a sister again. If not for her, Darcy thought Netherfield might almost be pleasant.

CHAPTER III

*T*here were several events of local society in the ensuing days, and those events always saw the attendance of the Netherfield party. Initially, Elizabeth was certain that their attendance was the work of Mr. Bingley and Lord Chesterfield, who were both clearly fond of society. Mr. Darcy, though he was still reticent, acquitted himself well, and Mr. Hurst appeared to be content wherever there was enough food and drink for his appetite, which Elizabeth quickly determined was vast.

The Bingley sisters, however, Elizabeth thought unappreciative of society, though of the elder she could not be quite certain. Miss Bingley's performance at the assembly suggested that she would only mingle with the locals with great reluctance. The woman, however, did not behave as Elizabeth might have expected.

"Miss Elizabeth," said she in greeting when the Bingleys arrived at the Goulding card party one evening about a week after their arrival in Meryton. "How are you this evening?"

"I am quite well, Miss Bingley," said Elizabeth when she had recovered from her surprise to be thus addressed.

"Your sister Jane, is present?" asked she, scanning the attendees for Elizabeth's eldest sister.

"Yes," replied Elizabeth. She turned and gestured toward where Jane stood, speaking with one of the Goulding ladies. "We have arrived ourselves not long ago."

Miss Bingley nodded. "I was hoping to speak with your sister tonight. She is a delightful girl, and I would like to know more of her."

"You will never hear me disagree with such a sentiment. I quite think the world of Jane, for she is my dearest sister."

A certain . . . something passed over Miss Bingley's countenance, but it was gone before Elizabeth could identify it or was even certain that it had appeared at all. Miss Bingley's eyes darted to the side, and Elizabeth, following her line of sight, noted that she appeared to have been looking at Lord Chesterfield. He responded to the sight of Elizabeth with a smile, but as he was speaking with Mr. Robinson at the moment, he did not approach.

"I hope you have settled into Netherfield?" asked Elizabeth, hoping to avoid an uncomfortable silence.

"We have," replied Miss Bingley.

"It is a fine estate, though it has been many years since I have visited."

Miss Bingley seemed to become more interested. "You have been to Netherfield?"

"Its owner is a Mr. Mason," replied Elizabeth. "He has not visited the estate for some years, but there was a time when he spent perhaps half of the year in residence. His daughter, Penelope, is one of my close friends, though I rarely see her now."

"That would explain it," replied Miss Bingley with an absent nod.

She stood there for a few moments seemingly in thought, before she excused herself. Elizabeth watched her approach and then greet Jane, wondering at the awkward conversation they had just exchanged. It was odd, she decided, but then again, perhaps she simply did not share much in common with Miss Bingley, rendering them unable to converse with much success.

"Is your temper yet intact, Lizzy?"

Pulled from her thoughts, Elizabeth turned and noted that Mary had approached her, and was watching with a grin. "I would have expected the woman to attempt to flay you with the edge of her sharp tongue. But I noticed no anger, no release of your wit in response. Might it actually be that she was pleasant?"

"It was uncomfortable, but not tense," replied Elizabeth. "Perhaps we have misjudged Miss Bingley."

Mary snorted. "I doubt it. Something has affected her and modified her behavior."

"Maybe her brother told her she must behave properly."

"It is possible. I will watch her, regardless. I do not trust the woman."

Elizabeth nodded in commiseration, and the subject was dropped.

Throughout those days, it was not to be supposed that Mrs. Bennet had given up her design of who of the Bennet daughters should be paired with which of the gentlemen. Indeed, it was often amusing to watch her as she attempted to rearrange the couples to her liking and with little success. One such occasion was playing out not far from where Elizabeth and Mary stood. They were near enough to overhear the conversation.

"My Jane is such a wonderful girl," said Mrs. Bennet to Lord Chesterfield. "She is always sought after, you know, for she is the mildest, kindest girl in the world."

"She is quite lovely, Mrs. Bennet," replied Lord Chesterfield. Though Elizabeth could see immediately that he was nothing less than honest, it was also clear he could see what Mrs. Bennet was attempting to do and was amused by it.

"I hope you are enjoying our society, my lord," said Mrs. Bennet, preening as if Lord Chesterfield's praise had been directed at her. "I know we have little to offer but small country gatherings. I hope you find it sufficient."

"Indeed, I do," replied he. "I have often had occasion to partake in many levels of society. I find that country manners are as estimable as what you would find in London."

"Thank you, my lord. You do us great honor!" Mrs. Bennet peered about, and noting that Jane was currently standing alone, she motioned toward her eldest. "But here I am, taking all your attention when I am certain you must be in want of a younger partner. Do not feel you must entertain me, sir. I am certain Jane would be pleased to speak with you."

"Ah, but Miss Bennet has a partner, madam." Elizabeth followed his gaze to where Mr. Bingley had just stepped close to Jane, two glasses of punch in hand, one of which he passed to her. "I would not interrupt them for the world. Instead, your two younger daughters are standing together without anyone attending them. I will take it upon myself to do so."

With a bow at the startled and confused Mrs. Bennet, Lord Chesterfield turned and approached Elizabeth and Mary. "Miss Elizabeth, Miss Mary," said he with a bow. "How are the loveliest

Bennet sisters this fine evening?"

Sensing the jest for what it was, Elizabeth caught Mary's eyes and they laughed together. "For shame, sir. Did you not just agree with our mother that Jane is the handsomest of the Bennet sisters?"

Lord Chesterfield grinned. "If you overheard everything, you might recall that I only agreed that your sister was *pretty*—not the *prettiest.*"

"But surely you must acknowledge it," said Elizabeth, who was firmly convinced of that fact. "Else, I must think you witless."

"The wonderful thing about this world we live in, Miss Elizabeth, is that there is something for everyone. For example, many men would undoubtedly agree that your sister is very pretty, indeed, and perhaps that might be the consensus view among the majority. But I am certain that there are gentlemen who might prefer you, or perhaps any of your other sisters. And they would not be incorrect, for it would be their opinion."

"Your words suggest you are one of those gentlemen," observed Mary.

The viscount returned his gaze to Mary, waggling his eyebrows, and she blushed in response. Elizabeth only laughed.

"Again, I did not say that. I will own that I find something estimable in each of you. But as for who is the prettiest? I should say nothing. If I choose between you, I will compliment one, but insult all the rest."

Mary and Elizabeth both laughed again. "Well played, sir! Well played, indeed."

It was to Mrs. Bennet's credit that she also noticed the attentions being paid to Jane by Mr. Bingley. They encompassed more than just the night at the Gouldings' home, and soon it became apparent that Mr. Bingley preferred Jane above all other ladies of the area. It was equally obvious that neither of the other two eligible gentlemen favored her, though it was not readily apparent whether that was because they did not wish to compete with their friend or because of other preferences. Though Mrs. Bennet attempted a few more times to have her way, eventually she confronted Jane about it.

"Jane," said she, one morning when the Bennet ladies were in the sitting-room, engaged in their sundry activities. "I wished to ask you a question."

"Yes, Mama?" asked Jane.

"It seems to me that you favor Mr. Bingley. Is that true, or is it simply because he is the one showing the most interest in you?"

The fact that it was a rational question, rather than Mrs. Bennet's usual overbearing manner, prompted Jane to throw her mother an even look. Elizabeth was as surprised as Jane, and she watched to see what would happen.

"I prefer Mr. Bingley, Mama," replied Jane. "He is an amiable man. I find myself drawn to him."

"But would it not be best for you to set your sights upon Lord Chesterfield?" asked Mrs. Bennet, a hint of her usual nerves beginning to appear.

"No, Mama," said Jane. "Lord Chesterfield is an estimable man, to be sure, but I am quite happy to allow him to focus on some other woman."

Mrs. Bennet was silent for several moments, considering what she had just been told. Several times Elizabeth thought she might object, but eventually, she sighed and nodded to herself, casting her eyes around the room. Her gaze once again rested on Elizabeth herself, as well as on Lydia. For her part, Elizabeth affected not to see it, though she wondered whether her mother had decided she would do for Mr. Darcy or Lord Chesterfield. Mr. Darcy, undoubtedly, for in Mrs. Bennet's mind, Lydia would be the more likely to capture the viscount.

"Can you believe it?" asked Mary, who was seated by Elizabeth's side. "Did Mama actually accept Jane's preference for Mr. Bingley?"

"I am certain she feels that a bird in hand is worth an entire flock in the bush," replied Elizabeth. "If Mr. Bingley seems to favor Jane, why interfere when her ambitions appear to be on their way to being fulfilled?"

"Why, indeed? Be warned, however—I am certain she means to push you toward Mr. Darcy, for Lydia is obviously for Lord Chesterfield."

Elizabeth laughed. "You have mirrored my thoughts quite exactly."

"At least I will not be required to bear her machinations," said Mary.

"For now, perhaps," replied Elizabeth, feeling a little smug. "But once Jane is married to Mr. Bingley, and Lydia and I have captured the two cousins, I am certain Mama will turn her attention to you and Kitty. And I have no doubt she will set her sights even higher, for our husbands will be in a position to introduce you to other rich men!"

Mary attempted a dark look at Elizabeth, but soon she joined in the laughter. "I wish I could refute your statement," said she.

It was a surprise to Elizabeth, but she found she was not at all averse to her mother pushing her toward Mr. Darcy, though Mrs. Bennet's methods were, as always, suspect. Mr. Darcy, though he continued to be reticent, seemed to Elizabeth to be a man who, when he said something, said it with absolute conviction, and while his opinions were not always aligned with Elizabeth's, he argued his points with intelligence. Furthermore, when they spoke, he did not speak down to her like so many men would. Instead, his words and the way he listened to her suggested the attention of an equal. It was not something Elizabeth often saw from gentlemen of her acquaintance, who typically regarded women as having little understanding.

On a night when the neighborhood was gathered at Lucas Lodge, the Bennets had, as was their custom and due to the proximity of Longbourn to the Lucas estate, arrived early to be greeted by the family. Elizabeth still felt her friend's absence keenly, and a few words with Lady Lucas informed her that Charlotte's mother was in similar straits. They spent a few moments consoling each other, after which Lady Lucas turned away to see to some of her guests. It was then an objectionable presence made himself known.

"I see you are still pining after my sister."

Elizabeth, who had been contemplating the gathering and considering with whom she wished to speak, turned to see the smirking visage of Samuel Lucas looking back at her. Instantly on her guard—she shared no cordial friendship with the man—she endeavored to end the conversation before it was even started.

"As does your mother, sir. Charlotte has been my friend for these many years. I think it is unsurprising that I should miss her. Now, if you will excuse me."

"I am happy she does not cling to romantic notions, unlike some I could name."

Elizabeth knew she should simply walk away. But she had never been able to resist piercing his puffed-up arrogance. The way he spoke of his sister, a woman beloved of Elizabeth, was enough to provoke her ire.

"I have no care for what you think of me, Mr. Lucas. As for Charlotte, I would think that *most* brothers would not wish their sisters to make such a desperate choice as Charlotte made."

"Then you would be incorrect," replied Mr. Lucas shortly. "The estate I shall inherit is by no means extensive. Clothing and feeding my unwed siblings would make it virtually impossible for me to have my own family. You may be assured that if Maria exhibits a similar tendency toward being unmarriageable, she will be required to fend for herself as well."

"I am certain that a man as self-centered as you will have no trouble throwing off siblings as if they were nothing more than old and worn garments, fit for nothing more than to be used as rags," said Elizabeth, a fire burning steadily in her heart.

Mr. Lucas only smiled faintly. "I have often had occasion to appreciate your lack of dowry. I would hate to be the one who must gentle your wildness and restrain your tongue."

"And I assure you, Mr. Lucas," said Elizabeth, "that even if I possessed fifty thousand pounds and you were a duke, there is nothing you could say which would induce me to marry you. Perhaps you should simply marry yourself. I am certain you are the only person you could ever love."

Then Elizabeth turned on her heel and marched away from the objectionable man, determined to stay away from him for the rest of the evening. If not for Charlotte's departure, she might have been able to ignore him. But he had spent years perfecting his ability to rile her, and with Charlotte unable to moderate their interactions, she found she had little patience with him.

"He is correct, at least to a certain extent."

The sudden voice surprised Elizabeth, and she took an involuntary step back, her eyes flying to the face of the man who had addressed her. It was Mr. Darcy.

"You sympathize with him?" demanded Elizabeth. "So, will you cast off your sister should she remain unmarried?"

Mr. Darcy smiled at her. "I have quickly come to appreciate your passion, Miss Elizabeth, for it is clear you are incapable of doing anything by half."

Not mollified in the slightest, Elizabeth only glared at him.

"Our situations are not at all similar. My sister, Georgiana, possesses a dowry of thirty thousand pounds. She will have no trouble supporting herself, should it become necessary, and as my heir is a distant cousin with whom I am not at all familiar, my early demise would bring about that end, though Chesterfield and his family would surely take her in.

"But in answer to your question, no I do not agree with your acquaintance, though I understand his position. In my situation, Georgiana will never be required to leave my house so long as I am master of my estate.

"But this estate, as the gentleman noted, is not nearly so large, and it appears Sir William has a large family. Is this not so?"

"Five children, the same as my family," replied Elizabeth.

"Charlotte, Samuel, Maria, and two younger sons."

Mr. Darcy nodded. "It *would*, indeed, be a trial to support so many while raising a family at the same time."

"Perhaps it would," replied Elizabeth, feeling frustrated at being challenged. "But I do not appreciate the ready manner in which Samuel Lucas throws his sisters off without a second thought. My friend is a good and sensible woman. Yet for the want of connections and fortune, she has been forced into service, raising another woman's children."

"I am certain, Miss Elizabeth, that any friend of yours must be estimable. It *is* unfortunate she has made such a choice. I do not say that I agree with Mr. Lucas's feelings or that supporting his unwed siblings is impossible. I only state that I understand his point."

Elizabeth heaved a sigh. "I understand it too, Mr. Darcy. It is just . . ." Elizabeth trailed off, and after a moment shook her head. "I am often unreasonable on the subject of my dear friend. She is too good for a life of service."

"It is quite understandable, Miss Bennet. I have taken no offense."

It was with some relief—likely for Mr. Darcy, as well as Elizabeth— that the subject was changed, and they spoke for some moments about other matters. Then Elizabeth noticed another event occurring in the room, and it brought her no small measure of amusement.

A company of militia, long rumored to be bound for Meryton to winter in the town, had marched into the neighborhood amid much fanfare only that week. As Sir William was an affable man, who lived to be civil to all, he had been eager to include them in the gathering. Thus, red-coated officers dotted the room, and though Elizabeth had yet to speak to any of them, they seemed to her to be a pleasant bunch for the most part.

"Is your cousin acquainted with the colonel of the regiment?" asked Elizabeth.

"A slight acquaintance, I believe," said Mr. Darcy. "He spent some years in the regulars, as you must know."

Elizabeth agreed that she did, but she did not question Mr. Darcy any further, though she longed to know. They were situated not far from where the colonel was speaking with the viscount, and they could hear much of what was being said. They spoke mostly of military matters, issues of training, and the state of the war. Elizabeth had little interest in the two former, though the latter was of concern to them all. But their conversation was largely unremarkable—or it was until Miss Bingley approached them.

"Lord Chesterfield, there you are," said she in what Elizabeth thought was too dramatic a voice. "I have been searching for you, but I see you have hidden in the corner here with the colonel."

"I am hardly hidden, Miss Bingley," replied Lord Chesterfield. "I dare say I am visible from most parts of the room."

"That is only because you are such a great, tall fellow," said Colonel Forster, he a man of slightly less than average height.

"Oh, his lordship is very tall, indeed," said Miss Bingley. Elizabeth could almost imagine the woman salivating like a dog over a bone. The soft snort from her companion told her that he had seen it himself.

"Height is not everything, Miss Bingley," replied Lord Chesterfield.

"No, but it certainly assists," said the colonel. "The men are much more likely to obey when their commanding officer is able to loom over them."

The two men laughed at his joke, but Miss Bingley appeared quite put out that they were speaking without her input. She continued to attempt to insert comments, but the men were equally adept at parrying them and continuing to speak. Soon she huffed and left.

"Is it my imagination, Mr. Darcy," said Elizabeth, "or does Miss Bingley . . . favor Lord Chesterfield?"

A chuckle was Mr. Darcy's response. "It is not your imagination, Miss Elizabeth. Would it surprise you to hear that until we came to Netherfield that *I* had been her target for several years?"

"No, Mr. Darcy," replied Elizabeth, sharing a laugh with the gentleman, "that does not surprise me in the least."

"Perhaps I should not speak in such a fashion about the sister of a close friend," said Mr. Darcy, his tone a little rueful. "But she has never been precisely subtle."

"Your secret is safe with me, sir," replied Elizabeth. "I shall not tell a single soul."

Mr. Darcy regarded Elizabeth, amused. "You are a keeper of secrets, are you?"

"Of course, I am, sir," replied Elizabeth, affecting a lofty arrogance. "I have five sisters, you understand."

"And that ensures your trustworthy nature?"

"It does. For you see, if I was to break one of my sisters' confidences, then I would open myself up to having *my* confidences broken in turn. That would never do."

Mr. Darcy laughed at Elizabeth's explanation, and before long she joined him. "Indeed, that would never do, Miss Elizabeth. Then I believe I have no choice but to trust you—and I thank you for that."

"It is no trouble, Mr. Darcy." Elizabeth paused and stepped forward, speaking softly: "I must own that I am no fonder of Miss Bingley than you are yourself, though I will say that she has been quite pleasant since that first night at the assembly. But I do not trust her transformation to last long."

A queer look came over Mr. Darcy's face, and Elizabeth realized at once that her action might be taken for flirting. Her cheeks bloomed, and she stepped back, refusing to look at the gentleman to whom she was speaking.

"I apologize, sir," said she, shame coloring her words. "I had not intended to be so forward."

"There is no need to apologize, Miss Elizabeth, for I did not suspect you of ulterior motives."

Elizabeth chanced a look up at him and noted he was smiling at her. Relief flooded through her—it seemed she had not lost his good opinion.

"If you saw my reaction to your words, it is only that I remembered something from the morning after the ball." He paused and smiled, though seeming a little uncomfortable. "I should not say anything further, for it truly is not proper to insult one's hostess behind her back. I will only say that you are correct to be wary of her offers of friendship."

"Thank you, Mr. Darcy. I believe I have taken your meaning. I will accept whatever gestures she makes, but will remain watchful."

Soon after Elizabeth withdrew from Mr. Darcy, returning to her sister Mary. There was something unsettling about her conversation with him, though she knew it was nothing to do with the man himself. They truly should not have been speaking of Miss Bingley in such a fashion, but when she spoke with him, their banter was easy, and the feeling of having known him longer than she had and trusting him had led her to say more than she should.

"Lizzy!" whispered Mary. "Is there something more between you and Mr. Darcy than you have told me?"

"No, Mary," replied Elizabeth. "But he is an estimable man, and I feel comfortable in his presence."

Mary looked skeptical, but she did not say anything further, for which Elizabeth was grateful.

Later in the evening, Elizabeth found herself close to the viscount, and she fell into conversation with him. He was an intelligent man, much like his cousin, and Elizabeth found that she was enjoying his company as much as Mr. Darcy's.

"I must own, sir," said Elizabeth after speaking with him for some moments, "I had not expected to find such affability in a member of the peerage."

"Oh?" asked the viscount, his eyebrow lifting in what she took as mischief. "You expect us all to be stuffy, proud, and above our company?" Then he winked. "I have never been called any of those things, but my cousin makes it a habit to give offense wherever he goes."

Surprised, Elizabeth frowned. "Mr. Darcy? But I find him to be quite agreeable, though it is clear he is reticent."

"That is because he has become comfortable with you. In fact, Darcy has a reputation in society for being fastidious and unapproachable. Those of us who know him are aware that he is only uncomfortable with those he does not know."

"Then I am happy he has taken to our society so quickly. He is quite welcome, I believe."

The viscount thanked her. "As for your question, as you know, I was a colonel for some years, and I have learned much of the nobility of character." Lord Chesterfield paused and then attempted a smile at Elizabeth, one which was fraught with heavy memories, she thought. "I have met foot-soldiers I consider to be better men than dukes. But if you attempt to betray my secret, Miss Elizabeth, I shall deny it all. I *do* have a reputation to uphold, you understand."

This last was said with a wink, and Elizabeth responded with a laugh. "I assure you, sir, that I am well able to keep secrets. In fact, I informed your cousin of my trustworthy nature not an hour ago."

"Oh?" asked the viscount. "Do tell."

"Come now, Lord Chesterfield. I just told you I would not betray your secrets. You would not expect me to betray your cousin's a breath later, would you?"

Lord Chesterfield laughed. "No, I suppose you would not."

"But I *am* curious, my lord," said Elizabeth. "I do not think most viscounts rise to be colonels in the army."

The viscount sobered immediately. "That is because I have not always been a viscount. You see, I was born a second son."

It was clear to Elizabeth that she had blundered, and she hastened to give her apologies. But the viscount would have none of it.

"You could not have known, Miss Elizabeth. I am not offended."

"That speaks well to your character, my lord," replied Elizabeth. "But I should not have asked such an impertinent question."

"I have no trouble answering it," replied Lord Chesterfield.

Elizabeth looked into his eyes, and seeing the truth of his words, acquiesced with a nod.

"Two years ago, my brother was killed in a carriage accident. It is because of his demise that I am now my father's heir."

"I am sorry to hear of it, Lord Chesterfield."

"Thank you, Miss Elizabeth. My brother was a good man, a father to a young girl. It has been hard. I never expected to inherit—I never *wished* to inherit. But life, as they say, is fragile. My family has had more than its share of tragedy—Darcy's mother passed when he was but twelve, and his father's heart gave out five years ago."

"My grandmother passed when I was six years of age," replied Elizabeth. "I had been particularly close to her, and her death was hard for me to understand."

Lord Chesterfield nodded in commiseration. "Somehow, Miss Bennet, what began as a happy conversation has turned maudlin."

Elizabeth nodded, though she did not feel like laughing. "I suppose it has, my lord. Perhaps we should speak of happier matters?"

"Agreed."

They changed the subject and spent the rest of the evening in pleasant conversation. When it was time to return to Longbourn, Elizabeth left with her head full of two men. Lord Chesterfield was an amiable man, to be sure, and she had enjoyed speaking to him. But Mr. Darcy was no less estimable, and she was equally happy she had made his acquaintance.

Chapter IV

"**L**ouisa, we have a problem."

Though she would much rather have attended to her book, Louisa Hurst looked up at her sister, wondering what bee had gotten into Caroline's bonnet this time.

"Our brother, Louisa," said Caroline, her annoyance bubbling over into her voice when Louisa did not immediately respond.

"What about Charles?" asked Louisa, though she knew very well why Caroline was angry.

"Oh, Louisa," said Caroline in a tone of longsuffering. She dropped down into a chair nearby with little elegance and sprawled there as she glared at Louisa. "Can you not open your eyes? Have you not seen how he cannot tear his eyes away from the eldest Bennet?"

"No, I have not missed them," replied Louisa, wishing to return to her book. "What of them?"

"She is unsuitable," snapped Caroline. "We will have to do something about it."

Louisa sighed and lowered her book. Her oblique inference that she did not wish to speak of the matter had not deterred Caroline a jot. With a deep breath, Louisa girded herself for an unpleasant conversation.

"Charles is his own man, Caroline. There is nothing you may do to direct him."

"I have directed him in the past."

"You *think* you have. But when has Charles ever listened to either of us when he believed himself to be right or when he truly wanted something?"

Caroline's returning glare was mutinous, but she did not reply. Though Louisa did not wish to encourage her sister, it was perhaps best to divert her.

"I do not think we need to concern ourselves, Caroline. You know how often Charles fixes his attention on a pretty woman for a few weeks before he loses interest. It is likely this is just another one of his infatuations."

"And if it is not?"

"Then there is nothing to be done."

"There is everything to be done," snapped Caroline. "Miss Bennet *is* an amusing sort of girl, but she is in no way suitable to be our sister."

"She is a gentleman's daughter."

"But she has no fortune or connections. She will not raise our position in society. Charles needs to think of these things, and if he will not, we need to consider them for him."

A headache was forming behind her eyes—Louisa was certain of it. It was often thus when speaking with Caroline. She had a way of taking a pleasant day, drawing a thunderstorm in by the force of her displeasure, and raining on the good moods of everyone in her vicinity.

"Charles may do as he pleases," said Louisa again, once again picking up her book. "If he decides Miss Bennet's worth is more than the sum of her dowry, then he has every right to make that choice. You cannot direct him, Caroline. I beg you do not even try."

Then, in a gesture which was a clear indication that the conversation was over, Louisa raised the book and began reading. For a few moments, she almost wondered if she had persuaded Caroline to leave the matter be—or at least induced her to take her complaining elsewhere. Then her sister spoke again.

"I think I might like to invite the Bennet sisters to dine with us, Louisa."

Taken aback by this non-sequitur, Louisa looked up at her sister. "I beg your pardon?"

"Oh, not all the Bennet sisters. The youngest are positively hoydens, and I will not endure them in this house. But perhaps Miss

Bennet and Miss Elizabeth might be invited. Brother has informed me that the gentlemen are engaged to dine with the officers two days hence. Without the gentlemen present, we would have the opportunity to become acquainted with the sisters without interference."

It was all Louisa could do not to roll her eyes. She knew exactly what her sister was about. Inviting them when the gentlemen were not to be present would allow Caroline to interrogate Miss Bennet without Charles's presence to monopolize her attention. She no doubt wished to discover something about the girl which was objectionable, which she could then use to ensure fascination with her was fleeting. Furthermore, she wished to avoid putting her in his company more than was necessary, and this would give her the opportunity to do so while obtaining the information she required.

"I think Charles would rather be present when Miss Bennet visited us, Caroline."

"Nonsense," said Caroline waving Louisa's concerns away. "He will understand. The gentlemen will have much to talk about with the officers. Surely he cannot begrudge us our ladies' conversation."

Louisa resisted the impulse to shake her head, no matter how sorely she was tempted. "I am certain he will not."

"Excellent!" said Caroline, rising to her feet. "I will write to Miss Bennet, inviting her and Miss Elizabeth to dine with us."

Then Caroline rose and quit the room, leaving Louisa watching her as she departed. Only when she was gone did Louisa give in to the impulse to shake her head. There had never been any chance of deflecting Caroline, she reflected. Caroline was all bluster and implacable will—she was not easily, nor quietly, defied.

But though the younger Bingley sister possessed a will of iron, so too was the elder possessed of that same core. Louisa's will was hidden, not openly displayed as was Caroline's. If Caroline was intent upon having the Bennet sisters to try to ferret out some embarrassing information, well, Louisa was equally capable of thwarting her sister. But it must be done delicately—Caroline would be impossible if she thought Louisa was going against her wishes.

It was only by chance that Fitzwilliam learned of the invitation. Despite his words to Darcy, Fitzwilliam knew well the danger that Miss Bingley posed to his bachelor state, and while he knew he would be required to marry one day, Miss Bingley was not a candidate for the position. Thus, he avoided the woman wherever possible, a determination he found easy to make but difficult to implement.

Netherfield was not one of the great estates. But it was a good challenge for a new estate owner such as Bingley. And, more importantly, for Fitzwilliam's—and Darcy's— peace of mind, it was a large house with many rooms and ample opportunity to escape its predatory mistress. The cousins made good use of it, relaxing with Bingley in his study while discussing the estate, playing billiards, or enjoying the library, such as it was, while hiding from Miss Bingley. It was also fortunate that Fitzwilliam's bedchamber was one of the only guest bedrooms in the house which also boasted a private sitting-room, one more location they could use to thwart the woman's matrimonial designs.

As the days passed, Fitzwilliam became more familiar with Bingley, and he was forced to agree with Darcy's assessment of the man. He was not the most diligent individual, a fact Fitzwilliam attributed to his being a young man and it being the autumn season when the harvest was already in and most gentlemen were engaged in their local societies—those who were not in London for the little season. But he was eager and friendly, and Fitzwilliam did not know how anyone could dislike Charles Bingley.

Thus, they whiled away their days, avoiding Miss Bingley, riding when the weather permitted, and indulging in their gentlemanly pursuits. It was, then, surprising that Fitzwilliam was in a position to learn something he was certain that Bingley himself did not know, and then only by chance. It was the name "Bennet" which caught his attention.

"Did I hear you correctly, Miss Bingley? Are the Bennet sisters to come to Netherfield for dinner tonight?"

Miss Bingley appeared guilty, and she attempted to obfuscate. "Why do you ask, Lord Chesterfield?"

"Because I heard you speaking with Mrs. Hurst, Miss Bingley." Fitzwilliam paused and made a show of thinking for a moment before he spoke again. "I do find it curious that you would invite them tonight when Darcy and I will be away with Hurst and your brother, dining with the officers."

Miss Bingley shook her head and made light of his comment, which also confirmed his conjectures. "Why should it be strange, my lord? The gentlemen will dine with other men, while we ladies also wish for some company which we will appreciate. It seems like the most natural thing in the world to me."

Though it was great fun to tweak Miss Bingley's nose, Fitzwilliam decided now was not the time to indulge in teasing. "I suppose when you put it that way, it makes perfect sense. Shall you invite *all* the ladies?"

This time Miss Bingley's disgust was clear. "I believe the youngest Bennets are too young to make good companions. I actually only considered asking the eldest two."

"Prudent," said Fitzwilliam, amused that in this, at least, he agreed with her. "You might reconsider Miss Mary, however. She is, as yet, quite young, but she struck me as an intelligent woman, one who would be well worth knowing.

"Then I shall take your suggestion under advisement, sir."

"Very well," replied Fitzwilliam. "Then I would be happy to further assist you this evening in promoting your friendships with the lovely Bennet ladies."

"That is not necessary, Lord Chesterfield," was Miss Bingley's quick response.

"Nonsense!" said Fitzwilliam, gesturing expansively. "I am quite happy to help."

It appeared Miss Bingley was curious in spite of herself. "Then what do you suggest, my lord?"

"Please offer them the use of my carriage, Miss Bingley."

"Will *you* not require its use?"

"The gentlemen will be traveling in your brother's carriage. Mine is quite free, I assure you."

"I do not believe that is necessary," the woman was quick to say. "I am certain the Bennets own a carriage. Surely they are not *that* poor."

Fitzwilliam suppressed a laugh—it seemed his hostess was desperate to avoid showing their neighbors *any* favor, no matter how trifling. "I insist, Miss Bingley," said Fitzwilliam. "It is only polite to do so since the invitation is coming from Netherfield. I am certain it will foster excellent relations between you, and I am happy to do my part to assist."

Since there was nothing she could do, Miss Bingley acquiesced. It was clear, however, that her thanks were as false as her rigid smile. "Then I will be certain to inform them of your largesse, Lord Chesterfield."

"There is no need, Miss Bingley. I am happy to be of service."

Fitzwilliam paused, his amusement with Miss Bingley and her airs having run its course. But the woman's attempt at mirth had prompted his annoyance, and he would not allow her to disparage a good family without response.

"I would, however, caution you, Miss Bingley, lest you espouse any misapprehension. Though I do not know the exact extent of Mr. Bennet's wealth, I suspect that Longbourn has an income of more than two thousand per year. That does not make Mr. Bennet wealthy, but it is not an inconsequential sum. I am certain that Mr. Bennet does, indeed, own a carriage.

"My offer to send a carriage for their benefit does not stem from a belief that they cannot afford it themselves, but because I wish to be neighborly and because it is good manners."

"You are quite correct, Lord Chesterfield," said Miss Bingley hastily.

"I am sure I am." Fitzwilliam paused and considered the woman, before continuing: "I also wish to thank you and your brother for extending the invitation to me to join you here, Miss Bingley. I am quite at home in such society and find it to be to my taste. The Bennets and the others of the neighborhood are good people, and I have been happy to make their acquaintance."

"We are happy to have you with us," replied Miss Bingley, though she appeared confused by his declaration.

With a bow, Fitzwilliam turned and left, intending to find his cousin. With any luck, Miss Bingley would now avoid any overt castigation of local society. Anything which limited her venom was welcome, in his opinion.

When the invitation arrived from the ladies at Netherfield, those to whom it was addressed received it with varying emotions. Jane, who had come to esteem them—and more particularly, their brother—was eager to go and become better acquainted with them. Elizabeth, though Miss Bingley had been pleasant the past several times she had been in her company, was nevertheless cautious, and not only because of Lord Chesterfield's words on the subject. Mary was only surprised to have been included in the invitation.

"There is no mistake," said Jane to Mary's request for clarification. "The invitation is for all three of us—Jane, Elizabeth, and Mary—to attend Miss Bingley and Mrs. Hurst at Netherfield for dinner tonight. The gentlemen are dining with the officers, and the ladies wish to come to know us better and request our attendance. The viscount's carriage is even to be dispatched for our use."

"That must be Lord Chesterfield's work," said Elizabeth.

Jane directed a level look at Elizabeth. "Why is that, Lizzy?"

Elizabeth laughed and touched Jane's hand. "Miss Bingley can hardly offer the use of a viscount's carriage without his consent, Jane.

I was not attempting to censure Miss Bingley or make any comment to her detriment."

Mollified, Jane nodded. "Please restrain your usual wit when it pertains to Miss Bingley, Lizzy. She has been all that is pleasant to us — that you must confess."

"She has," replied Elizabeth. "I know nothing ill of her, other than a slight haughtiness the night of the assembly. She has been quite civil since then."

With a beaming smile, Jane nodded, and the subject was dropped. Elizabeth had not told Jane of her conversation with Lord Chesterfield, and she did not intend to. Not only would her sister not believe any ill of Miss Bingley, but there did not seem any reason to try to sink the woman's character. She *had* been pleasant, after all.

"The question is, who will attend?" said Mary into the silence. "I am not truly known to Miss Bingley — I wonder why she has seen fit to invite me as well."

"You have spoken with Mrs. Hurst several times," said Elizabeth. "Perhaps she has influenced your inclusion."

Though Mary was skeptical, she bowed to the persuasion of her sisters and agreed to accompany them. Thus, Jane quickly applied to their father for permission, and with that in hand, the reply was swiftly dispatched. Now it fell to them to inform their mother.

It was fortunate that Mrs. Bennet had not been present when the missive had arrived. It was Mrs. Bennet's custom to retire to her rooms after breakfast to rest her nerves, as she termed it, before returning to the sitting-room to welcome any morning visitors. Whatever the reason, Elizabeth had a hearty respect for her mother's ability to meddle, or even worse, to insist on actions which were not at all proper. At the very least, she might have snatched the letter from Jane's hands to read herself, one of the numerous ways in which the Bennet matron showed her lack of understanding of polite manners. The communication would thus be made at luncheon.

"Invited to Netherfield for supper?" cried the woman when Jane informed her of it. "Oh, I knew how it would be. Mr. Bingley has taken a liking to you and has influenced his sister to invite you, so he may come to know you better. What wonderful news this is!"

"I do not think that Mr. Bingley has influenced his sister in this matter, Mama," replied Jane in her usual calm voice. "In fact, Miss Bingley informs me that the gentlemen are to dine with the officers."

Mrs. Bennet's face fell for a moment. "Mr. Bingley shall not be present?" She shook her head as if to clear her thoughts. "But this is still a good sign, for it shows Miss Bingley's favor for her brother's choice. And no doubt Elizabeth and Lydia have been invited as well by the influence of the cousins."

"Elizabeth has been invited, yes," said Jane. Elizabeth, though amused at her mother's antics and wishing she could speak herself, decided it was best to leave it to Jane. "But Lydia is not included in the invitation. Instead, Miss Bingley has invited Mary to Netherfield."

"Mary?" cried Mrs. Bennet. "Why, in heaven's name, would she invite Mary?"

Grasping Mary's hand in quiet support, Elizabeth shot an annoyed glance at her mother, the mirth of the previous few moments forgotten in the face of this new insult to her younger sister. Mary, for her part, seemed unaffected by her mother's ill manners—it was not as if she was not accustomed to them, after all.

"I do not know why I was invited, Mama," said Mary, her tone affecting unconcern. "Lizzy suggests that it is because I have become friendly with Mrs. Hurst."

But Mrs. Bennet was shaking her head, the motion becoming firmer by the moment. "No, no, no, this will not do at all! We cannot send Mary when Lydia is the focus of the viscount's attention. He will think she is slighting him."

Even Lydia found Mrs. Bennet's statement to be nonsensical, if her unladylike snort was any indication. Mr. Bennet only watched his wife from across the table, his amused grin testament to his enjoyment of the spectacle. He did not essay to correct his wife, leaving his daughters to the task.

"I am sure that Lord Chesterfield knows of the composition of the party which has been invited," said Jane, her tone reasonable. "It is *his* carriage which is to be dispatched for our use, after all."

It was clear that Mrs. Bennet was at a loss. "For Lord Chesterfield to send his carriage, it must be a compliment to Lydia." She paused and thought for a moment before her eyes widened. "It must also be a compliment to Jane. For Mr. Bingley's carriage must be in use to convey the gentlemen to their dinner, and he must have persuaded Lord Chesterfield to send it to take our girls to Netherfield.

"But Miss Bingley must be mistaken in her invitation, for surely Lord Chesterfield intended that Lydia be invited—not Mary." Mrs. Bennet nodded once, determination gleaming in her eyes. "Then we must inform them that Mary is indisposed tonight and that Lydia shall take her place."

"Mama!" exclaimed Jane, which was only a small portion of the cacophony which erupted at Mrs. Bennet's statement. "We cannot impose on Miss Bingley in such a fashion."

"Whether a mistake has been made, I cannot say," added Elizabeth, though privately she was certain there was no error. "But we cannot simply substitute another when the invitation is quite specific in including Mary. Lydia cannot go, or we will be imposing upon them."

"Nonsense, Lizzy," replied Mrs. Bennet. "My mind is quite made up. Lydia shall go in Mary's stead."

"Lydia shall not go."

All eyes turned to the Bennet patriarch. He was still watching the scene with amusement, but now there was a hint of resolve in his countenance, which set his wife to glowering. Elizabeth suppressed a sigh of relief—she knew her father took far more amusement in his wife's excesses than he should, but he usually acted to curb the worst of her improprieties, when it could affect the family's reputation.

"Lizzy and Jane are quite correct, Mrs. Bennet," continued Mr. Bennet. "The invitation specifies that your three eldest daughters have been invited to Netherfield, and it is they who shall go. Even if one of them should come down with a fever between now and this evening, you shall not substitute Lydia where she has not been invited."

"But, Mr. Bennet—"

"No, Mrs. Bennet. There is a point where even the desperation of securing husbands for your daughters must give way to the needs of polite behavior. Jane seems to be getting on with this Bingley fellow well enough." Mr. Bennet paused and smiled at Jane, which she returned, though not without embarrassment.

"You should allow matters to proceed naturally, Mrs. Bennet," said he, turning his attention back to Mrs. Bennet, who was sitting, watching him with the sullenness of a child of five. "If Jane is meant to marry Mr. Bingley, then I am certain she shall. Your other daughters, also, have charms aplenty. And you never know, Mrs. Bennet—it may be Mary who has caught our good viscount's eye."

Mrs. Bennet looked on Mary with evident skepticism, but Elizabeth had focused on Lydia, who she was certain could not allow such an assertion to pass her by. She appeared ready to comment, but she caught sight of Elizabeth's fierce scowl and restrained herself, though not without a huff of annoyance or contempt. For her part, Mary had turned to her father with a shy smile, while Mr. Bennet nodded. Though he did not pay much attention to Mary, he could be counted on to compliment her at the oddest times.

"Very well," said Mrs. Bennet, though there was no grace in her acquiescence. "I suppose it must be as you say."

"Thank you, Mrs. Bennet," said Mr. Bennet, his tone dripping irony. "I knew you would come to see my point of view."

The subject closed, Mr. Bennet rose and announced his intention to retire to his bookroom, departing with nary a glance back. If he had thought, upon exiting, that Mrs. Bennet's machinations were at an end, he would have been disappointed.

"Girls, go upstairs and put on your best frocks for an evening visit, but you should also wear stout boots. You will need to leave well in advance, for Netherfield is three miles distant."

"Why would we be required to leave so early?" asked Jane, clearly perplexed. "It will not take the carriage so much time to traverse the distance."

"Because, Jane, you must walk to Netherfield."

"Walk?" cried Jane. "Why ever would we walk?"

"Would you go to Netherfield and not see Mr. Bingley?" demanded Mrs. Bennet. "It looks like rain, and should you walk, you will not be able to return home tonight. Therefore, you will be at Netherfield tomorrow morning, and able to greet Mr. Bingley before you return home."

"We would look like beggars if we were to do such a thing," said Elizabeth with some asperity. It was times like this when she wondered if she were truly related to the woman in front of her.

"Besides," said Mary, interjecting when it appeared Mrs. Bennet was about to release a harangue, "If you recall, Lord Chesterfield has offered us the use of his carriage, which will retrieve us an hour before supper is to begin."

"He has—yes, of course," said Mrs. Bennet. "What a compliment this is, and how good of his lordship!"

Mrs. Bennet paused, and she looked from Lydia to Mary. Elizabeth could easily see the course of her thoughts. In the end, however, her husband's instructions won out, for she grunted with annoyance.

"Then you girls must make a good impression upon not only the sisters, but also Mr. Darcy and his lordship. The next invitation will, I am certain, include Lydia, for Lord Chesterfield was ever so attentive to her these past few events."

Soon the eldest Bennet sisters were able to escape, and they left, each relieved their mother had not managed to embarrass them. They took themselves up to Jane's room to choose dresses and prepare for their evening out. Contrary to Mrs. Bennet's instructions, none of them were of a mind to dress in an elaborate fashion, but they would need to wait until the last possible moment, so their mother could not interfere.

"Mama is determined, is she not?" asked Mary. Elizabeth instantly sensed that the question was rhetorical and did not require a response. She attempted to reply regardless.

"She is. But I have no notion that her ambitions with respect to Lydia and Lord Chesterfield will ever be realized."

"*That* is without question," replied Mary. "He has talked with her at times, but it is clear he views her as a child."

"Personally, I *do* think the offer of Lord Chesterfield's carriage is a compliment," said Jane. "But I do not think it is the one Mama dreams of."

"Oh?" replied Elizabeth. "Then what do you suspect?"

"I think it is a compliment to *you*, dear sister."

Elizabeth gaped at Jane. When her sisters started laughing between themselves, she fixed them with a severe frown.

"I cannot imagine of what you are speaking, Jane. Lord Chesterfield has no interest in me."

"Actually, I think Jane might be correct," replied Mary. "He does speak with you quite often, and it is clear he enjoys your conversation."

"Of course," added Mary, "if he wishes to pay her his addresses, he may need to vie with his cousin for that. It has not escaped my notice that Mr. Darcy seems to enjoy your wit equally well."

Mary and Jane exchanged a glance, and they burst out into laughter. For her part, Elizabeth did not know whether to be amused or angry. In the end, she chose to ignore her sisters' teasing.

"Both gentlemen are good men, I am sure, though they are quite different. But I do not feel any danger from either, and I am certain your teasing will come to nothing in the end."

"Danger?" asked Mary with a raised eyebrow, one which resembled an expression Elizabeth often used. "You consider matters of the heart to be dangerous?"

Elizabeth determined that ignoring their teasing was now the best remedy. But her sisters laughed nonetheless.

CHAPTER V

*W*hen the viscount's carriage arrived, it was hardly surprising that the inhabitants of Longbourn—one in particular—were impressed with it. It was a wide, spacious vehicle, black lacquered on the outside, and covered with sumptuous leather on the inside, a truly fitting vehicle for a member of the peerage. Perhaps the most impressive detail, however, was the coat of arms which decorated the rear of the conveyance, a heraldic emblem both elaborate and inspiring.

"What a beautiful carriage!" exclaimed Mrs. Bennet when it pulled up onto Longbourn's drive. "I have never seen anything so fine!"

"The very rich can well afford such luxuries," replied Elizabeth. "I am sure the earl must ensure his son has nothing but the best."

Mrs. Bennet eyed the carriage and then turned back to the sisters before finally looking directly at Lydia. She heaved a sigh, no doubt repining the exclusion of her youngest from the excursion. Then she straightened, evidently deciding there was no reason to focus her energies on what could not be changed.

"Off you go, then," said she, gesturing at the waiting coach. "Be on your best behavior and give every deference to your hostess and her sister.

"And, girls," said she when they had begun to file from the room. "Should one of you become ill and be required to stay the night, be aware that I can well spare you."

The accompanying wink was not in any way a subtle hint, any more than her words were. But they were not allowed to think on the matter any further, for Mrs. Bennet turned and sat in her usual chair, beckoning Kitty and Lydia to her, their attitude one of plotting.

Eager to be away from their mother's schemes, the three elder daughters exited the house and were assisted into the carriage by a waiting footman. The step was stowed, the door closed, and soon the carriage lurched into motion. It was only then that they gave into laughter.

"It is truly not proper for us to be laughing at our mother," said Mary.

"It is not," agreed Elizabeth. "But there are times when I feel that I must laugh, else I will surely cry."

"Mama does mean well," said Jane, trying to defend the indefensible as was her usual custom.

"She does," agreed Elizabeth. "But her execution leaves much to be desired. If we are to stay the night at Netherfield, I am certain it will not be because of our mother's plotting."

Her sister nodded in commiseration, and the subject was dropped for the time being. They spoke of inconsequential matters throughout the short journey to Netherfield, each avoiding the subjects which may have been of most interest, such as Mr. Bingley, the gentlemen who were his guests, or even their mother's actions. There seemed to be little reason to return to their initial subject, so they did not.

"Look, it has begun to rain!" said Mary when they were about halfway to their destination.

Jane and Elizabeth crowded around the window, looking out on the landscape. The rain had begun, and at the moment, it was only falling lightly, coating the earth beyond the carriage in a thin sheen of shining dampness. But in the distance, the sound of thunder rumbling reached their ears, and they looked at one another with interest.

"Perhaps our staying at Netherfield is not so impossible, after all," said Mary. "Should this weather worsen, it may be difficult for us to return tonight."

"Let us not put the cart before the horse," said Elizabeth. "It is possible that the weather will simply pass us by and all will be well."

Her sisters agreed that it was possible, and the subject was dropped. For the rest of the ride, they were silent, with only the odd comment passing among them. Elizabeth was grateful for the silence, for it allowed her the opportunity to think. She did not know why, but the thought of staying at Netherfield for the night filled her with apprehension. Perhaps it was her imagination of what Miss Bingley would think of them. But Miss Bingley would think of them what she thought, and Elizabeth knew there was little any of them could do to change her opinion, so there was clearly no need to concern herself on that account.

But the gentlemen . . . Elizabeth did not wish for them to think ill of the Bennet family. She told herself that it was because Jane seemed to be making such an impression on Mr. Bingley. But in the back of her mind, she knew that she also did not wish for Mr. Darcy and Lord Chesterfield to abandon their good opinions.

When at last Netherfield rose out of the surrounding trees, they disembarked from the carriage and, protected by umbrellas the footmen held over their heads, they made their way into the house. Elizabeth appreciated the protection, though it truly was not raining enough for them to worry overmuch about it. When they were shown into the vestibule, they were met by the housekeeper, who assisted in divesting them of their coats, and were then shown into the sitting-room where the Bingley sisters were waiting for them.

"Miss Bennet!" exclaimed Miss Bingley. "Welcome to Netherfield. And Miss Elizabeth and Miss Mary, of course. We are so happy you have joined us this evening!"

"Thank you for the invitation, Miss Bingley," said Jane, speaking for the sisters. "We were happy to accept."

They entered the room and sat down, and for a time, they indulged in general conversation among the five of them. Once again, Elizabeth was impressed with the way Miss Bingley attended them, with none of the supercilious condescension she had betrayed that first night in company. Mrs. Hurst, by contrast, had always been easy and pleasant—Elizabeth had never seen her in any other attitude. Elizabeth was still suspicious of Miss Bingley's motives, but she was determined to give the woman the benefit of the doubt unless otherwise provoked.

Before long, they were called into the dining room for dinner. The soup was served, and they busied themselves with the task of eating, interspersed with conversation. It was at that time that Elizabeth began to see through Miss Bingley's façade yet again.

"The dinner is excellent," said Elizabeth, speaking up when the main courses had been served. "Thank you once again for inviting us."

"We are blessed with the services of a wonderful cook," replied

Mrs. Hurst, "and are happy to have you."

"Do you not know that a whole evening's tête-à-tête with just the two of us might lead to disagreement?" asked Miss Bingley. "In inviting you to provide us company, we derive as much benefit as you do."

Elizabeth laughed at Miss Bingley's words. "For some sisters, that is quite true. However, I could never imagine being at odds with my dearest sisters. Jane is quite too angelic to provoke a disagreement."

"Do not praise me so, Lizzy," said Jane. "I am no more perfect than any other person."

"No, Jane," said Mary, her expression filled with mirth. "We have years of experience to inform us that you *are* nearer perfection than anyone else of our acquaintance."

Elizabeth and Mary laughed at Jane's obvious embarrassment, and in this, they were joined by Mrs. Hurst. Miss Bingley, however, only watched them, her expression unreadable.

"If only Caroline and I were so perfect as Miss Bennet," said Mrs. Hurst. "We are prone to disagreements, for, unfortunately, neither of us is so good."

"We have our disagreements," said Jane, shooting a quelling glare at Elizabeth. "Do not allow Lizzy and Mary to lead you to believe otherwise."

"Miss Bennet," said Mrs. Hurst, "I believe that we have all become well enough acquainted that we do not need to stand on ceremony. Shall we not dispense with formality and refer to each other by our Christian names?"

They all agreed to her suggestion, though Miss Bingley shot a look at her sister, suggesting displeasure. But she did not demur, so "Caroline" and "Louisa" they were. The conversation continued for some time after, and the subjects were interesting and more than a little laughter was shared. It was not until near the end of dinner that the tenor of their discussions changed.

"Now that we have all become such close friends, I would like to know more of you," said Caroline during a lull in the conversation. "You must not be all of the Bennets, surely—have you any aunts and uncles, cousins, and the like?"

"We are our only near Bennet relations," replied Jane. "We have a distant cousin on my father's side of the family, but his branch of the family assumed a new surname some generations back and now go by the name Collins. Our only other relations are on our mother's side."

"That is quite interesting," said Louisa. "The Bingley clan is much larger. We have so many aunts and uncles and cousins that it can be difficult to keep track of them all."

"We never have that problem," said Mary. "We are not close to Mr. Collins, and since our mother has only one sister and one brother, there are not enough of us to become confused. And only our uncle has children!"

"Oh?" said Caroline, her eyes gleaming with sudden interest. "They must not live in the neighborhood. Or perhaps we have not been introduced to them?"

"Our aunt lives in Merton, but our uncle does not," said Elizabeth.

"And where is his estate?"

There was something about Miss Bingley's tone of voice which put Elizabeth on her guard. It was a sort of eagerness in her tone, one which suggested she expected to hear some salacious gossip, the type which would be spoken of in whispers, with giggles and surreptitious looks included. Elizabeth could not help but wonder what the woman intended.

But Elizabeth responded with calmness, for the Gardiners were such fine people that there was no reason to be ashamed. "Our uncle lives in London, Caroline, and he is very successful."

"Shall we all retire to the music room?" said Louisa, interrupting the increasingly tense conversation. "I understand Mary plays the pianoforte?"

"I do," said Mary, her complexion assuming a rosy hue. That she had not immediately raced to the music room, eager to display her talents, was a testament to her recent growth. "But Lizzy plays with far more feeling than I do."

"But your technical proficiency is far greater than mine," replied Elizabeth.

"But Jane's singing is far more beautiful than either of ours," said they together, bursting into laughter after.

"Then I must insist on hearing you all," said Louisa, her smile showing her mirth.

Caroline looked on, her expression carefully devoid of any hint of her thoughts. Elizabeth was certain she was annoyed at being denied her inquisition, but she did not say anything to contradict her sister.

They rose together and made their way toward the music room, light conversation accompanying them as they walked. Elizabeth, whose attention had been captured by Caroline's suddenly changed behavior did not say much, and she noted the focus of the younger Bingley sister's attention was likewise occupied listening to Mary and

Jane as they chatted with Louisa. Elizabeth resolved to watch Caroline for the rest of the evening, for she was certain the woman was again showing her true colors.

Once they had arrived in the music room, Louisa indicated to the housekeeper that they were ready for tea to be served. When she had departed from the room, they gathered at the pianoforte. Though Elizabeth and Mary both displayed their talents on the instrument, it was quickly evident that Louisa and Caroline's talents far exceeded that which Bennet sisters could boast. It was not until Elizabeth and Jane sang a duet, with Mary accompanying, that the sisters' true talents were unleashed.

"You do have a lovely voice, Jane," said Louisa when they had finished singing. "And Elizabeth's voice complements yours quite well. Do you often sing at events of the area? I am only curious, for I do not think we have been blessed with the pleasure."

"We *do* sing at times," replied Jane.

"But not often," said Elizabeth with a grin at her elder sister. "Jane does not like displaying her talents before all the neighborhood."

"That is the truth," said Mary when Jane made to protest. Mary turned to Louisa. "But I can tell you both have had extensive access to masters, for your playing is very fine, indeed."

Louisa appeared a little embarrassed. "Caroline is the true proficient in the family, though I do my best."

"Do not allow her to deflect the praise," said Caroline, speaking for the first time since they had entered the room. "Louisa is very talented."

"You play very well yourself, Mary," said Louisa. "By your words, I assume you have not had much time playing with masters, but for all that, your talents are not insubstantial."

The two ladies stayed at the pianoforte, playing together and discussing their favorite composers, while Caroline invited Jane and Elizabeth to the sofas to partake from the tea set. They went along willingly, Jane eager to deepen her friendship with Caroline, while Elizabeth was merely curious as to how the woman would conduct herself. After Caroline poured, they sat for some moments, speaking of the sort of inconsequential nothings which often punctuated polite discourse. Before long, however, Caroline's questions once again became more pointed, and the opportunity was provided to her because of an innocuous question of Jane's.

"Do you see your family much, Caroline?"

"Louisa, perhaps, misspoke," replied she. "Hurst usually makes his home in London, as the family estate in Norfolk does not suit his need for society. Since her marriage, Charles and I often stay with Louisa and Hurst. Now Charles will make his home at his estate when he finds a suitable one for purchase. Our relations are more distant, and they are not truly of our sphere."

Poor Jane was not quite certain what to think of Caroline's assertions. Elizabeth was under no such limitation; she knew *exactly* of what the woman was speaking, and she was rather amused at Caroline's conceit—especially the suggestion that her brother was now a gentleman when he was only leasing an estate.

"What of your family?" asked Caroline with seeming nonchalance. "You said your aunt lives in Meryton and your uncle in London?"

"Yes, that is true," said Elizabeth, unwilling to distance herself from beloved relations, as she was certain Caroline was attempting to do to her own. "Uncle Phillips is a solicitor in Meryton—his practice is highly successful, as he handles the accounts of many gentlemen in the vicinity of Meryton and other villages nearby. Uncle Gardiner owns an import business in London and supplies many other businesses. He is quite well regarded in London circles."

That was clearly the information for which Caroline had been waiting. "He is, is he?" The woman's nose rose several inches in the air, and she looked down its length at Elizabeth. "With his success, I must assume then that he lives in a fashionable area of town?"

"He lives on Gracechurch Street," said Jane.

"My uncle could afford a more fashionable address," added Elizabeth, sensing the challenge and responding accordingly. "But the house he lives in is sufficient for his family, and lovely besides. And it also has the benefit of being near his business, which he finds convenient."

"I see," replied Caroline. Elizabeth, watching the woman's sudden transformation as she was, wondered if she would hasten to inform her brother of Jane's unfashionable relations that very night, or if she would savor her supposed triumph and wait until morning.

Feeling suddenly mischievous, Elizabeth assumed an expression of innocence and said: "Perhaps your father and our uncle were known to each other. Is your family's business in a similar industry?"

Caroline almost choked on her tea and glared at Elizabeth, her affront a living thing. "You are mistaken, Miss Elizabeth, for we are not involved with trade. My brother's fortune is unencumbered and unconnected with trade."

"But it has been accumulated through the auspices of trade, has it not?" asked Elizabeth. She affected a wide-eyed look of surprise. "Your brother is the first of your line to possess an estate—am I not correct?"

Her jaw working with affront, Caroline appeared to be mastering a great emotion. She did not reply for a short time, in which Jane looked back and forth between the sudden combatants, uncomfortable with the changed atmosphere. For Elizabeth herself, she only watched Caroline and waited for her response, never allowing her ingenuous smile to slip.

At length, Caroline responded with a clipped: "We are not connected to trade." And she fell silent.

At that moment, a crash of thunder echoed throughout the room, and the five ladies looked up in surprise, as none of them had known it had begun to storm. They rose together and crowded around one of the windows near the pianoforte, looking out on the landscape below. The inky blackness of the night sky made it difficult to see, but as they watched, a few flashes of lightning illuminated the earth, and they could see the rain coming down in waves.

"I am not certain I have ever seen a storm this wild," commented Louisa. "With such rain, I wonder if you will be able to return to your home tonight."

The suggestion was less than palatable to at least one of them. "Perhaps we should not be too hasty," replied Caroline. She shot a suspicious glare at her sister. "If we wait for some time, the rain should slacken."

"That is best," said Elizabeth, agreeing with her hostess. She had no more desire to stay the night than Caroline wished them to stay.

"Perhaps the gentlemen will arrive soon and inform us of the situation," said Louisa.

Caroline shot her sister a hard glance, but she did not reply. The housekeeper was sent for and instructed to refresh the pot of tea and speak with the butler about the weather. Then the ladies once again sat together, only this time the conversation was much less objectionable. They concentrated on their tea and spoke of the weather and how unusual it was to have a thunderstorm in November.

As they spoke, Elizabeth continued her vigil on the behavior of Miss Caroline Bingley. While the woman was as outwardly friendly as she had been at the beginning of the Bennet sisters' visit, Elizabeth was certain that the true woman had finally made an appearance. She did not speak much and she seemed to be considering a subject which had nothing to do with the conversation. No doubt, she was planning her use of the information she had learned that night. Elizabeth almost snorted—the truth of the Bennets' connections was well-known throughout Meryton. Caroline need not have obtained the information in such a manner, risking offending them all. Then again, Elizabeth was certain the woman did not worry about offending them. She likely now considered them beneath her notice.

At length, the night grew late, and the time for the Bennet sisters to return to Longbourn arrived and passed, and while the ladies checked the weather through the window, there seemed to be little change. Furthermore, when the butler was queried, he argued strenuously against their returning home. Caroline had just asked the man for the third time—it seemed like she was eager to be rid of them—when there was a commotion out in the hall, and the four gentlemen stepped into the room.

Elizabeth's quick survey of their countenances revealed that Mr. Bingley was surprised to see them, Lord Chesterfield was not, Mr. Darcy was unreadable, and Mr. Hurst uncaring. Mr. Bingley stepped forward as the spokesman and greeted them with his usual cheer.

"I had not realized you were to invite the Bennet ladies, Caroline," said he, turning his attention to his sister. "I am surprised you neglected to mention it."

"You had your amusement for the evening; we had ours," replied Caroline.

"We have been having a marvelous time, Charles," added Louisa. "But since it has grown late, we have just been discussing the possibility of their return to their home."

"Absolutely not!" exclaimed Mr. Bingley. "The night is not fit for man nor beast. Our evening with the officers was cut short for that very reason."

"Surely it is not so bad," said Caroline. "Lord Chesterfield's carriage is sturdy and fine—I am certain they may return to their homes in safety."

Mr. Bingley turned to the viscount. "You knew the Bennet sisters were to come tonight?"

"I did Bingley," replied Lord Chesterfield, "for your sister asked for the use of my carriage to convey them here. You have my apologies— I had completely forgotten the matter."

A frown was Mr. Bingley's response, but he did not pursue the subject any further.

"I will add my own opinion, though I have not been asked for it," said Mr. Darcy. The man glanced at Elizabeth, and she was utterly surprised when he winked at her. "You cannot return tonight. It would not do to risk your safety, and the comfort of the drivers and footmen is also to be considered."

"In that case, I extend an invitation for you to remain the night," said Caroline, though Elizabeth was certain the woman wished to do anything but.

"That is for the best, to be certain," said Louisa. She looked the Bennet sisters over. "Jane is taller than I—nearly as tall as Caroline—so perhaps my sister will agree to loan her a nightgown. Elizabeth and Mary are of a height with me, so I should have something which will fit each of you."

The sisters thanked their hostess and her sister and agreed to stay for the night. And with that, they made their way toward the stairs to retire for the evening. As she went, Elizabeth's mind was full of Mr. Darcy. She had always thought of the man as a sober, serious sort of individual. She would never have suspected he would actually wink at her. Suddenly, Elizabeth wished to know more of this enigmatic man from the north.

There were times when Louisa considered herself to be positively prophetic. She waited in her rooms before retiring, knowing Caroline would almost certainly seek her out, more than likely to complain about the presence and imposition of the Bennet ladies. Perhaps Louisa could not claim the talent given her knowledge of her sister, but she certainly felt like it.

"Those Bennets are so artful," exclaimed Caroline almost as soon as she had entered the room.

"How so, Caroline?" asked Louisa. "You can hardly accuse them of controlling the weather, so they may forward their nefarious purposes."

"Of course not!" snapped Caroline. "But did you see the way their eyes lit up in avaricious satisfaction when I issued the invitation?"

"The only thing I saw was relief that they would not be required to brave the elements," replied Louisa.

"Oh, it was there." Caroline's frown was very nearly a sneer. Louisa, who had always known that Caroline considered her to be a simpleton and a bore, ignored it as she usually did. There was little to be gained from taking offense, especially since Louisa had grown less concerned with her sister's opinion over the years.

By now Caroline was pacing the floor. "I wanted to keep Jane Bennet away from Charles! I am most put out by this turn of events."

"Then you should not have invited them," replied Louisa. "It is November and the weather is always unpredictable. Should we have been inundated by a snowstorm, or had the viscount's carriage developed a fault, the result would have been the same."

Caroline paused and seemed to think of something, then she sat down on the nearby chair, looking at Louisa with determination. "Perhaps Charles being in Jane's company again is not ideal, but I have gained the information I needed. The Bennets only have two relations worth any mention—both are Mrs. Bennet's siblings. Her sister is married to the solicitor in Meryton, and her brother is a *tradesman* in London!"

The way Caroline's lip curled in disgust at her mention of the Bennets' uncle suggested she found even the chore of pronouncing the word to be foul. Louisa almost shook her head—it seemed Caroline had forgotten yet again that the Bingleys were descended from a long line of successful tradesmen.

Then Caroline's countenance darkened again. "Do you know Eliza questioned me about our connections to trade? The impudent chit actually asked if our father might have been known to her uncle. How is such disrespect to be borne?"

"Our father was, indeed, a tradesman, if you will recall."

"But Charles's wealth is completely unencumbered from trade." Caroline's eyes bored into Louisa's. "We are completely unconnected."

"Except for our extended family, all of whom are all still heavily invested in the family business."

Caroline missed the wryness in Louisa's tone. Instead, she sniffed and turned her attention back to her original purpose in coming.

"The question is, how do we use this information? While Jane Bennet is a sweet sort of girl, her ties to trade make her completely unsuitable for our brother, even if her lack of dowry did not already disqualify her."

"I would caution you, Caroline," said Louisa, "not to make assumptions. We have no knowledge of the Bennets' circumstances. We have nothing more than suppositions—do not think you know of the extent of her dowry without firm information."

"One only has to look at them and to be in company with Mr. Bennet to know," sneered Caroline. "But be that as it may, this news of their connections seals the matter. Charles cannot be allowed to marry the girl. He must marry an heiress and assist in raising the Bingley family name in society."

"Oh, Caroline," said Louisa, shaking her head. "You may attempt to turn Charles away from her if you wish, but I have never known either of us to be able to sway him when he wished for something."

"We must!"

Louisa shook her head. "I have no notion how deep Charles's feelings for Miss Bennet run, but he will do as he likes, as he always has. I suggest you do not interfere."

For a moment, Caroline glared at Louisa, and then she rose with a huff and quit the room. Louisa watched her go, wondering at her sister. It had always been difficult to like Caroline, for she had been obsessed with their family's position in society since long before she should have thought about such things. Louisa had done her best to prevent Caroline from making a fool of herself, but it was difficult at times, especially when she set her sights on men who would never offer for her.

With a sigh, Louisa rose to her feet and quit the room, passing through the sitting-room to her husband's bedchamber. Caroline did not know she spent most nights with her husband—she would have berated Louisa if she had known, for fashionable couples *did not* sleep in the same bed.

"Your sister has gone to bed?" asked her husband when she slipped under the counterpane.

"She has."

"And was it as unpleasant as you thought?"

Louisa shrugged and settled into her husband's arms. "Nothing more than Caroline being Caroline."

Hurst grunted and fell silent. Soon Louisa had joined him in sleep, the concerns for her wayward sister forgotten until the next day.

CHAPTER VI

*W*hen Elizabeth awoke the next morning, the first thing she noticed was the sunlight shining in through the drawn curtains. Sitting up and being confronted with an unfamiliar bedchamber, the memories of the previous evening flooded back, but Elizabeth pushed such thoughts to the side for the moment. The storm of the previous night had given way to a beautiful November morning, and Elizabeth was eager to be out partaking in the glory of the new day.

Rising from the bed, Elizabeth quickly donned her dress from the day before and folded the borrowed nightgown with care, mentally noting to herself to thank Louisa. Then taking care to remain quiet, Elizabeth let herself from her room, down the stairs to the main door, and from thence out onto Netherfield's front drive, where she walked around the house and into the back gardens.

They were just as she remembered them, and for a moment she felt a pang of loss for Penelope Mason's company. They were of similar tastes and dispositions and had often enjoyed the gardens of Netherfield together or indulged in a hint of mischief. The departed Charlotte Lucas also entered Elizabeth's mind, and she spared a moment of longing for another dear friend, now making her own way in the world. The thought, of course, brought Elizabeth's mind back to her dear friend's brother, Samuel, and she indulged in a few choice thoughts for the unfeeling man.

But the brightness of the day was such that Elizabeth could not long remain in dreary thoughts, and she soon shook them off and concentrated on her walk. The air was crisp and cool after the previous night's rain, and the morning sun felt warm on her face. Elizabeth loved the feeling of the sun mixed with the chill in the air, and she strode forward, greeting each well-loved sight with delight, marveling in the beauties of nature to which only she seemed privy.

It was thus with surprise when Elizabeth noted the presence of others in Netherfield's back gardens, and she stopped when she saw them approaching her, surprised that any of the other inhabitants would be up as early as she.

"Miss Elizabeth," said Lord Chesterfield with a smile and a nod. "You are awake earlier I might have expected."

"And I might not have expected *you* to be out this early," replied Elizabeth, directing an arch look at both the viscount and his cousin.

Lord Chesterfield laughed. "I fear that my years in the army have ruined me for sleeping later than I ought."

"And what is your excuse, Mr. Darcy?" asked Elizabeth, turning her attention to the other man.

"Only that morning is my favorite part of the day," replied the man.

He did not make any attempt to further explain himself, and Elizabeth decided it was not proper to press. "Then I bid both of you a good day," said she. "I am certain I shall see you at breakfast before we return to our home."

"My cousin and I would be happy if you would walk with us," said the viscount. "Unless you wish to walk alone."

"No, indeed," replied Elizabeth.

They turned and proceeded together, soon coming to a wide path Elizabeth remembered walking with Penelope many times. It was not so wide as to allow more than their current number, and Elizabeth was grateful they had not come in the company of Miss Bingley, for surely she would have tried to exclude Elizabeth.

"Your sisters are not likewise early risers?" asked Lord Chesterfield after they had walked for several moments.

"None of us are prone to sleeping late," replied Elizabeth. "But I believe I am the most likely to be up early. That, however, is due to my love of nature and desire to be out of doors. None of my sisters share this predilection."

"I will own a love of the outdoors myself," replied Lord Chesterfield. "My pursuits, however, run more toward horses and hunting than walking. Darcy here is as avid a horseman as I am myself."

"Though I am largely indifferent to hunting," said Mr. Darcy, speaking for the first time. "I do hunt on occasion, but I am not nearly so interested in it as Fitzwilliam or even Hurst."

"Where are our manners?" asked the viscount, smiling at Elizabeth. "I have no doubt our words about hunting are boring you to tears. Tell me, Miss Bennet—do you ride?"

"I do ride a little," replied Elizabeth. "But I am not accomplished. Jane is the horsewoman in the family."

"I am astonished, Miss Bennet," said Lord Chesterfield, feigning shock, Elizabeth was certain. His cousin seemed to understand what he was about, for he looked at Elizabeth with interest. "But perhaps you have not considered the matter correctly."

"What do you mean?" asked Elizabeth.

"Why, that with your love of nature, you would have the ability to see so much more of it were you astride a horse." He grinned at her. "Unless, of course, you are able to run like the very wind itself."

Elizabeth was quick to laugh. "No, sir, I am not so fleet of foot as your trusty steeds. Perhaps you are correct that I might see more of nature should I ride more, but one of my reasons for walking is for exercise, which I also enjoy. Were I to allow a steed to serve as my legs, it would defeat the purpose. Do you not agree?"

"I do not know," replied Lord Chesterfield, turning to his cousin. "I seem to remember gentling some horses with nothing more than riding them provided all the exercise one required."

"And riding a horse is not devoid of movement," said Mr. Darcy, apparently ignoring his cousin's sally. "There is *some* skill involved."

"You are quite correct, sir," replied Elizabeth, enjoying the sound of the man's melodious voice. "But you must agree that walking provides more exercise than riding can."

The gentleman agreed, and they continued on their walk. Soon talk turned to Hertfordshire and the lands around Meryton, and as Elizabeth was quite acquainted with them—at least the paths which meandered through the landscape near Longbourn—she was quite happy to tell them what she knew. In turn, the viscount described some of the sights he had seen, both on the continent and in the various places in England he had visited. He even described some of the sights he had seen on his grand tour before he had joined the army.

Though Mr. Darcy interjected with comments here and there, he was, for the most part, silent, content to listen to Elizabeth and his cousin carry on the conversation. Elizabeth was feeling more than a little confusion at this enigmatic man. He had actually winked at her last night, showing more spirit than she had ever before seen from him, yet this morning he was as reticent as she had ever seen him. Who, therefore, was the true Fitzwilliam Darcy?

Then his reticence faded, as the subject turned to the gentlemen's own estates.

"Darcy's estate is in Derbyshire, close to the Peak District," said Lord Chesterfield. "Unfortunately, I do not think he can tell you everything, for there is not enough time. He is, you see, inordinately proud of his estate and can speak of it at great length."

"I do love my home," replied Mr. Darcy. "And my love for it is not much different from your family's affinity for Snowlock."

"You live near the peaks?" asked Elizabeth. "My Aunt Gardiner was raised in Derbyshire, not far from there. Have you heard of a little town called Lambton?"

"Lambton is not five miles from Pemberley," replied Mr. Darcy with more animation than Elizabeth had seen from him the whole time they had been walking.

"It must be quite beautiful," replied Elizabeth. "My aunt loved her years in Lambton, and she often talks of returning there when she has the chance."

"I can understand her love for it. It is a picturesque location, and one the locals always seem to remember when life calls them to other places." Mr. Darcy paused and then said: "Excuse me, Miss Bennet, but I wonder if I am acquainted with your aunt. Is she from one of the estates in the neighborhood?"

"No. She lived in the town itself. Her father was the rector of the church in Lambton until he passed suddenly when she was fifteen. Since then she has lived in London."

Mr. Darcy nodded, though slowly. "I remember the circumstances, though not the particulars. Pemberley itself is part of Kympton parish, and my family has always attended church there."

For the rest of their time walking the paths around Netherfield, they spoke of Mr. Darcy's estate, and Elizabeth found that though his cousin's words were spoken in jest, they were nothing less than the truth. It seemed like Mr. Darcy knew every rock and tree on his estate and was acquainted with everyone who lived there, down to the tiniest babe born only that summer. His cousin teased him, though with good-natured comments rather than jibes, and they passed a very agreeable time until they returned to the house.

When they returned to the house, it was immediately clear that Miss Bingley did not appreciate the company they had kept. Miss Elizabeth herself seemed to sense this, and rather than respond with annoyance or anger, as he might have expected, she only parried Miss Bingley's remarks.

"How kind of you gentlemen to entertain Miss Elizabeth!" exclaimed she when they escorted Elizabeth into the dining room for breakfast. Miss Bennet and Miss Mary were already there, as were the Hursts and her brother. Then Miss Bingley fixed her gaze on Miss Elizabeth. "Had I known you were to rise so early, I would have ensured there was someone to attend you."

"It is no trouble, Miss Bingley," replied Miss Elizabeth cheerfully. "The morning sun and a beautiful day are all I required to amuse myself."

"And we did not amuse Miss Elizabeth," added Fitzwilliam. "She seemed quite capable of amusing herself. But as we were all walking the grounds, we decided to walk them together."

Though the woman did an admirable job of keeping her countenance, the look she bestowed on Miss Elizabeth implied she suspected her of attempting to compromise both himself and Fitzwilliam at once.

"It is quite fortunate, then, that you were blessed with ready protectors and companions, Elizabeth. How ever did you manage it?"

"It was completely by chance, I assure you, Caroline. Nothing more than a fortunate crossing of our paths allowed us to be together this morning."

"You must be chilled," said Mrs. Hurst. "Please sit down and partake of a little breakfast."

"Thank you, Louisa," replied Miss Elizabeth.

She went to the sideboard and helped herself to a light breakfast before taking it to the table and sitting next to her sisters. Darcy and Fitzwilliam shared a look and Darcy knew that his cousin's thoughts mirrored his own—it was a rare woman who was able to ignore the incivility of another and parry her attacks with aplomb. He was grateful to Mrs. Hurst for deflecting her sister, who was now attending her own breakfast. The looks she directed at Miss Elizabeth when she thought no one was watching, however, spoke to her continued suspicion of the other woman.

It seemed like Miss Bingley had made the connection for the first time, though Darcy had noted his cousin's interest in the second eldest Bennet for some time. Darcy did not think Fitzwilliam's attentions tended to anything other than politeness, but Miss Bingley would not see it in such an innocuous way. To her, any other woman would be a rival, one she would be required to best in her pursuit of a wealthy husband.

"Are the selections this morning to your taste, Lord Chesterfield?" asked Miss Bingley after a few moments. "If there is something you would prefer, I would be happy to speak with the cook."

"There is nothing further I require, Miss Bingley," replied Fitzwilliam, his amusement barely held in check. "Your cook is to be commended, I think, for the meals at Netherfield thus far have been very fine."

"Thank you, sir," replied Miss Bingley, preening as if Fitzwilliam had just paid *her* the compliment. "We do our best to provide all our guests with the best." She paused and bestowed an unctuous smile on him. "Tell me, sir, does your mother intend to come to Netherfield to visit?" She turned to Darcy. "And your sister? I had understood there was some talk they would both join us?"

"I *did* mention it to my mother," replied Fitzwilliam. It was all Darcy could do not to snort—though the invitation had been extended, Darcy doubted the Countess of Matlock would agree to stay at Netherfield. She had met Miss Bingley, unfortunately, and did not like her. "But I believe she and my father—as well as Georgiana—are ensconced at Snowlock for the present and shall not leave it."

"Please give her my regards," replied Miss Bingley, "and ensure she understands she is welcome to come at any time convenient. We would be happy to have her."

"Thank you, Miss Bingley. I surely shall."

The conversation at the breakfast table continued to consist of that particular dance of huntress and unwilling prey. Miss Bingley asked after Fitzwilliam's comfort in minute detail, while Fitzwilliam parried and assured her he was quite well. No doubt he was thinking of certain times on campaign when his situation had been a matter of life and death, and such comforts were the furthest thing from his mind. Miss Bingley, by contrast, thought of nothing more than catching a titled husband.

Of the rest of the company. Mrs. Hurst quite obviously knew what her sister was doing, and if her pinched look was anything to go by, she was not amused. Miss Bennet and Bingley spoke quietly to themselves, with Miss Mary injecting a comment at times, and Hurst was, as usual, engrossed in his breakfast. It was Miss Elizabeth who caught his attention, as she was, as was Darcy himself, well aware of what Miss Bingley was about.

"Do you think your cousin enjoys the attention he is receiving?" asked Miss Elizabeth in a quiet voice when she noted his scrutiny.

"Knowing Fitzwilliam, I do not doubt he does," was Darcy's reply.

Miss Elizabeth chuckled. "Then I suppose there is no need to rescue him. He seems to be quite in his element, after all."

Darcy fixed a long and deliberate look on his cousin, and then with an exaggerated slowness, he turned back to Miss Elizabeth. "I had considered attempting to distract her—it is usually *I,* after all, who am the focus of her attention."

By now, Miss Elizabeth was grinning openly. "And why do you not?"

Shrugging, Darcy said: "Because I am enjoying the reprieve. Besides, my loyalty to my cousin only runs so deep, you understand."

It was admirable the way Miss Elizabeth avoided laughing with nothing more than a slight snort escaping. Darcy, however, could only see the way her eyes twinkled with mirth, even if her outward show of emotion was curbed. She picked up her glass and drank from it, Darcy was certain, to further stifle any reaction. When she put it down, she turned a severe look on him.

"For shame, sir," said she.

"Do you have anything, in particular for which to censure me?" asked Darcy blandly.

"It is not proper to force me to laugh at my hostess in front of her, sir, to say nothing of the inappropriate topic of conversation."

"I beg your pardon, Miss Bennet, but if you recall, it was not *I* who raised the subject."

Miss Elizabeth made a great show of thinking about it before she turned back to him. Darcy noted that her jollity had not subsided in the slightest. "I will grant you that, sir, though I declare you turned the conversation which provoked my mirth. I was merely asking a question."

"Ah, but did the question not invite me to respond with humor?"

"I can see I should not trade such words with you, Mr. Darcy. You are entirely too quick. I must warn my father—you are clearly not a man who may be the target of sportive comments without understanding."

"And your father enjoys doing so?"

"He does not make sport of others to make them ridiculous," replied she. "But follies and inconsistencies do amuse him. I must own that I find them diverting myself."

Darcy returned her look with as sober a cast to his countenance as he could manage. "Then I will guard against any seemingly silly behavior, Miss Elizabeth. I would not wish to be the target for you—or your father's—witticisms."

Unable to hold it in any longer, Miss Elizabeth broke into laughter, and Darcy found that he could not hold back himself, indulging in a few chuckles. Their laughter drew the attention of the others around the table. Her sisters were aware of her character and only smiled in an indulgent fashion before turning back to Bingley and their conversation, while Mrs. Hurst looked on with interest. Miss Bingley, however, seemed to sense a situation which would not be to her advantage.

"Would you share whatever prompted your laughter, Elizabeth? Few have been able to make Mr. Darcy laugh, for he is known as a sober, serious sort of man."

"I laugh as much as the next man, Miss Bingley," replied Darcy, speaking before Miss Elizabeth would be required to respond. "But I hope I do not do so in a frivolous manner."

"Then Eliza's words must have been quite diverting, Mr. Darcy, for I have already known this of you."

By her side, and apparently enjoying the cessation of the woman's focus for a time, Fitzwilliam watched them, merriment dancing in his eyes. Darcy speared him with a look, warning him not to speak, and Fitzwilliam grinned. It was clear he knew that at the very least their commentary had been concerning the woman at his side.

"It was nothing of consequence, Miss Bingley," said Miss Elizabeth before Darcy could speak again. "Mr. Darcy and I were speaking of follies and inconsistencies and how they may be amusing at times."

Miss Bingley's smile turned positively patronizing. "If you will recall, Mr. Darcy just spoke of not laughing frivolously. Surely you do not mean to teach him to laugh at silliness such as this."

"Oh, I would never dream of directing Mr. Darcy's humor," replied Miss Elizabeth. "I am certain he shall laugh whenever he feels it warranted. But for my part, I believe there is much in life at which to laugh. Provided we are not unkind to others, we may laugh away. I, myself, dearly love to laugh. It makes a world which is otherwise dreary at times much more bearable."

"Here, here!" exclaimed Fitzwilliam. "Having seen much in my life,

I cannot but agree with you, Miss Elizabeth. It is much easier to walk the path of life when you do so with pleasure, rather than sorrow."

Miss Bingley grunted, but she seemed to sense that the conversation was not proceeding in her favor, and she called Fitzwilliam's attention back to her. A wry grin was his cousin's response, but Fitzwilliam did his duty and turned back to his hostess. Darcy did not miss the frequent glances his cousin directed at Miss Elizabeth and Darcy himself. There was a quality inherent in them which Darcy could not quite make out; his cousin seemed to be watching Darcy askance, but Darcy could not quite determine why.

At length, when breakfast was consumed, the Bennet sisters insisted that it was time to return to their home, after apologizing for imposing upon their hosts. While the duty of response should have fallen to Miss Bingley, as the hostess, it was Mrs. Hurst who shouldered the burden.

"Nonsense! You cannot control the weather, after all—or if you can, I fear I have not given you nearly enough credit."

The Bennet sisters laughed, but it was Miss Mary, with whom Mrs. Hurst seemed to have struck up a friendship, who responded for them.

"No, you are correct in that matter, Louisa. We are not nearly well enough versed in the occult to exert such control."

The way Mrs. Hurst's eyes darted to her sister and the pinched look Miss Bingley gave her in response, suggested something behind that comment. But whatever it was, Darcy could not quite tell, and the demands of the present conversation forced it from his mind.

"Then it is no imposition. In fact, we were happy to have you with us. I hope we may do it again very soon."

"I agree," said Bingley. "It would be no imposition to have you stay with us longer. Shall you not remain until luncheon and then return to Longbourn after?"

Once again Miss Bingley's countenance darkened, but the woman was saved by the insistence of the Bennet sisters.

"Thank you all," said Miss Bennet. "But I believe we must be returning to our home. We appreciate your friendship and your hospitality, but we must depart."

With such a strong declaration, no one attempted to gainsay them further. Fitzwilliam called for his carriage to be made ready, and soon the Bennet sisters had entered therein for their short journey to their home. As he watched the carriage proceed down the drive, Darcy could not help but notice the sun shone just a little less brightly with their absence.

"How wonderful it is to have one's home to oneself again," said Miss Bingley as they re-entered the house.

It was clear that no one agreed with her. But no response was made, allowing the woman the illusion of the company's approval. For himself, Darcy certainly was not about to agree with her.

CHAPTER VII

*N*ever before had Elizabeth fully appreciated her mother's apparently adaptable nature, though, in her defense, she rationalized that her mother had never shown any hint of such abilities. Mrs. Bennet was essentially a simple soul. Gossip was her greatest joy, and while the subjects of her discussions with the neighborhood consisted of many things, inevitably her attention would turn back to her daughters. Of the five Bennet sisters, she could speak of with an unflagging zeal, and while her observations most often centered on her favorites—Jane and Lydia—she could boast of any of them without hesitation, regardless of the situation.

But in the days following the eldest sisters' visit and subsequent stay at Netherfield, she truly proved herself to be versatile, though Elizabeth had not ever expected to be in the position to make such a claim about her mother. Mrs. Bennet's first inclination, of course, was to pair either Jane or Lydia with Lord Chesterfield—whichever caught his fancy—leaving the other for Mr. Darcy, while Elizabeth was to capture Mr. Bingley. But she had surprised them all when she had accepted Jane's preference for Mr. Bingley, shifting the pairings in her mind so that Lydia would capture the viscount, leaving Elizabeth for Mr. Darcy. And then things changed once again.

"How do you do, Miss Elizabeth?" asked the viscount one morning when the Netherfield party visited Longbourn. It was the morning after their return to Longbourn, and Elizabeth thought it remarkably civil of them to visit so soon after. The entire company had come, Mr. Darcy following his cousin into the room, with the Bingley party trailing behind.

"I am very well, Lord Chesterfield," replied Elizabeth. "I am surprised to see you again so soon, sir. I had thought you and Mr. Darcy would likely be riding the grounds of Netherfield at all hours of the day. Or perhaps your penchant has led to walking, or perhaps there are too many birds on Mr. Bingley's estate, and you have been thinning their ranks?"

Elizabeth could easily hear Mrs. Bennet's strangled gasp at the sportive way in which she was speaking to the viscount, and the glare with which Miss Bingley favored her was not unnoticed. The man himself, however, laughed at her sally.

"Darcy and I did ride this morning, with Bingley in our company. For the present, however, the birds are safe from us."

"I am certain they will be happy to hear it, Lord Chesterfield."

They continued to speak in their sportive manner for some time, and Mr. Darcy, who was sitting nearby, joined in on occasion. Caroline's countenance became even more sour, as the woman no doubt thought Elizabeth was hoarding the conversation of the two gentlemen for herself. It was not long before she was not able to hold her tongue any longer.

"I hope your family is all well, Eliza," said she, her expression barely less than a sneer.

"We all have been quite well, Caroline," replied Elizabeth, refusing to rise to the woman's bait.

"And your extended family?" Caroline's eyes darted to the viscount and her smile became smug. "I am sorry, but you never did inform me where your uncle actually lives. Is it quite close to Mr. Darcy's house in Mayfair? Your aunt lives in Meryton, I understand."

"Yes, on both accounts. And they are all well. If you are all still in residence at Netherfield at Christmas, you shall meet my Uncle Gardiner and his family, for they usually spend the holidays with us."

"Your uncle is Mr. Gardiner?" asked Lord Chesterfield, his interest clear. "Mr. Edward Gardiner?"

"Yes, that is he," replied Elizabeth, surprised. "Are you acquainted with him?"

"Not personally," said Lord Chesterfield, "though he is quite well-known in town. Everyone with whom he is acquainted speaks of his business acumen and his manners, which I am told are sufficient for him to pass himself off as a gentleman."

"I do not think it proper for *anyone* to portray themselves as inhabiting a station which they do not possess," interjected Caroline.

Elizabeth goggled at the woman as if she had just stated that the moon was naught but a bit of dust in the sky, wondering at her hypocrisy. "It is interesting to hear you say that, Caroline. But I assure you that my uncle does not attempt to be taken for anything other than what he is. Much like your brother, it is his ultimate goal to purchase an estate and join the ranks of the landed."

"How fortunate for him."

The woman's tone was enough to set Elizabeth's teeth to grinding, but she was able to control her temper and refrain from snapping at her. Instead, Elizabeth contented herself with a stiffly spoken: "I fully agree with you, Caroline. One should definitely be required to portray themselves with honesty to all and sundry. Why, daughters of tradesmen might think themselves above those descended of gentlemen should that rule not be applied."

Caroline's eyes glittered at the insult—whatever the woman was, she was not senseless, and Elizabeth was certain Caroline had understood the thrust of her words quite well, indeed.

"If your uncle is to attend you," said Lord Chesterfield at that moment, breaking the tension between the two women, "then I would be happy for an invitation. He seems like a man well worth knowing."

"I certainly shall not dispute that, Lord Chesterfield," replied Elizabeth. "My uncle is a fine man—he and his wife are among the best people I know."

Their conversation wended on from there, and Elizabeth was grateful that Caroline fell silent, contenting herself with glaring while Elizabeth spoke with the two gentlemen. Lord Chesterfield proved himself to be a true gentleman, for he forwarded the conversation past Caroline's ill-temper and taunts, while Mr. Darcy performed equally well, ignoring the woman completely.

As they spoke, Elizabeth found herself wondering at the difference between the two men, the objectionable person of Caroline Bingley shunted to the back of her mind. The viscount seemed intent upon paying attention to her, and Mr. Darcy—with the possible exception of Mr. Bingley—seemed to be more comfortable in his cousin's company than anyone else in the room.

The viscount's words were playful and amiable, and at times

Elizabeth wondered if they strayed into territory which might be better referred to as flirting. But Elizabeth had seen enough of him to know that it was nothing more than the man's usual manners. In short, Elizabeth did not think he meant anything by it, and she certainly had no notion that he had any true interest in her.

By contrast, Mr. Darcy did not indulge in flirtatious comments or exaggerated statements designed to flatter. Whatever he said was done with a gravity she had associated with him since the earliest days of their acquaintance. She was not certain what it was, but she began to realize that she preferred Mr. Darcy's company, though it was strange that she should. Lord Chesterfield was, after all, like Elizabeth herself in character and manners.

It was while they were engaged speaking that the change in Mrs. Bennet was made manifest. Elizabeth had noted her mother watching her speaking with the gentlemen, though Mrs. Bennet's attention had also been on where Mr. Bingley and Jane had been speaking in quiet voices. Unfortunately, her mother could not suppress her improper streak for long enough to suit Elizabeth.

"Mr. Darcy!" said she suddenly, drawing the eyes of most of the company to her. "Perhaps you would prefer to see the back gardens of Longbourn? Though it is not as pretty as it will be in the summer, I dare say it is a sight well worth seeing. I am certain our Lydia would be happy to accompany you."

Miss Bingley's smile immediately became predatory, and she said: "Yes, Mr. Darcy. I am certain you will get on famously with Miss Lydia Bennet."

"It is too cold for walking in the garden, Mama," complained Lydia.

"In this instance, I believe I must agree with your daughter, Mrs. Bennet," said Mr. Darcy, apparently relieved to have been granted a reprieve. "The air is far too chilly to be out of doors."

Though seeming disappointed, Mrs. Bennet was by no means defeated. "Then you should sit here where you may speak much more easily."

Mr. Darcy appeared less eager to do anything than sit next to Lydia, but he seemed to sense there was no graceful way to demur, and he moved to the indicated seat, though not without reluctance. Elizabeth watched them, annoyed with her mother for showing the Bennet family to have little sense, but as Mary was seated near Lydia, she stepped in and began conversing with Mr. Darcy. The man himself appeared grateful, and he spoke with her, showing perfect composure, if not perfect comfort. For her part, Lydia continued to speak and giggle with Kitty. Mrs. Bennet only watched over them, her expression smug, seeming not to realize that Lydia and Mr. Darcy were not falling in with her grand designs.

"I sense, Miss Elizabeth," said Lord Chesterfield softly, "that your mother fancies herself to be something of a matchmaker."

Elizabeth turned and grinned at the viscount. "You have no idea, my lord. It is unfortunate for her that her daughters often have little appreciation for her efforts."

"Oh?" asked the viscount. "Is that so? I must own I am surprised, for my cousin has been a prime catch on the marriage market since he inherited his estate five years ago. Does your sister believe she can do better?"

Had the jest not been evident in the man's smile, Elizabeth might have thought he was being severe upon them all. As it was, Elizabeth grinned back at him and replied:

"That presupposes that the only consideration for any Bennet daughter is nothing more than a man's standing in society, and the extent of his holdings, of course."

"And what is the going rate for a Bennet girl, then?"

Elizabeth made a great show of thinking for a moment. "It depends upon the daughter in question," said she at length. "Jane and I are determined to marry for love and affection, while Mary is much like us, though perhaps a little more practical. As for Kitty and Lydia, they have stated their preference for the color red many times in recent weeks." Elizabeth looked at the viscount critically. "While your current jacket is not red, I am told you have worn one in the past. Perhaps you would do for our Lydia, should you only revert to your former habits."

Lord Chesterfield guffawed, but Caroline, who had been following their conversation closely only huffed and speared Elizabeth with a glare. "I suppose I must not be surprised that *your* family is so narrow-minded. A militia officer, indeed! I know not how to account for such inanity!"

"I believe, Miss Bingley," said Lord Chesterfield, "that Miss Elizabeth was making a jest at my expense. And quite well done, I should think.

"But if you would excuse me, Miss Elizabeth, I believe I will decline and continue with the current color of my jacket. Miss Lydia is, of course, an estimable lady, but she is yet full young and not ready for such weighty subjects as marriage. And, she is naught but half my age."

"Then I shall inform her, Lord Chesterfield," said Elizabeth, displaying a disheartened sigh for his benefit. "She will recover, I am sure, and go on to break many more hearts before she is finally induced to give up her single state sometime in the future."

"I am sure she shall," replied Lord Chesterfield. At the same time, Caroline let out another offended huff. At least the woman had the sense to remain silent.

When the Netherfield party left some time later, the Bennets accompanied them to the door to farewell them. While Elizabeth was happy to have such interesting visitors, she was relieved when they had left, for she was not certain she could bear the mortification of her mother's blatant scheming any longer. It was unfortunate, therefore, that Mrs. Bennet was not finished with them.

"I must apologize to you, Elizabeth, for ever doubting you."

Confused, Elizabeth gaped at her mother, saying: "I have not the pleasure of understanding you, Mama."

Mrs. Bennet clucked and led Elizabeth back to the sofa. "Your cleverness, of course. I thought it would always inhibit you from attracting a good man for a husband, but it appears I was incorrect."

A snort distracted Elizabeth, and she turned to see her father regarding them with open amusement. He had been present during the visit of the Netherfield party, but he had not spoken, for the most part, only sharing a few words with Mr. Darcy and Lord Chesterfield. Elizabeth glared at him, but he only grinned and waved her back to her mother.

"But now it is clear to me," continued her mother. "You have used your cleverness to attract the attention of Lord Chesterfield, and I have no doubt that his attentions are fixed on you, given what I was witness to in this very room. I had thought he would prefer Jane, of course, but with Mr. Bingley's quick actions in capturing our Jane's affections, I suppose he was forced to look elsewhere. How clever of you to have caught his eye!"

"I do not think it happened quite that way, Mama," said Elizabeth, feeling quite faint. "His lordship is only being polite."

"I am sure he is, my dear," replied Mrs. Bennet, patting Elizabeth's knee. "Now we have only to nurture that spark of interest Mr. Darcy displays in Lydia, and our family's fortunes shall be on the rise!"

A chuckle and a shake of his head preceded Mr. Bennet's announcement that he would retire to his bookroom, leaving Elizabeth at the mercy of her mother. She glared at his retreating back, but then her mother pulled all the girls back into her scheming. It was many minutes before Elizabeth was able to escape to her room. If her mother's blindness was not so amusing, Elizabeth might have felt put out!

There had been times when their visit to Longbourn had taken on the aspect of a spectacle, but Darcy found himself strangely unmoved by the family's eccentricities. They were not so different from some of the families of lower standing in the neighborhood in which he himself lived, and though the attention was irksome at times, as was the blatant matchmaking, there was no true harm in any of them. Mrs. Bennet was difficult to endure, but Darcy chose to see the love and concern for her children, rather than avaricious greed.

Fitzwilliam was likewise unmoved by some of the foibles to which they were witness, and he was not shy about stating his approbation. Fortunately, he chose to do so later that afternoon when they were not in company with Miss Bingley. Darcy shuddered to think of what the woman would say if she heard the Bennets—and in particular, Miss Elizabeth—referred to in such glowing terms.

"In short," Fitzwilliam was saying, "Miss Elizabeth Bennet is a gem, a rough one to be certain, having been raised in the hinterlands of the kingdom by a woman who possesses little sense. But even if it is for nothing more than her success in raising her most enchanting daughter, I must esteem Mrs. Bennet."

"I suspect that Miss Elizabeth's character might be more the influence of her father than her mother," replied Darcy. "They seem to think much alike, though Mr. Bennet is taciturn. Miss Elizabeth is anything but."

"Aye, you might be correct." Fitzwilliam stroked his chin. "She certainly inherited her intelligence from Mr. Bennet. In fact, it seems to me the only girls who inherited anything other than their looks from Mrs. Bennet are Miss Lydia and, perhaps, Miss Kitty."

Darcy allowed it to be so, but he did not say anything further. Fitzwilliam was more than ready to fill the void.

"Regardless, Miss Elizabeth is truly the brightest star among the Bennet sisters. I must own to some surprise that there are no men beating a path to Longbourn's door for the privilege of being admitted to her presence."

"You forget that Longbourn is a small estate and Miss Elizabeth likely does not possess a large dowry. Her person is enough to tempt many a man, but her situation is likely what keeps them away."

Fitzwilliam turned a critical eye on Darcy. "Is that the infamous

Darcy pride speaking?"

"No," replied Darcy, deciding it was not worth his cousin's teasing to correct him. "It is merely the realist. As you know, I think highly of Miss Elizabeth. But there are many men who would not consider her even for an instant due to the drawbacks of paying attention to her."

"Well, I am not such a one," declared Fitzwilliam. "She is as fine a woman as I have ever met. Any man would be fortunate to receive her favor in response."

Darcy was surprised. His cousin had given her his attention, but Darcy had thought it was nothing more than his typical playful and amiable nature at work. "Are you speaking of anything more than simple praise?"

"At the present, I know not," replied Fitzwilliam. "She is a gem— that much is certain. But how would she fit into the role of a countess? That is a question I cannot answer at present."

"I am sure she would take to it with aplomb," replied Darcy, surprising himself by meaning every word he said. "In fact, I imagine Miss Elizabeth could do whatever she wished without any hesitation at all."

Fitzwilliam grunted and fell silent, and Darcy was too caught up in his own thoughts to forward the conversation.

It was not to be supposed after witnessing Fitzwilliam's blatant interest in Miss Elizabeth that Miss Bingley would allow the matter to rest. The woman had invested several years of effort into the pursuit of Darcy himself. Her focus may have shifted to his cousin, but the tenacity with which she had applied herself to it suggested that she would not easily concede defeat when it came to the bigger prize.

"Oh, Lord Chesterfield," cried she when they entered the dining room for dinner, "I must commend you for enduring Eliza's impertinence during our visit today. It is the hallmark of a good and indulgent man to allow a young woman, inexperienced in higher society, to rattle on as she did."

"I did nothing more than any other man might have, Miss Bingley," said Fitzwilliam. "I find her to be quite enchanting."

Though the lines around Miss Bingley's eyes tightened, she found a new target for her witticisms.

"And you, Mr. Darcy. Shall we be wishing you joy with your own Bennet sister? If you should fall in with Mrs. Bennet's schemes, though, you may wish to house dear Georgiana in a different location from Lydia Darcy. I am not certain she would be the best influence on your dear sister."

"Miss Lydia *is* a lovely girl," said Fitzwilliam, joining in the teasing. "I am not certain, however, that Miss Lydia would have such a detrimental effect on our dearest girl. Georgiana could do with a little liveliness, after all."

For a moment, Darcy thought of reciprocating by teasing Fitzwilliam about Miss Elizabeth, but the very thought filled him with repugnance. Thus, he decided to simply parry their remarks, at least until he was able to determine the state of his own feelings.

"Miss Lydia is a vibrant girl, indeed, but I do not think she is for me." Darcy paused and considered the matter, before saying: "I have nothing against a lively girl, but I think one of a little more experience and restraint would be my preference."

Fitzwilliam directed an odd look at Darcy, but Miss Bingley only exclaimed: "Poor Mrs. Bennet! I am certain you are breaking her heart, Mr. Darcy."

Again, Darcy decided against speaking, and he was relieved when he had no need to do so, for Miss Bingley turned her attention back to Fitzwilliam. Not for the first time since arriving at Netherfield, Darcy was grateful for Fitzwilliam's presence. Since he was the higher placed in society, it was his duty to escort Miss Bingley—the hostess—into dinner. Consequently, withstanding the woman's attentions by her side at the dinner table was also his cross to bear.

Their conversation wound on, and Darcy was amused to see that Fitzwilliam, though he was not precisely baiting the woman, was paying her far more attention than Darcy might ever have considered doing. If Miss Bingley's self-satisfied smiles were anything to go by, the woman likely thought she was making progress in her quest to capture him.

If she did, she was a fool. Fitzwilliam would no more marry Miss Bingley than Darcy would marry Miss Lydia. But Darcy had more pleasant things on which to think, so he left them to it.

"The situation is worsening, Louisa. I simply must have your assistance in preventing Charles from making a catastrophic mistake."

Louisa sighed. She had been hoping she would be able to avoid Caroline's vitriol this evening. But it was not to be, as her younger sister had invaded her room before Louisa had been able to make her escape.

With a suspicious look, Caroline sat on a nearby chair. "Are you actually supportive of this madness? Is that why you are resisting me?"

"My support or lack thereof is irrelevant in the end, Caroline," replied Louisa, massaging her temples. "As I said before, Charles will do as he pleases, and I do not think there is anything you or I can do about it."

Though Louisa would have expected otherwise, Caroline did not respond. She seemed to be thinking of what Louisa had said. It had happened little enough in the past that Louisa was surprised by it.

"Charles *is* stubborn," replied Caroline. "We will be required to recruit Lord Chesterfield and Mr. Darcy to assist."

This time Louisa did respond, and the snort which made its way through her lips caused Caroline's ire to be raised. But Louisa did not care.

"You *have* seen both men in company with the Bennets, have you not? I doubt we can induce them to say anything against Jane — certainly not the viscount, whose attention seems to be fixed on Elizabeth." Louisa paused, wondering if she should have said that, and then turned a critical look on her sister. "In fact, I am surprised you are not here trying to determine how to induce the viscount to release *his* interest."

Caroline huffed. "Lord Chesterfield is much more discerning than to lose his head over an impertinent chit such as Eliza Bennet. I have no doubt I shall be victorious there. But while *my* victory is the most important, I will not allow the Bennets *any* triumph, if I can prevent it."

While she thought to inform Caroline that there was little she could do to prevent anything, Caroline rose at that moment and barked out one last imperious command: "Think on it, Louisa. I am counting on you to assist. Do not betray our father's memory by allowing our brother to drag our name down into the mud."

And then she was gone. Louisa, disgusted at her sister's airs, took the opportunity to retreat to her husband's room, where she was relieved to climb into bed. As usual, Hurst seemed to realize when she had received a visit from Caroline, and when Louisa explained it, his response was much as hers had been.

"I would wish your sister luck, but though I would appreciate it if she was in her own home, I cannot wish such a calamity on the heads of either Darcy or Chesterfield. But she has little chance of being successful. If Bingley wishes Jane Bennet for a wife, he will have her, and neither of the cousins has any intention of being captured by her."

"I know," replied Louisa with a sigh. "I just wish I could knock some sense into her."

"That also would require great fortune." Hurst turned over and settle himself into the mattress, but before he fell silent, he spoke once again. "As for the viscount, I doubt he is having as much of an impression on Miss Elizabeth as your sister fears. I would put my money on Darcy if anyone."

"Mr. Darcy?" asked Louisa, surprised.

"Yes. He is not demonstrative, but he thinks as much of Miss Elizabeth as his cousin. More, in fact."

Hurst fell silent, leaving Louisa to her thoughts. She was not certain of what her husband was speaking, but she decided to keep a close watch on them. Miss Elizabeth marrying Mr. Darcy would not impact Caroline's plans for the viscount, but she would certainly not wish for a woman she considered inferior to marry a man she spent years chasing. Louisa sighed with frustration—it would be so much easier had she been blessed with a sister of a complying temperament like her brother's.

CHAPTER VIII

*I*t is often said that every family contains at least one objectionable member, one who's behavior embarrasses the rest or who possesses eccentricities which make his presence a trial. Elizabeth had always assumed that her family's objectionable member was her mother; even Lydia, with the right guidance, would be more tolerable than she was at present. Unfortunately, Elizabeth was to learn how mistaken she was, for Mrs. Bennet could not hold a candle on a scale of what was objectionable to a man she had never met. Would that such circumstances could continue indefinitely!

The first indication any of them had that this man was to visit was when their father mentioned the matter only days after the eldest sisters' return from Netherfield. That he did it in a manner seemingly designed to cause his family to react was not missed by Elizabeth, but she did not expect anything different from him.

When Mrs. Bennet learned that the objectionable future master of Longbourn was to attend them, her reaction was entirely predictable. "Mr. Collins is coming here?" Her voice approached a shriek, and Elizabeth was witness to more than one wince in response. "Can he not wait until you are cold in your grave to come and gloat over us?"

"Apparently, he cannot, Mrs. Bennet," replied her husband. "If you were to read his letter, however, I suspect you may be a little softened toward his coming."

Mr. Bennet stood and approached around the dinner table, holding a folded sheet of paper in his hand. His wife looked at it as if she expected it to rear up and bite her. Eventually, however, she took it and opened it, albeit gingerly. Her daughters watched her with baited breath as she read through the missive, but at length when she set the paper down on the table beside her, she was calmer than she had been a moment later. For the rest of the meal, she remained silent and contemplative. Elizabeth was not certain whether this was a good sign. But since it silenced her mother's lamentations on the subject, she found herself content.

When Mr. Collins's carriage proceeded down Longbourn's drive the following day, the sisters were afire with curiosity concerning the arrival of the gentlemen. When the man stepped out, he revealed himself to be a tall, heavyset man of perhaps thirty years, his black hair balding in the back, his manners solemn and ponderous, and his conduct a curious mix of servility and pomposity. He had not been in the house for ten minutes before Elizabeth realized he was an abject dullard, who likely had not ever had an original thought during the entire course of his life.

"What a lovely home you have, Mrs. Bennet!" said he when they all gathered in the sitting-room later that evening. Dinner had been a tiresome affair, with Mr. Collins regaling them all with tales of his situation and patroness, proving his love for the sound of his own voice. After dinner would, no doubt, prove to be equally unpleasant.

"Thank you, Mr. Collins," replied Mrs. Bennet. "It is not much, but Longbourn is our home, and we are prodigiously fond of it."

"On the contrary, Mrs. Bennet," said the man expansively, "I have never seen such a happily situated home, and it is clear the décor you have chosen compliments your family very well, indeed."

Then Mr. Collins paused, and an expression of abject mortification stole over his features. He cast his glance about as if he expected someone to appear out of thin air and chastise him. When no one was in evidence, he turned his gaze back to the Bennet matron and gave her a sickly smile.

"I should say, actually, that Longbourn is *one* of the happiest homes I have ever seen, for no manor house could ever truly compare with the home of my patroness, Lady Catherine de Bourgh. Rosings Park, her home, is truly without equal in the entire width and breadth of all England."

"Is that so?" asked Mr. Bennet, his eyes gleaming with amusement. "A home even greater than Chatsworth or Blenheim? It must be a sight to see."

Mr. Collins's head nodded so swiftly that it seemed like it was attached to his body with a hinge. "It *is*! And her ladyship manages her home with the skill of a master artisan, always knowing exactly what must be done in any situation. I am truly indebted to her ladyship for the affability and condescension which I would never have expected from one of her greatness. My humble home is, you must understand, the result of Lady Catherine's beneficence and ability to make any location, no matter how humble its circumstances, so much greater by her attention."

On and on the man went, and if he was not speaking with awe of his patroness, he was commenting on Longbourn's appointments, the doings of his parish, or his expectations of future felicity with his newly reconciled family. It was his comments concerning this last subject which caused Elizabeth some worry, but she soon found out she need not have bothered.

When the evening had progressed far enough that Mr. Bennet felt the demands of hospitality had been met, he absented himself to his study, leaving the guest in the company of his wife and daughters. As was their wont, the Bennet ladies fractured into various groups dictated by their own interests. Lydia and Kitty occupied themselves by whispering and giggling between themselves concerning subjects about which Elizabeth did not wish to speculate. Jane busied herself with some needlework, while Elizabeth and Mary took up their books—Mary's a treatise of church doctrine, while Elizabeth contented herself with a book of poetry.

As a proper young woman, Elizabeth knew she should not eavesdrop on the conversations of others, but since her mother and Mr. Collins, who were sitting nearby, were making no effort to modulate their tones, she supposed she could not be blamed.

"What brings you to Hertfordshire, Mr. Collins?" asked Mrs. Bennet almost as soon as they were seated together. Mrs. Bennet was never one to speak in an oblique manner when directness was possible.

It appeared Mr. Collins was not put off by her pointed question. "It is the particular recommendation of my patroness, Lady Catherine de Bourgh, that I attend your excellent family and heal the breach between us. In fact—"

"Yes, yes, Mr. Collins," said Mrs. Bennet, her impatience betrayed by the cutting motion of her hand. "You have spoken much of this

Lady Catherine, and she does sound like a very great lady, indeed. But surely some motive, other than your patroness's command, has prompted you hither."

Though Mr. Collins appeared a little affronted at the term "command," he readily responded. "Yes, well, there was also the matter of Lady Catherine's advice that I marry as soon as may be. As a parson, I must set the example of matrimony for those in my parish."

Mrs. Bennet gazed at him for a moment, apparently considering his words before she nodded slowly. "Yes, I can see how that would be beneficial."

"And your daughters are, indeed, lovely and amiable, Mrs. Bennet," the parson was eager to say. "I have rarely had such examples of beauty, such a wide display of feminine virtue as I see here before me tonight. You are much to be praised for raising such excellent daughters."

"They *are* good girls," said Mrs. Bennet, her eyes roving across the sisters, a hint of affection displayed in her slight smile. Elizabeth's heart was warmed; the fact that Mrs. Bennet cared for her daughters was often hidden under her manic need to see them married.

"I believe your eldest daughter is perhaps the most estimable," said Mr. Collins. "She has such an air of sweetness about her which must render her beauty and other qualities enhanced because of it."

"Ah, yes, my Jane is a veritable angel, sir," replied Mrs. Bennet. She turned back to Mr. Collins, a determination in her countenance. "But I must warn you not to fix upon Jane. In recent weeks, she has been the recipient of the attentions of a man of the neighborhood, and I believe will be very soon engaged."

Though Elizabeth knew her mother was overstating the matter at this juncture, she was glad Jane would not be forced to endure Mr. Collins's pitiful attempts at wooing. Furthermore, Elizabeth was becoming convinced that outcome was not only likely but increasingly certain.

Mr. Collins, however, frowned at this intelligence. "Is there a courtship in place? Or is she already engaged?"

"Neither, sir."

"Then I cannot imagine it is an impediment."

"The man's prior claim and already existing attentions are not an impediment?" demanded Mrs. Bennet. "I am afraid I do not understand your meaning, sir."

"Only that my offer is before you, while this other man only *may* ask for her hand." Mr. Collins's manner was stiff as if he had been mortally insulted.

"Perhaps that might be the case, sir," replied Mrs. Bennet, "if our only concern was to accept the first offer which presented itself. But my daughter's happiness is not a matter of such indifference, I assure you. Jane's inclination for Mr. Bingley is clear. I would not ask her to give up that inclination for another."

Elizabeth could hardly keep her countenance, she was so surprised. Her mother protecting her daughter's right of choice? It was more than Elizabeth had ever expected from Mrs. Bennet, whom she had always assumed would insist on any of them accepting the first proposal from any eligible gentleman.

"It *is* surprising, is it not?"

Mary, who had spoken, and who had also, it seemed, been following the conversation, directed a wry smile at Elizabeth, who returned it, albeit hesitantly. "I would not have suspected her of it. It may just be because Mr. Bingley is wealthy, and it is *Jane* of whom she speaks."

But the continuation of their conversation put the lie to that supposition.

"I suppose when you put it in such terms," said Mr. Collins, though he was quite obviously disgruntled. His eyes found the sisters again, and he seemed to consider them one by one.

"Then perhaps Miss Elizabeth, the next to her sister, in both beauty and seniority?"

Chilled by his words, Elizabeth's eyes desperately sought her mother, but Mrs. Bennet was already responding to the parson. "I am sorry, Mr. Collins, but Elizabeth also has become the favorite of an illustrious gentleman. I should also warn you that my youngest, Lydia, I also believe will be very soon engaged."

Mr. Collins's mouth worked, though no sound came out, so great was his shock. Such a state of affairs could never continue long, given the man's verbosity, and shortly thereafter Mr. Collins's mouth curled into a scowl of disgust, laced with suspicion.

"I am all astonishment, Mrs. Bennet. How did you ever manage such a coup? Three daughters to be engaged at once—I know not how it can be fathomed!"

Though Mrs. Bennet could not fail to hear the contempt in his tone, her ability to ignore it was admirable. "You have already said yourself what admirable ladies my girls are, sir. Can you be surprised that they have attracted the attention of gentlemen other than yourself?"

His scowl darkened, but Mr. Collins was forced to own his words, and he grunted his agreement. Thereafter, his eyes found first Mary, and then Kitty. It was clear he did not like what he found in them.

"Might I suggest Mary as an alternative?" asked Mrs. Bennet.

Mary stiffened at Elizabeth's side, but Elizabeth only leaned toward her and whispered: "Do not worry, Mary. Did Mama not just say that her daughters would be allowed the power of choice?"

"I have no wish for that determination to be put to the test by one of them refusing a proposal of marriage; least of all, should *I* be the one to refuse!"

A giggle escaped Elizabeth's lips and soon Mary joined in. Together, however, they turned their attention back to Mr. Collins's response.

"I am not certain your middle daughter possesses the . . . attributes I would expect in a wife," replied Mr. Collins.

Elizabeth was immediately offended on her sister's behalf; she knew exactly to what Mr. Collins referred. Mary, however, only breathed a sigh of relief.

"On the contrary, sir, she is pious and knowledgeable and takes prodigious care of Longbourn's tenants. I am certain she would be a credit to any parson who might have her as his wife."

Mr. Collins grunted, but he turned his attention to Kitty. "And Miss Catherine . . . Well, I am sorry, Mrs. Bennet, but I am not certain she is ready to be a wife. Or her youngest sister, for that matter."

"Perhaps," said Mrs. Bennet noncommittally. "But I think Mary and Kitty might surprise you. Regardless, they are my only daughters whom I believe to be presently unattached. I am happy, of course, if you take some time to think on the matter and determine what you wish to do."

"Of course," replied Mr. Collins.

He was largely silent for the rest of the evening. Despite Mrs. Bennet's words, his gaze often fixed on Jane or Elizabeth as often as it did on either Mary or Kitty. When he retired, as he did early, he seemed in the midst of deep thought on the matter. Elizabeth was not certain what he would ultimately do, but she was at least heartened that she herself was not in the running for the dubious position of the man's favorite. She was equally relieved that any of her sisters who were not inclined to him—which included them all, by her estimation—would not be forced to marry him.

Elizabeth had always enjoyed studying those persons of intricate personalities. Though she could readily acknowledge they were no more estimable than those of a simpler character, there was always something new to discover, some new understanding to be gained. But while complex characters were always revealing new facets to her interested eyes, simpler people were easy to understand — sometimes painfully so. In the case of Mr. Collins, he fell into the latter category, a fact which could be deemed a blessing or a curse.

When the family members made their way to the breakfast table the morning after Mr. Collins's arrival, the man himself appeared, and it was immediately evident that he was sulking. His reproachful looks at Mrs. Bennet were punctuated by his equally petulant glances at both Elizabeth and Jane. When he looked at Mary, his expression soured further, a fact which Elizabeth, who had become protective of her younger sister in previous months, found offensive. Then he looked at Kitty and his expression became pinched, as if he was forced to contemplate some distasteful task.

For her part, Mrs. Bennet was ignoring the man, a surprising development, as Elizabeth might have thought her mother would be promoting a match with either Kitty or Mary fervently. Then again, the previous night's tête-à-tête between them had illustrated a facet to her mother's character she would never have expected. Perhaps she truly wished to consider her daughters' wishes before pushing them into marriage. Or perhaps she felt secure enough in the attention paid to them by the three Netherfield men. Regardless, she spoke with Kitty and Lydia — in their usual loud and laughing manner, and left Mr. Collins to his own devices.

"Denny is to return today, you know," said Lydia, speaking of the officers, as was usual of late. "He has been in town, but he should be returned by now. Kitty and I will walk to Meryton today to ask after him."

"Of course, you must, my dear," replied Mrs. Bennet. "I am certain he finds you enchanting, as all the officers must."

"And *I* am an especial favorite of Sanderson," said Kitty. It was Kitty's lot in life to be continually attempting to equal Lydia in her mother's eyes.

"I am sure you are, Kitty, my dear," said Mrs. Bennet. "But you must own that Sanderson is not nearly so handsome as Denny."

"I beg your pardon, Mrs. Bennet," said Mr. Collins, "but am I to understand this Mr. Denny is your daughter's suitor?"

Mr. Bennet snorted, and Elizabeth and Mary exchanged a grin. Lydia preened, but Mrs. Bennet only turned to Mr. Collins and said in an offhand tone: "Of course not, Mr. Collins. Mr. Denny is, after all, naught but a lieutenant, and as such, he is not able to afford a wife."

It was clear that Mr. Collins was confused. "Then who—"

"Mama, we wish to go as early as possible! We shall leave directly after breakfast."

Huffing because he was cut off, Mr. Collins hunched over his meal and stuffed a large forkful of food in his mouth, glaring at Lydia as she continued to prattle on. Then Mrs. Bennet proved that she was not completely relieved of the instinct to scheme for her daughters' supposed benefit.

"Mr. Collins," said she, pulling the man's unwilling eyes to her, "perhaps you would enjoy a bit of exercise? Meryton is only a mile distant, and it would give you the opportunity to come to know my daughters better."

As one, the Bennet daughters looked at their mother, appalled at her betrayal. Mr. Collins, however, blinked once, and then a slow smile settled over his face.

"Yes, indeed, Mrs. Bennet. I would find that agreeable, indeed." He paused and looked once between Mary and Kitty. In a weighty tone, he addressed Kitty: "Miss Catherine, would you do me the honor of walking into town with me?"

Astonished, Kitty looked at Mr. Collins as if he had sprouted a second head. At her side, Lydia giggled with glee, prompting Kitty to shoot her an injured glance. This, of course, only made Lydia giggle harder. In the end, Kitty muttered something which Mr. Collins took as agreement, and she and Lydia retreated from the room as if the very hosts of the underworld were on their heels.

When the sisters had gathered together with Mr. Collins to walk to Meryton, the man expected to command Kitty's attention. Unfortunately, he had not counted on her commitment to avoiding him. He soon learned.

"Miss Kitty!" exclaimed he when they stepped from the house. "I believe I asked you to accompany me to the town."

Though Kitty seemed to wish for anything else, she assented and set out with the rest of them. It was unfortunate that her good behavior lasted for about two minutes into the walk. The man insisted she take his arm for support, which she did, though reluctantly. When they set off, Mr. Collins's mouth kept pace, for he seemed to think they could not take two steps without him filling the air with his commentary. Unfortunately for the parson, he could not have designed his words to be less interesting to the fourth Bennet sister had he tried.

"What a charming land this is!" said he when they had left

Longbourn's drive. "Of course, it is not the equal of Kent, especially not the locale in which sits my patroness's great estate, Rosings Park. Indeed, that land seems to be have been designed with all the best parts of beauty, waiting for the eventual adornment to make it perfect, which is, of course, the great house her ladyship calls home.

"You shall see it someday, of course," continued he, blithely unaware of Kitty's growing horror. "In fact, if I may be so bold, I believe I may state that there is nothing there which shall not be to your taste. The parsonage, though small, is a handsome building, perfectly situated in a beautiful garden, and you will have the patronage of the great Lady Catherine de Bourgh, which must certainly be the most beneficent boon for any young bride."

Finally, Kitty could take no more. "Excuse me, Mr. Collins!" squeaked she, and she disengaged her arm from the parson's and scurried forward to where Lydia was walking in front of the rest of the group. Mr. Collins stopped and gaped at her.

Lydia, who had been enjoying Kitty's misfortune, welcomed Kitty with a giggle and a few whispered words, which turned into a conversation. Even Mr. Collins, dullard though he was, could not miss the gist of it, for even if he was so witless as to misunderstand the meaning of her hasty retreat, the looks Kitty shot him, which were not flattering in nature, could not be misunderstood.

Still, it could not be said the parson was not determined, for he hurried forward and attempted to put himself near Kitty to continue his wooing. When he came close, however, Kitty only turned and scowled at him. "I am speaking with my sister, sir."

That pointed dismissal still was not enough, for Mr. Collins hovered for several more moments, making several ineffectual comments, none of which were heeded. This lasted until about halfway to Meryton, when the man huffed in annoyance and gave up, casting his glance about at the other sisters. At this moment, Elizabeth's understanding of the man's character was proven, for she witnessed his calculating gaze and was certain he was pondering how he could steal one of them away from their supposed suitors. It was Elizabeth who was the fortunate sister to whom he spoke next.

"Your sister is . . ." Mr. Collins paused, searching for the words which would not reveal him to be completely unkind. "She is seventeen, is she not?"

"Kitty recently turned seventeen," replied Elizabeth.

Mr. Collins glared at Kitty's back. "If I may be so uncharitable, I wonder that she is already out. She still seems to lack maturity."

As it was, Elizabeth did not disagree with the parson in this instance. "She is still full young," said Elizabeth. "And Lydia is the same. We expect that with age and experience she will grow into an estimable young lady. But as you say, she is yet immature."

Mr. Collins grunted, but it was clear he did not wish to speak of Kitty. Instead, he turned to Elizabeth and pondered her for several moments, his thoughts so distracted he almost tripped on a tree root as they walked. Elizabeth stifled a laugh, and she imagined Mr. Collins's thoughts as a slow-moving river, one which was particularly shallow and lacking any complexity.

"I understand from your mother that you and your eldest sister have been courted recently by a pair of gentlemen in the neighborhood. In addition, your words of your youngest sister confuse me, for she intimated that Miss Lydia was also being courted."

Elizabeth had a dilemma. If she revealed her mother's words for the wishes she knew them to be, she risked turning Mr. Collins's ardor in her direction. But she did not wish to lie either. In the end, she decided that the viscount had paid her enough attention that she could prevaricate a little and not be telling Mr. Collins a falsehood.

"First, I should warn you that my mother's thinking with regard to Lydia is perhaps a little wishful. Lydia is, as you noted yourself, still too young to be married. Regardless, I do not think my father would give consent, even if someone did offer for her."

"And as for yourself?" asked Mr. Collins, his tone too eager. "And Miss Bennet?"

"I expect that Jane will soon be engaged, indeed," replied Elizabeth. "Mr. Bingley shows every sign of possessing ardent feelings for her, and Jane's are no less deep. As for myself—let us simply say that I am enjoying the society of a young gentleman. For anything more . . . Well, I am eager to learn what my future will be."

It was clear from Mr. Collins's gaze that he was not satisfied by her response, but as they strode into the outskirts of Meryton at that moment, he seemed content to ponder what he had heard for the present. Knowing he would almost certainly come to the wrong conclusion and thinking to echo what Mrs. Bennet had told him the previous night, Elizabeth made one more comment.

"But even if I am ultimately not pursued by the man who is currently paying attention to me, please remember that I will not marry unless I esteem the man who offers for me. My sisters are all of like mind with me, Mr. Collins. Our esteem is not easily bought, nor is it likely to be gained in a few days, with nothing more than a superficial acquaintance."

Mr. Collins frowned. "You would refuse a proposal from a man who has the power to give you a good home for nothing more than a whim?"

"I did not say that, Mr. Collins," replied Elizabeth, eager to be finished with this conversation. "All I said is that I require more than such things in a marriage partner. I wish for true esteem, as well as the means to keep myself in comfort. I certainly shall not know a man's character until I have known him for some weeks at the very least."

With these words, Elizabeth stepped forward and caught Jane's arm, smiling at Mary as she rolled her eyes. The three sisters stepped forward, following their younger sisters and keeping them close by. Mr. Collins seemed content to follow them at a short distance, and though Elizabeth could feel his eyes upon her, she ignored him. Let him puzzle out what she meant. Regardless, she was certain the man would not obtain a wife at Longbourn after only a week's stay.

As was always the case when the Bennet sisters—the youngest sisters, anyway—went to town, they flitted from one shop to the next, exclaiming about this ribbon or that bonnet, visited the sweet shop for sugar sticks, and stopped by their Aunt Phillips's house for a word with their aunt. Mrs. Phillips, unfortunately, was beset with a cold that day, and they could not stay with her long. Mr. Collins was not introduced.

The one thing missing from the early part of their time in town was the man for whom the youngest Bennets had been searching, and Elizabeth steadfastly refused to allow them to call at the officers' barracks to ask after him.

"No, Lydia. That is not done. You would appear to be nothing but a flirt if you were to go looking for Lieutenant Denny in such a manner."

"But, Lizzy!" exclaimed Lydia, exasperated by Elizabeth's intransigence.

"I agree with Lizzy," said Jane. "We shall not go to the barracks."

Lydia huffed, and Elizabeth happened to catch sight of Mr. Collins. The man was watching the youngest Bennets, a frown upon his features. If Elizabeth had not been annoyed with her sisters, she might have taken umbrage at what she saw in his countenance.

"Oh, look, Lydia!" exclaimed Kitty. "Is that not Denny there?"

Forgetting about the confrontation with her elder sisters, Lydia spun and looked where Kitty was pointing. "It is!" squealed she.

"Put your arm down, Kitty," said Elizabeth. "It is not at all polite to point."

"And you should not draw attention to us," added Jane.

Lieutenant Denny, however, spied the Bennet sisters, and he turned toward them, pulling along with him another man who was dressed in the usual suit of a gentleman. As soon as they caught sight of the newcomer, the attention of the youngest Bennets was caught by him, and poor Denny found himself quite ignored. For her part, Elizabeth could understand why, for the man was one of the handsomest men Elizabeth had ever seen. He was tall, erect of bearing, his shock of curly brown hair fell over his forehead, and his eyes were the bluest Elizabeth had ever seen in a man. He was almost as handsome as Mr. Darcy, Elizabeth thought to herself.

Of course, such a thought could not occur to Elizabeth without causing her embarrassment, and she was suddenly grateful that no one could read her mind. From where had that thought originated? She did not know, but thinking critically for a few moments, she was forced to acknowledge that it was true.

"Ladies," said Mr. Denny, bowing low when he stepped up to them. "You are all looking very well today."

At that moment, Elizabeth happened to be looking at the man with Mr. Denny, and she saw a look of overt interest on his face. Furthermore, she was also able to just make out his softly murmured: "*Very* well, indeed."

Confused, she almost stepped back a pace, wondering what this man had meant by his words. But Denny was continuing to speak, and Elizabeth was forced to attend his words. He exchanged a few pleasantries with Kitty and Lydia, followed by a few jovial words with the elder sisters, then turned to his friend, begging leave to introduce him.

"Ladies, I have the distinct pleasure of introducing you to my good friend, Mr. George Wickham. Wickham, these ladies are the Bennet sisters: Miss Jane Bennet, Miss Elizabeth, Miss Mary, Miss Catherine, and Miss Lydia."

The clearing of a throat behind her reminded Elizabeth that they were accompanied by another that morning, and she rose to the occasion, introducing her cousin to them. Mr. Collins's bow, however, was so shallow and stiff, that Elizabeth was certain that he considered himself to be quite above a militia officer and his friend.

"Are you to stay here long, Mr. Wickham?" asked Lydia as soon as she could, impatient for details about their new acquaintance.

"All winter, actually," said Mr. Wickham. They were the first words he spoke, revealing a higher tone than Elizabeth might have expected, though not at all unpleasant. "You see, I have taken a commission in Colonel Forster's regiment. I have only just arrived now."

"And we are happy to have you, sir," said Elizabeth, though she was not at all certain that was the truth. "I am certain you will lend the regiment much distinction."

Mr. Denny laughed. "Please, do not inflate Wickham's opinion of himself, Miss Elizabeth. He already possesses enough swagger for any two other officers."

"You misrepresent me, Denny," said Mr. Wickham. But his tone was all confidence, and Elizabeth could immediately sense that he was pleased by the attention. What this meant about his character she was not certain, but she felt it prudent to be on her guard.

"It is unfortunate that our aunt has caught a cold," said Lydia, "else we could become acquainted with you immediately. But she has canceled her card party, and we are left without amusement this evening."

"I am certain we shall become acquainted before long, Miss Lydia," said Mr. Wickham. "There is plenty of time before the regiment moves on in the spring."

"I certainly hope so, Mr. Wickham," replied Lydia.

For Elizabeth's part, she did not like the way the conversation was progressing, but before she could speak up, the sound of voices hailing them caught their attention. They turned to see Lord Chesterfield, Mr. Darcy, and Mr. Bingley approaching them. They were leading their horses, having just dismounted, and Elizabeth, whose eyes sought out Mr. Darcy, noted that he was looking past her. His gaze was fixed upon Mr. Wickham, and his expression was not friendly. For that matter, Lord Chesterfield's eyes appeared to have been chiseled from diamond, so hard were they.

"How fortunate we are!" said Mr. Bingley, the only man not affected. "We were to go to Longbourn to call on you. How do you do, Miss Bennet?"

Jane replied that she was quite well, but Elizabeth had no time at present for the amiable Mr. Bingley. She turned instead and focused on Mr. Wickham, noting the man's pale countenance, the way he regarded Lord Chesterfield and Mr. Darcy with something akin to dread.

"Ladies," said Lord Chesterfield, his eyes never leaving Mr. Wickham's countenance. "How do you do this fine morning?"

"We are quite well, my lord," replied Elizabeth. Then a sudden thought came to her mind, and she blurted it out before she could think on the matter. "We were just making a new acquaintance when you arrived."

"Ah, yes, Mr. George Wickham. Darcy and I are quite familiar with Mr. Wickham, you see.

"Darcy, Fitzwilliam," said Mr. Wickham, finally finding his tongue. "It has been some months, has it not?"

"It has," said Mr. Darcy, his tone implying it had not been nearly long enough.

"Indeed," said Lord Chesterfield. He turned back to Elizabeth and addressed her, though she had the distinct impression that he was aware of everyone else in the party and making certain they could all hear him. "You see, Wickham is the son of the Darcy family's former steward, so the connection goes back many years. Wickham played with Darcy — and myself when I was at Pemberley — when we were all young." He turned back to Mr. Wickham. "I do not think we have seen you since your father and Darcy's passed away." The viscount snorted. "Of course, I am well aware of the fact that Darcy has *heard* from you."

Mr. Wickham swallowed. "Of course. I try to keep in contact with the dear companions of my youth."

"As do we all, Wickham," replied Lord Chesterfield.

Then he turned and began to speak with Elizabeth directly. Mr. Bingley was speaking with Jane, while Kitty and Lydia were conversing with Mr. Denny, Mary keeping a close eye on them. Mr. Darcy, however, had not taken his eyes from Mr. Wickham, and his gaze was distinctly unfriendly. After a moment of this, he stepped close to Mr. Wickham and said something to him in a low tone, and while Mr. Wickham did not respond, he watched Mr. Darcy as if he expected him to turn feral and attack at any moment.

A moment later, anger seemed to come over him, and he glared back at Mr. Darcy. But Mr. Darcy did not give an inch.

"Denny," said Mr. Wickham, his tone clipped, "I believe the colonel is waiting for us."

It seemed that Mr. Denny had seen nothing amiss, for he only agreed and made his farewells. The two men left soon after, leaving the Bennet girls in the company of the three gentlemen from Netherfield and the unwanted presence of Mr. Collins. Elizabeth wondered what had happened. It was not in her nature to not wish to know all, little though she thought it likely her curiosity would be gratified.

CHAPTER IX

*T*he moment the militia officer and Darcy's personal nemesis left, Miss Lydia rounded on him.

"What did you say to Mr. Wickham?" demanded she. "The poor man fled because of your incivility."

Surprised, Darcy turned on Miss Lydia, a retort springing to his lips. He restrained himself, but before he could speak, Fitzwilliam stepped in.

"I can well imagine what Darcy said to Wickham, Miss Lydia. But now is not the time or the place for *that* discussion. Come—let me escort you back to your home."

Lydia regarded the viscount for a moment, her gaze straying to Darcy himself again before she nodded and accepted Fitzwilliam's arm. The rest of the Bennet sisters had realized something was occurring, for they had all turned their attention to their youngest sibling. That was when Darcy realized that the sisters were not alone that day; they were accompanied by a tall portly man whom Darcy had never met.

"Ah, yes," said Miss Elizabeth, correctly sensing the train of his thoughts.

Before it became awkward—she could not introduce the man until

Darcy requested it, after all—Darcy smiled at her and nodded. "We would be pleased if you would introduce your friend to us, Miss Elizabeth."

With obvious relief, Miss Elizabeth said: "Please allow me to introduce our father's cousin, Mr. William Collins. Mr. Collins, this is Lord Anthony Fitzwilliam, the Viscount Chesterfield, and Mr. Fitzwilliam Darcy, his cousin."

Darcy and Fitzwilliam bowed to the man, but Mr. Collins did not respond, for there was a look of such stupefaction on his face that for a moment he could not respond. At length, however, he found his tongue. Darcy wished he had not.

"Did I hear aright? Am I in the august presence of *two* of Lady Catherine de Bourgh's esteemed nephews, including—though I never thought I would be in the presence of a peer—the honorable Viscount Chesterfield?"

"I believe you have it all in order, old man," replied Fitzwilliam. He shot an amused grin at Darcy, but Darcy only shook his head. They were both aware of the kind of man with whom their aunt liked to surround herself. "But perhaps it would be best if we escorted the Bennet ladies home. Do you not agree?"

"Magnificent suggestion, your lordship!" agreed Mr. Collins with alacrity, completely misunderstanding Fitzwilliam's sardonic tone. "Perhaps we could speak more as we are walking, for I have much to tell you. I have but recently come from Kent, from the parish your aunt in her gracious condescension has bestowed upon me, and I am sure I must have more recent intelligence as to the health and happiness of your excellent aunt and cousin. I would be happy to share it with you."

"Trust me, Mr. Collins," said Fitzwilliam, "I am sure your intelligence cannot be greater than that which we already possess."

Darcy turned away to hide the smile which threatened to break out at Fitzwilliam's overt mocking of the man, and he noticed that Miss Elizabeth was in similar straits. Eager to avoid being forced to walk with the parson, Darcy offered his arm to the young woman. Miss Elizabeth quickly accepted it, proving that she had no more wish to be beset by the parson than he had himself. Thus, with Fitzwilliam escorting Miss Lydia, Miss Bennet and Bingley paired up, and with Miss Mary walking close by Miss Catherine, they began to walk toward the edge of town and toward Longbourn.

It was several moments before Darcy heard the sound of hurried footsteps as Mr. Collins overcame his stupefaction and avoided being left behind. They all walked for some time in relative silence while

Darcy considered his aunt and her penchant for surrounding herself with those who would never dare challenge her, wondering if she had not outdone herself in this instance.

"Mr. Darcy?"

The sound of his name on his companion's lips brought Darcy from his reverie, and he looked to his side to see Miss Elizabeth watching with evident curiosity.

"I apologize, Miss Elizabeth. It seems I was wool-gathering."

"It is no trouble, sir," replied she. "I was simply curious—I had the distinct impression that your association with Mr. Wickham is not a happy one."

"There is *no* association between us, Miss Elizabeth," replied Darcy shortly. "There has not been since before my father passed away, and there never shall be again."

Miss Elizabeth nodded, though slowly. "It is as I suspected. I could easily see that you were not happy to see him." She paused and then looked up at him. Darcy was surprised to see the determination in her eyes, though he knew he should not. "Can you tell me about him? I do not mean to pry into your private affairs, sir, but I would not remain ignorant if a viper has slithered into our midst."

"It is not a secret, Miss Elizabeth," replied Darcy with a sigh. "My association with Mr. Wickham has not been a happy one since our childhoods. There are many who could tell you of him if you knew where to ask.

"He was my father's favorite, you see since Wickham has always had the talent of recommending himself to those of greater consequence. My father, thinking highly of him, was his patron at school and later at Cambridge, and it is by his actions that Wickham has been educated. Unfortunately, my father was never privy to the other side of Wickham, never knew that underneath the charm and sense of humor existed a man of little morals and a proclivity for unsavory habits."

Miss Elizabeth watched him, seeming to see right through him. It made Darcy more than a little uncomfortable, to own the truth, as did her next question. "I do not doubt you, sir. He struck me as someone who should not be trusted almost at once. But I wonder why you did not inform your father of his character. Might he not have taken steps to reclaim Mr. Wickham, or at least withdrawn his patronage?"

"You see clearer than I might have thought," replied Darcy, turning to look up the path at those who were walking in front of them. "I have often asked myself that question, and while I have many excuses I told myself over the years, I have few real answers. Perhaps at the root of it, I wished to believe there was something left of my childhood companion. Perhaps I wished to believe him redeemable."

The feeling of a hand covering his arm brought Darcy's attention back to the woman at his side, and he noticed how she had brought her free hand up, to circle his arm. It was incongruous to the moment, but he noted how small and delicate her hands were. He almost fancied he could feel their heat through the fabric of her glove and his shirt, jacket, and overcoat, though he knew that was silly. Her eyes were solemn as she looked up at him, and he noted compassion in their depths directed at him. A warmth welled up within him. This was a woman of rare mettle and worth above the price of rubies.

"I understand, sir. You have my apologies—I should not have questioned you in such a manner."

"On the contrary, Miss Elizabeth," replied Darcy, "you asked nothing that I have not asked myself." Darcy brought his own hand up to cover hers. "I am certainly not offended, especially when your sympathy comforts me. Please take heed of my words: Mr. Wickham is not a good man, and I would not see you hurt."

"I shall take care." She paused and then said: "So your words to him were a warning?"

"Indeed," replied Darcy. "I informed him that not only was Fitzwilliam acquainted with his commanding officer, but that he had better not run up debts in town, or it will go ill with him."

Miss Elizabeth's eyes widened. "He is a debtor?"

"Far more than you know. I myself hold enough of his debts to see him in prison for the rest of his life."

"Then I shall warn my father. I am certain he will speak with the merchants about offering credit."

"There is no need. As soon as we arrive at Longbourn, Fitzwilliam and I will speak with your father. Furthermore, I do not doubt Fitzwilliam will visit Colonel Forster and warn him, and he will, in turn, warn the shopkeepers. Fitzwilliam still has many contacts in the army, and if Wickham steps out of line, he may just discover that joining the militia was the worst mistake he has ever made."

Miss Elizabeth grinned at that moment, and though such talk was not the sort of subject to inspire glee, Darcy thought he understood. This was a young woman who lived in this town and who would be in danger because of Wickham's habits. Furthermore, Darcy knew first hand that her two youngest sisters, still silly and immature, would be prime targets for a libertine such as Wickham. She would naturally wish them to be protected.

"While I cannot wish for the ill fortune of another," said she, "I hope Mr. Wickham is not here long."

"I agree with you, Miss Bennet. It would be best for all concerned if he would simply resign his commission and leave. But Wickham has never been prudent. I expect we will be required to suffer his presence for at least some time." Darcy turned and regarded her, attempting to impart exactly how serious he was. "You should take great care when you are near Mr. Wickham. He is not a good man."

"I will do so, sir. I thank you for the warning."

"Cousin Elizabeth!"

The sound of the parson's voice startled them all, and they stopped walking, Darcy turning to look at the man askance. He was watching them, his eyes a little wild and filled with condemnation for the woman by Darcy's side. What was the meaning of that?

"Perhaps you should not be walking so closely with Mr. Darcy," said Mr. Collins. "I would be happy to escort you instead."

"I believe I would appreciate Miss Elizabeth's company myself," said Lord Chesterfield.

It was clear that Mr. Collins desperately wished to object, but equally evident he was not capable of gainsaying anything so great a man said. He watched with suspicion as Elizabeth took the viscount's arm, but he did not object. But he put himself into position behind them—behind Lord Chesterfield's horse, actually, who was plodding along obediently after them. Lydia went to walk with Kitty again, while Mary took up a new position on Mr. Darcy's arm.

"I hope you were not reluctant to walk with me, Miss Elizabeth," said the viscount. "I apologize if I seemed officious, but it seemed that you—and Darcy, for that matter—required rescuing from your father's cousin."

Elizabeth turned an arch look on his lordship. "And why would Mr. Darcy require rescuing from an unassuming parson such as Mr. Collins?"

"I don't know that I would call him unassuming," replied Lord Chesterfield with a laugh. "Perhaps it is more appropriate to say that *Mr. Collins* required rescuing from *my cousin*. Darcy does not suffer fools easily, and though I have only just made your cousin's acquaintance, he did not strike me as a man Darcy would willingly endure."

This time it was Elizabeth's turn to laugh. "I believe, sir, you have just referred to my cousin as being a fool, though in an oblique way."

The viscount grinned. "That is *one* interpretation of my statement, yes. However, in my defense, I will state that as I know my aunt well, I understand her preferences. I have often seen the likes of Mr. Collins in her employ, so it took no great discernment to understand his character."

It was much the same as the thoughts Elizabeth herself had espoused, and she found it more than a little diverting. "If Mr. Collins possessed a deep, intricate character, I might accuse you of judging hastily. Fortunately for you, however, he does not. I cannot claim your likeness of him is incorrect."

They walked on for several more moments, Elizabeth sneaking a surreptitious look behind to ensure that Mr. Collins was not close enough to have heard their conversation. The man appeared to be attempting to find some way to bypass the viscount's horse, but when he saw Elizabeth looking at him, he scowled at her and moved to the side. Soon he was walking directly by their side and not far distant.

"It *is* kind of you, Lord Chesterfield, to favor my poor cousins with your presence. And Mr. Darcy, of course. But I would be happy to relieve you of the burden of escorting Cousin Elizabeth to her father's home."

"What burden do you call it, Mr. Collins?" asked Lord Chesterfield. "In fact, I find the Bennet ladies to be engaging and interesting. It is no burden at all to be in the presence of such estimable ladies."

"And it does you credit, sir," said Mr. Collins, blithely unaware of the note of censure in the viscount's voice. "But I am aware of the ways of great men. You may withdraw without any stain of your honor or of any of us thinking any ill of you."

"I believe, Mr. Collins, that I am much more aware of the ways of great men, as you call it, than are you. Though I would not presume to call myself great, I know my own purposes. I do not care for the insinuation in your tone or your words. I suggest you be silent before you anger one of your patroness's nephews."

Mr. Collins gaped at the viscount, for the anger in his words could not be mistaken, even by one such as the parson. While his attempt to pull Elizabeth away from Lord Chesterfield was foiled, it seemed he still did not wish to leave her in the man's company. Instead, he turned the subject and began to speak of his patroness and her daughter, informing the viscount of every piece of information concerning their doings which he thought to be of interest. It was with the droning of his voice that they passed the remainder of the walk.

*   *   *

By the time they reached Longbourn, Fitzwilliam was ready to strangle a certain parson. The man's ability to speak was positively without limit, and his words were so pompous, though mixed with a curious level of servility, that Fitzwilliam did not quite know what to make of him. There was something happening here, something Fitzwilliam could not quite understand, but which concerned Miss Elizabeth. Whether the man was attempting to court her — which was strange, as Fitzwilliam was certain they had only just become acquainted — he was not sure. But he seemed intent on pulling her away.

The Bennet sisters invited them to come inside, which was accepted with alacrity. Darcy shared a look with Fitzwilliam, and he understood it quite well — Mr. Bennet was to be warned about a certain officer who had joined the local regiment. Bingley entered the house and went with Miss Bennet into the sitting-room to entertain their mother. Fitzwilliam was grateful for the man's amiable nature, for it allowed Fitzwilliam and Darcy to attend to the more important task.

"May I assume that you wish to see my father?" asked Miss Elizabeth, when Darcy came near.

Surprised, Fitzwilliam turned a questioning glance on his cousin. Darcy nodded. "Miss Elizabeth and I spoke something of Wickham when we were walking together."

"Prudent," replied Fitzwilliam. "Very well, then, Miss Elizabeth. Please lead us to Mr. Bennet."

"Cousin Elizabeth!" exclaimed Mr. Collins at that moment. "Shall I escort you into the sitting-room?"

Fitzwilliam was reminded of the eagerness of a puppy, though Mr. Collins was certainly not so cute. He was also not amused by the parson's continued attempt to interfere. "That will not be necessary, Mr. Collins. My cousin and I must speak with Mr. Bennet, and Miss Elizabeth is to guide us to him. You may go to the sitting-room. Miss Elizabeth will join you there after she returns."

Though chagrinned, Mr. Collins did as he was bid. Fitzwilliam, however, did not miss the hardness of his glare at his cousin. Incensed, Fitzwilliam decided he had had enough of this man's idiocy.

"I do not know what your issue is with Miss Elizabeth," hissed Fitzwilliam, stepping close to Mr. Collins, "but I suggest you temper it, sir." Mr. Collins stepped back in alarm, but Fitzwilliam only followed him. "I have witnessed your dark looks at her. I suggest you be a little more aware of the impression you are making to others and cease this objectionable behavior."

Then Fitzwilliam turned and motioned to Miss Elizabeth to guide them away. She did so without comment, but Fitzwilliam thought he saw a glimmer of thanks in her eyes. What an odious relation the Bennets had!

Mr. Bennet's study was near the vestibule, down a short hall which led to the back of the house. Miss Elizabeth led them to the door and knocked. When the command was given, she opened it and ushered them inside. The master of the estate was sitting behind a sturdy oak desk with a book in his hand. It was evident he was a great reader on the order of Darcy, for his collection was impressive.

There was also obvious affection between father and daughter, for the man smiled and set his book down when he spied his daughter, though he did look at her askance. "Lizzy, my dear. I might wonder why my most sensible daughter would suddenly appear in my doorway with *two* gentlemen in tow. Though I would hardly accuse *you* of silliness, I might wonder if they have both seen your worth and have come to blows over you."

"Oh, Papa!" said Miss Elizabeth. It was clear this was a common reaction to his teasing. Darcy appeared a little shocked at the man's sportive words, but for Fitzwilliam's part, he could only grin at the warmth between father and daughter.

"Actually, Father," said she, this time speaking with a slight warning edge in her voice, "Lord Chesterfield and Mr. Darcy have, indeed, requested the opportunity to speak with you. I believe the subject of which they wish to speak is an important one."

"Then by all means, please have a seat, gentlemen." Mr. Bennet directed a shrewd look at his daughter. "Might I assume that Elizabeth knows something of your reason for seeking me out?"

"She does, sir," replied Darcy.

"In that case, as she is the most sensible of my daughters, and assuming you do not mean to speak of matters unsuitable for a young lady's ears, I would suggest she stay with us for your communication."

Fitzwilliam turned to Darcy and arched an eyebrow at him, which Darcy returned with a shrug. It would be easy enough to gloss over the details sufficiently to keep the subject matter appropriate. Thus, Fitzwilliam turned back to Mr. Bennet and nodded. Fitzwilliam and Darcy sat on the chairs in front of the desk, and when Miss Elizabeth had retrieved another from the side of the room, they began.

"As I am the one most acquainted with the *gentleman* in question, I suppose the burden of this communication falls to me." Fitzwilliam did not miss the emphasis in Darcy's words, and he could not agree more on the content of the man's character. "When we met your daughters in Meryton today, they were making the acquaintance of a man known to me. It appears he has purchased a commission in the army and is to join the regiment."

Darcy paused and turned to Fitzwilliam. "That in itself is odd, I suppose. I know for a fact Wickham has not possessed the means to make such a purchase for at least the past two years. I wonder where he obtained it."

"He is not unknown to other men of means," replied Fitzwilliam. "Maybe he persuaded one of them to purchase it for him to be rid of him, or perhaps he won it in a game of chance. Regardless, it is not germane to the subject."

"True," replied Darcy. He turned back to Mr. Bennet. "As my cousin has stated, Wickham's means of coming to Merton is not relevant. The fact that he is present at all is."

"Of what do you have to accuse him? Why is his coming of such concern?" asked Mr. Bennet. Fitzwilliam watched the man, wondering at his manner. His countenance was difficult to read, and he almost wondered if Mr. Bennet was listening with the appropriate level of gravity.

"His presence must be of concern when a man has young daughters and Wickham is known as a seducer of women."

A pregnant silence ensued. Mr. Bennet seemed reflective for several moments during which he made no response, until, at length, he nodded. "Yes, Mr. Darcy, I can see where that would be a concern. If I may clarify, is this Mr. Wickham of whom you speak merely a fortune hunter, or do his proclivities go beyond such mundane endeavors."

There was just enough sardonic disdain in Mr. Bennet's voice to tell Fitzwilliam that though his manners might not be what he might have expected, the man was listening carefully.

"You are correct in that Wickham primarily seeks a way to enrich himself," replied Darcy. "But that does not take into account, for example, the maid who works on my estate he seduced. No, Mr. Bennet, while one might take comfort in the lack of fortune preventing his depravities, in fact, that is no protection at all. Wickham cares not— all he concerns himself with is his own gratification.

"Furthermore, Wickham is a debtor and a gamester. I myself have direct knowledge of his proclivities, for I have made good his debts both in Cambridge, where we attended university together, and in the town of Lambton, which is near my estate."

"If he is all this, Mr. Darcy," said Mr. Bennet, "then why is he not in prison even now?"

Darcy instantly became defensive, but Fitzwilliam, who had often counseled Darcy in the same way, only nodded at Mr. Bennet. "I could not agree more, sir."

"He was my late father's favorite," replied Darcy. "I have stayed my hand for my father's memory."

"If you will excuse my saying so," said Mr. Bennet, "I believe your father would be disappointed in what this Mr. Wickham has become." Mr. Bennet sighed. "But I cannot gainsay you in this matter. I will, of course, see that my girls are warned against him. I will also attempt to do something with the merchants. An unscrupulous man such as you are describing may ruin the economy of the town and leave the shopkeepers without means to feed their families."

"We will do something on that front, Mr. Bennet," said Fitzwilliam. Darcy turned to regard him, and Fitzwilliam nodded at his cousin, to which Darcy responded tightly. "I am known to the colonel of his regiment. I will ensure Colonel Forster knows *exactly* what kind of man has joined his ranks. A further warning to the merchants should ensure he is unable to run up debts as he usually does. With any luck, when the neighborhood is warned against him, he will flee for greener pastures."

"Thank you, Lord Chesterfield, Mr. Darcy. Your warning is greatly appreciated."

"It is no trouble, Mr. Bennet," replied Darcy. He paused and seemed to struggle with what response to make for several moments before he sighed. "It may be that it will not be much longer before I use his debts against him. For many years I held out hope that Wickham could be induced to change his ways. In the past few years, however, I have settled for simply washing my hands of him. That was not the best way to handle the situation, I know."

"I do not mean to chastise you, sir," said Mr. Bennet. "But I am grateful all the same."

They spoke for a few more moments before Fitzwilliam and Darcy excused themselves to make their way to Meryton for an urgent appointment. Miss Elizabeth, who had stayed silent the entire time they were in the study, showed them to the door, sending a maid to summon Bingley. When they were prepared to depart, she turned to them.

"Thank you for your warning, sirs. I will ensure my sisters and friends are alerted against Mr. Wickham."

"It is no trouble, Miss Elizabeth," replied Fitzwilliam warmly. "Please give our regards to your mother and sisters."

Then they left. For Fitzwilliam's part, he could not wait to spike Wickham's wheel. The man was a snake. Fitzwilliam was anticipating a bit of well-deserved retribution.

CHAPTER X

*A*fter the gentlemen from Netherfield left Longbourn, Elizabeth thought to return to her bedchamber. Not only had the day been full of revelations, of meeting a man and immediately learning he was a libertine, but a full morning in the company of Mr. Collins's company had left her wishing for a respite. It was now clear to her that he was all that was objectionable and, furthermore, he seemed intent upon pulling one of the Bennet sisters from their suitors. While Elizabeth was not even certain she *had* a suitor at present, she was determined that she would *not* gain one in the person of her father's cousin.

It was, unfortunately, with this determination in mind, that she was spied by the man himself as she made her way to the stairs. Elizabeth was certain he had been watching for her appearance, as he presented himself out of nowhere, and faster than a man of William Collins's bulk should have found it possible to do so.

"Cousin Elizabeth! Come, sit with us in the sitting-room, for I have matters of which I would ask you."

It was all Elizabeth could do not to snap at the man, but her manners overcame the crossness she felt at his persistence. Her sense of propriety also informed her that it would be churlish to take herself up to her room now when he had already spied her. With a longsuffering sigh she could not quite suppress—and she need not have bothered trying, for she was certain the parson would have remained oblivious of it—she entered the sitting-room, though she steadfastly refused to sit near Mr. Collins.

The sofa she chose was a small one on which Mary already sat, giving Elizabeth the opportunity to avoid having the gentleman beside her. Lydia and Kitty were nowhere in sight, and Jane was not far away, attending to some sewing, though she took the entrance of her sister and their guest with a frown. Mrs. Bennet also was not present, and a quick and low query of Mary revealed their mother had been summoned by Mrs. Hill to deal with some matter of the house.

"I had not thought to meet such illustrious personages as Lady Catherine de Bourgh's nephews here, Cousin," said Mr. Collins without preamble. "What curious chance has brought them here at precisely the time that I may be of use to them?"

Elizabeth was certain the question was rhetorical in nature, and while she could not think of what possible use Mr. Collins could be to them, she essayed to respond, regardless.

"The timing *is* curious, Mr. Collins. Mr. Bingley is leasing Netherfield Park, the estate which borders Longbourn to the east. Lord Chesterfield and Mr. Darcy have come to assist him since he is unfamiliar with estate management."

"Ah, then he could not have asked anyone better to teach him than her ladyship's nephews." Mr. Collins paused, and he said as if he felt it required: "Except for her ladyship herself, of course. For I know of no one who manages an estate with such skill, such natural aptitude as her ladyship. Rosings must be the envy of Kent, and I am certain that her ladyship's nephews' properties must be similar.

"Excuse me, but where are their estates located?"

"I *am* surprised, Mr. Collins," replied Elizabeth, unable to resist teasing the silly man. "I would have thought you would already know, considering how deep in her ladyship's counsels you are."

A slight snort from Mary nearly prompted Elizabeth to burst out laughing with her sister, but Mr. Collins took no notice. "Lady Catherine *does* rely on me—yes, it is true. I was to meet her nephews next spring, you understand, for they attend her ladyship every year at Easter. But her ladyship has never raised the subject of the location of their homes."

"Ah, that would explain it," replied Elizabeth, saying nothing more.

Mr. Collins looked at her, expectation evident in his manner, and when she did not say anything further he frowned. By contrast, Mary was shaking, her handkerchief held to her mouth as she held the book in front of her, trying to keep her composure.

"And where might that be, Cousin?" asked Mr. Collins at length.

"Oh, of course!" cried Elizabeth. "Mr. Darcy's estate is in Derbyshire, quite near the Peak District, or so I understand. Lord Chesterfield's estate is also in the same county, though exactly where I do not know."

"You appear to be quite well informed, Cousin. In fact, it seemed to me that you were quite friendly with both his lordship and Mr. Darcy."

"They *have* been in the neighborhood for some weeks, Mr. Collins. I am accounted by some to be a witty conversationalist. I do not think it is strange that Mr. Darcy or Lord Chesterfield—or Mr. Bingley, for that matter—would seek me out to converse with me."

Mr. Collins's gaze flicked to where Jane sat, ostensibly concentrating on her sewing. In fact, Elizabeth was certain Jane was listening quite closely to what they were saying.

"You speak with Mr. Bingley? I had thought his gaze was fixed upon your elder sister."

"So it is," replied Elizabeth pleasantly. "But that does not mean he spends every waking moment glued to Jane's side." Mary snorted and raised her book even higher. "Mr. Bingley is a pleasant, amiable man. I find great enjoyment in speaking with him when he is not making love to my sister."

"Then you do not have any designs on any of these gentlemen?" asked Mr. Collins.

"I think you have forgotten something, Mr. Collins," replied Elizabeth. "As a woman, I must wait for the man to indicate his interest. I have no designs, as you call them, on anyone. Whether *they* have designs on *me*, I cannot say. I can assure you that Mr. Bingley has no designs on me, for his focus is largely on Jane."

The parson considered that for several minutes, and then he fixed his gaze on Elizabeth, his expression faintly demanding. "I fear I must be direct, Cousin, for there is no other means by which I may obtain the answers I seek. Your mother suggested you were all but being courted by a gentleman. Though I know the gentlemen in question are above reproach, I am aware of the stratagems young ladies employ to draw men into their webs. Thus, I would warn you that her ladyship's nephews are not men with whom to trifle. Any attempt to draw them in will surely lead to failure. I hope you are not attempting such, for if you are, I fear that you are destined to receive the severest of censure. Young ladies of your station do not become countesses."

All teasing of the silly man aside, Elizabeth was now becoming annoyed with him. "I am sorry, Mr. Collins, but I did not hear a question in your words.

"Before you speak further, however," said she when he opened his mouth to respond, "I must inform you that what you are insinuating is impertinent, and I have no intention of answering. You should be careful to refrain from disrespect yourself. Young ladies of *my* station may not become countesses, but young men of *yours* do not question viscounts, lest they receive the severest of reprimands."

Elizabeth stood. "I am sorry, sir, but I have nothing more to say on this subject."

With those words, Elizabeth left the room with Mary on her heels. Feeling all the offense of the questions of a stupid man, Elizabeth climbed the stairs and entered her room, and therein she began pacing, muttering imprecations under her breath at the parson. Mary sat on her bed and shot Elizabeth a sympathetic smile.

"I believe I have never felt so fortunate to be beneath a man's notice because of my beauty as I do now," said Mary. "Seeing you parrying the man's comments and the looks he throws at you and Jane both when he thinks no one is looking is enough to put a woman off men for a lifetime!"

"Oh, Mary!" exclaimed Elizabeth. "As I have told you before, any man who cannot see your worth and, I dare say, your beauty, is not worthy of the wonderful woman he is missing. In Mr. Collins's case, I am certain he would not recognize it if we beat him over the head with it."

"Thank you, Lizzy." Mary paused and then addressed Elizabeth seriously. "I do not know what either his lordship or Mr. Darcy is about, but I am certain I see more interest in you from *both* men than you will acknowledge."

Elizabeth huffed, but Mary only continued. "You *do* speak with both men frequently, Elizabeth. You know that Mr. Collins will not appreciate it. I have little faith that he will hold his tongue, and every expectation he will speak when he ought to remain silent and embarrass you at every turn."

A groan escaped Elizabeth's lips, and she flung herself onto the bed, lying on her back with her legs hanging down the side. "That is what I am afraid of. I do not think there is any stopping him."

"Short of inducing Papa to throw him from the house," replied

Mary.

The thought was tempting — oh, so tempting!

"Papa finds Mr. Collins too amusing for the present," said Elizabeth. "Besides, he cannot simply evict Mr. Collins without a reason. I shall never hear the end of his teasing if I make such a request."

"I was not serious in my words, Lizzy. But the fact that you even considered them informs me how much you loathe Mr. Collins's presence."

"I thought, my dear Mary, it was already evident."

Margaret Bennet, nee Gardiner, was not the senseless, nervous woman everyone thought her to be. Or, to a certain extent, she was. But she was mostly concerned — frightened silly might be a more apt description — of the future and what should happen to herself and her daughters should Mr. Bennet leave the earth before their futures were assured. Her nerves were, therefore, real, though she would readily own, if asked, that she made more of them than she should. But she was not *completely* without sense.

In the matter of Mr. Collins, Maggie knew that he was not the brightest specimen. He was portly and homely, possessed of a streak of haughtiness which would put a duke to shame, and yet sniveled and groveled when presented with one above him in society. He also possessed an exalted notion of exactly what his position in society was. But Maggie knew that a simple parson was not of a high level of society, though they *were* generally respected.

Of the matter of his suitability for her daughters, Maggie was of two minds. He was, undeniably, a single man, one in possession of an apparently fine living. He was also the heir of Longbourn, and the thought of continuing to live at the estate when her husband was gone, should Mr. Collins marry one of her daughters, was a powerful lure.

On the other hand, Maggie was certain he would not make any of them a good husband. Elizabeth was too intelligent and would not tolerate the man for more than a few moments, and Jane, too beautiful — it was fortunate, indeed, that they were both already the focus of other gentlemen. Kitty and Lydia were too lively and too young, in actuality. Though Maggie had visions of Lydia making a match with Mr. Darcy, she thought the man would be forced to wait a few years for Lydia to mature. And though Maggie had suggested Kitty as a potential bride, she had thought Mr. Collins would see her immaturity and turn his attention to Mary, having no other choice.

That he had spurned Mary showed him to be truly shallow.

One weakness Maggie knew she possessed, however, was the ability to speak of her daughters, and she often did so without any provocation. She was not blind to the looks Elizabeth and Jane sometimes gave her, but she could not help it. She had been blessed with girls who possessed every good virtue, and she felt it right that they be lauded for it. Thus, when Mr. Collins approached her on her return to the sitting-room, he hit on the exact topic which would encourage her to be articulate.

"Mrs. Bennet," said he, "I must own that I am curious concerning what you told me yesterday evening. I, myself, was witness to Mr. Bingley and your eldest when we walked back to Longbourn from Meryton."

"Ah, yes!" exclaimed Maggie her excitement taking over her tongue. "Mr. Bingley has been so very attentive to Jane. Why, he spends every moment he is able to manage in her company every time they are at the same gathering."

Maggie continued to prattle on, and her excitement was such that she did not notice the fact that Mr. Collins said little and added nothing to her comments. But she was in her element, and the lack of a response did not bother her. Had she thought to look at the parson, she might have seen the impatience written upon his brow. As it was, she did not see anything at that time which might have given her pause.

"Yes, yes, your eldest is fortunate!" interjected Mr. Collins just as Maggie was cataloging the benefits such an alliance would bring to the Bennet family. Maggie gaped at him, thinking it was unconscionably rude for a parson to interrupt a woman when she was speaking. He should wait his turn! Did he behave this way with the people in his parish?

"While I congratulate Miss Bennet on her fortunate conquest, I must own that I am more interested in your second daughter."

"I am sorry, Mr. Collins," said Maggie, wondering that he had forgotten already, "but Elizabeth is not available."

Nor would she accept you if she were, thought Maggie.

"That is unfortunate," replied Mr. Collins. "For I have come to appreciate her liveliness and wit. It seems to me that with the correct training, and the silence which my patroness's exalted station will most surely excite, she would be an excellent parson's wife.

"I would never presume to interfere," said Mr. Collins, putting his hand up to halt her tirade, "but I will own that I am curious. Can you tell me about the man who is making love to her? Perhaps I might learn from it and refine my approach, so that I may not be disappointed again in the future."

"Of course!" said Maggie, thinking it was the most sensible thing the man had said in her presence. "Why did you not ask?"

"I believe I did, madam."

The stiffness in his tone suggested annoyance, but Maggie could not understand it. The thought was soon thrust from her consciousness by other considerations. Here was another opportunity to discuss her daughters at length, and Maggie could hardly wait to do so.

"It was clear from the beginning that Mr. Bingley favored Jane," said Maggie, warming to her subject. "That match was made on the very first night they met. My other girls, however, took a little longer to make their own conquests. That makes sense, of course, as they are not nearly so beautiful as my eldest.

"At first, I thought Mr. Darcy favored Elizabeth, but it quickly became clear that it is actually Lord Chesterfield who is in love with her. You should see them when they are together, sir, for they are inseparable! And he is such a wonderful man; so tall and broad-shouldered and handsome. He is much like my Lizzy, you know; he is always jovial and happy, and he says the kindest things about us.

"As for Lydia, well when Mr. Darcy realized that Lord Chesterfield had captured the heart of my second daughter, he turned his attention to my youngest, who is much like me in temperament. He is a bit of a taciturn man, but I am certain Lydia's liveliness will soon bring him from his cocoon. She will teach him to laugh if anyone can. Now, Lydia is still full young, but I am certain in another year or two she will be ready for Mr. Darcy. And a better wife he could not find."

As Maggie was speaking with great animation on the topic, she happened to catch sight of Mr. Collins. Though the man should have been listening to her with an unwavering fascination, the silly man was shaking his head, his movements becoming more pronounced and violent by the moment. What was he doing now?

"No, no, no," said Mr. Collins, each repeat of the word louder. "It cannot be. I am sorry, Madam, but these fantasies you possess—for fantasies they are!—cannot ever come to pass. The nephews of my eminent patroness, marrying the daughters of a country gentleman? It cannot be! Her ladyship's nephews are destined for much more illustrious matches than your daughters."

"Are you suggesting my daughters are not good enough?" demanded Maggie.

"Your daughters are all that are lovely and amiable," said Mr.

Collins, the stiffness increasing by the moment.

"So they are," replied Maggie. "I am certain there can be no impediment."

"Surely you must see this is not sound, Mrs. Bennet," said Mr. Collins. "They have not the lineage, the fortune. They do not possess the connections, the nobility of spirit which would be demanded by Lord Chesterfield and Mr. Darcy. No, I am certain this all must be nothing more than your imagination."

"Do not tell me what I have seen," said Mrs. Bennet. She stood and glared down at the parson. "We are a respectable family, Mr. Collins. My girls are good enough for any man. Even a viscount and a gentleman with an ancient name, if it comes to that."

Maggie turned and marched away from him. It appeared Elizabeth was quite correct about Mr. Collins; a little of his society went a long way, indeed.

When Elizabeth descended for dinner in Mary and Jane's company—Jane had joined them soon after they left the sitting-room—she was certain something had changed. For one, her mother, while normally voluble and loud, was quiet and watchful. In fact, rather than simply maintaining silence, she carried an injured air, much as she often did when her husband teased her. But on this occasion, though Mrs. Bennet shot injured glances, they were not directed at her husband, but at their guest.

For his part, Mr. Collins was watching Mrs. Bennet with exasperation, which turned to disapproval when Elizabeth entered the room. Furthermore, she noted that when Kitty and Lydia entered, his looks were also directed at *them*, though Elizabeth was amused to note that the bulk of them were reserved for herself. Elizabeth sighed—it seemed he had learned that the cousins had supposedly fixed on Lydia and Elizabeth as prospective brides.

It was evident that Mr. Collins meant to have his say, and equally obvious that Mrs. Bennet was not of a mind to allow him. Mr. Collins tried to speak several times, but Mrs. Bennet cut him off, not allowing him to say what he wished. Though it was a display of poor manners, Elizabeth could not criticize her mother in this instance, as she had no desire to hear the parson's rants on the subject. Her father also noticed, and if his grin was any indication, he was diverted by what was happening before him.

When the family was called into the dining room, they sat in their usual places, and the food was served. It seemed Mr. Collins was not about to be denied again, for he was speaking almost as soon as they sat in their chairs.

"It has come to my attention, Cousins," said Mr. Collins, glaring at Elizabeth and Lydia in turn, "that there is a travesty occurring beneath this very roof. Though I flatter myself that I am uniquely qualified to intervene in this matter, my presence here seems like a blessing from on high. Indeed, I must consider it to be that fortunate, for I am in a position to prevent a grave error in judgment from taking place."

"That is, indeed, fortunate, Mr. Collins," said Mr. Bennet, his amusement with the parson cracking and showing more than a hint of impatience. "This, however, is the dinner hour, and I think we would all appreciate it if you would leave your sermons for Sundays."

"Have you no care for the mockery of all that is right and just which is being perpetrated under your roof and, I dare say, under your very nose?"

"So far as I am aware, Mr. Collins, the Bennets are mocking no one." Mr. Bennet winked at Elizabeth. "At least, we do not mock anyone at present."

Mr. Collins stared at Mr. Bennet, and when it became evident he would say nothing more, the parson sniffed with disdain. Then he turned his attention to Elizabeth.

"You are setting your sights too high, Cousin. As I informed you before, Lord Chesterfield is destined for a much more illustrious bride. Only humiliation awaits you if you stay this course." Then without allowing her to respond, Mr. Collins turned to Lydia. "And you, Cousin. You should hardly be out of the schoolroom, let alone chasing after a man of the consequence and position of Mr. Darcy. I cannot even begin to fathom what you are all thinking to be pursuing these two gentlemen in such a shameless manner. Does the credit of this family mean nothing to you all?

"No!" exclaimed Mr. Collins, his hand slapping down on the table, a loud punctuation of his words. "It shall not be. My patroness shall never allow such unsuitable matches to be made, if, indeed, this is not all just a matter of your imaginations. Lord Chesterfield will marry a woman of high character and position, and I do not doubt her ladyship will have some say in whom he marries. As for Mr. Darcy, I am afraid he is not available for you to prey upon, for he is already engaged to his cousin, Lady Catherine's daughter, Miss Anne de Bourgh!"

Mrs. Bennet gasped and Elizabeth, shocked, gaped at Mr. Collins. Could it be true? Was Mr. Darcy already engaged? In indefinable pang of loss pierced Elizabeth's heart.

But she had no time to consider her feelings, for Mrs. Bennet cleared her throat. At first, Mrs. Bennet had appeared as stricken as Elizabeth had felt herself, but after a moment, she seemed to come to some determination.

"That is interesting, indeed, Mr. Collins, for I have it on good authority that Mr. Darcy admires at least one of my daughters."

"He is only being kind," snapped Mr. Collins. "He can have no more thought of one of your daughters than he might of marrying one of his dogs."

"We have heard nothing of it."

"Do you expect a great man to share his business with all and sundry?"

"No, indeed, we do not. But Mr. Darcy is not the type to make love to young ladies indiscriminately. Are you certain you are not mistaken?"

"I have had the matter from Lady Catherine's own lips. From their cradles, Mr. Darcy and Miss de Bourgh have been intended for each other by the will of their mothers."

"Ah, a cradle betrothal!" exclaimed Mrs. Bennet, triumphant. "Have the marriage articles been signed? Has the proposal been offered? Has the church been booked and the day chosen? Is this agreement of which you speak legal?"

Mr. Collins's mouth worked though nothing came out. Mrs. Bennet appeared like the cat who had got into the cream, and she smirked at the parson. It was clear he did not like her expression, for he fixed her with one so haughty that Elizabeth wondered if he thought himself to be a duke.

"It is by her ladyship's design, Mrs. Bennet. Are her designs to be thwarted by a family of much less consequence in the world?"

"Her designs are irrelevant, Mr. Collins," snapped Mrs. Bennet. Mr. Collins stared at her, and Elizabeth could not call herself any less surprised—she had never heard her mother speak so, nor had she ever witnessed Mrs. Bennet striking to the heart of any matter in such a way.

"What matters is if the engagement is legal," continued Mrs. Bennet. "If a contract has not been signed, then her ladyship's designs are naught but wishes."

"I am afraid she has you there, Cousin," said Mr. Bennet. All eyes swiveled to the patriarch, and it was clear he was once again enjoying himself thoroughly. "If there is no marriage contract signed, then Mr. Darcy is free to do whatever he likes, regardless of your patroness's demands."

By the time Mr. Bennet finished speaking, Mr. Collins was shaking his head rapidly. Elizabeth wondered if he should not be more careful, for it seemed likely to come loose at any moment.

"Her ladyship cannot be gainsaid!" cried he, desperation evident in his tone.

"Mr. Collins," said Mrs. Bennet. "I know nothing of your patroness. But I am familiar with Mr. Darcy and Lord Chesterfield and am convinced they will act in a manner they see fit. Furthermore, my girls are good enough for anyone. I would thank you not to disparage them while you reside in my home."

"Mrs. Bennet, I am certain you do not understand. You see—"

"I assure you, Mr. Collins, I understand perfectly. I do not wish to repeat myself."

"Mrs. Bennet—"

"It is fruitless to argue with a woman, Mr. Collins," interjected Mr. Bennet. "You will understand this when you marry. For now, I suspect it would be best to avoid becoming involved. In the end, what Mr. Darcy or Lord Chesterfield do is none of your concern, I should say.

"Now, if you will oblige me, I believe we should concentrate on our dinner."

Clearly, Mr. Collins wished to do anything *but* oblige Mr. Bennet, but when he looked around the table to find nothing but unfriendly countenances, he subsided with a huff. Dinner was mostly silent thereafter, except for Lydia and Kitty giggling together and the occasional comment from one of the other diners. Mr. Collins, however, said nothing of note for the rest of the evening. But his dark looks told them all he had not relinquished his objections.

CHAPTER XI

*I*t is the curse of a man possessing a weak understanding to value his own abilities at a level which is far out of touch with reality.

Perhaps few captured this truth more than Mr. William Collins. Mr. Collins was a member of the family who had long been sundered from the Bennets living at Longbourn and would not even have been the heir of Longbourn but for the inability of the Bennets to produce many children in recent generations, and of the present property holder producing only girls. And that did not even count a great uncle, who had left England to go to the New World; any male progeny of that member of the family would be the rightful heir, though there was little chance of ever discovering them.

Mr. Collins, however, did not see this, as he did not see the limitations of intelligence and sense under which he was forced to operate. In Mr. Collins's mind, he was the heir, and as such, should be afforded the respect of his position. He also had an inflated sense of his position in society as a parson, which led to his curious mixture of haughtiness and servility.

Having come to Longbourn to heal the breach with his cousin's family, Mr. Collins had expected to be welcomed with open arms and to have the pick of his cousins for a wife as Lady Catherine had demanded. That three should already have suitors had not pleased him, and with the other two unsuitable to be the wife of a parson, he had begun to feel rather aggrieved.

But that was nothing compared to the information he had gleaned about those supposed suitors. Mr. Collins was now faced with a dilemma. It was without question that Lady Catherine would not be happy to learn that her nephews were fraternizing with such unsuitable ladies. But Collins was not certain what he could possibly do concerning the matter. He could possibly woo one of the girls away from them, but a man did not bestow his favors on two young ladies at once.

For the present, he did what he could—he dispatched a letter to Lady Catherine as soon as he rose the morning following the disagreement at dinner. Her ladyship would no doubt journey to Longbourn to make her sentiments known and pull her wayward nephews back from the calamity they were entertaining, if that was, indeed, what they were contemplating. Though they had paid attention to Elizabeth in particular, Collins was still not convinced they were at all serious in those attentions. But prudence demanded he confront the matter with the seriousness it deserved.

But until instructions arrived from Lady Catherine, he was alone in a hostile environment. Lady Catherine would be displeased if he did nothing. Thus, he would need to do what he could.

After sending his letter to Lady Catherine, Mr. Collins made his way back to Longbourn, arriving as the rest of the family was descending the stairs to partake of breakfast. Miss Elizabeth alone was returning to the house the same time he was, and he wondered at it. It seemed she had been out for some time as her cheeks and nose were red.

"Cousin Elizabeth!" exclaimed he as he approached the house.

She whirled in surprise, evidently not having known he was there, and relaxed when she saw him.

"Mr. Collins," said she by way of greeting, before making to turn back to the house.

"I would be very happy, Cousin, if you would allow me to escort you to breakfast."

A rush of gratification accompanied his cousin's acceptance of his arm, and as they walked into the house, Mr. Collins began regaling her with tales of Rosings Park and the parsonage which was his home. And he fancied that he might be able to pull her from her contemplated improprieties with Lord Chesterfield.

* * *

Unfortunately, Mr. Collins once again overestimated his abilities.

"I am surprised to see you out of doors so early this morning, Mr. Collins," said Elizabeth when they had entered the house.

"I had a matter which required my attention," was his blithe response. "I must own that I am surprised that *you* were outside."

"It is not unusual for me to walk out in the mornings," replied Elizabeth. "I do so almost every morning when the weather permits. It is one of the reasons why winter is my least favorite season, for I am often denied."

"Walking about the park in the back of the house is beneficial exercise," replied the parson with a sage nod. "I often walk about my own gardens. I believe you will enjoy them, Cousin, for they are beautiful, and the grove in which stands my home is delightful."

Elizabeth ignored the assertion that she would one day see his gardens. "The back wilderness is all I am afforded at times. But as this morning is quite mild, the gardens were not my destination. I walked the path which follows Longbourn's border with Netherfield."

The way Mr. Collins's head suddenly swiveled to look at her with horror told Elizabeth that she had made an error. "You walked so far already this morning?"

"I am an early riser, Mr. Collins. As I said before, it is not unusual."

"But surely there is no call to walk so far."

"It is one of my favorite activities, Mr. Collins. I have been doing so for many years. I do not know how you could possibly object."

Mr. Collins was silent. He glared at her for several moments, considering her words, and when he spoke, his tone was all suspicion. "I hope you were not walking in that specific direction in hopes of an accidental meeting along a secluded path."

"I do not appreciate your insinuation, Cousin," said Elizabeth. She placed her hands on her hips and returned his glare. "I walk for enjoyment, exercise, and the ability to be alone with my thoughts. I do not go searching for men to arrange some assignation with them. I would highly appreciate it if you would not make such insinuations."

With those words, Elizabeth turned on her heel and made her way to the dining room, the heavy tread of Mr. Collins following her thither.

When they arrived, Mr. Bennet looked up and smiled at Elizabeth, but when he saw her countenance, his expression became one of annoyance. The parson, though he was the recipient of her father's censure, seemed unaware of it, so focused on Elizabeth herself was he.

"Mr. Collins," said Mr. Bennet. The parson started, his forkful of food flying into the air when he jerked, falling on the sleeve of his black coat. Mr. Collins remained oblivious as he turned to Mr. Bennet, though Elizabeth was near to laughter at the spectacle. She dearly needed a laugh.

"Yes, Cousin?"

"I hope we do not need to repeat the words we exchanged last night. Do we?"

Apparently, Mr. Collins saw something in Mr. Bennet's countenance he did not like, for he only shook his head and muttered: "I believe that is not necessary."

"Excellent!" said Mr. Bennet, and he turned back to his breakfast.

While one might have thought the inanities would be finished for the day, only one who had never met Mr. Collins would have entertained such a hope. Enter the Netherfield party and the silliness was destined to increase.

They were led into the room by Mrs. Hill and welcomed by the company. Mr. Bingley, as was his wont in these situations, went to Jane immediately, greeting her with the ardency of a suitor, and Elizabeth could watch with nothing but pleasure. Then she found herself being addressed by those who had increasingly become of interest to her.

"Miss Elizabeth," said Mr. Darcy, leading his cousin to where she stood. "How are you this fine day?"

"I am very well, Mr. Darcy," replied Elizabeth. "I thank you for asking. And you? Everyone at Netherfield is well, I expect?"

"All very well," replied Lord Chesterfield. He leaned in as if imparting a secret. "Miss Bingley is not best pleased by the reason for our errand today, but you shall discover the reason for that anon."

"Cousin Elizabeth!"

Elizabeth closed her eyes briefly in mortification at the sound of the detested voice. She did not need to turn around to know the parson was scurrying toward them, and with resignation, she turned to him, plastering a smile on her face.

"Mr. Darcy, Lord Chesterfield, I must thank you profusely for paying attention to my poor cousin. But I assure you, she has no need of such attention, for I am happy to attend to her myself."

The way both gentlemen regarded Mr. Collins suggested they considered him to be less than an annoying bug. For his part, Mr. Collins seemed oblivious, for he beamed at them as if he had just said something worthy of being passed down by sages.

"I was not aware that a man could not greet a woman with whom he is acquainted without sparking censure, sir," said Lord Chesterfield.

The smile fell away from Mr. Collins's face. "I only mean to remind my cousin to remember her place, Lord Chesterfield. It is not seemly that she should attempt to seduce the attention of such illustrious gentlemen as yourselves."

"Your choice of words is suspect, Mr. Collins," said Mr. Darcy. Elizabeth darted a glance at the gentleman, and she could see he was not pleased by Mr. Collins's silliness. "If a man enters a room and approaches a woman for the purpose of greeting her, there is no reason to suppose it is anything more than acquaintances exchanging civilities."

"You are quite correct, sir," said Mr. Collins, dropping into a series of hasty bows. "I had not meant to insinuate anything more."

Though Mr. Darcy clearly did not believe him, he proved himself to be a true gentleman by allowing the matter to drop. For the next few moments, the two gentlemen carried on a conversation with Elizabeth, mostly consisting of the aforementioned courtesies, while Mr. Collins took every opportunity to interject. It was something of a relief when the demands of civility asserted themselves, and the two Netherfield gentlemen turned to the other members of the family and greeted them. As soon as they left, however, Mr. Collins turned to Elizabeth. His countenance was severe.

"You must desist in this course, Cousin!" hissed he.

Elizabeth turned and glared at him. "Really, Mr. Collins, I think you must acquire spectacles, for your eyesight appears deficient. The gentlemen entered the room and approached *me*, not the reverse. Did Mr. Darcy not say as much?"

Then Elizabeth turned her back on the man and walked away. Though she paid him no more heed and attempted to ignore him, she was not unaware of the heat of his gaze upon her back.

Mr. Collins was, without a doubt, one of the most curious creatures Darcy had ever had the misfortune to meet. Had that fact not been sufficiently established during the walk from Meryton to Longbourn, Darcy would have known without a doubt during a half-hour in his company in the Bennets' sitting-room.

Furthermore, Mr. Collins's purpose for acting as he did was only a secret to one who was, like him, completely bereft of wit. Darcy did not know how Lady Catherine did it, but she consistently managed to find lackeys who would protect her interests as if they were their own. In the case of Mr. Collins, his zeal was beyond anything Darcy had seen in her ladyship's previous underlings.

After greeting Miss Elizabeth, Darcy and Fitzwilliam both turned to the rest of the room and made the required salutations to the family, and then they sat with them for the required visit. Bingley, though the purpose of the visit was his, sat by Jane Bennet and could not be moved from the object of his devotion. Darcy watched them for a few moments. Bingley's preference was clear for all to see, but Miss Bennet's serene countenance was not one to be easily understood. At first, Darcy had been inclined to warn his friend to be cautious, but a conversation with his cousin had changed his mind.

"Miss Bennet is a good sort of girl, Darcy," said Fitzwilliam when Darcy had voiced his concerns. "It is true that she may not have much in the way of fortune, but she is a steady influence on your sometimes temperamental friend, and in matters of society, she would be a step up for him. She *is*, after all, the daughter of a gentleman, whereas he is naught but the son of a tradesman."

"I had not thought *you* to espouse such opinions, Fitzwilliam," replied Darcy. "Even with your elevation to the status of a viscount, I had thought you to be of a more liberal mind."

"And you would not be incorrect," replied Fitzwilliam, unoffended by Darcy's words. "Some attention must be paid to such matters, of course, but if it does not concern Bingley, what is it to anyone else?"

"True," said Darcy. "But I do not object to the girl because of her situation."

"So you *do* object?"

The grin accompanying Fitzwilliam's question told Darcy his cousin was attempting to make sport with him. Darcy only shook his head—at times his cousin was rather predictable.

"I only wish for the best for my friend," replied Darcy. "Bingley is, as you have seen, a jovial soul. I do not think he would be happy with a woman who did not return his regard."

"You do not believe Miss Bennet does?"

"It is more that I am unconvinced. She is serenity personified, and that leads me to believe her heart will not be easily touched. Furthermore, you know what Mrs. Bennet is—I am not certain Miss Bennet would be allowed to refuse any offer which came her way."

"I think Mrs. Bennet—and Miss Bennet, for that matter—might surprise you, Darcy. But be that as it may, I suggest you watch Miss Bennet the next time you see her in company with Bingley. She is not indifferent to him; quite the opposite, in fact."

And so, Darcy had taken his cousin's advice to do just that, and what he found filled him with shame for the mistake he had almost committed. Darcy, who was universally judged to be reticent, or even taciturn, should have seen such reserve in another. Miss Bennet behaved as properly as any young woman he had ever seen. She accepted Bingley's conversation with pleasure and responded with as much animation as she was capable of offering. She did not throw herself at him, unlike some others he could name.

That settled in his mind, Darcy felt free to turn his attention away from the couple, knowing that Bingley, if he did decide to propose, would live a happy life with his angel. After all, that is all Darcy had ever wished for his friend.

It was while Mr. Collins was distracted that Miss Elizabeth approached Darcy, and after greeting him broached the subject of the previous visit with a gravity with which he usually did not associate with her.

"My father warned us all about Mr. Wickham," said she, cutting through to the heart of the subject. "Even Lydia, who was fascinated by Mr. Wickham's good looks, has promised she will not associate with him." She paused and directed a faint smile at him. "Mary and Jane and I have agreed to watch her to ensure she makes good on that promise."

"That is prudent," replied Darcy. "If you will forgive me, your sister appears to be a little . . . immature, perhaps? She is the kind of girl on whom Wickham loves to prey."

"She is flighty and silly and has not the sense God gave a goose," was Miss Elizabeth's assessment.

Darcy could not help but chuckle. "I shall not agree with you, Miss Elizabeth, for fear of appearing censorious toward your sister. I shall simply say it is prudent to be watchful."

"Thank you, sir." Miss Elizabeth paused and seemed to be considering something. "Might I be correct in supposing that you and Lord Chesterfield visited Colonel Forster concerning the matter?"

"We did, and as you may expect, he was not pleased to learn that such a man was to join his regiment. He plans to inform the shopkeepers that they should not extend credit to his men, or if they plan to do so, that it should be limited to small amounts."

"That is excellent news, Mr. Darcy. I know my father spoke with Sir William Lucas briefly this morning. Since he is aware of the situation, I do not doubt it will be known throughout the neighborhood without delay."

It was, of course, then that Mr. Collins espied them speaking together, for he let loose a desperate-sounding "Cousin Elizabeth!" and scurried toward them as if his very life depended on his attendance. Thus, Darcy was forced to endure the man's simpering attentions, not to mention his dark looks at Miss Elizabeth. Had it all not been so very pathetic and amusing, Darcy might have been put out with the parson.

But then, sometime later, Darcy noticed that his cousin was speaking with the youngest Miss Bennets, and when his cousin laughed with the two giggling girls, Mr. Collins turned white. His reaction was much the same as it had been when he had first seen Darcy and Miss Elizabeth together.

"Cousin Lydia!" exclaimed he, and off he went to interrupt their conversation. Fitzwilliam, who seemed to have been enjoying himself — though Darcy could not know of what he could speak with such silly, immature girls — appeared more than a little put out over Mr. Collins's actions.

A huff of exasperation from his side pulled Darcy back to his companion. She was watching the parson, no friendly expression in her dark eyes. Had she been a man, Darcy thought she might have called the man out for stupidity. When Miss Elizabeth noticed his scrutiny, she shook her head.

"You informed me you were aware of the type of man your aunt employs. Might I assume that Mr. Collins has acquitted himself as you might expect in every particular?"

"He has exceeded my expectations," replied Darcy. "My aunt has outdone herself on this occasion. But there is one thing I do not understand."

Miss Bennet cocked her head to the side and regarded him through dark, mysterious eyes. Darcy had rarely seen such a fetching mannerism. "Perhaps I might assist you in shedding some light on the subject?"

"I well understand Mr. Collins's actions toward *me*." Darcy snorted. "Given my aunt's unrelenting expectations concerning my future felicity, I am not surprised she would have shared it with him. Hoping she will be more circumspect is a fool's hope.

"But Mr. Collins seems eager to prevent any interaction between my cousin and members of your family, particularly your youngest sister, even when he is not in company with you. Where you are concerned, Mr. Collins's reason may easily be discerned. But Miss

Lydia? I cannot fathom that he would suspect any danger on *that* front. She is, as you said, full young, and not ready to marry."

Miss Elizabeth's cheeks bloomed with embarrassment, but she did not scruple to reply. "My mother may . . . have some hopes in that direction for my youngest sister."

"Truly?" asked Darcy, eyes wide. "But she is naught but a child!"

"Yes, but she is also my mother's favorite." Miss Elizabeth fixed a tight smile on him. "Furthermore, Mama thinks that if one of you fall in love with her, that you will be content to wait until she matures and is ready for marriage to secure your bride."

"There are several fallacies in that line of thinking, Miss Elizabeth," replied Darcy. He was not certain whether he should laugh or throw up his hands and depart the madhouse that was Longbourn forthwith.

"Yes, but it is so like my mother." Miss Elizabeth paused, and then directed a beseeching look at him. "Please do not fault my mother, sir. She loves us all prodigiously, but her fear for our future often overrides her judgment."

"Fear for the future?" asked Darcy.

"You have not heard that Longbourn is entailed?"

Understanding bloomed in Darcy's mind. "Of course. I was not aware, but it now makes sense." He directed a glance at Mr. Collins, who was still annoying Fitzwilliam with his interference. "Might I assume that your father's heir is in this room?"

"You may."

"Then the mystery is solved." Darcy paused, thinking about what he should say. When he saw her anxiety, he fixed her with a smile. "Your mother is no different from many other mothers I have met in the past. I am not offended. As for Mr. Collins, I assume that he is attempting to direct your youngest sister away from my cousin because he thinks his patroness will not approve."

Miss Elizabeth nodded. "Perhaps, then, you may take the opportunity, should it present itself, to inform your mother — allowing Mr. Collins to overhear — that neither Fitzwilliam nor myself have any designs upon your youngest sister. She is yet a child; gentlemen of thirty years of age do not fall in love with children. If they do, they are not fit for the appellation."

A relieved look stole over Miss Elizabeth's face. "I will do so, should the opportunity present itself. I should warn you that my mother will likely not believe me."

"Then perhaps a passage of time will convince her."

"I hope you are correct, sir."

They changed the subject and continued an interesting conversation thereafter. Mr. Collins, for his part, hurried between himself and Fitzwilliam, attempting to intervene with both conversations. Now that Darcy knew what he was about, he could only be amused by the situation. Or at least he would have been amused had he not found Miss Elizabeth so fascinating.

When the thirty minutes of their visit had almost elapsed, Bingley roused himself to make the communication which had been the purpose of their visit.

"Mrs. Bennet," said he, "I am pleased to announce that my family and I will hold a ball on Tuesday next to thank you all for the welcome we have received." Producing a card, Bingley stepped forward and handed it to the Bennet matron. "I hope we can anticipate the attendance of your family."

"Of course, Mr. Bingley," said Mrs. Bennet, her reply *almost* restrained. "We would be delighted to attend. We thank you for your civility and generosity."

"Excellent!" cried Bingley. Then he turned to Miss Bennet. "If I might be so bold, may I ask, Miss Bennet, for your hand for the first two dances?"

Had Darcy still had any doubts about Miss Bennet's feelings, her rosy countenance and smile of utter pleasure would have put them to rest. She accepted with alacrity, which set Bingley to beaming. Darcy had often informed his friend in a jesting manner that he appeared quite ridiculous when he smiled in such a way, but on this occasion, it was appropriate. Bingley seemed near to finding his angel, and Darcy could not be happier for him.

Mr. Collins, who had been flitting about the room, watched them with grave attention and then nodded. It seemed like he had come to the same conclusion as Darcy had. If he had espoused any hopes in Miss Bennet's direction, they were now well and truly extinguished.

Turning back to his companion, Darcy noted her pleasure for her sister's good fortune and a powerful feeling stole over him. Before he even knew what he was about, Darcy caught her eye and addressed her thus:

"Miss Elizabeth, perhaps this is a little precipitous, but I believe that Bingley has set a good example for us all. Might I request *your* first sets of the evening as well?"

CHAPTER XII

No one could have been more astonished at Mr. Darcy's application than Elizabeth was herself. Though she had noticed that Mr. Darcy had become comfortable speaking with her, she had not had any notion of any partiality from the gentleman.

Silly goose! Elizabeth berated herself. *Just because a man asks for a dance, does not make him in love with you!*

For an instant, Elizabeth imagined what it would be like to be the object of such exquisite feelings from such a man as Mr. Darcy. Then she pushed those feelings to the side and focused on the man who was, after all, waiting for her response. But she could not suppress the thought that having a handsome man like Mr. Darcy make love to her would be very pleasant, indeed.

"Of course, Mr. Darcy," replied she at length. "I would be happy to dance those sets with you."

"Thank you, Mr. Darcy!" Elizabeth jumped a little when her mother appeared at her side, seemingly moving from one space to the next in the blink of an eye. But though Elizabeth might have expected her to be silly with excitement, Mrs. Bennet managed a credible level of restraint. "You and Mr. Bingley do us much honor in bestowing your kindness on my girls."

Mr. Darcy appeared no less surprised at Mrs. Bennet's manners, but he was every inch the gentleman. He bowed and smiled, saying: "I believe, Mrs. Bennet, that you have every reason to be proud of your daughters. They are some of the brightest ladies I have ever met. I am anticipating dancing with Miss Elizabeth keenly."

They had attracted much scrutiny by that time, and Elizabeth looked about, hoping her sisters would not display a lack of sense and exclaim over Elizabeth's good fortune. But whereas Lydia and Kitty were obviously amused at the scene, they did naught but whisper and giggle between themselves, while Mary only gave Elizabeth a soft smile.

It was the gentleman who stood near her youngest sisters who caught Elizabeth's attention, for she noted the look of utter surprise and stupefaction on Lord Chesterfield's face. Then she noted when his attention turned on his cousin. In fact, Elizabeth was put out a little because of the suspicious way he regarded Mr. Darcy, and Elizabeth wondered the reason for it. He had never shown himself to be a proud man—could she have been mistaken?

Then her attention was caught by Mr. Collins and his inanities. Whereas the viscount's feelings on the matter were complex beyond Elizabeth's ability to understand, Mr. Collins's were not. When he whirled and approached them at a quick pace, Elizabeth took a step back, certain he had some physical response in mind.

"Mr. Darcy!" exclaimed he. Anyone with any sense at all could hear the consternation in his tone. "You are too kind to honor my cousin in such a manner. But I beg you to reconsider, sir. Do you not think dancing the first with her will make a statement which you cannot possibly mean to make?"

"There is nothing anyone could misunderstand," replied Mr. Darcy, the haughty mask Elizabeth had not seen since the first night of their acquaintance covering his countenance like a veil. Then Mr. Darcy looked at her, and his entire manner softened. And Elizabeth felt herself melt in response to this new suggestion of regard.

"But the first dance, sir! Surely dancing the third or fourth with my cousin would be more appropriate. I offer myself as a substitute should you choose to reconsider."

Mr. Collins's tone suggested that he was certain Mr. Darcy would reconsider. Elizabeth, by now completely exasperated with the parson's inanities had a retort poised at the tip of her tongue when Mr. Darcy answered first.

"It is the height of rudeness to withdraw once a request has been made. Dancing with Miss Elizabeth makes no more or less of a statement than I wish to make."

What an ambiguous answer! thought Elizabeth, though she supposed he truly could not say anything more clear. Mr. Collins, however, treated it as if Mr. Darcy had made a declaration of everlasting love for Elizabeth.

"Surely you *must* reconsider! What would Lady Catherine think? What would Miss Anne de Bourgh, that fair flower, even now pining for you in Kent, think of your attention to another woman?"

"Mr. Collins!" barked Mr. Darcy. The parson positively jumped at the sound of his harsh voice. "I would ask you to refrain from speaking of things of which you have no knowledge. My aunt has nothing to do with a simple request for a dance with a young lady. Do not forget yourself, sir."

Then Mr. Darcy turned away and deliberately ignored the parson, thanking Elizabeth for accepting his request. A few moments later, the Netherfield company departed. But before they left, Mr. Darcy approached Mr. Collins and hissed a few words in his ear. Whatever they were, Mr. Collins's countenance paled, and he darted a glance at Elizabeth. Then Mr. Darcy was gone.

"I do not know how we can tolerate your presence much longer, Mr. Collins," said Mrs. Bennet. Elizabeth had forgotten that her mother was close by when she was accosted by Mr. Collins. "Perhaps it would be best for you to spend the afternoon in your bedchamber studying the Bible. It seems to me you could benefit from the wisdom the holy book would impart. At the very least, you would be out of our hair."

Mr. Collins was clearly offended by Mrs. Bennet's words, but she did not pay him any heed. In the end, though he shot an aggrieved glance at Elizabeth, he stalked from the room and was not seen again until supper. Elizabeth was certain she had not heard the end from him. Mr. Collins clearly had no ability to stay silent and clearly held a determination to forward his mistress's interests regardless of how many times Mr. Darcy berated him.

"What was the meaning of that display, Cousin?"

Darcy, who had retreated to Netherfield's library—a pitiful collection of uninteresting tomes, completely undeserving of the appellation—started in surprise and looked up. Fitzwilliam stood just inside the door, looking at him, his expression accusing. Though Darcy had seen his cousin's reaction to his request for Miss Elizabeth's hand for the first two dances at Bingley's ball, he had been engaged in much more agreeable thoughts during the journey back to Netherfield. And as the topic of discussion was dominated by Bingley's raptures of Miss Bennet, Darcy had been at liberty to consider her younger sister.

It was strange that Miss Elizabeth was affecting him so much when one considered how many others had tried—and failed—to make an impression. And she had done it with so little effort! Darcy was certain she was genuine, nothing hidden and nothing feigned. She was a ray of sunshine, one which Darcy could now confess intrigued him. Yes, indeed—he was far more partial to the dark, mysterious sister than the light, demure one.

"Well, Cousin?" Fitzwilliam's voice interrupted his musings, bringing Darcy's mind back to the present. "Will you answer my question?"

"To what display are you referring?" asked Darcy. Though he knew well to what his cousin referred, he was not about to answer such a query phrased in such a way. Fitzwilliam's tone suggested he had not acted properly.

"The matter of Miss Elizabeth Bennet," said Fitzwilliam from between clenched teeth. "You, who have yet to be moved by *any* woman, ask a young country miss of little consequence in the world for the first dance at a ball? I do not believe you have danced the first with *any woman* since your first season!"

"You are correct about that," replied Darcy. His thoughts were once again sliding to his contemplation of Miss Elizabeth, and he was forced to turn them back to his cousin, who was now grinding his teeth in frustration. "It was something of an impulse of the moment."

Fitzwilliam regarded him with open suspicion. "You *never* do anything by impulse, Darcy. You always think any matter over, deliberating all angles before coming to a decision."

A chuckle escaped Darcy's lips. Yes, his cousin knew him well, indeed. "I cannot deny that.

"But in this instance, that is exactly what happened. I felt a . . ." Darcy paused, struggling to find the words to explain what was happening to him. He was grateful to his cousin for giving him the chance to think, though Fitzwilliam was obviously still angry. "I do not know what prompted me to make the request I did. But I have come to consider Miss Elizabeth as one of the most estimable ladies of my acquaintance, and the feeling has only grown the longer we have been in Hertfordshire."

"That is tantamount to a ringing endorsement from *you*, Darcy. But I still do not understand what you mean by it."

"What I mean by it?" asked Darcy with amazement. "Am I to understand that you agree with the estimable Mr. Collins? Am I declaring my intentions openly by asking Miss Elizabeth for a dance?"

"Do not compare me to that simpleton," growled Fitzwilliam. "I know you are aware of his designs. My concerns regarding the matter are much different from that buffoon's."

"Then perhaps you should state them directly," said Darcy, beginning to feel vexed by his cousin's manner. "Or would you have me continue to guess your meaning?"

"Just answer the question, Darcy," said Fitzwilliam.

Darcy was astonished. His cousin was behaving in a manner which he had never seen before. Since they were young boys, they had been the closest of companions. He could not remember the last time they were seriously at odds. He could not account for Fitzwilliam's behavior.

In the end, however, he decided it was best to simply oblige his cousin. "The fact is that I have no ready answer to give you, Fitzwilliam. I do not intend to be glib. But when I said that I asked Miss Elizabeth for the dances on impulse, I was merely stating the truth.

"If you are asking what my intentions are toward Miss Elizabeth, I am afraid I cannot answer at present." Fitzwilliam's countenance darkened, but Darcy ignored him and continued to speak. "What I do know is that she is an estimable lady, one who would be a blessing to any man who was fortunate enough to win her favor. But at this time, I stress I do not know her well enough to know the extent of my intentions. I am, however, anticipating coming to know her better."

If anything, his cousin's countenance became even more forbidding. "I am surprised at you, Darcy. Not only would I have never thought it likely that *you* would favor a woman in such a situation, but I am shocked you would interfere in this manner."

"I am sorry, Fitzwilliam, but I have not the pleasure of understanding you." Darcy stood and glared at his cousin, wondering where the jovial man he had always known had gone. "Are you accusing me of playing with Miss Elizabeth's affections?"

"Of course not!" snapped his cousin.

"Then say what you mean!"

They stared at each other for a few moments, and it was ultimately Fitzwilliam who broke the impasse. "Then you shall have it. I wonder why you would seek the hand of the woman to whom *I* have been paying attention these past weeks."

"The woman to whom you have paid attention?" asked Darcy,

nonplussed. "Of what are you talking?"

"Come now, Darcy, I know you are not obtuse. You are very observant. Surely you have seen *my* preference for Miss Elizabeth."

"I assure you I have seen no such thing. Since we have come to Hertfordshire, it seems to me you have dispensed your civility to all and sundry, as is your usual habit. I have seen no particular notice given to Miss Elizabeth."

"Then you have been blind," snarled Fitzwilliam. "I have, in fact, showed her far more interest than any other woman I have ever met. I can hardly believe you have not noticed this."

"Well, then you have played *my* part to perfection, Cousin." If this conversation had not been so tense, he might have almost found it amusing. "I have had no notion of any interest on your part. Nor, I might add, has Miss Elizabeth seen anything of it."

"Well, I have. I suppose I shall have to be more overt."

"You may, of course, do as you wish."

Fitzwilliam's eyes narrowed. "It would be best if you stepped back, Darcy."

"You have my apologies, Cousin, but I shall not. If you will pardon my saying, I was not aware you were courting her. As I am certain you are not, I find my path is clear before me."

Then Darcy stepped past his cousin and departed the room. He almost expected Fitzwilliam to chase after him to continue their argument, but the door closed behind him and did not open again.

It was beyond belief, this argument they had just had! Rarely had they been in conflict with each other, so close had their relationship been. That Fitzwilliam would demand — *demand!* — that he step aside showed a haughtiness Darcy had never seen from his cousin. He would not have thought Fitzwilliam, of all people, would be affected by such feelings.

"Oh, how I hate Eliza Bennet!"

Once again, the calm of Louisa Hurst's chambers was rent by the entrance of her ranting sister. Louisa, who had enjoyed the past days since the sisters had left Netherfield, and especially Caroline's good mood, could only shake her head in dismay. She wondered why Caroline did not abandon hope of Louisa's support in her schemes. Louisa had never given her any reason to hope — but she stubbornly insisted on bringing her petty concerns and plots to Louisa.

"What is it now, Caroline?" asked Louisa in a tone of longsuffering. It was lost on Caroline, however — she paced and muttered and threw her hands in the air, ranting like a madwoman.

"She is drawing both Mr. Darcy and Lord Chesterfield in by her flirtatious and impertinent manners."

"I am sure she is doing no such thing."

"Then you are wrong." Caroline spun and turned on Louisa, and for a moment Louisa wondered if her sister meant to attack her physically. "I just overheard a conversation between Lord Chesterfield and Mr. Darcy which confirms it!"

"Oh, Caroline," said Louisa. "Tell me you did not eavesdrop on a private conversation between gentlemen."

"Of course, I did," snapped Caroline. "How else am I to discover what happened at Longbourn? I was only just able to escape detection when Mr. Darcy left the room." Caroline's snarl deepened. "Oh, how I wish Charles had not chosen this backwater county to lease an estate! How could he possibly do this to me? I cannot believe he was so stupid as to ask Miss Bennet for the first dances at his stupid ball. I am sure he is considering throwing everything for which we have struggled away on that chit!"

"Miss Bennet is a good woman, Caroline. Should Charles marry her, she would be the making of him."

"But that is not the worst of it!" exclaimed Caroline, completely ignoring—or likely not even hearing—Louisa's reply. "Mr. Darcy asked Eliza for *her* first dance at the ball."

"He did?" asked Louisa with some interest. Perhaps Hurst was correct about Mr. Darcy and Elizabeth.

"Yes! And while I may rejoice in the fact that she is attracting Mr. Darcy, leaving Lord Chesterfield for me, the viscount man is also interested in her. I swear they are like dogs in heat, fighting over the bitch of the pack!"

"Caroline!" scolded Louisa. "Do not use such language."

"It is no less than the truth!" snapped Caroline.

At length she gave way, sensing that Louisa was not about to be denied in this instance. Instead, Caroline threw herself on a nearby sofa and sat in silence for some time, brooding. Louisa watched her sister, disgust staining her mind, and not for the first time. Her sister was approaching the point of being ungovernable, and Louisa had never possessed the temperament necessary to make her obey or affect her improvement. Perhaps it was time to consider sending her away to their aunt. Miss Amelia Bingley was a no-nonsense woman, and if anyone could improve Caroline's behavior, it was their aunt.

"Mr. Darcy and Lord Chesterfield exchanged angry words, you

know." The words, when they came, were contemplative, Caroline's rage of a few moments before completely forgotten.

"That is strange," said Louisa with a frown. "I have never seen so much as a cross word pass between them."

"I know," replied Caroline. "It is that which gives me some hope that this situation might be salvaged."

Louisa regarded her sister, suspicious of Caroline's meaning. "Oh?" was all she said, hoping to prompt Caroline to be more explicit. Caroline, of course, obliged readily.

"With the cousins at odds and Mr. Darcy focusing on Eliza, it is possible I can use that to ensure Lord Chesterfield turns to me. If he thinks that Eliza has betrayed him with his cousin, it will make him that much easier to influence."

"Oh, Caroline," said Louisa, shaking her head, a wave of sadness passing over her. "I do not know by what convoluted reasoning you think that a schism between cousins would cause his lordship to turn to you."

"Because I will be his sympathetic ear," said Caroline, her manner still distracted. "And if I can fan the flames of his disgust for her, I improve my position as the only other eligible female in his current sphere." Caroline made a disgusted noise at the back of her throat. "To think of Eliza Bennet as an 'eligible female' is more than I can bear. But I will use Mr. Darcy's attraction for her to my benefit.

"There is still the matter of Charles," continued she. "We cannot allow him, of course, to continue with his fascination for Jane Bennet. Though my marriage to a viscount would be a step up for our family, Charles would merely pull our name down again should he marry such an unsuitable woman."

This time Louisa decided against disagreeing with her sister openly. None of the other times she had done it had Caroline so much as heard her, so it was fruitless.

"I must make plans," muttered Caroline, standing and moving from the room without even a glance back.

Louisa watched her go, grateful when the door closed behind her. Caroline was becoming a serious problem, and Louisa did not know what to do to mitigate the damage she might potentially do to their reputation. Perhaps she should speak further with Hurst.

CHAPTER XIII

The rain began the day after the visit of the Netherfield gentlemen to Longbourn. November was often a time when the weather could be fickle, a time when Elizabeth attempted to be out of doors to store up as much of the serenity of nature as she could for the winter months when she was largely confined to the house. This year, however, it was more of an imposition than ever, largely because of the Bennets' visitor, who was quickly wearing out his welcome.

With the rain falling as it was, turning the landscape around them into a sodden mess, the Bennet girls were confined to the house. If the promise of amusement had not been there to prop up flagging spirits and calm short tempers, they might not have survived. As it was, they spent much of their time preparing for the ball: dresses were pressed, wraps prepared, and the little extra effects which enhanced a lady's appearance were considered, chosen, discarded, and, occasionally, fought over. But in the end, Elizabeth believed the sisters were all happy with what they would be wearing.

"Are you certain this dress is appropriate?" asked Mary, proving that her previous severe opinions of proper dress and adornment were not completely abandoned.

"Of course, Mary," replied Kitty. Her tone was offhand, prompting pursed lips from Mary, though she decided not to reply. Kitty had always had a good eye for what colors and styles suited them, and she had taken to assisting Mary with a certain zeal which Mary did not always know how to take.

"That style suits you marvelously, and I dare say the dress looks better on you than it ever did on Lizzy."

"Thank you," said Mary, mollified by Kitty's praise.

"I told you it would," added Elizabeth. "When the gentlemen at the ball see you, they will line up to dance with you. Perhaps father should hire a few footmen to stand about you looking menacing at those who will surely vie for your hand. Otherwise, he will have a ▓▓▓▓ of a time keeping them all away."

Mary swatted at Elizabeth, who ducked out of the way, while Jane and Kitty laughed. Only Lydia was not present—she could not be trusted to keep her remarks kind, especially where it concerned Mary, and she deemed it all a tedious waste of time anyway. Elizabeth was happy to dispense with Lydia's company, for she truly was a thoughtless girl much of the time.

The dress Mary was to wear was one of Elizabeth's old dresses, but she had never felt that it flattered her, and as it was purchased when Elizabeth was in the middle of a growth spurt, she had only worn it two or three times. Mary, who was a little smaller of stature and form than Elizabeth, fit into the dress as if it were made for her. In a certain sense, it seemed like it had, for the pale yellow suited her much better than it ever had Elizabeth.

"Then I suppose I shall wear it," said Mary. Though she affected an unconcerned attitude, Elizabeth could see that she was excited. Most of Mary's dresses in the past had been of somewhat dull colors, as she felt that was demure and proper. It had taken much coaxing to induce Mary to see that she could dress in a more flattering style and still be a proper young woman.

It was in pursuits such as these that they spent their time during those days—that and avoiding Mr. Collins wherever possible. In the confines of a house the size of Longbourn, they were not always able to stay away from the man. As such, Elizabeth would often retreat to her room when she was feeling particularly vexed with him.

"Cousin Elizabeth," he would say to her whenever he had the chance, "I think we have much of which to speak. There are many things I would share with you concerning my home, which, I flatter myself, you shall see before long."

"You *do* flatter yourself," said Elizabeth on one of these occasions, prompting the parson's mouth to fall open. "I cannot imagine how I would possibly see the parsonage in Kent, for I know no one else there. Do you mean to invite my family to stay with you?"

"There is not enough room in the parsonage for all your family."

"Then there is little chance of my ever seeing it."

Mr. Collins gaped for several moments, but then a sly smile came over his face. "I believe you are misunderstanding my meaning, Cousin. I have no intention of inviting your family to Kent. I merely suggest that *you* will see the parsonage before too much longer."

"In that case, Mr. Collins, I understand your meaning perfectly." Mr. Collins beamed. "I simply tell you that I disagree with you. For such a reason as you suggest, I will *never* visit the parsonage."

"But, Cousin, you cannot mean it!"

"I cannot?" asked Elizabeth, completely uncaring of the parson's consternation. "I assure you that I can, sir."

Then Mr. Collins's countenance turned grim. "I suppose you hold out hope you can impose upon Mr. Darcy or Lord Chesterfield? *That* shall never happen, I assure you."

"I cannot say what my future holds, Mr. Collins," replied Elizabeth, unwilling to debate with the man. "But I can assuredly state without equivocation that I shall *never* view your parsonage as my home."

With those final words, Elizabeth spun on her heel and removed herself from the parson's presence. Even sitting in her room for hours with nothing to do was better than enduring Mr. Collins's silliness!

On the third day, the rain slackened and, for a short time, it ceased altogether. The clouds remained threatening, however, and Elizabeth reluctantly determined that not only would the paths of the estate be too muddy, but it would also start raining again before long.

All was not lost, however, for though it seemed unlikely, Longbourn was the recipient of several visitors. When Lydia and Kitty saw the red coats of the visiting officers, they squealed and scurried to greet them, welcoming them to their father's house. Elizabeth was also happy to see them until the smirking visage of Mr. Wickham came into sight.

"Miss Elizabeth, I believe?" greeted Mr. Wickham. "How do you do?"

It was only Elizabeth's innate sense of polite behavior which allowed her to respond. "Very well, Mr. Wickham. I thank you for asking."

The officers entered in and soon Mrs. Bennet had sent for tea and cakes, and conversations began all over the room. Mr. Wickham, though he could not have missed Elizabeth's disinclination for his company, seemed to fix upon her as the target of his civility. Elizabeth could easily have dispensed with the man's presence.

"I thank you for your gracious welcome, Miss Elizabeth," said he, his smile seeming designed to charm. "Though I have not yet had the opportunity to taste much of society here in Meryton, it seems to me that you are all very welcoming."

For some reason, Elizabeth did not appreciate the way Mr. Wickham said the word "taste," but she ignored it in favor of fending the man off.

"I believe we all take pride in our hospitality, Mr. Wickham."

"That much is clear. Is there something you can tell me about your neighbors? I *am* new to the neighborhood, after all."

Elizabeth directed a disarming smile at him. "I am certain it would be best if you were to meet them and make your own judgment, Mr. Wickham. My perception is mine alone, and it may not meet yours. Regardless, I am certain others can tell you more about themselves than I can."

Though he regarded her, his expression even, Elizabeth had the distinct impression he was not happy with her answer. Of course, she was aware of what he was truly asking, though the man seemed to think he had been subtle.

"Then I shall do that." Mr. Wickham paused and then continued: "I *am* curious, however, as to the Netherfield party. I understand that Mr. Darcy and Lord Chesterfield have been in residence for some weeks now?"

"They have," was all Elizabeth would say.

"And do you know if they mean to stay long?"

"Come now, Mr. Wickham. You cannot expect me to have any knowledge of the plans of men such as Mr. Darcy and Lord Chesterfield."

"You are correct, of course," said Mr. Wickham with what Elizabeth thought was a false joviality. "I am afraid I made the wrong assumption in light of what I saw the first day we met of your interactions with them. It seemed to me like you were quite friendly with them."

"I *am* friendly with them, but only in the manner of an acquaintance. If you insinuate any other connection, then I must disabuse you of that notion, sir."

"That is not necessary, Miss Elizabeth, for I mean nothing more than I said."

Elizabeth nodded at the man and, seeing Mary out of the corner of her eye, used that as a reason to excuse herself from his company. She went to the sofa on which sat her sister, knowing that Mr. Wickham was watching her as she walked away, feeling an unaccountable itching between her shoulders where she thought his eyes rested.

"Are you well, Elizabeth?" asked Mary.

"I am," replied Elizabeth, speaking softly to her sister. "But I wonder if we should not call Papa."

Mary directed a pointed look at Elizabeth. "Did Mr. Wickham say anything improper to you?"

"No. But he was *very* interested in my friendship with certain gentlemen of our acquaintance, even going so far as to ask if I knew their plans."

The look Mary bestowed on the militia officer was one which could not help but make a man uncomfortable. Mr. Wickham, however, was surveying the room and did not see it. Soon, however, he seemed to note that Mrs. Bennet was not being attended by any of the officers, and he made his way thither.

"Mrs. Bennet," said he, bowing low before her. "I wish to thank you for your hospitality, madam. You have much of which to be proud, for I have rarely seen such welcome as I have experienced here in Hertfordshire."

"Thank you, Mr. Wickham," said the Bennet matron, apparently forgetting, for the moment, the warning they had received concerning this man. "This *is* a friendly neighborhood, I am sure. We are happy to have the officers here, for it gives us a much greater variety of society."

"Yes," replied Mr. Wickham with a laugh. "I suppose it does."

They carried on a conversation for some few moments, Elizabeth and Mary listening carefully, though at times they were also obliged to speak with other officers who approached. Most of Mr. Wickham's words with Mrs. Bennet seemed to be of a banal nature. But then they changed when he was able to bring it around to the subject about which he had previously importuned Elizabeth.

"And they are so elegant, fashionable, and far friendlier than I ever would have expected from anyone of such an exalted station." Mrs. Bennet favored the militia officer with a surprising amount of restraint. "Netherfield Park has sat empty for so long that we have longed to have someone in residence. We are fortunate, indeed, that those who have taken the lease are so amiable and have fit so well with our society."

"It is interesting that you say so, Mrs. Bennet," said Mr. Wickham. "I know nothing of this Mr. Bingley, and I have heard that Lord Chesterfield is an amiable man. But I know no one who would call Darcy 'amiable.' Our circle of friends is quite similar, and though there are some who will give him a good name, adjectives used to describe him are usually in the nature of 'reticent,' 'taciturn,' or even 'proud.'"

Mrs. Bennet regarded Mr. Wickham. "I doubt there is anyone here who would use such words to describe Mr. Darcy, sir. We know who our friends are, and Mr. Darcy, though he has not been here long, has earned that appellation."

"Of course." Mr. Wickham's reply was both expansive and magnanimous. "Darcy is well able to please where he wishes, of course. When it is worth his while."

Elizabeth almost gasped at the blatant innuendo in Mr. Wickham's statement, but Mrs. Bennet only watched him, for once her countenance unreadable. Mr. Wickham took this as a sign for him to continue to speak.

"Darcy, you see, has been known to me for many years. I grew up in the same house with him and was favored by his father, my patron. I owe much to Mr. Robert Darcy and have always striven to uphold his memory with honor and respect. His son, however, is cut from a different cloth, somehow becoming prideful and arrogant, dismissive of those below his station. I have felt the hard edge of his contempt on more than one occasion."

Mr. Wickham stopped short, and he seemed to become more than a little embarrassed. "I am sorry, Mrs. Bennet; I should not speak in such a fashion."

"No, you should not," replied Mrs. Bennet quietly.

It appeared that Mr. Wickham did not even hear Mrs. Bennet's words. "I become so incensed at the wrongs I have suffered from the present Mr. Darcy that I forget myself. I have vowed not to speak ill of the son, for I cannot forget the father and all he has done for me."

"Then it seems you have failed in that resolve," said Mrs. Bennet.

For a moment Mr. Wickham was taken aback, but he quickly recovered. "It appears I have." His countenance was mournful. "I *am* sorry, Mrs. Bennet. When I think of what lies between us, the benefits designed for me which have been withheld, my good judgment escapes me, and my indignation takes over."

"It is clear that your indignation *does* take over, sir," said Mrs. Bennet. "But as I said before, I suggest you temper your outrage, for it will not be well received in this neighborhood. Mr. Darcy is well respected in Meryton. He was a little quiet when he was first in company, but he has proven himself to be a good and amiable man who has become like one of us. Let us hear no more of Mr. Darcy."

Mr. Wickham feigned astonishment. "I cannot be more surprised to hear you say such things, Mrs. Bennet. Darcy is many things, but amiable is not one of them. Furthermore, if you only knew the extent of his actions toward others not of his station, I am certain you would judge differently."

"Mr. Wickham, do you consider *my* family to be of Mr. Darcy's station?"

This unexpectedly astute question surprised Mr. Wickham. Elizabeth found herself no less shocked, and when she looked over at Mary, she found her sister in similar straits.

"I think your family is all that is good, Mrs. Bennet," replied Mr. Wickham. "There is no deficiency in any of you."

"That is not what I asked, Mr. Wickham, and you well know it."

Again Mr. Wickham goggled at Mrs. Bennet. For her part, the Bennet matron watched him placidly. Elizabeth thought, however, she detected more than a hint of steel in her mother's gaze.

"The fact of the matter, Mr. Wickham," said Mrs. Bennet when Mr. Wickham did not speak again, "is that Mr. Darcy inhabits a higher sphere than the Bennets of Hertfordshire can boast. My husband's family *has* had stewardship over this land for many generations, but we have never been rich or important. Mr. Darcy, however, possesses connections to the peerage, an old and respected family name, and great wealth, from what I understand. Would you not agree?"

"I would," replied Mr. Wickham. It seemed to Elizabeth the man was having difficulty holding his amiable countenance.

"Then I cannot understand what you mean when you say that Mr. Darcy looks down on those of a lower station. We have already established that *my* family is below his in society and consequence. And yet, I have seen none of these tendencies you describe. He has always been friendly and affable to my daughters and me, as well as to Mr. Bennet."

"Perhaps he has," said Mr. Wickham, clearly attempting to salvage the situation. "But you are also gentlefolk, and that must carry some weight. For those such as I, it is a different situation. Tell me, do you think a man should withhold advantages designated for another due to nothing more than jealousy?"

"No, Mr. Wickham, I do not. And I doubt Mr. Darcy would either."

"But—"

"No more, Mr. Wickham!" exclaimed Mrs. Bennet. Mr. Wickham fell silent, but his countenance was overset by a sullen frown. "As I said, we will hear nothing against Mr. Darcy. If you feel you have been misused, then you must appeal to those who are in a position to obtain justice for you."

"It is not that easy, Mrs. Bennet," replied Mr. Wickham. "Darcy is a powerful man, while I am merely the son of his father's steward."

"Perhaps it is as you say. But even the son of a former steward—which, I might add, is information you conveniently forgot to mention earlier—must have the ability to appeal to the law for what is rightly his."

Mr. Wickham's cheeks bloomed, but Mrs. Bennet took no notice. "For the final time, you will keep your grievances to yourself. I will not have you importuning my girls with them nor spreading them throughout the neighborhood, little good though that will do you. Now, I do not wish to call for my husband to ensure you are removed from my house. Please, desist in your attempts to defame Mr. Darcy. You will not find any sympathy here."

So saying, Mrs. Bennet rose and crossed the room, joining a conversation her youngest daughters were having with a pair of officers. Mr. Wickham glanced about surreptitiously, paling when he noted that Elizabeth and Mary were close enough to have heard everything said between himself and their mother. With a scowl, he rose and stalked to a corner of the room where he stood in aggrieved silence.

"Was that truly our mother?" asked Mary, eyes wide in surprise.

"It seems to be so." Elizabeth stopped and paused. "She seems to have become a little less flighty since Mr. Bingley focused his efforts on Jane."

"And perhaps Mr. Darcy's attentiveness to you?"

Elizabeth turned and regarded her sister, noting that Mary was not teasing or jesting—she seemed to be completely serious.

"Perhaps, though I do not know much of that yet. Could it be that she has been so frightened of the entail for so long that it has altered her behavior?"

"It is possible," allowed Mary. "If so, I hope she will be more proper if we are able to find husbands."

"I hope so too, Mary," replied Elizabeth.

Rare was the occasion when Wickham had found his manners and ability to charm women of all ages insufficient to ensure he was believed, especially when it involved vapid wives who possessed little sense. On the contrary, such women he could usually charm with little trouble. In fact, many such women he had been able to take to his bed—or hers—it truly did not matter to him. Mrs. Bennet was one he would likely not bother with, for though she was still a handsome woman, she was the kind who would drive him to Bedlam before he could take his pleasure from her.

Her daughters, however, were another story. Wickham had been all over England, and rarely had he seen a family of such comely daughters. It was true the youngest were silly and would compete with their mother for the title of most vexing, but the eldest girls were exquisite and ripe for the plucking. Even the middle girl, who was not the equal of the others, would be worth a roll in the hay, in Wickham's estimation.

They should be his for the taking. Except they were not. With difficulty, Wickham refrained from grinding his teeth in frustration. How had he had the poor fortune to come to the exact location which housed that prig Darcy and his equally detestable cousin? Wickham could hardly fathom it. When he had seen the two men in Meryton, he considered refusing the commission and leaving the area. But he was out of money and needed a place to hide from his creditors—Meryton was as good as any place for such an endeavor.

What he truly wished to do was sell the blasted commission and use the money he gained to start anew in the New World. Surely there were opportunities for an enterprising man to make his fortune with the colonists. The situation in England had become too hot for his tastes. Since there were men one did not cross seeking payment from him, flight seemed the best option. It was for that reason he did not attempt to sell the commission—it might bring attention to him. And that, he could not risk.

So he was stuck in this town, and he well knew his stay would not be a pleasant one. Not with Darcy and Fitzwilliam in residence. The fact that he had already been called into the colonel's office and told he would not be allowed credit would curtail his usual activities drastically. And he had no doubt Darcy had already told the Bennets about him if the mother's reaction was any indication. Without a doubt, it would be heard throughout the neighborhood before long.

Wickham burned for vengeance before he left the dust of this insignificant town behind. He had thought to attempt to make off with Darcy's sister and claim her dowry, but that scheme had fallen through when Darcy had not hired his accomplice, Mrs. Younge. But the matter was not forgotten—Wickham owed Darcy for all the misery the other man had caused him. And this time, he was not willing to accept the expedience of escape before vengeance.

Certain something would present itself, Wickham watched the Bennet sisters as they spoke with his fellow officers, noting who seemed to favor whom, the mannerisms and personalities of the girls. Miss Elizabeth, he thought, had been particularly favored by both men—what a delicious irony it would be if they came to blows over her! Perhaps she was the one who would provide the means for his revenge. If only it was Darcy who was paying attention to her, then ruining her would be just the thing. It was unfortunate that she was already wary of him. Then again, any one of her sisters would do. Surely the youngest girls, being silly and ignorant, would not know they were being used until it was too late.

As Wickham watched the room, he noticed a large, heavyset man standing to the side, looking out over the party. By the cast of his countenance, Wickham could see he was unhappy with what he was seeing. In particular, it seemed he was watching Miss Elizabeth, though at times he would also glare at Miss Lydia.

Pondering whether this man might lead him to his vengeance, Wickham made his way around the room. As he drew closer, he realized it was the parson to whom the Bennet sisters had introduced him on the street the first day they had met. What was his name? Clovis? Connor? No, Collins! Yes, that was it.

"How do you do today, sir?"

When Mr. Collins turned to Wickham and eyed him with distaste, it was all Wickham could do not to widen his eyes in surprise. He did not think he had offended the parson.

"I have no desire to speak to you, Mr. Wickham. I heard what you were saying of Mr. Darcy. I will not deal with a man who defames my patroness's nephews in such a manner."

Wickham's mind worked quickly. Patroness? Aunt? That would be either Lady Susan Fitzwilliam or Lady Catherine de Bourgh—Darcy had no relations from his father's side closer than a great uncle. No, not the countess, for Fitzwilliam was her son, not her nephew. Wickham suppressed a grin—Lady Catherine was a termagant, it was true, but she was also a silly woman, thinking far more highly of her own abilities than she had any right. That would make it easier.

"I am sorry, Mr. Collins, was it?" When the parson gave him a stiff nod, Wickham continued: "I am afraid you have completely misunderstood my purpose. The grievance between myself and Mr. Darcy is entirely my fault, and I own it without disguise. But having been brought up among the family, I find that their concerns are necessarily my concerns. Lady Catherine, in particular, has always been a favorite, though her ladyship does not know me well."

It was apparent that Wickham could have chosen no better approach than to praise the stupid man's equally senseless patroness. "She *is* the most perfect example of all that is good," agreed Mr. Collins. He watched Wickham, his eyes still betraying a hint of suspicion. "And necessarily, any family of hers must be of the highest character and nobility. I am convinced Mr. Darcy has not misbehaved in whatever lies between you."

"As I have already stated, Mr. Collins," said Wickham smoothly. "I must own that I *am* curious, however. I have noted your . . . less than friendly looks at Miss Elizabeth. She impressed me as an intelligent, lively girl. Might I ask after your dispute with her?"

A scowl settled over the parson's countenance, and his eyes once again found Miss Elizabeth where she stood across the room, speaking with Carter. The liveliness in her eyes was a magnet to Wickham, and he wondered what would be seen within them if she was in the throes of ecstasy.

"She will not cease her attempts to distract Mr. Darcy," said the parson shortly.

"Oh?" asked Wickham, keeping his tone casual. "If you will forgive my saying so, I believe Darcy could use a little distraction. He is so fixed on his duty to the exclusion of all else that I sometimes wonder if he has time to live."

Mr. Collins shook his head vigorously. "In this matter, Mr. Wickham, Mr. Darcy's duty must be his *primary* concern."

"What matter would this be?"

"Why the expectation of marriage between Mr. Darcy and the fair flower who is his cousin, Miss Anne de Bourgh."

Wickham almost lost his composure. Miss de Bourgh was many things, but fair? A *flower*? Many adjectives came to mind to describe her, but those two were well, well down the list. Wickham had given some consideration to attempting to elope with Miss de Bourgh as a means of gaining her wealth, but he had immediately discarded the idea. She met every criterion—rich, sickly, listless, would no doubt not even notice his activities, even should he carry on under her very nose. But Lady Catherine was a serious impediment to any such plan, for Wickham was certain her ladyship would make his life a living hell should he succeed in marrying her cross, sickly little daughter.

"It is a matter which has occupied my mistress's mind." Mr. Collins had continued speaking while Wickham was attempting to suppress his disgust. "It is the wish of every member of their family, and a splendid match it will be. Why, Mr. Darcy might even become the wealthiest man in England, should their two estates be joined together."

"You suspect him of wishing to escape his duty?" asked Wickham.

"Of course not!" snapped Mr. Collins. "I am certain Mr. Darcy means to abide by his aunt and late mother's wishes."

"Then I do not understand the problem, Mr. Collins."

The parson waved his hand ineffectually in Miss Elizabeth's direction. "It is clear my cousin's daughters mean to do everything in their power to distract him. I cannot allow it to happen. I must prevent their scheming!"

Privately, Wickham thought Darcy would be as little affected by a pretty woman as a stick. But it seemed to Wickham that fate had smiled upon him this day. Here was a chance for a little fun and retribution before he quit this insignificant town.

"Then, Mr. Collins, what you must do is distract the Miss Bennets before they can distract Darcy."

"But how can I do that?" wailed Mr. Collins. "My cousin's wife informs me that she intends Miss Elizabeth and Miss Lydia for Lord Chesterfield and Mr. Darcy. I am but one man—how can I prevent both?"

"You could start by informing me of all the details," replied Wickham, annoyed with the stupid man. "It is clear you cannot woo two women. But we are two men, and it seems to me that we match the Bennet sisters in question quite perfectly."

Mr. Collins turned wide eyes on Wickham. "You would assist?"

"As I said, Mr. Collins, I have been at fault in the matter between Darcy and myself, but his family's concerns are my own. If I assist in this matter, then perhaps I expunge some small part of my guilt for what has come between us."

The parson's eyes lit up, and he began to thank Wickham profusely for his assistance. Wickham did not need his thanks. He needed the man to play his part and not ruin Wickham's plans. With a little luck, he might gain some revenge and even pluck a few Bennet sisters at the same time.

CHAPTER XIV

When Mr. Collins renewed his efforts to distract Elizabeth, it did not take much to discern that something significant had happened. The question, of course, was what. Elizabeth had thought she had put the parson off enough to ensure he would step back for at least some little time. How wrong she was.

"Cousin Elizabeth!" exclaimed he, interrupting an interesting conversation she was having with Captain Carter. "Cousin Elizabeth! I believe I must speak to you concerning a most important matter."

Though loath to give up her current discussion, Elizabeth was left with no choice when the captain grimaced and shrugged, turning to one of his fellow officers—who was speaking to Mary—and joining their conversation. Elizabeth glared at him for his betrayal, but then Mr. Collins was in front of her.

"I have had an epiphany, Cousin—a notion surely provided from on high. You see, I was thinking of the situation before us, and it occurred to me that you are not truly attempting to steer Mr. Darcy away from his rightful bride."

"Of course, I am not," replied Elizabeth, disgusted with the parson for once again bringing this matter up. "I have been telling you all along."

"Marvelous!" exclaimed he. "I tender my apologies, Cousin, for I had not thought of the matter properly. Moreover, since I have now seen the situation for what it is, and I am certain you do not wish to be misunderstood, I believe it would be best to encourage Mr. Darcy to give me your first dance at the ball. You would not wish for Mr. Darcy to misunderstand, I am sure."

"And I am sure there is no misunderstanding," snapped Elizabeth, her patience exhausted with the silly parson. "Mr. Darcy asked *me* to dance, Mr. Collins—not the reverse. I will not be so rude as to refuse to dance with him now, nor will I be so improper as to insist he pass those dances to another."

Mr. Collins opened his mouth to retort when he paused, a look of deep thought settling over his face. At length, he said, though grudgingly: "It *would* be rude, I suppose."

"Indeed, it would," said Elizabeth, hoping this would be the end of the matter."

"I did not consider it in that light, Cousin. No, I would not wish you to be rude to such a great man."

"I am happy you have seen the light, Mr. Collins."

"Indeed, I have. Now, since I certainly cannot obtain the first, I believe I would like to ensure that I have your second, Cousin, if you will promise it to me."

Elizabeth felt the desire to gnash her teeth, and she wondered if she could somehow induce him to sprain his ankle, thereby relegating him to the side of the dance floor. But there was nothing for it, so she agreed to his request. The beaming smile which appeared on his ugly countenance gave Elizabeth the irrational desire to slap him.

"If you will excuse me, Mr. Collins," said Elizabeth, thinking to escape from him.

"I *have* seen the light," said Mr. Collins, and when Elizabeth began to walk away, the parson only followed her. "It is clear to me that you are clever, my dear cousin. When I take you to the parsonage, I do not doubt I will be gaining the most exquisite jewel. I can hardly wait."

A longsuffering sigh escaped Elizabeth's breast, but she had not the stamina to withstand his proclamations again. She instead settled for simply ignoring him, hoping he would go away soon enough. But the parson was indefatigable and could not be moved from her side. So Elizabeth resigned herself to his continued presence. But she did not take a seat—she would not allow him to claim the intimacy of sitting together.

It was as they were standing in this attitude, Mr. Collins speaking without cessation and Elizabeth ignoring him, that she noticed another change she had not noticed earlier. Lydia, who had been speaking with Lieutenants Sanderson and Denny in Kitty's company, was now the recipient of Mr. Wickham's attention. And from the look of things, the man was flirting outrageously with her. Stupid Lydia, having forgotten her father's edicts at the first sign of attention from the man, was flirting in return.

"I see you have noticed the lieutenant's attentions toward your sister," said the voice of Mr. Collins, piercing Elizabeth's annoyance. "He is such a respectable man. Do you know he owned his culpability in the matter which lies between himself and Mr. Darcy? Few men possess the courage to accept their portion of the blame, even when deserved, so readily."

"I am sure he has, Mr. Collins," said Elizabeth.

She directed a withering glare at Mr. Collins, which caught the parson by surprise, Elizabeth crossed the room to where the housekeeper was speaking with Elizabeth's mother.

"Mrs. Hill, would you please have my father summoned here at once?"

The housekeeper noted the serious cast of Elizabeth's countenance and nodded. Mrs. Bennet looked at Elizabeth curiously.

"I believe, Mama, we should have called Father when Mr. Wickham first arrived. Now he is flirting with Lydia."

Whatever discussion her mother had been having with Mrs. Hill, it was apparent it had distracted her. She turned to look at Lydia, and a frown settled over her face. A moment later the door to the sitting-room opened. Mr. Bennet had come.

It was not often that Bennet was called from his bookroom. His family knew of his disinclination for company, and while he attempted to endure society for their sake, the calls of visitors were not something he enjoyed. Mrs. Hill had brought him word of the officers' coming, but Bennet, knowing his youngest daughters — and likely his wife — would be in full-throated raptures over their coming, had decided not to make an appearance himself.

A summons from Elizabeth, however, was not a trifling matter. As the most sensible of his daughters, he had a healthy respect for her judgment. If she thought he was needed, he knew he should attend his family as quickly as possible.

As it was, the worry in his daughter's mien was enough to raise his concern, and he hurried to her to find out what was the matter. His toad of a cousin was hovering about her, but Bennet knew she was more than capable of handling *him*, so he simply ignored the man.

"What is it, Lizzy?"

In response, Elizabeth nodded to the other side of the room and said: "Your youngest is behaving quite inappropriately, and the subject of her attention is none other than Lieutenant Wickham."

Following her gesture, Bennet turned and looked at the gentleman. He was partially turned away from where they stood, but Bennet could easily see that he was tall and lean, dark-haired, likely handsome enough to catch the eye of his youngest and silliest daughter. And their flirting was far more than Bennet could tolerate. His mouth tightened when he saw Lydia lean forward and brush her hand against this Wickham's. The silly girl! And this after he had already warned her against the man!

Filled with determination, Bennet stalked over to the oblivious couple and cleared his throat. Lydia's eyes found him and must have immediately remembered, for her countenance turned pale. For his part, Wickham only turned lazily with an insouciant and uncaring look of boredom.

"Lydia, I can see you are enjoying the company of our guests. Will you not do me the honor of introducing me to your friend?"

The girl perked up at the request. "Of course, Papa. This is Mr. Wickham, newly of the regiment. Mr. Wickham, my father, Mr. Bennet."

"Good day to you, Mr. Bennet," said the militia officer. His tone of voice was all amiability "I am happy to make the acquaintance of the enchanting Miss Lydia's father."

Bennet directed a faint smile at the officer, then turned back to his wayward daughter. "Lydia, it seems to me that you have forgotten the matter we discussed only a few days ago. Can I assume this man approached you?"

"Yes, Papa."

She was chastened; at least that was something. "Have you anything else to tell me?"

Though she appeared to wish otherwise, she sighed and said: "Mr. Wickham asked me for the first dance at Mr. Bingley's ball."

"Did he?" asked Bennet, his gaze returning slowly to Mr. Wickham. The man was cool, for he only smiled at Lydia, prompting a wary look in response.

"Lydia, please go to your sister, Elizabeth. I believe I need to speak with Mr. Wickham."

Lydia curtseyed and fled. It was an unfortunate trial on Bennet's nerves when her place was taken by his senseless cousin.

"May I be of assistance?"

"No." Mr. Collins started at the curt response. "I have no need of your assistance, Mr. Collins. I will speak with Mr. Wickham alone."

It seemed Mr. Collins was thinking of insisting, but he turned away, which was fortunate for Bennet's peace of mind. Putting the silly man from his thoughts, Bennet turned his sights on Mr. Wickham, noting the man's look of polite interest. He had clearly played the game for many years, for his expressions were practiced and easy.

"Now, about this matter of your asking my youngest for her first sets at Mr. Bingley's ball."

"The first sets!" screeched his wife. Unbeknownst to Bennet, she had also followed him to where he was speaking to Mr. Wickham and was now watching the man with mixed loathing and consternation. "But I was certain she would be asked by Lor—" Mrs. Bennet swallowed thickly. "I mean she already has someone with whom to dance the first."

"Mrs. Bennet," said Bennet with exaggerated patience. "Please allow me to handle this matter. You will not be displeased with the outcome."

His wife regarded him for a moment before she nodded and returned to her chair. Bennet glared about, noting the position of his daughters, along with the visiting officers. While his girls likely knew what he was about, the interruptions had brought the attention of the officers to them.

But there was nothing to be done on the matter, so he turned back to Mr. Wickham. "Well, Mr. Wickham? Am I correct?"

"You are, sir. Is there some problem? Your daughter *is* out, is she not?"

"She is," replied Bennet, "though I must own that I am questioning the wisdom of that state of affairs. In answer to your question, however, yes, there is a problem."

"And what might that be?"

"The fact that it was *you* who asked her, sir." Mr. Wickham feigned affront, but Bennet was not about to allow him to claim ill use. "Come, sir, let us be open. I am aware of your history and your offenses in the other neighborhoods in which you have resided. I would advise you not to attempt such behavior in Meryton."

"It seems another has attempted to besmirch my good name," said a mournful Mr. Wickham. "I might have thought Darcy would leave me be now that he has reduced me to this state."

Bennet was amused by the man—not fooled. "Mr. Darcy offered to provide proof of his assertions, including references who would vouch for his trustworthiness. If you would prove his words false, all you must do is provide similar proof."

"And you would believe me before you believe a rich man?"

"I am not blinded by wealth, sir. I believe I am as objective as the next man and would be forced to give your words the consideration they deserve, should they prove to contradict with what I have already been told. So I ask again: are you prepared to provide proof against those allegations which have been made against you?"

"Spurious documents may be produced which will say anything such a wealthy man wished them to say."

"In other words: no." Mr. Bennet fixed Wickham with a sardonic grin, and the other man's lips tightened in response. "Now that we have that out of the way, let us return to our original discussion. As I said, I know how you have conducted yourself in other neighborhoods, sir. But you will not have the opportunity to do the same here. I require you to leave my girls strictly alone. They have been instructed not to speak to you, not to respond when you speak, and to avoid you at all times. In these prohibitions, I include any dancing at any function. Lydia will not be dancing with you at Mr. Bingley's ball, sir. Do not ask any of my other daughters to dance either."

Mr. Wickham's eyes glittered his hate and fury. "The request has already been submitted and accepted, sir. Would you have your daughter sit out the entire night?"

"As her guardian, I am forbidding it," snapped Bennet. "As such, there is no requirement for her to sit out. I am certain she will have no trouble finding other young men with whom to dance. She has a talent for dancing—is one of Meryton's finest dancers, I am sure."

"I beg you to reconsider, sir. I mean your daughters no harm."

"I have no notion as to what your intentions tend, sir. But I will not take the chance."

Quite deliberately, Bennet reached down into his waistcoat pocket and pulled out his watch, noting the time. "Now, if I am not mistaken, I believe the time for your visit has elapsed."

"I believe it has," replied Captain Carter, who had approached them at the sight of the tense standoff. "Pardon me, Mr. Bennet, but though I have heard something of Wickham's character, I hardly think this is required. Can you not tell me what you have against Lieutenant

Wickham?"

"Please ask your commanding officer, Captain," replied Bennet. "He has been provided with all the particulars. The sooner he disseminates the details to you and your colleagues, the better."

Captain Carter was obviously not happy, but he nodded once, a short, clipped motion. Bennet was not concerned with the captain's displeasure; his attention was once again focused on Lieutenant Wickham. The lieutenant must have more than his share of luck, for it was clear he had never been challenged in such a manner.

"When you leave Longbourn, Mr. Wickham, do not return. I have tried not to make a scene, but I will not tolerate your presence here. If you attempt to darken my door again, you will be denied entrance."

Wickham gave a jerky nod, and when a subdued group of officers said their farewells, Mr. Wickham only stood and glared at all and sundry. Bennet stood nearby, ensuring the man's good behavior. When the officers left the sitting-room, Bennet followed them. Though perhaps it was not necessary, he wished to ensure Wickham was gone and would not return.

Charles Bingley was a man who despised conflict of every sort, which was why that night at Netherfield was a trial for his sensibilities.

"Darcy," greeted Bingley when he met the others of his party that evening before dinner. "It has been a lovely day, has it not?"

Bingley had always been able to determine when his friend was amused at his ability to see the best part of any situation, for his countenance assumed an indulgent smile, which he wore at present. It was not patronizing, but an expression of true amusement and pleasure. Bingley relished the fact that he was able to lift his friend's spirits.

"I suppose the lessening of the rain for a time was welcome," replied Darcy. "It did, of course, begin to rain again soon after, so I suppose any benefit we derived was fleeting."

On the other side of Darcy, the viscount snorted. "Trust you, Darcy, to put a damper on any measure of bright spirits."

"Merely an observation," replied Darcy, seemingly unruffled by his cousin's harsh words.

Bingley frowned and looked between them. The viscount was watching Darcy with a certain level of asperity, shaking his head at Darcy's answer to Bingley's comment, while Darcy was doing a credible job of ignoring it. Bingley had never so much as seen the cousins exchange anything remotely unfriendly. And yet here was

Lord Chesterfield sniping at his cousin as if they were enemies.

"Well, I am assured that the weather will improve tomorrow," said Bingley. It was best if he just ignored what passed between the two men. "It is only two days until the ball. I would hope it will dry out a little before then."

"That sounds suspiciously like a wish rather than an expectation," said Lord Chesterfield.

"Perhaps it is," replied Bingley, not affronted in the slightest. "But I have often found that if I find reasons to be happy, life is much easier to bear. Would you not agree?"

It was curious when Lord Chesterfield's gaze shot to Darcy before he answered. "Perhaps it makes life easier to bear, Bingley. But it does nothing to improve the present."

"No, you are correct there. But then, my attitude is much better, which makes all the difference."

Into this peculiar mix of ill feelings between the cousins, Bingley's own family entered, Caroline sweeping in as if she were a duchess, while Louisa followed with Hurst, watching her sister warily. That Bingley could well understand—Caroline needed to be watched at all times, for she was almost always contemplating some intrigue.

"Mr. Darcy, Lord Chesterfield," said she in greeting, "how do you do today?"

"Miss Bingley," said Darcy, while Lord Chesterfield only nodded and informed her that he was well. Caroline did not seem to hear them, for she began to speak, regaling them with tales of her day, what she had done to prepare for the ball, all likely designed to show them what a wonderful hostess she was. Darcy was outwardly attentive, while his faraway gaze clearly showed him to be thinking of something else. Nor did Lord Chesterfield even bother to make any pretension toward attending Caroline's words. It did not matter to Bingley's sister, however, for she kept speaking as if every word which emerged from her mouth was eagerly anticipated by both gentlemen.

When they were called into dinner, Caroline rose and directed a sly look at the viscount. "Shall we, my lord?"

"Of course, Miss Bingley," said he, rising and offering his arm.

They entered the dining room, and dinner was served. Through it all, Caroline continued her monologue, albeit neither man appeared to hear one word in ten. But the little undercurrents between Darcy and Lord Chesterfield were still there as the men directed surreptitious glares at each other regularly. Or maybe it was correct to say the glares were mostly on Lord Chesterfield's side, for Darcy ignored them more often than not.

Though Bingley could not understand it, he decided that it did not signify. Their closeness was such that they would soon move past any disagreement, Bingley was certain. Instead, there were far more pleasant subjects of which to think, particularly the upcoming ball and the dances he would share with Miss Bennet. Now that was a much more agreeable topic to snare a man's attention.

It seemed the one person at Longbourn who did not understand that Lydia had been forbidden from dancing with Mr. Wickham was Mr. Collins. Of course, that was not exactly surprising, considering the man's general inability to understand much of anything. Thus, when he learned the truth of the matter, he made a scene of it, as Elizabeth might have expected.

"I am certain you will enjoy it very much, indeed, Cousin," said Mr. Collins as they were in the sitting-room before being called to dinner. "Though I have not known Mr. Wickham for long, I flatter myself that I am a good judge of character. He is an exceptional man, one who would be a good match for a young woman of your station."

Though Elizabeth was wondering if the parson was jesting, Lydia only shrugged and turned back to Kitty. It was clear that she felt a little distressed at being forbidden to dance with such a handsome man, but Elizabeth thought she would recover when she was once again in the company of the officers.

"It seems to me like you have missed an important communication, Mr. Collins," said Elizabeth.

Mr. Collins turned to Elizabeth and fixed her with that superior smile he always wore. "I assure you, my dear cousin, that I am fully cognizant of *everything* which is happening in this house. Indeed, though, perhaps, you and your family have attempted to keep certain facts from me and ignored me at other times, I am far more aware than you can imagine."

"Ah, so you know that Mr. Darcy himself informed us of Mr. Wickham's untrustworthy, immoral nature."

"Nothing but a misunderstanding, Cousin," said Mr. Collins. He waved his hand as if swatting ineffectually at a gnat. "My patroness's nephews are the best of men, and that includes a spirit of forgiveness which inspires those for whom true nobility is a gift given from God. In fact, I have heard of this matter which lies between them, and I am confident in asserting that it is in the past. Mr. Darcy, perhaps, does not wish to be in company with Mr. Wickham—which is understandable—but you cannot expect so great a man to be anything less than forgiving to a childhood companion."

"That is interesting, for, as I said, Mr. Darcy told us himself that Mr. Wickham was not to be trusted."

"You must have mistaken his meaning. I am convinced that Mr. Wickham is sorry for his former conduct and eager to re-establish his character. Cousin Lydia could do little better than an alliance with such a man."

"Is that so, Cousin?"

Mr. Collins missed the dangerous note in Mr. Bennet's tone, but Elizabeth did not. Her father was watching the parson, but there was little of joviality or friendliness in his manner. In fact, her father was as displeased as Elizabeth had ever seen.

"Of course, sir. It is a match more of her station than others to which she has aspired. And Mr. Wickham is affable and kind—a true gentleman, in spirit, if not in standing."

"Let me see if I understand, Mr. Collins," replied Mr. Bennet. "You think my daughter, who is the scion of a long line of gentlemen, is a 'good match' for a young man who is not only a libertine and rake, but naught but the son of a steward. Is that what you are saying?"

Though belatedly, it seemed Mr. Collins had finally realized that Mr. Bennet was not amused. He also seemed to understand that his assertions were not so perfect as he had contended.

"Well . . . You see . . ." Mr. Collins ceased his stammering and looked at Mr. Bennet, then cast his gaze upon the entire family. He obviously did not like what he saw, for he turned away and muttered to himself.

"I am sorry, Mr. Collins, but I did not quite hear what you said. Might I trouble you to repeat it, so we all may hear? I find your observations fascinating."

"Perhaps I was a little hasty," replied Mr. Collins. "He is, indeed, a good young man, but I suppose your daughter is in a position to expect more from a marriage."

"The second part of your speech is the first sensible thing you have said since you arrived. The first does not bear discussion, for I believe Elizabeth has already informed you, and you refused to hear." Mr. Collins scowled, but Mr. Bennet took no notice. Instead, he regarded his youngest daughters and bestowed a soft smile on them. "My youngest girls are a little trying at times, but they are good girls. I wish them to be happy in marriage, Mr. Collins, and I am assured they will *not* be so should one of them be so unfortunate as to marry Mr.

Wickham. Either way, they are far above him in society's eyes, and I will not have them make so unequal a marriage."

"Of course, sir," replied Mr. Collins, seemingly eager to leave the conversation behind. "Then my dear cousin will simply need to be content with enjoying Mr. Wickham's company at the ball."

"Again, Mr. Collins, you are incorrect. It appears you have heard nothing my Lizzy has said."

"I cannot understand what you mean, Cousin," replied the parson. "Why would I listen to her, when she is obviously holding some grudge against Mr. Wickham?"

"Because she has been telling you the truth, Mr. Collins. Though I find it difficult to understand, it is clear to me that you are the only person at Longbourn who does not know that I forbid Lydia from dancing with Mr. Wickham."

"Forbid?" demanded Mr. Collins aghast.

"*All* my daughters have been forbidden from dancing with him."

"But, Mr. Bennet, have you not heard what I have told you?"

"I have heard far too much of what you have to say," replied Mr. Bennet. "It is unsurprising, I suppose, since your conversation is nothing less than ubiquitous."

Mr. Collins appeared lost for words, the first time Elizabeth had ever seen him in such straits. He glanced at Lydia and then at Elizabeth herself. She scowled at the man, knowing exactly what he was thinking. Then his countenance changed, and he appeared to brighten.

"In that case, I shall submit my request to partner for your first set, Cousin Lydia, since you are not to dance with Mr. Wickham. I myself am free, as I am to dance the second with your sister, Elizabeth."

"Ugh," said Lydia, an expression of utmost disgust coming over her countenance. "I would not wish to dance with you—"

"You may wish to rethink your words, Lydia," interjected Mr. Bennet. "You are aware that if you refuse a dance, you must sit out for the rest of the evening."

Elizabeth almost laughed at the utter consternation which came over Lydia, even as Mr. Collins appeared more than a little smug. Elizabeth shook her head—why one would think it a victory to have a woman's guardian force her to dance with him was beyond Elizabeth's understanding.

"But, Papa!" exclaimed Lydia. "You did not make me dance with Mr. Wickham!"

"That was a different situation, as you well know. Mr. Wickham has no business being in the company with *any* young lady. My cousin, though you may not favor him, can at least be trusted with you for a dance. Do you still wish to refuse?"

It was clear Lydia wished for nothing more than to refuse to dance with Mr. Collins, but understanding her father was implacable, she only shook her head and turned back to Kitty. Mr. Collins, for his part, had an expression of satisfaction when he looked at the girl. Elizabeth could not understand him. Therefore, she did not even attempt it.

CHAPTER XV

The curse of having a voluble, fatuous man in one's company was the requirement to listen to him speak without ceasing. This Elizabeth knew to be the truth, for the example of Mr. Collins proved it beyond any hint of doubt.

While the day after the officers' visit had continued without any deviation from the three wet days preceding it, Elizabeth found herself considering ignoring the rain and going outside, if only to avoid the odious man. While he had considered himself quite clever and fortunate to have secured the youngest sister's hand for the first dances at the ball, his imposition on Elizabeth herself never ceased. When the day of the ball arrived, she was on the point of strangling him with his own long-winded soliloquies.

The short carriage ride to Netherfield was no exception. Elizabeth, who was situated on one side, sitting with Mary, Kitty, and Lydia on one seat, looked out the window at the passing darkness, seeing the ghostly figures of trees, rocks, and signposts slip by the moving coach. In the background, Mr. Collins kept droning on about whatever crossed his mind at any given moment, most of his comments made to Elizabeth herself. Her father rode on the box with the driver, as even seven in their carriage had been a tight fit. Besides, though it was cold outside, even that must be preferable to riding with Mr. Collins. Elizabeth almost wished she could herself.

At length, when the manor at Netherfield came into view, Elizabeth felt a momentary pang for one of her absent friends. Her time with Charlotte would have been characterized by witty remarks and intelligent conversation, with no little light teasing at the expense of the silliest of the company. Elizabeth had no doubt Charlotte would find Mr. Collins silly, indeed. And Elizabeth and Penelope would have been thick as thieves on a night such as tonight, dancing, talking, laughing, and breaking hearts without regard for the gentlemen they were spurning. It was, of course, nonsense, for Penelope had always been very well behaved. But thinking of such things, even if they were childish, was much preferable to listening to Mr. Collins.

The house was bedecked with lanterns at regular intervals along the long drive, providing light and a sense of festive welcome for those invited to the ball. Along the entrance was a line of carriages waiting to debark their passengers, and as Elizabeth gazed up toward the front of the line, she noted gentlemen and ladies making their way from the drive up the stairs and into the house, their finery fairly shining in the light of the lanterns and of the candles inside the house spilling out through the open doors.

"I must compliment Miss Bingley on her arrangements," said Mr. Collins, as he looked out the window to the approaching house. "For a small society such as this, it is clear she could not have done much better.

"Of course, that which would adorn my patroness's home on such an occasion would far outshine that which I see before me. Perhaps I should see if Lady Catherine would agree to provide Miss Bingley with advice. The assistance of so great a personage could only assist her as she makes her way through society."

Elizabeth did not even bother to shake her head or roll her eyes or respond with any other indication of exasperation. The parson had not halted speaking the entire distance between the estates.

Mrs. Bennet, however, showing more discernment than Elizabeth would ever have guessed, turned to the parson. "Oh? Does her ladyship entertain often? Does she give balls which are anticipated by the majority of Kent society?"

Mr. Collins blinked. "She has not given one in the time that I have been her parson."

"And how long has that been, Mr. Collins?"

"Nearly eight months, Mrs. Bennet." He was attempting to make it sound impressive, but no one gave him the awed response for which he had hoped.

"I see," replied Mrs. Bennet. "And what of the years before you became her parson? I dare say that if her ladyship is so generous and free with her advice, that she would have hosted many such events. Surely because she informs you of her nearest concerns, she would not have stinted to regale you with tales of her exploits."

Elizabeth fairly gawked at her mother, an action which was mirrored by Mr. Collins.

"I have not heard of any."

A raised eyebrow met his admission. "Not a one?"

"No, madam."

"Then perhaps you would refrain from delighting us with tales of events which are, it seems, nothing more than your fancy speaking."

Mr. Collins sputtered, obviously offended. "Lady Catherine de Bourgh is a lady of high society and one who possesses all the best virtues and capabilities. I would ask you not to denigrate her, Mrs. Bennet."

"I do no such thing," said Mrs. Bennet. "But the entire journey from Longbourn, we have been forced to listen to you jabber on about this and that. You will forgive me if I receive your words as idle boasts and so much drivel. Your patroness may be from a prominent family, but I am afraid I do not see in her that height of nobility which fuels your imagination."

"How—"

"Be silent, Mr. Collins!" commanded Mrs. Bennet. "And allow us a little peace from your continual monologues."

The parson's mouth snapped closed, and he glared at Mrs. Bennet. The rest of the girls only watched him, their own countenances unfriendly, and when confronted by their unity, Mr. Collins did the only sensible thing Elizabeth had ever seen from him: he was not silent—his muttering prevented that blessed state of affairs—but at least he was not speaking in a voice loud enough to be heard in Meryton.

When the carriage finally stopped in front of Netherfield's stairs, Mr. Bennet alighted from the box and opened the door himself, handing out his wife and daughters one by one. The way he smiled at his wife and his softly spoken "Well done, my dear" informed Elizabeth that he had likely heard his wife's set down. Mr. Collins's scowl was ignored, and after they alighted from the conveyance, the man himself was as well. Eager to escape from him, the family hurried up the stairs and into the house.

There was a lull in the receiving line, and the Bennets, after they shed their coats, went in directly and were greeted by the family. Jane was welcomed by Mr. Bingley, who clearly had eyes for no one else, and Elizabeth and her sisters received the welcome of Mrs. Hurst, who appeared truly delighted to see them. It was at this moment that Mr. Collins approached.

"Come, let me escort you into the ballroom, Cousin," said Mr. Collins, attempting to catch Elizabeth's arm.

"I am quite capable of walking on my own," said Elizabeth with more asperity than good manners. Unfortunately, their exchange caught the attention of another, who shot a knowing smirk at Elizabeth.

"Is this your cousin, of whom I have heard, Eliza?" simpered Miss Bingley. "What an excellent catch for you! When am I to wish you joy?"

"On the contrary, Miss Bingley," replied Elizabeth, "Mr. Collins is not pursuing me. But if you are interested, I will be happy to provide an introduction."

A fierce scowl settled over the woman's face, but Elizabeth had already turned away toward the ballroom, denying her the opportunity to respond. Jane shot her a disapproving look, and Elizabeth was forced to acknowledge that she had been less than kind to both the parson and the hostess. She could not bring herself to repine her action, however, for both had been deserving of it.

Near the entrance of the ballroom, Elizabeth caught sight of Mr. Darcy approaching her. He wore a smile, which he bestowed liberally upon her before he caught her hand and bowed over it.

"Miss Elizabeth," said he in his deep, vibrant voice. "How enchanting you look tonight. Would you allow me to accompany you into the ballroom?"

"Of course, Mr. Darcy," said Elizabeth. As she tucked her hand into the crook of his arm, she was struck by just how handsome he appeared in his suit and marveled at the exquisite attention he paid to her.

Then Lord Chesterfield also approached, bowing when he reached her. As he rose, he shot a look at Mr. Darcy which Elizabeth could not quite understand. Mr. Darcy looked back at his cousin, and to Elizabeth, it seemed like his expression was carefully blank. There was nothing of the camaraderie or playful jests between the cousins that she had become so accustomed to.

"Miss Elizabeth," said Lord Chesterfield. "I have been most remiss in securing a dance this evening. Would you be so good as to allow me the second set tonight?" His eyes flicked to his cousin, and when he spoke again, his tone was harder, almost accusatory. "I understand that my cousin has already secured your first."

"Yes, he has," replied Elizabeth. "But unfortunately, while your cousin has secured my first, *my* cousin has secured my second, and as such, I cannot cede that dance to you."

"Mr. Collins?" asked Lord Chesterfield with a frown.

When Elizabeth confirmed that it was so, he cast his eyes around. Mr. Collins had just stepped away from the receiving line where Elizabeth suspected he had been regaling Miss Bingley with anecdotes of his patroness and imagined finery at her balls, for Miss Bingley stood behind him, glaring at him with contempt. He appeared to be looking for them. Elizabeth turned her attention back to the viscount and noted his narrowed gaze in Mr. Collins's direction. She thought for a moment that he would go to Mr. Collins and ask him to give up the set he had already asked for. While Elizabeth thought it would be somewhat officious, in the end, she decided it would be a relief, for she suspected she would not enjoy a dance with the parson.

"Then I would like your third, if I may be so bold," said Lord Chesterfield at length, when he turned back to her.

"Of course, Lord Chesterfield," replied Elizabeth. "It is yours."

"Then let us enter the ballroom," said Mr. Darcy.

He guided her into the room, his cousin falling into step with them on Elizabeth's other side. She did not miss the exasperated glance he threw in Mr. Darcy's direction, though when Elizabeth turned to the man escorting her, he did not give any indication that he noticed anything amiss. Elizabeth was confused. What had happened to provoke the two cousins to behave in such a manner?

They entered and stood on the side, speaking among themselves while the musicians tuned their instruments. The ballroom, which Elizabeth had not seen in some years, was decked out with finery and candles, thoughtfully placed in out of the way locations to spare the guests from dripping wax. Elizabeth was forced to own that whatever else she was, Miss Bingley seemed a competent hostess.

They had only just begun to speak when the parson hurried into the room and, espying them, shot Elizabeth a nasty look and rushed to join them. When he came within a few strides, Mr. Darcy turned, bringing him to a halt with a single imperious glance. Elizabeth was grateful—she knew the parson would not have done anything in a crowded ballroom, but he seemed like an angry father about to take a young lady to task.

"Mr. Darcy," said the groveling minister, "it is very good of you to escort my poor cousin into the ballroom. But it was completely unnecessary, for I would have done it myself. Do not, I implore you, allow her to impose herself upon you, for a great man such as yourself has no need to put himself out in such a way."

"Mr. Collins," said Mr. Darcy, mimicking the parson's mode of address, "Miss Elizabeth did not 'impose upon me,' nor did I consider it any trouble to escort her into the room. In fact, as I have the first dance with her tonight, I felt it my privilege to have the good fortune to enter the ballroom with her on my arm."

Elizabeth colored at his obvious words of approbation, but Mr. Collins, as was his custom, missed the dangerous note in Mr. Darcy's voice.

"Ah, yes, I wished to speak to you of that. You are very good to favor my poor cousin. It speaks to your noble upbringing and character, I am sure. But it is also not necessary. If you feel you have made an error in judgment by offering to partner Miss Elizabeth for the first sets, I would be happy to step in for you."

"Are you not to dance the first with Lydia, Mr. Collins?" asked Elizabeth.

"Perhaps I am," replied Mr. Collins. "But I am certain Cousin Lydia would be happy to dance with Mr. W—" Mr. Collins checked himself at the last moment. "With one of the officers instead."

"Yes, Darcy," said Lord Chesterfield, a note of sardonic amusement in his tone. "Give up your sets to the inestimable Mr. Collins."

Mr. Darcy did not even bother to glance at his cousin. "No, I will not give them up. A gentleman, Mr. Collins, does not renege on an offer to dance by giving his sets up to another." When the parson attempted to speak again, Mr. Darcy cut him off. "Do not ask me again, sir. Miss Elizabeth has agreed to dance with me, and I will not disappoint her by withdrawing."

The thought crossed Elizabeth's mind that she *would* be disappointed if Mr. Darcy had decided against dancing with her. She was not able to pursue that thought, however, as the music for the first sets began, and before the parson could say anything further, Mr. Darcy escorted her to the floor. Elizabeth left to the sight of two men, both glaring after them—Mr. Collins at her and Lord Chesterfield at Mr. Darcy. Mr. Collins, however, suddenly seemed to recall that he was to dance with Lydia and hurried off in search of her. Lord Chesterfield only continued to watch them.

*   *   *

It should not be supposed that Louisa Hurst would be able to escape her sister's ill humors, even at such an event as a ball hosted by their brother. No, in fact, Caroline was in fine form that evening, and as Hurst was generally not inclined to dance much—and to own the truth, Louisa was not very fond of the activity herself—she found herself standing by the side of the dance floor with her sister for company. In fact, Louisa had been behaving more like the mistress of the estate than her sister, as Caroline was too busy watching the cousins, annoyed that she had not been asked to dance by either.

"Look at her!" sneered Caroline, gesturing vaguely at Elizabeth. "Looking about her with smugness because she somehow managed to trick Mr. Darcy into dancing the first set with her."

Louisa knew Caroline was upset because *she* had never managed the same feat with Mr. Darcy. The man had stubbornly refused to even look her way, and only danced with her, Louisa suspected, because he felt it his duty to pay respect to his friend's sister, whether she deserved it or not.

"Why should it bother you if she dances with Mr. Darcy? Have you not set your sights on the viscount?"

Her eyes shifted to Lord Chesterfield, and her expression soured further. "Perhaps I have not given him enough of an opportunity," mused Caroline.

Privately, Louisa suspected that Lord Chesterfield simply did not consider her to be a potential bride. Oh, he engaged her much more than Mr. Darcy ever did, but it was all superficial, with no true depth or meaning.

"And all these officers," said Caroline with a disgusted wave at the crowd dotted with red coats. "Why would Charles invite all this riffraff to our ball?"

"Army service is a respectable occupation, Caroline."

Caroline grunted but changed the subject. "Look at that man over there."

Following her sister's motion, Louisa saw a single officer standing by the side of the room, watching the proceedings. He was tall and handsome, Louisa supposed, though not truly the type of man she would consider especially attractive. Furthermore, he seemed to exist in a kind of a bubble, with no one standing nearby. Several times as they watched, officers would either walk past him or glance at him before looking away in disgust. And he was alternately looking between Mr. Darcy, dancing with Miss Elizabeth, and Lord Chesterfield, standing alone, watching the couple, his expression showing clear revulsion.

"I wonder if he would be a useful acquaintance," mused Caroline, only moments after referring to the officers as "riffraff."

"I think you would do well to leave him be," said Louisa.

But Caroline did not listen. She wandered away, ostensibly to mingle with the crowd of local gentry when in reality she was making her way toward the lone officer in a manner which could only be called open stealth. Louisa shook her head—she did not know what the man was about, but if the other officers shunned him, it would be best to leave him be. But Caroline would be Caroline, and Louisa could do nothing about her sister. Indeed, she was long past the point of even trying.

Instead, Louisa began mingling among the crowd herself, asking after the comfort of their guests, speaking, listening, and generally being a good hostess. It was what Caroline should have been doing.

When the music started, Elizabeth began moving the steps of the dance with Mr. Darcy, gliding through the motions so well known to her. While she noted that Mr. Darcy was a skilled dancer, indeed, her thoughts were fixed upon other matters, and his prowess was nothing more than a minor thought in the back of her mind. She was much more interested in considering what she had seen, particularly between the cousins, that evening, wondering at their behavior. It was so out of character from what she had seen of them previously that she could hardly make any sense of it.

But one did not simply ask such questions of one's partner. Mr. Darcy, Elizabeth had come to realize, was a good man, but his patience would be tested by an overly curious dance partner. So she stayed quiet and danced with the man, noting his own quietude, the way he regarded her with his calm interest. Was there admiration in that gaze? Elizabeth could not be certain. But she thought she saw a glimmer of interest. Perhaps that was enough for the present.

"I must say, Miss Elizabeth," said Mr. Darcy when they had been dancing for some minutes, "I am quite surprised and perhaps a little worried."

"Oh?" asked Elizabeth, his sudden comment surprising her. "Why would that be, sir?"

"Only that I witnessed you dancing at the assembly the night we first met, and I cannot remember you remaining silent for this long."

Elizabeth could not help but laugh. "Perhaps you are correct. But why are you worried?"

"There are only three things which I can think of to which to attribute your inability to speak, and two of them could be construed as an indictment on your partner."

Though she protested, Mr. Darcy only smiled and winked at her. Elizabeth was in awe—Mr. Darcy appeared to be flirting with her!

"I shall tell you my conjectures, and you may inform me if I am correct." Elizabeth grinned and nodded. "The first possibility is that you simply do not know me well enough and do not know what to say. That is likely, as those men with whom you danced at the assembly must be known to you. The second is that you find me either a bore or not worth expending the effort to converse. The third is that you actively dislike me, and do not wish to speak. If it is the second or third, then I must apologize for imposing my presence upon you."

Again, Elizabeth laughed. "Perhaps it is simply that my mind wandered to some other subject, Mr. Darcy."

"Is that not also a mark against me?" asked Mr. Darcy. "Am I so dull that you cannot even talk to me about the weather?"

"No, indeed!" cried Elizabeth. "It is none of those things. Perhaps there are those who talk without cessation about nothing at all, but I hope that *I* am not one of those. I think we have spoken enough to know that I do not find you one I cannot esteem. I believe we have simply not hit on a subject about which we may converse with any degree of skill."

"Hmm, then perhaps it is incumbent upon me to provide us with the appropriate material."

Elizabeth opened her mouth to respond, but at that moment there was a sharp cry down the line and confusion reigned for a moment. Still continuing in the steps, Elizabeth looked down to the other end and noticed that a young woman was being helped off the floor, the black crow-like form of her cousin hovering over her. It was Lydia and Mr. Collins.

"Did you see what happened?" asked Elizabeth, turning back to her partner. With the departure of the couple, the line had once again settled into the rhythm of the dance.

"I am afraid I did not, Miss Elizabeth. I found myself rather busy, contemplating a young lady nearby, one who makes even the most mundane subjects the most interesting I have ever heard."

"And who is this young lady?" asked Elizabeth with an arch of her eyebrow.

Mr. Darcy showed her a mysterious smile. "Ask me another time, Miss Elizabeth. It is possible I have underestimated her appeal. I would not wish to do her anything other than the justice she deserves.

"Now, I understand you are a great reader. May I ask after what you have read recently?"

"Books in a ballroom, Mr. Darcy?" asked Elizabeth. "Do you not find your mind too full to consider such subjects?"

"My mind *is* full, Miss Elizabeth. But I believe I can carry on such a conversation credibly, as long as it is with you."

The inference in his words set Elizabeth to blushing. But she would not be overawed—thus, she answered his question, and they began to speak. And what a conversation it was! They were largely inattentive to anything else happening in the room as they spoke of their likes and dislikes, gave their opinions of what they had read, and informed each other of some works they had not read.

Elizabeth had been a member of society since she was fifteen, and now that she was twenty, she had attained a reputation for cleverness and wit. Even so, she still noticed that many men listened to her with the indulgent smiles of an adult for a child, or used patronizing words, complimenting her for her wit. At times it almost seemed to her like the praise of a boy for his dog.

Mr. Darcy did none of those things. They often agreed, and when they did, each shared insights that perhaps the other had not considered. Elizabeth came away feeling like she had learned something new and thought Mr. Darcy experienced the same. And when they disagreed, they each stated their opinion rationally, the other listening carefully. Once, Elizabeth was even able to elicit the comment that her reasoning had caused Mr. Darcy to reconsider his position. She had never had such an experience before, even from those who claimed to be the most impressed with her intellect! By the time the strains of music fell silent, Elizabeth was surprised the time had passed so quickly and was not eager to lose the company of this man.

"Thank you for an enlightening time, Miss Elizabeth," replied Mr. Darcy. "I believe I shall go back and read that passage in *Paradise Lost*, for I suspect your interpretation might be the superior."

"At least you own it," said Elizabeth, shooting him an arch grin.

Mr. Darcy only laughed. "I have the feeling, Miss Elizabeth, that life could never be dull when in company with you." They halted at the side of the room. "I believe there are a few moments before the next dance begins. Shall I fetch us both cups of punch?"

Elizabeth gave him a shy smile. "I believe I would like that, Mr. Darcy."

He bowed and turned away, moving toward the refreshment table, Elizabeth watching him go, wondering what his manners tonight could mean. For the first time, she felt the fluttering in her heart and wondered if it was being touched by this man. And his feelings? Did his manners show anything other than polite interest? Did she dare even hope?

The confused muddle set her head to spinning, and she turned her attention to other matters, deliberately deciding to leave such ruminations behind. Not far from where she stood, she noticed that Lydia had taken a seat on a nearby chair, her foot propped up on another chair with Mrs. Bennet in attendance. Not far away, Mr. Bennet stood speaking with Mr. Collins, and from what Elizabeth could see of their conversation, her father was not happy about something.

"Oh, Lizzy!" cried Lydia when she saw Elizabeth approaching. "It is in every way horrible!"

"What happened, Lydia?" asked Elizabeth.

"Mr. Collins is a truly ghastly man; that is what happened!"

Elizabeth looked at her mother, but Mrs. Bennet only grimaced and turned her attention back to Lydia. She massaged Lydia's ankle through the girl's stockings. Lydia winced a little, but she was far too incensed to give much thought to her mother's ministrations.

"Perhaps you would clarify your meaning, Lydia. What happened?"

"Mr. Collins is what happened," hissed Lydia. The girl was so angry that tears began to leak out of the corners of her eyes. "He is the worst dancer one could possibly imagine! He moved wrong and seemed to think it was necessary to stop and apologize every time he did so, which meant he never did truly dance. Then when I tried to correct his movements, he berated me for presuming to instruct him. Then he stepped on my toes and caused me to fall."

"She seems to have a bit of a sprain," said Mrs. Bennet.

Lydia keened her frustration. "Now I shall be forced to miss the fun of the dancing."

"There, there, my dear," said Mrs. Bennet, patting Lydia's knee. "I dare say it will improve quickly, though you will need to take care when you move."

Elizabeth looked at her mother gravely, and when Mrs. Bennet shook her head, Elizabeth sighed. She knew there likely would not be any more dancing for Lydia that night, and the girl would be almost unbearable for the next several days because of it.

"Well, what do we have here?" asked Mr. Jones the apothecary, as he approached from the other side of the ballroom, trailing Kitty who had obviously been sent to fetch him.

When directed, Mr. Jones knelt beside Lydia and asked her a few questions. Mr. Bennet approached, an obviously chastened Mr. Collins hanging back looking anywhere but at Lydia, and said a few words to Mr. Bennet, after which Mr. Bennet signaled for a nearby footman to bear Lydia to another room so her foot could be examined properly. Elizabeth watched them go, but her mind was on another matter altogether. Mr. Collins had been so insistent about Lydia and Elizabeth reaching above themselves. Had he somehow contrived to injure Lydia to prevent her from dancing with either man?

CHAPTER XVI

$\mathcal{A}$s Elizabeth stood thinking of Lydia's situation, she did not notice the approach of two men, one welcome and one not. The first to speak was Mr. Darcy, and when she heard his voice, Elizabeth turned without thought and smiled at him. His countenance, however, was all concern.

"Was that your sister who was carried from the room?"

"It was," said Elizabeth. She accepted the cup of punch from Mr. Darcy and took a sip from it. Her anxiety must have been evident on her countenance, for Mr. Darcy looked at her with grave concern before he edged closer and spoke in a soft voice:

"Is something wrong, Miss Elizabeth? Beyond what happened to your poor sister?"

Elizabeth sighed and turned her gaze up to his eyes. "I do not know, Mr. Darcy. I should not say it . . ."

"Do not think you need to be circumspect with me."

A sigh escaped Elizabeth's lips. "I cannot help but wonder — Mr. Collins has been so insistent about you and your cousin that I must question if he contrived a way to injure my sister, so she could not dance with you or Lord Chesterfield."

It is the mark of a truly senseless man that he interrupts a private conversation at the worst possible moment and in the worst possible way. Before Mr. Darcy had an opportunity to respond, the sound of Mr. Collins's voice interrupted him.

"Cousin Elizabeth!" exclaimed he. "You must stop this insistence on imposing upon Mr. Darcy! He is not some servant, to wait upon your every whim."

Once again, before Elizabeth was able to respond, Mr. Darcy spoke, his tone hard and unyielding. "Mr. Collins! I would ask you not to presume to misinterpret everything which passes between Miss Elizabeth and myself. For your information, sir, it is the mark of a gentleman to inquire after a lady's comfort and provide her with refreshment, should she require it."

"Of course, Mr. Darcy," said the parson, almost groveling at the gentleman's tone. "I only . . ."

"Step this way, Mr. Collins," said Mr. Darcy, beckoning to the parson. "I have something I wish to say to you."

Though Mr. Collins appeared like a man being led to the guillotine, he followed Mr. Darcy to where the man led him some few feet away. What followed was, to Elizabeth's eyes, nothing less than a stinging rebuke from Mr. Darcy, which had Mr. Collins ringing his hands and bowing ever lower—at least until Mr. Darcy reached out and prevented the man from bowing, presumably accompanied by an admonishment to that effect. Elizabeth could hear little of what he said, but a few phrases found her ears, including the strongly worded demand that she emerge from her dance unharmed.

By the end of the lecture, Mr. Collins was mopping his face with a handkerchief he had produced from a pocket. Elizabeth was certain the poor square of fabric was soaked by the time Mr. Darcy bowed with curt contempt to the parson and made his way back to Elizabeth. Of course, Mr. Collins followed him.

"Thank you, Mr. Collins, but I was speaking with Miss Elizabeth," said Mr. Darcy when he noticed the parson hovering nearby. "You may come and collect her when your dance begins." Mr. Darcy then turned a harsh glare on Mr. Collins, causing him to step back in alarm. "Remember what I have told you, sir."

Mr. Collins bobbed twice and then scurried away. Elizabeth noted, however, that he did not go far, and that he scowled at Elizabeth when he thought Mr. Darcy was not looking. Picking up his own cup of punch, which he had set down on a nearby chair, Mr. Darcy tossed it back and then handed the cup to a nearby maid.

"I do not know how your father can tolerate that man," said Mr.

Darcy in a low voice. "I would have thrown him from my property two minutes after his arrival!"

Elizabeth stifled a laugh. She agreed with her whole heart. "Papa *is* amused by follies and inconsistencies. Mr. Collins diverted him at first, but I think you will find that Papa has almost reached the end of his patience."

Following her eyes, Mr. Darcy noted where Mr. Bennet had entered the room and was standing not far away, glowering at the parson. For his part, Mr. Collins was oblivious to that fact; the frown which almost always adorned his mien when he witnessed Elizabeth and Mr. Darcy standing together was present once again.

"Come, let us leave such a disagreeable subject, Mr. Darcy," said Elizabeth, drawing the gentleman's eyes back to her. "I judge there are only a few minutes before the second set will begin." She grinned at him. "Are there any other passages of books which you have misunderstood? I would be happy to correct you if there are."

Though Mr. Darcy appeared surprised for a moment, soon he grinned. "I confess to no such thing, Miss Elizabeth. Furthermore, I am determined to prove you wrong."

"Then do your worst, sir."

As Elizabeth had suspected, there were only a few minutes left before the strains of the second dance floated through the air, but they spent an agreeable time until she was forced to leave. Lydia was brought back into the room just before Mr. Collins came to collect her, and Elizabeth went to her sister, attempting to soothe her glumness—the verdict from the apothecary was that she should stay off her foot for the rest of the evening and for a week after. Lydia's night—as far as the dance was concerned—was over.

When Collins led Miss Elizabeth to the dance floor, Darcy watched closely to ensure his instructions had been carried out to the letter. In fact, Darcy thought her concerns about the parson and her sister were perhaps a little sensational, though he understood why she worried about it. Still, to give her the peace of mind, Darcy had instructed the parson that she should emerge from the experience of dancing with him in the same condition as she began it. The parson, though at first a little offended, had given Darcy his assurance.

A few moments' watchful contemplation of the parson's steps revealed that he was not vicious, only clumsy. It was clear he had no idea whatsoever of the steps of the dance. He was able to follow the other gentlemen to a certain extent, but more often than not, he was in the wrong place at the wrong time. Darcy could see the mortification Miss Elizabeth was feeling, and his heart went out to her. That so bright a light should be the focus of the attention of such a buffoon was no less than a travesty.

As he was engaged in the pleasurable activity of watching Miss Elizabeth, a voice spoke, bringing his attention to a much less welcome individual.

"Mr. Darcy," said Miss Bingley, "I see you are watching Miss Elizabeth Bennet dance with her cousin." The woman let out a less than ladylike sniff of disdain. "He appears to be . . . less than impressive, does he not?"

Though Darcy agreed with her, he was not about to state that opinion openly. It would just induce the woman to more observations, which would decrease in acceptability and kindness the longer she continued. Instead, he only shook his head and returned to his contemplation of the ballroom.

"Still, I suppose it is nothing more than she can expect," said Miss Bingley. "I understand he has been paying much attention to her. It would be an eligible match, I dare say."

"I doubt she favors him," replied Darcy. "I think I know enough of Miss Elizabeth that she would refuse any offer when she cannot respect the one extending his hand."

"Then she is a fool," said Miss Bingley. Darcy turned and regarded her, but Miss Bingley did not seem to notice, so intent was she upon watching Miss Elizabeth. "A woman in her situation has not the privilege of holding out hope for anything better."

"Are you suggesting that a woman should take whatever offer comes to her, regardless of whether the man in question will make her happy in life?"

Miss Bingley's eyes found Darcy's, her expression unreadable. "I would never have thought that *you* would hold to such sentimental notions, Mr. Darcy. Have you not been raised, as are most in your set, to consider fortune and connections before such transient considerations of the heart?"

"It appears there is much you are unaware of me. My parents made a love match. Why would I wish for anything less for myself?"

"Then I apologize, sir," replied Miss Bingley. "I did not mean to offend."

"It is quite all right, Miss Bingley," replied Darcy.

The woman stayed near him for several more moments, a faintly expectant air about her. But when Darcy refused to speak to her — or more importantly, ask her to dance—she huffed and went away. Darcy paid no notice, and he decided in that moment he would not in the future. He had been thinking of asking her to dance, a duty akin to a task one knows must be completed but wishes to do anything else. But when Miss Bingley began speaking of Miss Elizabeth and her misunderstanding of what Darcy wished in marriage, he reconsidered. Never had the difference between them been displayed in such stark terms. Hopefully, she would not consider a marriage between them possible when she failed with Fitzwilliam.

Another objectionable presence made itself known to Darcy soon after, as he noted that Wickham, whom Darcy had seen at times that evening, was standing by the dance floor, watching the proceedings. That the man was not dancing was a testament to how different his stay in Meryton would be from any other place he had imposed his presence. Most of the neighborhood now knew of him, and though Darcy could not know for certain, he thought it likely that Wickham would be refused should he ask to stand up with one of the local ladies. That supposition was confirmed when he happened to notice Mr. Bennet also watching Wickham closely.

"Thank you, Mr. Darcy, for making us aware of Mr. Wickham's character," said Mr. Bennet when he noticed Darcy standing nearby. "The man has a countenance which would lead us all to believe his tales, had we not already known what he is."

"It is no trouble, Mr. Bennet," replied Darcy. "I would not have him importuning your daughters when I had the power to prevent it."

"Even then, I was forced to convince him not to importune them." Darcy looked at Mr. Bennet askance. Mr. Bennet shook his head. "Two days ago, a group of officers came to Longbourn to visit. Mr. Wickham was one of their number. When he asked Lydia to dance, I intervened, informing him that none of my girls would be allowed to dance with him and that he was not to return to my estate."

Darcy grunted. "He has never been prudent. He should have remained as inconspicuous as possible and left as soon as was expedient. But he has always had too much confidence in his ability to extract himself from trouble."

"I dare say he has seen much of that," replied Mr. Bennet. "Either way, he will not dance with any of my girls, and they all know to stay away from him. With that, I must be content."

The men drifted apart after that, Darcy continuing to watch Miss Elizabeth, though he attempted to avoid giving the appearance of being focused on her. Mr. Bennet, from what Darcy could see, watched

Mr. Wickham with all the intensity of a man protecting his daughters. Darcy's original estimation of the man had been that he was slothful and indifferent. But what he was seeing of Mr. Bennet tonight informed him that though he might be a little odd, he cared for his girls and would exert himself in their protection. Darcy appreciated that Miss Elizabeth had an able protector.

Being released from the dance floor was akin to a soul's entrance in paradise, or so Elizabeth imagined. A more disagreeable partner she had never had. While she had quickly understood Mr. Collins was only clumsy and unpracticed, that did not change his limitations as a dance partner. Elizabeth escaped as soon as she could to her next partner, Lord Chesterfield.

Of course, she did not miss the dark looks thrown at her by Mr. Collins, who seemed to think she was attempting to attract *two* men to her with the voice of a siren. With any luck, however, she would be free of the odious man's presence for the rest of evening. It was perhaps a vain hope, for she had no faith in his ability to make himself scarce.

When the viscount collected her for their dance, Elizabeth smiled and greeted him, allowing herself to feel pleasure at the attentiveness of such a prominent man. He led her to the line, and they set to it with a will. Their conversation flowed more quickly and easily — at least at first — than her conversation with Mr. Darcy had.

"Miss Elizabeth, I do not think I have mentioned it yet, but you are positively divine tonight," said Lord Chesterfield as soon as they began to dance.

Once again, Elizabeth was flattered at his attention, and she felt her cheeks heat up in response to his words. "I believe there are many who are looking their best tonight, my lord. An occasion such as this is a reason for us all to display whatever charms we possess to their best advantage. Do you not agree?"

"Oh, aye," said the viscount. "Ladies are always at their best at any event where they may be seen. But you outshine them all, I dare say. I challenge any man to disagree."

"Are you suggesting vanity on my part, Lord Chesterfield?" asked Elizabeth, arching an eyebrow at the man. "This talk of ladies being at their best smacks of artificial charms designed to capture a man."

Lord Chesterfield laughed and shook his head. "No, indeed, Miss Elizabeth."

They separated slightly due to the dance, and when they came together again, they clasped right hands and moved in a circle together. When they were thus engaged, Lord Chesterfield leaned forward and said in a low tone: "Courtship is a matter of showing the best of oneself to a potential mate, is it not?"

Though surprised at his choice of words, Elizabeth maintained her composure and allowed that it was. But she could not allow his words to pass without a challenge. "But I would not call this a courtship, sir. It is naught but a ball given by a good man to those in the area in which he resides."

"Perhaps there is no official or explicit courtship, Miss Elizabeth. But are events like this not the beginnings of courtship? Some might say, for example, that Bingley and your eldest sister are all but courting even as we speak."

Elizabeth darted a glance at where Jane was dancing with one of the local gentlemen—Samuel Lucas, Elizabeth noted with a look of annoyance at the objectionable man. But it appeared she was paying him no attention, and he was not even trying to turn her eye. In fact, her gaze rarely strayed from the figure of Mr. Bingley, who danced with Mary several couples away. It warmed Elizabeth's heart to see her sister so enamored with a man.

"Perhaps you are correct, my lord," said Elizabeth, turning back to the viscount, who was watching her with an intensity that reminded her of Mr. Darcy. "But you still have not answered my initial question."

"Then I shall do so directly. In fact, I was not speaking to the vanity of anyone, though it is possible that a certain amount exists. But that may be true in almost every setting, and not only the ballroom. We all, I am certain you would agree, wish to be respected and esteemed by those of our acquaintance. Being admired for how we look can be a facet of that wish. Do you not agree?"

"I am afraid I must yield to your arguments, my lord," replied Elizabeth.

"I am glad to hear it."

Once again, they were forced to pause their conversation because of the demands of the steps. When they came together again, it seemed like Lord Chesterfield had more he wished to say.

"I *will* inform you of this, Miss Elizabeth: I do believe there exists a certain level of 'artificial charms,' as you call them, in most of those one meets. Indeed, it can often be difficult to determine the true person behind the façade we all put up before the world.

"Having said this, I believe I may safely say that *you*, Miss

Elizabeth, are one of the most honest and genuine young ladies I have ever met."

Elizabeth could not help but blush before the man's praise, but he was not finished. "It is clear you are in the habit of stating your opinion without pretense or obfuscation, and while other ladies might preen in front of a mirror to ensure their appearance is exactly so, you do not need to put any effort in such endeavors. You are natural, wholesome, and good, and you do so without conscious thought. I find that quite intriguing, I assure you."

"I thank you, my lord," replied Elizabeth, wondering if her cheeks were giving off light, so warm did they feel. "But you ascribe far greater virtues to me than I actually possess. I am not so estimable as all this."

"Those who demur are those who are most estimable," replied Lord Chesterfield. "I find that those who consider themselves beautiful and desirable are often those who are the vainest. They expect the adulation of the masses and, particularly, anticipate the gentlemen to fall at their knees and worship them. You do no such thing."

Elizabeth peered at him suspiciously. All this talk of vanity and pretension and sincerity was pushing her embarrassment away, and she now wondered what his purpose was. In her experience, men would often flatter a little to show their appreciation. But a man who flattered excessively usually wished something from the woman. Elizabeth did not think that the viscount was the kind of man who would improperly importune a woman — particularly a gentlewoman — but prudence dictated she be on her guard.

Throughout the course of their dance, the viscount continued to speak, and while Elizabeth enjoyed his conversation and their banter, the little niggling feeling of being excessively praised continued to build within her mind. And the more he praised, the more she parried and backed away. Lord Chesterfield did not appear to recognize her increasingly defensive stance; he spoke and flattered and bantered without pause, and by the end of the dance, Elizabeth was grateful for the opportunity to retreat from him a little and think.

When she was back on the side of the dance floor waiting for the next set to start and the arrival of her next partner, Mary approached. She grasped Elizabeth's arm, pulled her to an area of relative privacy in the busy ballroom, and fixed Elizabeth with a serious look.

"What is it, Lizzy?" demanded she.

Elizabeth, surprised at her sister's forceful nature, could only stare. This prompted an annoyed huff.

"I was not so engaged in my dance with Mr. Bingley that I could not see what was happening between you and the viscount."

The mention of the man caused Elizabeth's eyes to flick to where he was standing on the other side of the dance floor, speaking with Colonel Forster.

"You began the dance with your usual level of repartee," said Mary, drawing Elizabeth's attention back from the viscount, "but it seemed to me you became more defensive as time wore on."

"I hardly know what to think," replied Elizabeth. "He has always been friendly and engaging. But tonight, he seemed determined to flatter, and he did so without ceasing." Elizabeth glanced about and decided the particulars could not be disseminated in such a place without risking being overheard. "I do not wish to say much at present. But I am struck by a vast difference in two of the men with whom I have danced tonight."

"You are not speaking of Mr. Collins."

It was not a question, but Elizabeth shook her head anyway. "No. I am speaking of Mr. Darcy and Lord Chesterfield. Whereas Mr. Darcy is quieter and does not possess the animation of his cousin, he spoke to me in a friendly manner, debating various topics like he was speaking to an equal, listening to what I had to say with true interest. I felt like my opinion was valued and my intelligence respected. Lord Chesterfield wished only to flatter my vanity, even while he protested that I was far too genuine for such conceit. Their manners were so different. I almost felt . . ."

"What, Lizzy?" asked Mary when Elizabeth did not speak further.

Elizabeth ducked her head in embarrassment. "I assure you I have no reason to believe the viscount meant it in such a way, but I almost felt like a woman being considered for the position of the man's mistress."

Mary's eyes widened and her nostrils flared. Elizabeth put a hand on her sister's arm to calm her.

"As I said, Mary, I do not believe that was his intention. But I also must wonder why his manner with me is so changed tonight. We have often spoken in congenial terms, and I know he is a good man, one who does not look down on others and speaks to them as equals. I simply do not know why he was so insistent upon flattering me."

"The contrast *is* striking," said Mary, as she worried her lower lip with her teeth. "Perhaps it would be best to maintain a little distance from the viscount. He may not mean anything by it, but it would be best to be certain."

"I agree," replied Elizabeth. "I shall not slight him, but I will not go out of my way to attract his attention either."

With that, the conversation between sisters ended, as a pair of militia officers approached them for the next sets. The rest of the evening was a whirlwind of dances, conversations, refreshments, laughter, and other enjoyments. Elizabeth was not forced to dodge the viscount much — while the man did approach her on several occasions and seemed intent upon flattering her, the demands of the dance were such that she never had much time to devote to his blandishments.

Mr. Darcy, on the other hand, also approached her several times. His conversation, however, consisted of more of what they had indulged in during their sets together, and on one occasion, he informed her that after due consideration, he thought one of her assertions about a text they had both read was correct. Elizabeth felt quite gratified at his attention and spoke with him easily on several occasions.

The third gentleman who seemed intent upon intruding upon her notice was Mr. Collins, but he did not act the suitor. He seemed more determined to interrupt whenever she was speaking with one of the other two men, though a harsh glare from either was enough to send him scurrying away. As such, Elizabeth was only required to avoid him whenever Mr. Darcy or Lord Chesterfield were not present, which, as it turned out, was easy enough for her to do.

It was approaching the supper hour when Elizabeth was forced to stand up with the second objectionable man of the evening. She had not been prepared to dance with Samuel Lucas, and he usually avoided her at events such as this, which was no hardship for Elizabeth. Thus, when he approached her not long after her arrival, asking her for a dance, she had scowled at him, before acceding, knowing she would not be allowed to do otherwise.

"I must own, little Eliza," said he in his usually patronizing tone, "that I might have underestimated you."

"By my account, little Sammy," said Elizabeth, attempting to be as insulting as he was himself, "you have made it a habit of underestimating me. I have no notion of what you mean in this instance."

The detestable smirk, which Elizabeth had often wished to remove from his countenance forcibly, was once again in full view. "Why, in your determination to avoid being forced to follow my sister into the circumstances of her new life. I had thought that with your proclivity for clever words and tendency to overwhelm potential suitors with your intelligence, you were destined to end in service. Perhaps I was mistaken."

"Are you accusing me of acting improperly, Mr. Lucas?" asked Elizabeth. She wondered that he was not frostbitten by the coldness in her tone. As was his wont, he only laughed and shook his head.

"I do not mean to be so cruel, my dearest little Eliza. I only mean to congratulate you. Why, given what I am witnessing before me, I should not wonder if you will have Mr. Darcy and Lord Chesterfield engaged in fisticuffs by the end of the evening for the privilege of your favor. I know not how you have managed it, but well done, I say!"

Elizabeth opened her mouth to reply, intending to flay the objectionable man where he stood. But suddenly there was a disturbance and a loud voice rose over the room, audible even above the sound of the music and general conversation.

"Where are they? Where are my nephews? I demand to see them at once!"

CHAPTER XVII

*D*arcy could hardly believe his ears. There was only one person in all of England who could speak in such a loud volume with such force, expecting to be obeyed by all within range of her strident proclamations. What he could not quite determine was why she was in Hertfordshire and how she had come to be here at this late hour.

There was no time to be lost, however, lest she stain the family name irreparably. The door through which she had entered was not far from where Darcy stood, and he approached at a quick walk, intending to quell her demands as soon as may be. In the corner of his eye, Darcy noted the Fitzwilliam was moving in her direction as quickly as was Darcy himself.

"Where are they?" demanded she again. "And where are the Jezebels determined to make them forget all they owe to the family? I insist on being satisfied this very instant!"

When Darcy broke clear of the crowd which had gathered to watch the spectacle, he noted that Mrs. Hurst was attempting to placate Lady Catherine and not having much success. While Mrs. Hurst's comments were soft enough that Darcy could not overhear them, of course, that was not the case with her ladyship.

"No, I will not wait. I will see Darcy and Chesterfield this instant! Do you not know who I am?"

"Lady Catherine," said Darcy, shifting her attention to him and away from his friend's sister. "What a surprise this is. How came you to be here, this late at night?"

"I have come to bring you to your senses!" came the lady's haughty reply. "As for the time, we wasted much of it attempting to discover the location of this insignificant house and then more of it calling at that wretched estate of those Jezebels who are determined to ruin you."

Darcy paled. Had Lady Catherine gone to Longbourn first? He could only be thankful the family had been at Netherfield rather than been forced to deal with Lady Catherine's ill humors and demands. He would no doubt be forced to apologize to Mr. Bennet on her ladyship's behalf for her treatment of his servants.

"Your ladyship!" exclaimed Mr. Collins as he approached at a quick trot. The silly man almost prostrated himself at her feet, so low was his genuflection. "I had not thought I would see you here tonight. You are, of course, very welcome here. We are, indeed, all privileged to be in your majestic presence. Shall I introduce you to the master of the house?"

"I have no desire to be known to him," said Lady Catherine with a sniff. "I will be leaving with my nephews in tow immediately, so there is no need."

A shared glance with his cousin revealed them to be thinking the same thing: it was imperative to remove Lady Catherine from the room before she offended everyone within. As such, they both stepped forward at the same time.

"Come, Lady Catherine," said Darcy, "let us take this conversation to another room, so we may speak privately."

"I shall not go," protested their irascible aunt when the cousins grasped her arms and began to lead her from the room. "You both will leave with me at once. I shall accept no other outcome!"

"You will come along with us both at once," snarled Fitzwilliam softly, causing her to look at him with surprise. "If you do not, I will personally see that you are thrown from this house." When Lady Catherine's eyes hardened, Fitzwilliam tugged at her arm again, forcing her to begin walking, with Darcy on her other side. "For heaven's sake, Lady Catherine, are you determined to offend everyone in attendance tonight?"

Lady Catherine sniffed with disdain. "There is not a single person here whom it would give me an instant's hesitation should I offend them."

"Perhaps not," said Darcy. "But our host is a good man, one whom I have counted as a friend for many years. I will not allow you to insult him."

Once again Lady Catherine reacted with a disdainful sneer. "It would be better if you would. Staying at the house of a tradesman? How can either of you countenance such a thing? It is beyond all decency!"

"No, Lady Catherine," growled Fitzwilliam. "*You* entering an event to which you were not invited, screeching at the top of your lungs with insulting remarks on your lips is what is beyond the pale. Now, be silent until we have reached the library!"

It was a wonder, but Lady Catherine did fall silent, though her glare at Fitzwilliam did not lessen a jot. Fitzwilliam, a large and imposing man, had often succeeded in quelling her excesses where Darcy had failed. She also knew that Fitzwilliam was an implacable enemy, which surely helped the matter. Furthermore, she seemed to show more deference to him since his elevation to the peerage on his brother's death.

Soon, they had reached Bingley's library, and there they entered in, Fitzwilliam escorting Lady Catherine while Darcy held back and made certain the door was closed so their discussion would not be overheard. Then, all pretense of restraint was done away with. Lady Catherine stepped away from Fitzwilliam and pulled her arm from his grasp, whirling, and facing him with implacable determination in her eyes.

"I will brook no opposition from either of you. I expect you both to leave this room at once, to instruct your valets to pack your belongings, and for you to attend me in my carriage within the next thirty minutes, so we may return to London. Staying with this Mr. Bingley has clearly addled you both. I shall not stand by and witness the fall our noble house to the wiles of such Jezebels as my parson reports his cousins to be. Furthermore, I shall demand Mr. Collins return to Kent where I may find him a proper wife since his cousin's daughters are so clearly unsuitable."

"I find it fascinating that you can declare them such, Aunt," said Fitzwilliam, "when you have not even met them."

"I do not need to meet them," snapped Lady Catherine. "I am aware of girls of their kind. There are many grasping, artful females in the kingdom, and I know of the stratagems they will employ to entrap wealthy young men. I am only surprised you have fallen for such base arts and allurements. I had thought better of you both!"

"Then I shall correct you, Lady Catherine," replied Fitzwilliam. Darcy wished to speak, but he was so angry by now that he could not trust himself to say anything. "There is no one objectionable here. These artful women of whom you speak are daughters of a respectable gentleman. In my opinion, your parson is a dolt, who is only upset that the woman to whom he wishes to attach himself sees him for the fool he is and wishes to have nothing to do with him."

"Collins is my hand-picked parson! I trust his judgment implicitly."

"More is the pity for you, Lady Catherine," replied Fitzwilliam, a whole host of sardonic undertones in his voice. "I doubt the man would be able to lace his shoes if he did not have you to instruct him on the best way to do so."

"That is enough of Mr. Collins! You will now oblige me by informing your valets of our immediate departure."

"Fitzwilliam may do what he wishes, Lady Catherine," replied Darcy. "But I will not go anywhere."

"Darcy!" screeched the lady. "You will obey me!"

"I will not!" Darcy grasped the tatters of his composure like a man holding onto a cliff face. "I am not beholden to you. I will do as I please. Bingley is a friend of longstanding, and I will not insult him."

"Heavens, Darcy, how can you tolerate the friendship of such a base lout? Have you no care for your position in society, the credit and honor of your family?"

"I have every care in it, Lady Catherine," replied Darcy. "As I ever have. But I do not see people as the sum of their lineage or the enormity of their holdings. Bingley is a good friend, one who is loyal, honest, and true, and the Bennets, whom you have decried tonight on the word of your idiotic parson, are good people, as are the others of this neighborhood. I shall not submit to such unreasonable demands as yours."

"Nor shall I," added Fitzwilliam. "You have wasted your time, Lady Catherine."

The lady's look could have broken through granite, so angry was she. Darcy, however, decided that it was time to once and for all end the delusion he knew was the reason for her insupportable actions.

"Let us be blunt, Lady Catherine," said he, pulling her gaze back to him. "We all understand why you have come here tonight. Perhaps you do not wish Fitzwilliam to be entangled with those you deem of a lower level, but the true reason is that you are afraid of losing me as a potential groom for your daughter."

"I have no fear of any such thing," said Lady Catherine, holding her head high. "Though you have been stubborn about it, I know in the end you will do your duty and marry Anne as your mother intended."

"In fact, I doubt my mother ever intended that I marry Anne." Lady Catherine raised her voice to reply, but Darcy was quicker. "You may have spoken of it, but since my mother did not say anything to me, I know of no such thing. Regardless, I have informed you before that I will not marry Anne. Whether my mother wished for it is immaterial. I do not wish for it. I will not relent."

"Have these ladies so thoroughly infested your senses that you would neglect your duty?" demanded Lady Catherine aghast.

"As I have stated, I do not consider it to be my duty," replied Darcy. "My mother made no mention to me of any desire that I marry Anne, and my father openly decried the very thought. As I am my own man and may make my own decisions, there is nothing you can do. Unless you can produce a contract which compels me to make your daughter my wife, there is nothing more for us to say."

"Before you scream any longer," interjected Fitzwilliam when Lady Catherine appeared about to do just that, "you should know that my father has no interest in attempting to force Darcy in this matter. And should you have any notions concerning *me*, you should know that I am also my own man, as well as a future earl. I am not about to listen to your threats or your harangues demanding I oblige you. I believe it is time for you to leave."

"I have never been so insulted in all my life!" cried Lady Catherine. "Have you both no decency, no sense of the credit of our family names, all of which would be dragged through the dust should you go through with an alliance with this family? Heaven and earth, of what are you thinking?"

"Of nothing more than my own happiness," replied Darcy. He wished for this conversation to be finished, so he may be about settling ruffled feathers and apologizing for Lady Catherine's affronts. "No one will say anything, even should I choose to tie myself to one of the Bennet sisters, though I have not yet made any such decision. Perhaps you should advise your parson to avoid reading novels and concentrate on the Holy Book, for he is seeing plots where none exist."

"You will both oblige me!" It was one last desperate attempt, and both cousins knew it.

"Come, Lady Catherine," said Fitzwilliam. "It is time for you to depart. I am certain you will be able to find a good inn nearby to stay, for I do not think it would be wise for you to return to London tonight."

"We will not attempt to impose in Bingley," added Darcy. "I am certain you have offended him too much for that."

"This is not over," hissed Lady Catherine. "I will know what is to be done."

"You may try," replied Darcy, as he opened the door in time for Fitzwilliam to usher their aunt through it. "But I will not be moved. Further discussion on this matter is pointless."

Lady Catherine did not respond. She removed her arm from Fitzwilliam's grasp and walked with her head held high. Darcy doubted she would go away quietly, but there was nothing she could do. He would not concern himself with her machinations.

"Well, little Eliza, I suppose you are *not* to have your choice of wealthy gentlemen after all. His lordship's relation, unless I miss my guess, has come to save them both from you. I fear you will be required to strive against her for your comfortable situation."

Elizabeth, who had been watching the scene until the men left with the woman in tow, turned back to her partner and fixed him with a withering glare. Mr. Lucas was not cowed—in fact, he seemed rather amused. Elizabeth only shook her head and turned her head away. It was surprising, but he did not essay to tease her any further, for which Elizabeth was grateful.

The dance had started again with the removal of the harridan, but the line was ragged, and most were concentrating on whispering amongst themselves of the spectacle they had just witnessed. It was fortunate, in Elizabeth's estimation, that the dance was soon complete, for she could not wait to escape from her partner and did so at the earliest opportunity, not even allowing him to escort her to the side of the room. What was not so fortunate was the abundance of objectionable men in attendance that evening.

"Cousin Elizabeth," said Mr. Collins as he approached her almost as soon as she had left Mr. Lucas on the dance floor. "I am certain you must have noticed that my patroness, Lady Catherine de Bourgh, has come to Netherfield."

"Indeed, Mr. Collins," said Elizabeth. "I doubt her coming went unnoticed by anyone within five miles."

Behind Mr. Collins and to his left, Mr. Bennet snorted in laughter from where he was standing. Mr. Collins, however, preened as if she had just flattered his patroness to the heavens.

"Yes, she does possess the magnificent presence, the nobility to carry herself effortlessly and stun the room with the force of her character. I dare say there is not another person in all England like her."

By this time Mr. Bennet was shaking with suppressed mirth, and Elizabeth wondered if he might do himself harm if he did not let it out. For herself, she had had about enough of this man for an entire lifetime. "I believe, Mr. Collins," said she, "that there can be no other like Lady Catherine. For that, we may all be grateful."

Though Mr. Collins continued to preen, he seemed not to know what to make of her second sentence. In the end, he seemed to decide it was not important.

"Now that her ladyship is here, I am certain all will be set to rights. Surely you must now see that your endeavors have no chance of success."

"Mr. Collins," said Elizabeth, her tone such that the man visibly forced himself not to take a step back. "I am certain I have no notion of what you speak. Mr. Darcy and Lord Chesterfield are their own men and may do what they please, regardless of the edicts of an elderly relation. As for your inferences regarding *me*, I may only state that I have no intention of being ruled by your patroness, any more than either of the two gentlemen. Furthermore, I am not attempting anything with regard to either man. Once again, you have assumed where you should not.

"Now, if you will excuse me."

Then Elizabeth brushed past the stunned parson and stalked away from him. What perverse misfortune had resulted in Mr. Collins being related to them! Elizabeth wished for nothing more than the stupid man to retreat to Kent and never darken their doorstep again.

As she walked toward the refreshment table, Elizabeth happened to notice a young woman seated on a chair just inside the door through which Lady Catherine had entered the ballroom. She was small and slight, pale of complexion, her head drooping with weariness. She was also dressed in a similar fashion to that of Lady Catherine, which led Elizabeth to believe that this woman was her daughter. Louisa Hurst stood some distance away, her manner all affront, and while Elizabeth could well understand why, she also knew that it would be considered rude not to ask after the newcomer's comfort. Thus, she endeavored to do it herself.

"Hello, Miss?" asked she as she approached and sat in the chair next to her. "Are you quite well?"

The woman was possessed of keen blue eyes, belying her sickly appearance, and she looked up at Elizabeth, though seeming to see her but little. "I am only quite tired. It has been a long journey."

"Might I obtain some punch for you?" offered Elizabeth. "Perhaps a little refreshment would help?"

"Thank you," replied the young woman. "That would be heavenly."

The strains for the supper set began as Elizabeth rose and made her way to the refreshment table. She was not yet engaged for the supper set and moved in such a way as to inform the gentlemen in the room that she did not intend to dance it. It must have worked, for no one approached her, and she soon returned, the requested cup of punch in one hand, which the young lady accepted with seeming gratitude.

"This seems like a lively little party," observed the young lady as she sipped from her cup.

"I believe it is," replied Elizabeth. "Netherfield is the principal estate in the neighborhood, and we are all grateful for the presence of the family here. It has sat unoccupied for far too long."

That penetrating gaze was once again fixed on Elizabeth. "I understand the family who lives here are descended from trade. Would you not find their presence objectionable? Or does your family have less than impressive roots also?"

Yes, that this was Lady Catherine's daughter, Elizabeth was certain, even though she had never met the lady nor had any experience with her other than listening to her from across the room. Miss de Bourgh had been tutored at her mother's knee—of that there was no doubt.

"No, I am a gentleman's daughter," replied Elizabeth. "My family has owned our land for centuries now. But regarding Mr. Bingley, I must say that I attempt to judge others based on their merit. Mr. Bingley may be descended from tradesmen, but he carries himself as a gentleman both in manners and demeanor."

Miss de Bourgh seemed to consider that for a time, and then she nodded, though it was almost imperceptible. "In such a society as this, I suppose he must be acceptable. My mother informs me that it must be different in London, especially amongst those of the first circles. They are much more discriminating than small, local societies."

"I must assume you are correct," said Elizabeth. She wondered at the woman's words. Her mother had informed her? Had Miss de Bourgh not any experience among higher society herself? Surely Lady Catherine, the daughter of an earl, would not have neglected to display her daughter for the peacocks of the first circles.

When Miss de Bourgh finished her cup of punch, Elizabeth felt it incumbent upon her to inquire after her comfort. "Shall I obtain another cup for you? Or perhaps a little sustenance would be welcome? I believe we are to go to dinner after these sets, but there are refreshments aplenty laid out on the table."

"I am well, I thank you," said Miss de Bourgh. Then she turned a querying eye on Elizabeth. "I believe we have not been introduced, Miss, an oversight we should correct, though there are no mutual acquaintances to perform the task. Might I ask you to introduce yourself to me?"

"Of course," replied Elizabeth. "And you have my apologies. I should have realized it myself. I am Elizabeth Bennet of Longbourn, which is quite near to Netherfield. I am the daughter of Mr. Henry Bennet, and the second of five sisters."

Though curious as to how she would be received, not knowing what Mr. Collins had told his patroness to induce her to come all this way, Elizabeth was not surprised when Miss de Bourgh's countenance hardened. She glared at Elizabeth, fire in her eyes, her jaw chiseled from granite.

"So it is *you* who have brought us hither," said Miss de Bourgh. The words were spoken softly, and while they were not without venom, they were not so forceful as Elizabeth might have expected. "You and your youngest sister, unless I remember incorrectly."

"I know not what you have heard," replied Elizabeth, "but I had nothing to do with your journey here."

"I doubt that. Mother has told me of young women of your ilk."

"Having never met your mother, I am certain she knows nothing of me. Please allow me to say that you should not listen to anything your mother's parson says. He sees much where nothing exists, and his perception of matters is not reliable. He is not the most intelligent specimen."

Miss de Bourgh was taken aback for a moment, likely because Elizabeth's statements of Mr. Collins had rung true, regardless of whatever her mother said concerning the man. But she soon shook it off and fixed her implacable stare on Elizabeth. It would have been impressive coming from Lord Chesterfield. From a mousy, thin waif of a woman such as Miss de Bourgh, it was nothing more than comical.

"You will *never* have my cousin. Darcy is to be *my* husband, and even if he was not, you are not of his sphere. Young ladies who reach above their sphere to grasp hold of prominent men are the most despicable creatures in existence. You should be ashamed of yourself."

A hundred retorts sprang into Elizabeth's mind at that moment, but she pushed them away. There was no cause to anger this woman further and create another scene. Therefore, Elizabeth endeavored to remove herself from an objectionable conversation.

"If Mr. Darcy is to marry you, then I wish you both joy. I hope the rest of your stay is comfortable."

With that, Elizabeth rose to depart. But she was forestalled by the return of the two gentlemen and their aunt. They walked on either side of her, watching her through wary eyes, clearly expecting her to make some other scene. As for herself, Lady Catherine walked with her head held high, her nose even further in the air than Miss Bingley could manage. As she approached, she took in the sight of those who were still dancing, the spectators who were rapidly turning their attention away from the dance floor to where she walked. Her sniff of disdain told all within reach of the contempt she held for them.

"Come, Anne," said the lady in imperious tones. "We shall depart. I have pressing business in London. We will return at a later time when my nephews are more reasonable."

Miss de Bourgh rose at her mother's command. But rather than follow her immediately, she shot a look at Elizabeth and addressed her mother.

"Mother, I think you might be interested in an introduction to this young lady. She is Miss Elizabeth Bennet, whom I believe we came to see."

"So *this* is the little baggage who has attempted to steal my nephews' attention away from where it rightfully belongs." Lady Catherine's eyes raked Elizabeth's form from head to toe. "I wonder at your taste, for she does not appear impressive at all."

"No, your ladyship," said a new voice, and they all turned in astonishment to see Louisa Hurst glaring at Lady Catherine. "Miss Elizabeth Bennet is the woman who approached your daughter and saw to her comfort, all the while knowing she would be castigated when her identity was revealed. You will not accost anyone else in this house."

"I will do as I please," snapped Lady Catherine. "I require a room and privacy to speak with Miss Bennet. You will oblige me."

Out of the corner of her eye, Elizabeth saw her father approaching, no doubt to deny the lady's request. He need not have bothered, for it appeared the lady's nephews' patience was exhausted.

"No, Aunt," said Lord Chesterfield. "It is time for you to leave." When she opened her mouth to speak, he stepped forward and looked down at her, his manner relentless. "*Now*, Lady Catherine."

"This is not over, Fitzwilliam," hissed the lady. "I am not to be cast aside with so little consideration."

Then she turned on her heel and stalked from the room, Mr. Collins and Miss de Bourgh scurrying after her. His lordship and Mr. Darcy followed behind, intent upon seeing that she was gone. The music continued and those on the dance floor continued in the patterns, but Elizabeth could hear none of it. She could never have imagined such incivility as the lady possessed. How was such a thing to be imagined?

"Elizabeth, I hope you have not been unduly distressed."

Turning, Elizabeth noted the concerned countenance of Louisa Hurst and endeavored to reply in an unaffected manner.

"No, I am well. Thank you, Louisa, but I hope that I am made of sturdier stuff than to be offended by Lady Catherine's ill humors."

"It is I who should thank you," replied Louisa. "I should have seen to the comfort of Miss de Bourgh."

"But it fell to you to receive the first lashings of the storm that is Lady Catherine," replied Elizabeth. "It is not a wonder you should be out of sorts when confronted by such a woman. I was happy to help."

They two women laughed together. "I thank you nonetheless," said Louisa. "Come, let us forget about such an objectionable presence."

Elizabeth agreed, and she turned back to the ball, standing beside Louisa for some time. But how was such a display to be forgotten? Indeed, Elizabeth thought it would be many days before she could successfully put it in perspective.

CHAPTER XVIII

*I*t came as no surprise, least of all to Elizabeth, who had played some small part in the event, that the coming of Lady Catherine and her daughter dominated the conversation at dinner. At first, Elizabeth wondered if the lady's loud comments had resulted in gossip regarding her and her sisters. But then she realized that the lady had not said much of them, only referencing some nebulous "Jezebels" who were tempting her nephews. The Bennets were well enough regarded that such words would not affect their standing, regardless of the looseness of the gossips' tongues.

Chief among the diners who held court and spoke with great fervor concerning Lady Catherine's coming was, of course, Mrs. Bennet. But whereas most of their neighbors would not understand of what the lady spoke, Mrs. Bennet was not insensible to the insult of the woman's words toward her progeny, nor was she apt to let it pass.

"It is scarcely to be believed," said she to Lady Lucas and some of the other ladies nearby. Mary was also seated with her, no doubt to attempt some moderation of their mother's words should it become necessary, while Kitty—somewhat subdued due to the indisposition of her closest sister—and Lydia, still immobile because of her injury, were also within range of their mother's voice.

"That such a loud, proud, termagant of a woman could be related to Lord Chesterfield and Mr. Darcy is beyond my ability to understand. They are everything good and kind. To be burdened with such a relation must be a cruel cross to bear!"

"It *is* difficult to understand," agreed Lady Lucas. "But, Maggie, you should lower your voice. Despite a less than desirable relation, I do not think the gentlemen would appreciate hearing her spoken of in such a manner."

Few things were certain in life, but the ability of Mrs. Margaret Bennet to speak in a loud voice and ignore all reason had always been one. But in this instance, Mrs. Bennet was stopped short, and she cast about, looking for the gentlemen unless Elizabeth missed her guess. When she turned back to Lady Lucas, her manner was almost furtive.

"Right you are. Though my girls have suffered much insult because of this Lady Catherine's coming, I shall overlook it. The gentlemen deserve our approbation, for they have been everything good."

"I cannot agree more, my friend."

And with those words, the two women fell into quieter conversation with other nearby ladies, and though Elizabeth witnessed more than furtive glances about the room, she heard nothing more from them. Lydia's injury had resulted in her inability to run amok as she usually did, which limited Kitty's will to embarrass them too. With her mother's seeming new-found restraint, it was quite possible the family would emerge from the night without any stain on their reputation. There had been enough occasions in the past where such a conclusion was not assured to leave Elizabeth in a state of relief.

As her mother was checked for the present, Elizabeth turned away and noted the approach of Mrs. Hurst. Not having had much chance to speak to the other woman thus far this evening, Elizabeth greeted her with pleasure, which the other woman returned with equal enjoyment.

"Again, I wished to thank you for seeing to Miss de Bourgh," said Louisa, the first words to issue from her mouth. "My sister, as you can see, does not have much interest in acting as she ought, and I was still fuming from Lady Catherine's demands. That is no excuse, of course, but I am grateful nonetheless."

A quick glance at where Miss Bingley was sitting revealed the woman to be watching all and sundry with a look of utmost distaste. She caught Elizabeth's eye and sneered at her, but it did not contain the woman's usual measure of superiority. In fact, Elizabeth suspected Miss Bingley had, for the first time, been made aware of the possibility that her chosen target's family would not welcome her with open arms as she had thought and was revising her plans accordingly.

"It was no trouble, Louisa," said Elizabeth, turning her attention back to her true hostess. She smiled at the other woman and continued: "Perhaps it would have been best had I considered better and kept myself separate from Miss de Bourgh's disdain."

Louisa laughed. "I cannot dispute your words. But you acted to see to a guest's comfort, and I appreciate your support."

"Think nothing of it, my friend. I am happy to assist."

They stood in that attitude speaking for several minutes until finally, Elizabeth espied the gentlemen returning with Mr. Collins trailing along behind. Mr. Darcy's expression, though carefully controlled, was easily seen as fury, while Lord Chesterfield appeared more exasperated. As for Mr. Collins, he displayed a measure of shock, no doubt because his patroness had not been treated like a queen when she had swept into the room. Then he saw Elizabeth, and his countenance darkened. Elizabeth thought he might have approached to castigate her, had Mr. Darcy not started toward her first, with a warning look for the parson to keep away. Mr. Collins did so, but not without a scowl at Elizabeth.

"Miss Elizabeth," said Mr. Darcy. He bent in a low bow before her. Elizabeth could see Mr. Collins gasping at his actions from behind. "I would like to take this opportunity to apologize most humbly to you for the behavior of my aunt. Lady Catherine does not speak for me in any way. I would not wish for you to think I espouse any of her beliefs, for I do not."

"I do not blame you for your aunt's behavior, sir," said Elizabeth. She dared look up into his eyes and noted they were fixed upon her in earnest appeal. "It is clear that your opinions are quite different from Lady Catherine's. There is no one who could possibly blame you or your cousin for her words or actions."

"But her vitriol was directed toward you and would have been even more pointed, had she known who you were earlier."

"And is *my* cousin not equally to blame?" Elizabeth glanced at Mr. Collins. The man was too far away to hear what they were saying, but his distress was evident in the wringing of his hands. "I presume it was he who summoned her, after all."

Mr. Darcy turned slightly and regarded the parson. Though he was turned away from Elizabeth, it was clear from the sudden pallor in Mr. Collins's countenance that Mr. Darcy's look was not at all friendly.

"I believe he did. But she would have come at some time or

another." Mr. Darcy paused and grimaced. "You have likely heard from your cousin, but my aunt has long maintained the delusion that I will marry her daughter. Her assertions are without foundation; I am *not* engaged to my cousin, nor are my wishes restricted in any manner."

Though Elizabeth wondered at the forceful nature of his statement, she could only assure him that she was unharmed. "Then I think I must congratulate you, sir. I should think that the prospect of having Lady Catherine as a mother-in-law would make strong men quail. It must be a relief to be spared such a fate."

At first, Mr. Darcy gawked at her, seeming unable to credit Elizabeth's sportive comments of his aunt. Then he laughed, allowing Elizabeth to release the hint of hysterical mirth which had been building while she waited to see if the man would take offense at her thoughtless jest. It was clear her glib tongue would land her in hot water if she did not take care.

"Your humor, more than anything else, informs me you are unharmed," said Mr. Darcy as he shook his head. "Your resilience is truly awe-inspiring, Miss Elizabeth. I have rarely seen its like."

"Perhaps you have not looked," replied Elizabeth, feeling the embarrassment of his approbation all over again. "I do not think I am so special."

"And I will assert you *are*," replied Mr. Darcy. His earnest expression had made a reappearance. "There are few who would not be offended at such caustic words as my aunt directed at you. And I am sure my cousin was no kinder."

Mr. Darcy paused and seemed to consider her. Elizabeth did her best to simply wait for him to speak again, though the appearance of fluttering wings in her midsection did little calm her. Why she should feel this way in Mr. Darcy's presence she did not know, but it was there nonetheless.

"If you will oblige me, Miss Elizabeth," said Mr. Darcy at length, "I believe I would like to request another dance of you if you have one available."

Elizabeth gawped at the man, the word surprised not even close to what she felt about his application. "Another dance?" asked she, though the words were weak to her own ears.

"Yes," replied Mr. Darcy, his tone and purpose firm. "I am fully aware of the implications of such a request, and I do not make it lightly. I find you are an estimable woman of whom I wish to know more. Furthermore, I wish to show the room that whatever my aunt's opinions are, I do not share them. Will you do me the honor?"

Some reply must be made, and though Elizabeth was bemused at the impossibility of it all, she could only respond to this man's entreaty in a like manner. "The only dance I have left is the final dance of the evening."

"Then I will claim that dance, if I may be so bold."

Hardly aware of what was happening, Elizabeth nodded her acceptance. Mr. Darcy took her hand and bowed over it, and for a moment Elizabeth thought he might kiss it. In the end, however, he chose the lesser form of regard, thanked her, and went away. Elizabeth could not tear her eyes away from his back. What would her neighbors think? To dance the first *and* last dance with the same woman was an unmistakable sign of favor. Was it not?

"Louisa!" hissed Caroline. Louisa felt her sister's hand, as she reached out and grasped her arm, pulling her to a nearby door and out into the hall. "Of what were you speaking with Eliza just now?"

"I was thanking her for seeing to a guest in our house in our stead," said Louisa, pulling her arm from Caroline's grasp and glaring at her sister with contempt. "*We* are the hostesses for the evening, are we not? It should have been *our* duty to see to Miss de Bourgh's comfort, no matter how objectionable her mother's behavior. Yet *Elizabeth* saw fit to do so herself when we could not be bothered."

"I am certain it was nothing more than an attempt to ingratiate herself with the cousins," sneered Caroline. "She is an artful woman. I am certain she intends to snap one of them up from under my very nose."

Louisa regarded her sister, wondering how Caroline had become so conniving and selfish. In fact, Louisa was certain that *both* men were enamored with Elizabeth, and it was obvious to all but Caroline that neither would ever pay any attention to her as Charles's sister beyond what was required by civility. It was a great pity—more than ever, Louisa wished to be free of the burden Caroline had always been. But she could not wish her shrewish sister on such fine men.

"Caroline," said Louisa, her patience almost exhausted, "do you not see that you have not been acting as a good hostess ought? You have seen to little of our guests' comfort and have spent your time watching Lord Chesterfield and speaking with objectionable militia officers."

Caroline's sneer was once again evident. "Perhaps I would take greater care if the opinion of these country savages concerned me even a jot. Why should we concern ourselves with the opinions of such people?"

"Because they are our brother's neighbors," replied Louisa. "And because they are good people. How can you think to act properly when hosting the higher-ranking members of society from London when you cannot even be bothered to do so in a smaller society?"

"I am sure I will know how to act," replied Caroline with an airy wave of her hand.

"Then I suppose I should speak to our brother," said Louisa. "If you cannot be bothered to be his hostess, then perhaps I should take up the reins of that position. At least he would not be looked down on by his neighbors for an overly haughty woman presiding over his house."

With those words, Louisa turned and stalked away. Caroline could try the patience of a saint, and Louisa was feeling far from saintly that day.

"You have asked Miss Elizabeth to dance again?" demanded Fitzwilliam.

"I have," replied his infuriating cousin. "It was the least I could do to apologize for our aunt's behavior."

"I believe it may have been *my* right and obligation," said Fitzwilliam. "As the higher ranked between us, you should have stood aside and allowed me to tender our apologies. And I hardly think it necessary for you to offer to dance with her as compensation for being ill-used by the likes of Lady Catherine, especially when it is largely because of you that she was so treated!"

Darcy turned to regard him, his countenance forbidding. Such tactics had never worked on Fitzwilliam — he could be as forbidding as Darcy when he chose — and of late, they had only irritated him.

"Such a limit cannot be placed on good manners, Fitzwilliam. If you wish to apologize to Miss Elizabeth yourself, I am certain you have the opportunity to do so, should you only take it. As for my request to dance with her, that is *my* business, is it not? And I shall not even dignify your comments regarding Lady Catherine's behavior with a reply."

And Darcy stepped way, leaving Fitzwilliam watching him, feeling the need to gnash his teeth in frustration. That fastidious Darcy should pay such attention to naught but a country girl — the country girl in which Fitzwilliam found himself interested, no less — was a circumstance Fitzwilliam could never have imagined. And he was not about to tolerate it either.

His purpose clear, Fitzwilliam scanned the room for Miss Elizabeth, finding her speaking with some ladies of the area not far away. Fitzwilliam judged it likely the dancing would begin again quite soon. Consequently, he knew he had best step to it. Thus, he approached and bowed low in front of the three ladies, noting that while Miss Elizabeth was looking at him with curiosity, the others were giggling behind their hands. Fitzwilliam ignored them—Miss Elizabeth was the true prize.

"Miss Elizabeth," said he, "if you are not engaged, might I ask for another set this evening? I wish to apologize for my aunt's actions."

"I thank you for the apology," replied Miss Elizabeth. "But I am sorry to say that my dance card is full."

"You do not have another dance available?" asked Fitzwilliam, the feeling of anger wending its way through his mind. Darcy had snapped up her last dance!

"I do not. You have my apologies, Lord Chesterfield."

"Then another time, perhaps," replied Fitzwilliam, not caring that his words and tone were more than a little short.

He turned away removed himself to the side of the room, watching the dancers as they moved through the steps of the sets. But he had eyes only for Miss Elizabeth, as he fumed at being denied what he wanted. Fitzwilliam did not even consider dancing. He was too angry to ask any other lady for the pleasure.

As the viscount walked away from them, Elizabeth watched him, astonished at his reaction. He took up position by the side of the dance floor and refused to speak to anyone, his gaze roving over them all with seeming contempt. Elizabeth knew he did not feel that way—he had proven his character time and again. But the way he was carrying himself this evening, he reminded her of Mr. Darcy's demeanor that first night at the assembly in Meryton.

By contrast, Mr. Darcy was in another part of the room speaking with Mr. Goulding, and while he would never be so animated as his cousin, he was acquitting himself well. It was odd, Elizabeth decided, but it appeared as if the cousins had exchanged characters, or at least they had exchanged positions. The viscount had seemed angry when Elizabeth had informed him she could not dance with him. Was that enough to render him unsociable for the rest of the evening?

A little later, as the dancing was about to begin again, Elizabeth found herself beside her youngest siblings, and she was privy to their conversation about all that had happened that evening.

"Did you see Lady Catherine's dress, Lydia?" Kitty was saying. "The material from which it was constructed was positively divine." Kitty sighed. "If only Papa could afford to clothe us in such costly materials. I might never leave the modiste!"

"Yes, yes," replied Lydia in her usual caustic tones. "It is unfortunate the woman wearing the gown was so objectionable."

"What do you mean?" asked Kitty, seeming confused. Elizabeth shook her head — Kitty always had more than a little oblivious.

"Only that she treated Lizzy horridly," exclaimed Lydia. "If that is how all members of high society behave, then I think I want no part of it."

"There are surely objectionable characters in *every* society," said Elizabeth. As she was speaking, her eyes caught sight of Mr. Wickham, and she noted how he was watching them with keen interest. Suppressing a shudder, Elizabeth turned her attention back to her sisters. "But not everyone of higher society is objectionable. Lord Chesterfield, for example, is everything that is good and amiable. Is he not?"

Her sisters allowed that she was correct and began speaking of other matters. Soon they were joined by Mary who, it appeared, had been close enough to hear their conversation.

"I am surprised you held the viscount up as a paragon to our sisters, Lizzy," said she in a soft tone. "By your own admission, you have begun to have questions about his lordship."

"I am merely cautious, as we discussed. I could hardly speak of Mr. Darcy to Lydia. While she does not think ill of him, she does consider him to be too taciturn and stuffy for her taste."

Mary nodded. "I suppose that is true."

But the question Mary had posed stayed with Elizabeth, and she wondered at it. She had felt distinctly uncomfortable when confronted with Lord Chesterfield's behavior and warmed by Mr. Darcy's. Why, then, had she praised Lord Chesterfield to Lydia rather than Mr. Darcy? Did she, in some way, view them both through the eyes of prejudice? She had always been of a sociable nature herself — might that cause her to unconsciously esteem the man more like her?

When her next partner came to collect her for the next dance, Elizabeth was no closer to answering her own question as she had been at the start. But she was determined to try to see past whatever prejudices she possessed and view both men as they were. Perhaps most importantly, she was resolved to see Mr. Darcy as an amiable man, one who was, perhaps, not so open as she was herself, but no less estimable nonetheless.

It was much later in the evening, during the lull between the previous dance and the final one of the evening, when Elizabeth found herself on the side of the dance floor with Jane nearby. Jane was to stand up for the final set with Lord Chesterfield, who seemed to have roused himself from his thoughts. Much as Elizabeth herself, Jane had danced twice with her beau, though her dances had been the first and the supper. Elizabeth could not be happier for her sister and was not above indulging in a little teasing of her elder sibling.

"Mr. Bingley has been very attentive toward you this evening, Jane."

Jane, as Elizabeth might have predicted, blushed. "I am certain he is only being kind."

"If there was a man as kind to me as Mr. Bingley is to you, I would order my trousseau," said Elizabeth.

When Jane's color became even more prominent, Elizabeth laughed and enfolded her sister in an affectionate embrace. "Oh, Jane, it is rarely amusing to tease you, because you present such an inviting target!"

"Stop it, Lizzy!" exclaimed Jane, fixing Elizabeth with a stern glare.

Elizabeth could see right through her, however, and only grinned in response. "Very well. I shall leave you be, regardless of how sorely I am tempted to continue. I will only say this: be certain of your heart, my dearest sister. And when you *are* certain of it, take care to make *him* certain of it. He carries on quite charmingly, it is true, but a man needs a little encouragement."

With a smile, Jane turned away at something Mary said. The void was immediately filled by the tall man who was to dance with Jane.

"Miss Elizabeth," said Lord Chesterfield, "I have realized that though I said I wished to apologize for my aunt's behavior, I did not actually do so."

"It is quite unnecessary," replied Elizabeth, hoping to forestall another uncomfortable conversation. "As I informed your cousin, I do not hold you accountable for Lady Catherine's actions. I pray you will think no more of it."

Though the viscount's expression tightened, he bowed low to her. "It is a measure of your goodness that you can think so, Miss Elizabeth. Regardless, I will beg your pardon. Lady Catherine had no business speaking to you in the way she did. And for that, I apologize."

"Thank you, my lord," replied Elizabeth. "I appreciate your words."

Lord Chesterfield paused for a moment before he fixed her again with his attention. "Miss Elizabeth, I hope I am not speaking out of turn when I say that I find you the most intriguing young woman I have ever met. I believe I would like to know more of you if you will allow it."

It was these words which finally gave Elizabeth a little clarity on what was happening between the cousins. She did not like the implications at all.

"I am quite happy to converse on any occasion which presents itself, Lord Chesterfield," replied she. "At present, however, I believe I had best find my partner for the final dance of the evening."

She turned away, but not before she had seen the flash of irritation from his lordship. But Elizabeth was, by now, feeling more than a little annoyance with the man *and* his cousin. She was not about to allow herself to be the prize of their little rivalry. Perhaps she should control herself better, but the fact that she was to dance with Mr. Darcy presented an opportunity to allow her grievance to be heard.

By the time they started the dance, Mr. Darcy seemed aware of Elizabeth's less than congenial attitude. They moved in silence for several moments, Mr. Darcy regarding her as if trying to puzzle her out, Elizabeth attempting to bring her pique under control lest she say something she ought not. It was Mr. Darcy's opening sally which burst the dam holding Elizabeth's temper in check.

"It appears the evening has proven a trial on your patience, Miss Elizabeth," said he when they stepped close together. "If required, I once again offer my unreserved apologies for my aunt's behavior."

"You and your cousin are both intent upon apologizing repeatedly," replied Elizabeth. Her ire was leaking out despite her attempts to control it, and her tone was more than a little testy. "I will inform you again that you need not do so. I appreciated your first apology, but anything else is unnecessary."

Mr. Darcy nodded. "Then might I ask if your ire is reserved for me in particular?"

"Not for you, in particular, sir. I am equally frustrated with your cousin. Though I would not presume to accuse either of you of anything underhanded, I wish you both to know that I will not be the unwitting award of a rivalry between cousins."

"Miss Elizabeth," said Mr. Darcy, "I would not have you think that *I* see you in such a manner. It is clear to me you are nothing less than a treasure."

Mr. Darcy paused and though everything within Elizabeth

screamed to reply to his words, something kept her silent. She had always known Mr. Darcy was a careful man, one who, when he spoke, did so with the greatest of care, using words which were well worth hearing. Perhaps it was this which stayed her tongue and harnessed her wit. Either way, for those few, brief, awful minutes, she waited with bated breath to hear what he wished to say, wondering if she ought to fear it.

"I am not skilled at this, Miss Bennet," said Mr. Darcy at length, shooting her an apologetic smile. "I have not the talent for speaking which some possess, and I have never paid attention to a woman before. I have not, I would have you know, because I have never found a woman who intrigued me, who spoke to me directly to my heart as you have.

"While my behavior and that of my cousin might have led you to believe that we vie for your attention as a sort of contest between us, I would have you know that I have no such thoughts. I cannot say what Fitzwilliam feels, and I will not attempt to indict or vindicate him—I will leave that to him. For myself, I believe I may say that my interest in you is unalloyed and unstained by any thought of besting my cousin. You are an estimable woman; any man would be fortunate, indeed, to be able to claim your regard. A man who gained your love would be the luckiest man on earth."

Elizabeth gasped. "You speak of love, sir?"

"I do, but only in the sense of what I believe is possible." Mr. Darcy smiled and Elizabeth felt liable to swoon. "It is clear to me that loving you would be the simplest task to which I would ever set myself. But let us not put the cart before the horse, shall we? I understand your caution has been roused by what you have witnessed tonight, and I certainly cannot blame you for it. I am content to take it slowly, to earn your trust and regard, if you will allow me."

"How could I refuse such a heartfelt appeal, Mr. Darcy?" asked Elizabeth, though she hardly knew what she was saying. "I will not agree to anything at present, but I am happy to receive you whenever you call."

And it was true, Elizabeth decided. He had proven himself true by not demanding a courtship or the like immediately, so as to prevent his cousin from doing so first.

Suddenly, Elizabeth could imagine falling in love with this man. She could imagine it very well, indeed!

CHAPTER XIX

$\mathcal{I}$t is the fate of a man who does not possess a furtive bone in his body to appear silly when attempting that state. It was diverting, indeed, to see Mr. Collins returning to Longbourn the morning following the ball, and when Elizabeth saw him through the window, walking up the drive, she almost burst into laughter at the sight, for it appeared he was close to tiptoeing! Elizabeth neither knew nor cared where he had been, but she indulged in a laugh at his expense nonetheless.

When he entered the breakfast room and took his seat, he did so with little fanfare, merely sitting in his usual spot and helping himself from the dishes placed on the table. As the night before had been a late one, most of the family had slept late as well, such that the breakfast of which they were partaking was more the hour they usually sat down for luncheon.

Lydia and Kitty appeared weary, drooping before their plates and eating by rote; Elizabeth was certain they would retire once again to their rooms when the meal was completed. Lydia, it seemed, had not hurt her ankle enough to make her unable to navigate the stairs, though it would be at least two weeks before she could walk into Meryton. While the girl would likely rail against her forced

202 ✤ *Jann Rowland*

confinement, Elizabeth was anticipating the freedom from embarrassment her lesser mobility would engender.

As for the rest of the diners, Jane was contemplative, no doubt thinking of Mr. Bingley and perhaps even of what Elizabeth had told her the previous evening, while Mary was watchful, not only of her sisters, but her wary gaze settled on Mr. Collins more often than not. Mrs. Bennet was as lethargic as her youngest daughters, while Mr. Bennet focused on his meal. It was not long before he finished and excused himself, freeing his daughters to depart to their own activities as well.

As expected, Lydia and Kitty were soon gone to their rooms, and Jane excused herself as well. Mary and Elizabeth went to the sitting-room, Mary to read a book while Elizabeth thought to write a letter to her Aunt Gardiner. Mrs. Bennet seemed likely to follow three of her daughters above stairs when she was accosted by Mr. Collins.

"Mrs. Bennet," said he, "might I have a word with you? I have something I wish to say which I think will be of great interest to you."

The Bennet matron had never thought well of Mr. Collins—everyone in the family had known this since the first day of his arrival. Elizabeth knew her mother had espoused some hope of attaching Kitty or Mary to the parson, but when he had fixed on Elizabeth instead, she had quickly grown exasperated with him. Mrs. Bennet watched him, suspicion radiating from her in waves. In the end, however, she gave him a clipped nod and sat in her usual chair, the parson attending her close by, and speaking in a low voice.

"What do you suppose that is all about?" asked Mary.

Elizabeth, who had been watching the man through wary eyes, shook her head. "Likely some insipid entreaty again regarding Lady Catherine's nephews," replied Elizabeth. "I do not doubt we shall know before long, for Mama is not likely to oblige him."

In the end, Elizabeth's words proved to be prophetic, for it was not five moments later when the conversation became heated.

"No, Mr. Collins," said Mrs. Bennet, shaking her head with vehement denial. "What you ask for is nonsensical. I will not allow it."

"But Mrs. Bennet," pleaded the parson in what sounded more like a whine. "Surely you must see this is for the best. It is the particular—"

"I care not for anything you or your patroness wish!" exclaimed Mrs. Bennet. "I do not know how you think you can impose your will upon us, but I will not yield. Can you not see that my daughter does not favor you?"

"No," sniffed Mr. Collins, his tone filled with disdain. "She favors men who are far above her in consequence and lineage and, furthermore, those who are already claimed by other women. Your daughter will one day be mistress of this estate if you will only oblige me!"

"For that last time, I will not!" cried Mrs. Bennet. She jumped to her feet and glared at Mr. Collins, who rose with her and regarded her with haughty affront. "I would not agree to your request if you were the prince regent himself! My daughter has no care for your demands, and neither do I. I wish you had never come to Longbourn!"

And with those words, Mrs. Bennet marched from the room, the door through which she exited fairly slammed behind her. For a moment, silence reigned in the room. And then Mr. Collins turned his attention to Elizabeth.

"Cousin Elizabeth, I will speak with you," demanded the parson. "You will attend me this instant."

"I apologize, Mr. Collins," replied Elizabeth, "but I have no intention of hearing anything you say." Mr. Collins's jaw worked in his anger, but Elizabeth did not concern herself with his petty ire. "If I am not mistaken, my mother just denied you whatever you asked, and as such, I have no compunction against doing the same."

"You *will* hear me!" cried Mr. Collins.

He rushed toward Elizabeth, and in her sudden fear, Elizabeth rose herself, managing to put the sofa between them. He had always been such an ineffectual dolt that Elizabeth had never been frightened of him before. But now, with his dander up, she was forced to recognize that he was a large man, towering above her more diminutive height. He had never seemed vicious, but she could not predict what he might do in his offense for how she was speaking to him.

Mr. Collins glared at her from the other side of the sofa, but he made no attempt to follow or reach for her. Instead, he huffed his contempt and began to speak.

"Then I shall speak regardless. It is quite clear to me that you would make a most unsuitable wife for a man in my situation, for your brazenness is quite beyond anything I have witnessed.

"Be that as it may, my patroness has demanded this of me, and so I shall obey, as shall you. Lady Catherine has decreed that we shall wed. Therefore, I propose marriage to you, knowing that you have no offer before you and confident that you have no other option than to accept."

Whatever Mr. Collins had expected, he was clearly shocked by the sight of Elizabeth's sardonic laughter. Mary, who had risen from the sofa at the same time as Elizabeth, watched her sister with astonishment. But Elizabeth was heartened to see that while Mary was unable to laugh as Elizabeth did herself, she watched the parson, determination evident in her manner.

"I believe, Mr. Collins, that your proposal must be the worst which has ever been offered by any man in all the history of mankind. What care I for your patroness's demands? She is naught but a prideful woman seeking to impose her will upon her grown nephews."

"You will not speak of Lady Catherine in such a way!" snarled Mr. Collins.

"I will speak of her however I please," retorted Elizabeth. "Despite what you seem to believe, she is not deity. I commit no blasphemy by castigating her as the silly, stupid woman she is."

"Enough!" roared Mr. Collins. "If you say one more word, I shall not be responsible for my actions!"

"Mr. Collins," growled Elizabeth, "let me once again say that I have no concern for your patroness's whims. I would not marry you were you the only man standing between me and a life of poverty. And let me say that even if I was removed from the equation, it would make it no more likely Mr. Darcy would be compelled to marry his cousin. I cannot think he has any inclination toward her, for if he did, he would already have married her!"

"You will obey, Cousin Elizabeth," snarled Mr. Collins. "You will be made to marry me."

"No, she will not."

The words, spoken in a slow and deliberate cadence surprised the three combatants, none of whom had heard anyone enter the room. Mr. Collins whirled about in his shock, while Elizabeth and Mary only looked up to see their father standing inside the door, his countenance suffused with such a look of fury as Elizabeth had never before seen. By his side stood Mrs. Bennet, her contempt for the parson clear for them all to see. The disturbance had also drawn Jane, who watched with wide eyes of shock, while their footman, John, also stood at Mr. Bennet's shoulder, scowling at the parson.

"Mr. Collins," said Mr. Bennet, "I understand from Mrs. Bennet that you requested her permission to pay your addresses to Lizzy. Ignoring, for the moment, that it is to *me* you should make such a request, I have been informed that you were denied permission. Is that so?"

The parson drew himself up to his full height and glared at Mr.

Bennet, his patroness's haughtiness reflected in his manner. "I have come to offer honorable marriage to your daughter, Mr. Bennet, despite her clear lack of respectability."

"Did my wife *deny* your appeal or did she not?" enunciated Mr. Bennet.

"It matters little—"

"You are a fool, Collins," interjected Mr. Bennet. The parson goggled at him, but Mr. Bennet only shook his head. "Your father was perhaps the most objectionable man I have ever met. Rough and uneducated, yet haughty and determined he knew best, some of the arguments we exchanged were truly sights to see. It is clear to me that you have learned at the man's knee, for I find myself disgusted by your behavior."

"My father told me all about you, Mr. Bennet," spat Mr. Collins. "And yet I have offered you this olive branch to mend the rift, knowing how badly you treated him. And this is the thanks I receive?"

"Whatever fantasy your father spun for you, Mr. Collins, it does not give you the right to attempt to impose yourself on my family or my daughter in particular. There are rules of society to be met in any such offer. The woman's father must be petitioned, for example, and her favor must be obtained. You seem to believe that you are above all these things by virtue of your position as a parson. Or perhaps because of your perceived impression of how high your patroness is in society. Neither is true, sir."

"Very well, then," said Mr. Collins. "I hereby ask your permission to marry your daughter."

"Denied," replied Mr. Bennet. He fixed the shocked parson with a thin smile, one which did nothing to hide his contempt. "How you can think my Lizzy would be yours for the asking is quite beyond my comprehension, sir. She—all my daughters are precious to me. I would no more force her into marriage with *you*, of all men, than I would marry her to one of the pigs on the farm."

"Mr. Bennet—"

"No, Mr. Collins!" exclaimed Mr. Bennet. "You have disrupted my house quite enough. It is time you departed. I want you gone by this afternoon at the latest."

Mr. Collins gasped. "You would betray me in such a way? How am I to make my way home?"

"I care not, Mr. Collins. Your behavior has rendered the question moot. If you hurry quickly enough, perhaps you may catch your patroness as she flees the county with her tail between her legs. At the very least, I expect you have money for a night at the inn, if required, and money for the post coach to return you to your home."

It was clear Mr. Collins was not about to move, as he gaped at Mr. Bennet, unable to fathom what he was hearing. Mr. Bennet's patience, however, we clearly exhausted.

"John!" commanded he, bringing the footman to his side. "Please escort Mr. Collins above stairs to retrieve his belongings. He is to pack his trunks and depart from the estate. If he refuses, you may do whatever you wish with his belongings and call in the stable hands to evict him forcefully. I want him gone within an hour."

"This way, Mr. Collins," said John, approaching the parson and gesturing toward the open door.

Mr. Collins watched them all, attempting to gauge their will and, more particularly, John. The footman was tall and lean, and Elizabeth had seen enough of him around the house to know he possessed strength in his frame. Furthermore, though Mr. Hill—the butler—was an older man, the stable hands were both young and burly men and would have no difficulty seeing Mr. Collins evicted. In the end, Mr. Collins came to the correct conclusion himself.

"I see your betrayal, Cousin," hissed he. "I hope your wife and daughters are prepared to live on whatever pittance you will leave them, for they will receive no charity from me."

"Whatever our dispute, sir," replied Mr. Bennet, "it has never been clearer that you are not fit to wear that collar. Regardless, I shall not continue to bandy words with you. Be gone at once!"

With little choice, Mr. Collins glared at them all with contempt and exited the room, John trailing behind. The sound of his boots on the stairs informed them he was, for the moment, at least, obeying her father's edicts. Mr. Bennet waved to the butler, who appeared in the door, gave some instructions, which Mr. Hill hurried to carry out. Then he turned his attention to Elizabeth and Mary.

"Well, girls, how was that for a bit of excitement?"

Elizabeth shook her head—trust her father to find humor in such a situation! "Far more excitement than I might have wished to experience. What an odious man he is!"

"He is at that," said Mr. Bennet, his mercurial moods once again settling into seriousness. "I have sent for Lydia and Kitty. You all shall remain here with me until Mr. Collins is gone. I would not put it past him to attempt something with you. His desperation to do as his patroness bids might drive him to it."

The sounds of the stable hands entering the house soon reached their ears, along with Kitty and Lydia entering the room, protesting at being roused from what was surely their slumber. Mr. Bennet, with a patience he did not often possess with his youngest daughters, explained what had happened and why they had been summoned. Their complaints were then reserved for the loathsome parson.

"Are you well, Lizzy?" asked Jane when she sat beside Elizabeth, turning to her with concern in her eyes.

"I am, Jane," replied Elizabeth. "I will own that Mr. Collins showed much more bite than I had ever attributed to him, though his bark was as loud and obnoxious as ever."

"Lizzy!" exclaimed Mary, though quietly. "How can you make sportive comments of such an event? I truly feared for you in the face of *that man's* actions."

"I must laugh, Mary. Else I shall surely cry."

The three sisters laughed at Elizabeth's words. "Perhaps we shall be quite fortunate to receive the Netherfield party's visit this morning to distract us," continued Elizabeth. "The sight of Lord Chesterfield and Mr. Darcy now would be welcome, I dare say. And I am certain Jane wishes to see Mr. Bingley again, though she was hardly parted from his side last night, even by the demands of the dance!"

Both of her sisters realized this was Elizabeth's way of moving past an objectionable event, and they only shook their heads. It was for Jane to say: "Though I do not know if the cousins will come, I know that Mr. Bingley will not. He informed me last night he had some matters of business in London which required his attention. He was to depart today, intending to return in four or five days."

"Then we shall have to comfort you in your bereavement, dearest sister," teased Elizabeth. "I cannot bear the thought of you pining after your beau, so it shall be my purpose to induce you to laugh!"

When Mr. Collins came down the stairs, it was to the sound of the Bennet sisters' laughter, and had he not been so closely followed by Longbourn's employees, he might have gone into the sitting-room to confront Elizabeth again. As it was, the three men ensured he understood that no detours were to be tolerated and that he was to leave directly.

"You should all remember that when *I* am master of this estate, you will all be put out without reference," said he to the three men.

"But you are not the master yet, are you?" replied the footman. "The current master requires your absence. It is him we obey."

Mr. Collins only sniffed in disdain. "Regardless, you should not expect any charity from me when I inherit. I remember those who betray me."

"His effects have been gathered?" asked the butler, who appeared in the vestibule before them. When the footman nodded, the butler turned to Mr. Collins. "If you wish it, Clive will take you to Meryton in the wagon. But you are not to return—the door will be barred against you should you attempt it."

"I need no such assistance from the likes of you," said Mr. Collins. "I am able to make my own way."

The butler did not speak. He only nodded and opened the door, and Mr. Collins felt all the insult of being unceremoniously forced from the house which would one day be his. By the time he was halfway to Meryton, he regretted refusing the offer to see him to the town, for his arms ached from the strain of carrying his effects over the uneven ground.

"I will know how to act," muttered Mr. Collins. "Mr. Bennet will rue the day he betrayed me."

The events at Longbourn that morning were unknown to the inhabitants of Netherfield. But that did not mean they were not beset by their own trials. That their trials were perpetrated by the erstwhile mistress of the estate was not a surprise to Darcy. The woman had become more desperate the longer they had been in residence without the achievement of her designs.

"I am off to London this morning," Bingley had said when he greeted Darcy and Fitzwilliam earlier than Bingley had any right to be awake. He had always been a late riser, and though Darcy had known of his intended journey to London, he thought Bingley might have waited until later in the day.

When he made that observation, Bingley only laughed. "Under normal circumstances, you might be correct, my friend. But today I am impatient to be gone, for the sooner I leave, the sooner I will return. I find myself quite eager to return, I assure you."

Darcy grinned at his friend, feeling quite light-hearted. Bingley returned his gesture, but then his countenance became almost stern.

"I should also inform you that last night Louisa asked for permission to assume the position of my hostess at Netherfield, and I have accepted. I have no doubt Caroline will attempt to assert her authority, but with Hurst supporting her, Louisa will fend our sister off."

"Oh?" asked Fitzwilliam, the first time he had spoken since Bingley arrived.

Bingley shook his head, his exasperation evident. "Surely you saw Caroline's performance last night? She had little interest in behaving in a manner befitting the mistress of the estate. Louisa pointed this out, quite correctly, and I agreed.

"I am also certain Caroline will attempt to induce you all to follow me to London. I know the calendar is turning late in the year, but I hope you will consent to stay for a few weeks longer."

"Of course, Bingley," replied Darcy, resisting the urge to glance at his cousin. "I am quite happy to stay."

"As am I," added Fitzwilliam.

Darcy did not attempt to divine his cousin's purpose and Bingley did not see anything untoward in their interactions.

"Excellent! Then I shall depart, for I have already called for the carriage. I shall return anon, as I have promised."

Betting against Bingley's characterization of his sister was a fool's wager—had Darcy not already understood this, he might have thought his friend's words were prophetic. As it was, Darcy had anticipated Miss Bingley's performance. In fact, he was interested to see what form it would take.

After breaking his fast, Darcy settled himself in the library for some time, choosing a book which interested him from Bingley's pitiful collection. There he stayed for most of the remainder of the morning. When the time for luncheon approached, he made his way to the sitting-room, where he found Fitzwilliam in the company of the Hursts. Of Miss Bingley, there was no sign. It was unfortunate that state of affairs did not persist long.

Only moments after Darcy entered, Miss Bingley waltzed into the room. She greeted them and then set about the business of fulfilling Bingley's predictions.

"It has become a little late in the day," said she, "but if we are about the business of packing, we should be ready to leave by tomorrow morning. I find that I am eager to be in London once again, as I am sure you all are."

"Then you would be incorrect, Caroline," replied Mrs. Hurst. By her side, Hurst watched with amusement evident in the sardonic sneer he directed at his sister by marriage. "I know of no such plans to depart for London tomorrow. In fact, our brother was quite specific about his intention to return within five days."

"Oh, you know Charles," said Caroline, an airy wave of her hand swatting her sister's words away. "Once he is in London, he will be in no hurry to depart. There is no need to wait until he summons us — we should simply join him now."

"On the contrary, my *dear* sister," said Hurst, "I am quite settled at Netherfield at present."

"As am I," added Louisa. "It is a pretty estate; do you not agree? And the people of the neighborhood are friendly and obliging. Charles could not have found a better estate had he tried."

Miss Bingley glared at her sister, before she turned to Darcy, a forced smile adorning her countenance. "Surely *you* are eager to leave, Mr. Darcy. As a member of a much higher strata of society, these people must grate on your nerves. And your dear sister, Georgiana! I am certain you must be wild to see her!"

"I would need to go north if I wished to see Georgiana," replied Darcy. "She is at my uncle's estate in Derbyshire at present. I am in no hurry to depart, for I am quite enjoying myself in Hertfordshire."

Miss Bingley glared at him as if he had delivered her some mortal insult. But Darcy hardly noticed. Instead, he was contemplating a young woman of his acquaintance, one whom he had begun to see as a special young lady. Her dark, beautiful eyes haunted his dreams and thrilled his senses. Was it too late in the day to visit Longbourn? Perhaps visits were discouraged the day after a late ball, but he could not suppose Mrs. Bennet would object to his coming.

"What of you, Lord Chesterfield?" asked Miss Bingley. "Are you as tied to Netherfield as my relations and yours?"

Interested to see how his cousin would respond, Darcy pushed his musings to the side. Fitzwilliam, for his part, darted a glance at Darcy — the significance of which Darcy did not miss — and nodded.

"I am quite happy to stay here, Miss Bingley."

"Very well then, my lord," cooed she. "Then we are happy to have you. I am certain we shall all have a merry time here, assuming we manage to avoid the locals." She tittered at her own jest, laughing alone, as no one else joined her. "Perhaps you might even be induced to stay for Christmastide!"

The woman continued to prattle along, seeming intent upon maintaining the fiction that she was still the mistress of Netherfield. Darcy did not hear one word in ten, for he was considering her capitulation and what it meant. In short, she had surrendered far too quickly for his taste. She was becoming desperate. Darcy knew he needed to take great care.

"Louisa! How dare you betray me!"

It was all Louisa could do not to turn and snap at her sister. "As I informed you last night, Caroline," rejoined she through clenched teeth, "if you had behaved in the manner you should, you would still be mistress of this estate."

"I do not know what has happened to you," snarled Caroline. "Have you forgotten our determination to climb society's ranks so quickly?"

"That was always *your* ambition, Caroline. Not mine. I have no desire to be anything more than I am."

"Then you are as dull as I always thought you were. I shall know how to act!"

And Caroline went away, leaving a relieved Louisa behind. Her sister was becoming all but ungovernable. They would need to do something about her before long.

CHAPTER XX

While the residents of Longbourn might have preferred a more sedate remainder of their day, it was not to be. Elizabeth had suspected how it would be, given the characters of the people who were involved. It had all depended on how far Mr. Collins was forced to go before he was in a position to send word to his patroness, and how far away the woman herself lurked. That she arrived only three hours later informed them all that she had still been in the neighborhood as her father had suggested.

The lady descended on Longbourn with all the fury of a gale, pushing her way into the house, screeching at the top of her lungs, demanding satisfaction. Elizabeth neither knew nor cared where her lackey was. Knowing, as had his daughter, that the lady's appearance was likely, Mr. Bennet was on hand to confront her.

"I demand to speak with Miss Elizabeth Bennet!" These were the first words out of Lady Catherine's mouth, as she eschewed even the dignity of a greeting. "Where is she? I will speak with her at once!"

"Lady Catherine," replied Mr. Bennet, rising and standing between the woman and his family, "I will ask you not to rush into my home making demands of us all. You are a guest here, and an unwelcome one at that. It would be best if you would simply depart before I have you forcibly removed."

"I shall not go away until I have obtained the assurances I require! How dare you think to contradict me? Do you not know who I am?"

"You are a loud and obnoxious woman who has invaded my house and disturbed the tranquility therein."

Lady Catherine regarded Mr. Bennet with fury, clearly unaccustomed to be spoken to in such a manner. For Elizabeth, it was all she could do not to laugh—she could never remember such a thing as tranquility existing at Longbourn. Her younger sisters and their antics made such a state unlikely in the extreme!

But Elizabeth was not about to allow her father to take the onus of confronting the lady on himself, not when she was the principal reason for the woman's visit. As such, Elizabeth rose from the sofa on which she sat and approached the lady, her head held high.

"You!" cried Lady Catherine when she caught sight of Elizabeth. "Since your father is so unreasonable, I must appeal to your better sense. I require you to keep your distance from my nephews and cease this objectionable attempt to induce them to forget their duty. You will oblige me!"

"I have no notion of what you speak, Lady Catherine," replied Elizabeth. "I have never attempted anything with either of your nephews. They are good and amiable men who have been welcome in the neighborhood because of their characters."

"Of course, they are!" snapped Lady Catherine. "Their lineage will demand nothing less. But I am not unaware of stratagems employed by ladies of your station. You will desist at once!"

"Again, you are misinformed. I have done nothing improper, nor will I descend to such behavior."

Into this whirlwind of heightened emotions and harsh words entered Mr. Collins, once again proving his propensity for arriving at the worst possible moment.

"Cousin, you must listen to Lady Catherine! Have you no care for decency or the credit of your family?"

"Collins, I told you not to return," growled Mr. Bennet. "Shall I have Clive and Gordon run you off the estate?"

"I am here with Lady Catherine at her request," replied Mr. Collins. Had his nose been any higher in the air, a bird may very well have perched upon it.

"He is my parson, and I trust his judgment," said Lady Catherine with a sniff. "I will bring whomever I like wherever I go."

"Your ladyship," said Mr. Bennet, "I would not care if you were the

214 "2 Jann Rowland

Duke of Devonshire himself. You are on my land at present, and you are subject to *my* will. You will leave—both of you!"

"Not until I receive that assurance I require. You will give it to me now!"

"I would not give you a glass of water if you were dying of thirst!" exclaimed Elizabeth.

"How dare you speak to Lady Catherine in such a way!" cried Mr. Collins.

He stepped forward, his hands extended as if to grasp at Elizabeth, but she was ready for him and moved nimbly to one side, evading the enraged man. She was not forced to dodge him a second time, for the footmen and one of the stable hands seized Mr. Collins by the shoulders and held him tight, dragging him from the room. Mr. Bennet followed them to the door.

"If you so much as set foot on Longbourn's land while I am still the master, I will turn you over to the magistrate," said Mr. Bennet. Mr. Collins was screaming obscenities as he was dragged from the room, but the men holding him were inexorable, and for all Mr. Collins's bulk, he was a weak man, struggling ineffectually against their strength. Soon, he was gone.

Lady Catherine, however, was not idle. She used the distraction of Mr. Collins's actions to step up to Elizabeth, looming over her in a most intimidating way. She was a tall woman, was Elizabeth's idle thought. She shook her cane in a threatening manner at Elizabeth, punctuating each word with a thrust of its wooden length.

"I will have your solemn promise, Miss Elizabeth. You *will* oblige me, for I am not in the habit of being contradicted. If my nephews approach you to speak, you will turn away from them. You will have no more contact with either."

"I will do no such unreasonable thing," said Elizabeth, glaring back at the lady. "It is foolish for you to think the cessation of such imagined attentions from Mr. Darcy to me would make it more likely that he would marry your daughter. Has he not already had ample time to come to such a determination?"

"He knows his duty," cried Lady Catherine. "It is only you who is preventing him. You will promise me now!"

"I have done nothing wrong and will make no such promise!"

The lady's eyes widened at Elizabeth's refusal. Then they hardened in fury. But before she could take any further action, Mr. Bennet was once again there. He stepped in front of Elizabeth and looked down on Lady Catherine—he was several inches taller, Elizabeth noted—and his countenance, unlike the genial and sometimes sardonic father Elizabeth had always known, was anything but friendly.

"Lady Catherine, you will leave my home this instant, without any further harassment of my daughter. I give the same edict to you that I gave to Mr. Collins—if you so much as set foot on my estate again, I shall call the magistrate."

The look the lady bestowed on him was anything but cowed. "Do you not know who I am Mr. Bennet? Do you not know the weight of the social and legal pressure which may be brought to bear against you?"

"You are naught but a trespasser who refuses to leave," said Mr. Bennet. "I fear nothing you can do. No court in the land would do other than laugh at your claims should you make them, and since my family has the friendship of both Lord Chesterfield and Mr. Darcy, I doubt your brother would support you, even should you make an appeal to him. Your situation is untenable and your demands unreasonable. You will leave now, or I will have my men remove you."

They stood toe to toe, neither giving an inch. Whatever Lady Catherine saw in Mr. Bennet's face, it was clear she did not like it, for she grimaced and turned her glare on Elizabeth, shaking her cane.

"Do not imagine your ambitions will *ever* come to fruition. When I am finished with you, you will wish you had never met my nephews."

And with that, Lady Catherine spun on her heel and stalked from the room, Mr. Bennet following to ensure she left. A moment later, the ladies remaining in the sitting-room could hear the sound of her carriage wheels rolling over the gravel of Longbourn's drive, which soon faded away into the distance.

Unable to fathom what had just happened, Elizabeth sank down onto a nearby sofa. Her action was noted, as soon she was surrounded by a pair of most beloved sisters, who brought Elizabeth from her shock.

"Elizabeth, are you well?"

The question came from her mother, who stood in front of her, watching with concern. Elizabeth attempted a smile. "I believe I shall be, Mother."

Mrs. Bennet nodded and patted Elizabeth's knee. "I shall send for some tea. I dare say you could benefit from it."

While Mrs. Bennet left the room to speak to the housekeeper, Jane and Mary leaned in close, providing comfort to Elizabeth. She was no closer to a resolution to her dilemma, and the weight of all that had happened that morning pressed down on her, threatening to crush her until she was no more.

"I hope, my dearest sister, you are not listening to anything that odious woman said."

Surprised, Elizabeth turned to Mary, who had spoken, and raised an eyebrow. Mary only smiled and shook her head before turning a pointed and expectant look back on Elizabeth.

"I seem to remember a younger sister who was not quite this forceful." Elizabeth attempted a chuckle but suspected it did not fool anyone.

"Then you have yourself to blame for changing me," said Mary. "Now, shall you not answer me?"

With a shake of her head, Elizabeth said: "I do not give credence to anything Lady Catherine says. She is obviously a bitter termagant who has rarely been forced to yield in her entire life.

"But I cannot help but wonder . . ."

"What is it, Lizzy?" asked Jane when she did not speak again. Elizabeth shook her head, attempting to clear her thoughts.

"I simply wonder if it is all worth it."

"*What?*"

"The attention of a man of high society. Surely this is but a taste of what I will face should I marry a high-ranking gentleman."

Her sisters' eyes widened together. "Has something happened of which we are not aware?" demanded Mary.

Elizabeth felt her cheeks grow hot. "Last night Mr. Darcy all but declared his intentions."

"He is to speak to Papa?"

"No. He did not ask for a courtship. But he was very clear in stating his admiration and his wish to know me better."

Both sisters regarded Elizabeth in silence for a moment, though to Elizabeth that moment was long and tense. When she could not bear it any longer she demanded: "Will you both not tell me what you are thinking?"

The answer came from an unexpected source. "They are likely thinking what I am thinking, Lizzy."

Startled, Elizabeth looked up to see her father standing close, regarding them all. He grinned at her surprise, but it soon gave way to the seriousness of the subject. "For myself, I am wondering what has happened to my indomitable daughter."

"She still exists, Papa. But more is required than courage in the face of trials. Would I be subjected to similar behavior from those of Mr. Darcy's set at every turn?"

"You overestimate the ability of society to do you harm, Lizzy. Yes, there will always be those who are objectionable, but I hardly think they will all share Lady Catherine's scorn. Furthermore, you are correct that more than courage is required. A good beginning would be the love and support of a good man. If you believe Mr. Darcy would stand by and allow others to slander his wife, I must wonder if you even know the man."

"Papa is correct, Lizzy," said Mary. "He is not the kind of man to allow any foolishness."

"But a wife must stand on her own."

"I am certain you are capable of it," said Jane.

"Your sisters are correct, Lizzy." Mr. Bennet smiled, leaned over, and kissed her on the head. "Allow a little time to pass and the shock to settle. I am certain you will rediscover your courage."

The ordered tea service arrived shortly after, and Elizabeth began to feel like herself again, with the help of beloved sisters. Lady Catherine was, Elizabeth decided, an aberration, and while there would be others in society like her, she could hardly be representative of them all. Furthermore, few others would have a connection to the Darcy family such that they would protest so vehemently.

All this was mere supposition, though, for regardless of his words the previous night, Mr. Darcy had not asked for a courtship. The desire to know a young woman better did not necessarily precede a declaration of undying love. It was this, as much as anything else, which settled Elizabeth's nerves and calmed her fears. She would allow events to unfold as they would. There was no need to be afraid.

By the time the next objectionable visitor arrived, Elizabeth was quite recovered. It was nearing the end of visiting hours when a coach made its way up the driveway. Kitty, who was situated nearest the window, pushed the curtains aside and looked out at the conveyance, reporting that it was a large chaise and four. But when the visitor stepped from it, her identity was surprising to them all.

"It is Miss Bingley," said Kitty. "I did not know the Bingley carriage was so large and grand."

"Mr. Bingley is gone to London today," replied Jane. "She must have used Mr. Darcy's or Lord Chesterfield's carriage instead."

Mrs. Bennet gazed long at Jane, clearly not having heard of Mr. Bingley's departure from the neighborhood. But though Elizabeth wondered if a hint of her old hysteria was creeping into her mother's manner again, Caroline was soon led into the room. Mrs. Bennet had the sense to hold her tongue, for which Elizabeth was grateful.

"Miss Bingley," said Mrs. Bennet, greeting their guest. "How good of you to call. I trust everyone at Netherfield is well?"

"All very well, Mrs. Bennet," replied Caroline, her supercilious disinterest evident for all to see. "But they are not all at Netherfield. My brother, you see, has left for London this morning, because of some business which could not be put off."

Mrs. Bennet glanced at Jane. "Yes, we had heard something of that. Please accept my wishes for your brother's safe journey and return."

While Caroline's fixed smile tightened at Mrs. Bennet's observance, she did not reply. For the second time, a tea service was ordered and the ladies sat down to visit. It was clear within moments that Caroline had come to speak with Jane, though her purpose was not evident at once. Their amiable conversation passed the first few moments of Caroline's presence until the tea service arrived. Mrs. Bennet served them all and then sat back and allowed Jane to converse with her friend, Mary and Elizabeth nearby to offer support if required.

"Do you expect your brother back soon?" said Jane after a few moments, asking after the woman's brother as politeness dictated.

"His business, he informed us, is to take four or five days," replied Caroline. The woman paused, and then spoke again, her countenance suggesting the imparting of some great secret. "Of course, you must understand that Charles is quite impulsive. He is, you see, apt to change his mind on a whim and without any previous notice. He stated his intention to return, but I expect he will be in no hurry to leave London when he is there."

Jane's face fell at the woman's words, and Elizabeth was certain the woman noticed it, for there was a faint hint of satisfaction about her manner.

"In fact," continued she in a blithe manner, "I would not be surprised should a summons arrive for us to join him there. Accordingly, I have already ordered some of our belongings packed and some of the secondary rooms closed in the expectation of it. There are many benefits to our removal to London for Christmas, not the least of which..." Caroline paused, appearing as if she had reconsidered her words, before she said: "Well, as nothing is settled, perhaps I should not speak of it."

Jane opened her mouth, most likely to absolve Caroline of any obligation to speak further. Elizabeth, however, would not allow this woman to lie—for she was certain there was naught of truth coming from her lips.

"You may be assured of our secrecy, Caroline."

"I have no doubt of it," replied Caroline. Her self-satisfied smile suggested she thought she had obtained what she wished. "It is only that Charles has always possessed a tender regard for Mr. Darcy's sister, Georgiana.

"Have I told you of Georgiana?" asked Caroline, feigning ignorance of the way Jane's smile had turned brittle. "She is a wonderful girl. She is intelligent, handsome, and so accomplished. Why, I declare Charles could sit and listen to her play the pianoforte all day and not tire of it!

"And Mr. Darcy is eager, of course, to return to London and see his sister. And the dear viscount as well, for he is Georgiana's other guardian, you understand. Yes, I expect that by the end of the week we shall all be gone to London. When we will return to Hertfordshire, I cannot say, but I do not think it would be soon."

"That is quite interesting to hear you say that, Caroline," said Elizabeth. "I fear there must be some misunderstanding, however, for Mr. Darcy was very clear in informing me last night that he has no intention of leaving Netherfield at present."

Caroline turned a glare on Elizabeth, but to Elizabeth's surprise, Jane frowned and spoke next. "And Mr. Bingley was careful to inform me that he would return within five days. I do not think he would have spoken in such a way if he meant to do otherwise."

"I am certain he did," said Caroline, but not before sniffing at Elizabeth and then ignoring her. "But I know my brother. I am certain how it will be. And if he does decide to stay in London, I can only applaud him, for I cannot think he could do better than Georgiana Darcy for a wife. She is everything lovely and amiable and, equally important, a member of our strata of society."

Elizabeth could not hold in her snort of disgust for this woman, which prompted a malevolent glare in response. Having faced Lady Catherine, Elizabeth would not allow the likes of *this* woman intimidate her.

"You have my apologies, Miss Bingley, but I did not know the Darcy family had any near ancestors involved with trade. I shall have to ask Mr. Darcy about it, for I would be interested to hear of what manner of business they owned."

"What nonsense do you speak?" demanded Miss Bingley—for Miss Bingley she was. All pretense at intimacy was being dissolved with their tense confrontation. "The Darcy family have owned Pemberley for centuries. There is no hint of trade to stain their background."

"No, but your brother is descended from tradesmen."

Miss Bingley's head whipped around to look at Mr. Bennet who had spoken. Elizabeth's father was watching her, a faint hint of disgust hovering in his eyes and about his mouth.

"I am sorry, Miss Bingley, but I must dispense with pleasantries, for it has been a trying day. Though you may look down on my family for our modest circumstances, you should know that *my* ancestors have been gentlemen for as long as Mr. Darcy's have. Furthermore, for you to claim a level of society equal to that family's is absurd, given your family's background.

"I have no quarrel with your brother, for he is a good man. But do not attempt to lord over my daughters, who are daughters of a gentleman. That is one thing *you* will never be."

Miss Bingley's expression was all offense.

"Now, please return your conversation to acceptable comments for a morning visit. If you feel you have been insulted, you may, of course, depart."

It was a surprise to no one when Miss Bingley chose the latter, though not without sweeping them all with a contemptuous glare. She rose without a word and nary a curtsey, and made her way from the room, leaving them all watching her with feelings no friendlier than her own.

"Good riddance," said Elizabeth. "Her false friendship is exposed and dispensed with, and I, for one, cannot be happier." Elizabeth turned to Jane. "I do not pity you, Jane, for the prospect of having such a sister as she."

Jane, incapable as ever of speaking a negative word about anyone, chose to focus on another subject. "But what if she is correct? What if Mr. Bingley does not return?"

"I will eat my bonnet if he does not," muttered Mary.

It struck Elizabeth as diverting, and she laughed, soon joined by her younger sister. Jane, however, just watched them, a hint of crossness appearing in the firm set of her mouth.

"I agree with Mary, Jane," said Elizabeth, fondly laying a hand on her sister's arm. "Miss Bingley's purpose was obvious. I cannot state with any certainty Mr. Bingley's feelings for Miss Darcy, but I doubt Mr. Darcy would allow any attachment at present. I understand she is naught but fifteen! He is not a man who would allow his sister to be the focus of *any* man when she is so young."

It was clear Jane was still uncertain, so Elizabeth and Mary spent the rest of the afternoon cheering her. Whatever the case may be, Elizabeth was determined to ask Mr. Darcy about his sister when she next saw the man. Though Elizabeth was convinced Mr. Bingley would, indeed, return when five days had passed, any peace she could give her sister would be welcome.

As was typical, the sound of Lady Catherine's voice preceded her into the house, and Fitzwilliam, ensconced as he was with Hurst in the billiards room could hear her long before he could see her. It was apparent the Darcy was also made aware of her presence the moment she arrived, for he was on hand to confront her.

What followed was as tiresome as ever, for the discussion had played out between them more times than Fitzwilliam cared to remember. Most of those previously held, of course, had not been with such . . . animation.

"I have never been subjected to such treatment in my life!" The lady's words were spoken in the approximation of a scream. Fitzwilliam winced. He did not know how Sir Lewis had withstood this woman for a wife while he had lived.

"Those Bennets are artful, spiteful people, and they intend to ruin our family's reputation forever! I absolutely insist you break off all contact with them and come directly to London with me. We shall quit this place at once!"

"You went to Longbourn?" asked Darcy.

Fitzwilliam did not miss the dangerous quality in Darcy's voice, but Lady Catherine, as obtuse as ever, continued as if she had not heard. "Of course, I did! That little baggage refused Collins's proposal, insisting that she must have *you*! I went to demand her obedience, though she — and her odious father — were as disobliging as ever."

"Lady Catherine, I have often thought you senseless, but I never expected you to be so lost to good behavior as this. Mr. Bennet is not about to bow to your demands, and I would think much less of Miss Elizabeth if she agreed to marry your loathsome caricature of a parson. Are you completely mad?"

"How dare you speak to me in such a way? I am your nearest relation. Of course, I will do this to protect your reputation."

"Madam, I have no need of your protection, and I am quite certain your brother would take exception at your characterization of being my nearest relation, to say nothing of my own sister! If you had any sense at all you would leave and never return."

"I shall not!" Lady Catherine was beyond reason. "We will leave at once and I shall publish the notice of your engagement to Anne. I insist upon being satisfied."

"And I have no intention of satisfying you. I will not marry Anne, and if you send notice to any reputable paper, they will not print it, for I have already notified them that to do so will bring the threat of a suit against them."

Lady Catherine stared at him, appearing dumb and unable to respond. Darcy took that moment to grasp her arm and march her from the room. The woman regained her wits, demanded he release her, and struggled against his grip, but Darcy was inexorable.

"You will leave this instant, Lady Catherine." He stepped through the door, pulling the recalcitrant woman with him, his words floating back through it as they retreated through the halls. "Do not return, and do not try my patience any further. I will break all connection with you if you persist."

"Your aunt is beyond belief," observed Hurst.

Fitzwilliam nodded, but he did not respond. He was engaged in thinking of the matter of Lady Catherine and Darcy, and though he was not certain, a thought had occurred to him. For if Darcy *did* marry Anne, it would leave the field wide open for Fitzwilliam to swoop in and catch the fair Miss Elizabeth Bennet himself.

Chapter XXI

Winter had, indeed, always been a trial on Elizabeth's patience. But in present circumstances, the season, perhaps, served as a check on Elizabeth's impatience. It had long been her custom to seek solitude on the trails of her father's estate, for a long walk with naught but the trees to provide company allowed her the time to work difficult matters out in her own mind.

At present, however, they could not be certain Mr. Collins had left the area, and though Elizabeth did not wish to ascribe any danger to the man, his behavior at the end of his stay at Longbourn had suggested prudence. And that did not even take into account what Lady Catherine might do.

Thus, Elizabeth remained close to home those days, and as frigid temperatures had descended over the land, and an inch or two of snow had even fallen, she found herself largely confined to the house. There was no society and the Bennet sisters were forced to be content with one another's company. Even the officers did not visit, a circumstance which was lamented at length by Kitty and Lydia.

Three days after the ball, the gentlemen from Netherfield finally appeared at Longbourn, and while Elizabeth had always enjoyed their company, on this occasion she wondered if she could not more cheerfully do without it. Mr. Darcy was as friendly as he had ever been, but the feeling of rivalry between the two cousins was stronger than ever.

"Miss Elizabeth," said Lord Chesterfield, hurrying to greet her as soon as they entered the room. "I am happy to see you again. I trust you have been well?"

"I have, thank you," replied Elizabeth.

"We are all quite well, Lord Chesterfield," said Mrs. Bennet. "We thank you for visiting and inquiring after us. My Lydia, in particular, has been quite desolate without you, for after being injured by Mr. Collins's clumsiness, she has not had much company."

"Ah, yes," replied Lord Chesterfield, little though he appeared eager to greet Lydia. "I hope your injury is healing, Miss Lydia."

Lydia, fractious as ever, only complained: "Not quickly enough to suit my tastes. I swear I shall never dance with another parson again!"

"Perhaps you would sit with her for a time, Lord Chesterfield," said Mrs. Bennet. "I am certain she would appreciate your company."

Left with no way to politely refuse, Lord Chesterfield sat in Lydia's company, though he directed a long look at Elizabeth as he did. Elizabeth and Mary shared a look and each stifled their laughter. Regardless of whatever changes had come over Mrs. Bennet of late, she was still their mother and matchmaking was in her blood.

Elizabeth's attention was caught, however, by the sight of Mr. Darcy directing a faintly victorious glance at his cousin, and she was annoyed all over again. When he sat by her and turned to her, whatever he was about to say died on his lips, for he could see her displeasure.

"I hope you are not descending to rivalry, sir," said she in a soft voice.

Mr. Darcy was immediately chastened. "I apologize, Miss Elizabeth, but that was not my intent. It is only . . . Well, let us say that Fitzwilliam has been a trial on my patience of late. He has been making subtle statements these past few days concerning my cousin, Anne, and I cannot quite make him out."

Then Mr. Darcy turned a penitent look on Elizabeth. "It seems, however, that I must apologize for my aunt yet again. I understand she came here the day after Bingley's ball."

"She did, but I will inform you once more that you are not required to apologize for her. My father dealt with her and warned her against returning. It is not your fault."

"And Mr. Collins?" Mr. Darcy's manner was probing and not a

little apprehensive.

"Also departed." Elizabeth paused, wondering what she should share. "Mr. Collins, in fact, proposed marriage to me, even after being expressly denied permission to do so. My father decided he had experienced enough of Mr. Collins's foolishness and evicted him from the estate.

"He returned with Lady Catherine when she came to confront us, and my father evicted him once again, warning him that the magistrate would be called should he come here again."

"Did he harm you?" This time Mr. Darcy's hands flexed into fists, and Elizabeth might have feared for Mr. Collins's life had he been present.

"No, though he did reach out for me. But he was prevented, so there is no need to worry."

Mr. Darcy was silent for several moments, attempting to master his fury. While Elizabeth was not certain of this entire situation in which she found herself, she had never been more certain of his regard than she was now. He appeared almost ready to throttle Mr. Collins, should he see him again, for nothing more than the insult the man had given to Elizabeth.

"There was one other visitor that day," said Elizabeth, her eyes darting to Jane, hoping her sister would not overhear.

"Oh?" asked Mr. Darcy.

"Miss Bingley came to Longbourn," said Elizabeth, returning her attention to the man by her side. "She had some interesting things to say, though I am certain most of them were falsehoods."

Mr. Darcy did not speak, but his countenance demanded her to explain. "She informed us that Mr. Bingley was ever-changing in his moods and would undoubtedly call you all to London before long. She also waxed eloquent of his attachment to your sister and how she expected them to make a match."

To anyone with any wit, it was easy to see that Mr. Darcy was seriously displeased. "I hope you do not give credence to anything *that woman* says."

"No. But Jane is not so ready to discount the words of one she sees as a friend. I understand that I am prying into your private affairs, Mr. Darcy, and that of your friend. I merely wish to spare my sister the heartache of believing the man she admires does not return her feelings."

"Bingley has not confided in me to that extent," replied Mr. Darcy. "But though he *can* be impulsive and *has* paid attention to pretty women in the past, he is not fickle. We have received no word of him asking us to attend him in London, and he was explicit in his intention to return. I expect him the day after tomorrow.

"Furthermore, Miss Bingley's words concerning my sister are nothing more than those of a desperate woman wishing to ascend to the heights of society by any means possible. Georgiana is full young, and I will not be parted with her for some time yet. *If* Bingley was to fall in love with her, I would not prevent a match between them, regardless of any opinion of society. But he has shown no inclination toward her. In fact, he has informed me himself that he sees her as a much younger sister. I must also suppose that Miss Bingley spoke so in an attempt to dampen your sister's enthusiasm for my friend, for she wishes Bingley to make a match of high society."

"Much of that I told Miss Bingley myself, with my father and sister's assistance."

Mr. Darcy's eyebrow rose. "Oh? Is that why she was in such high dudgeon that afternoon?"

"I can only suppose it must be," replied Elizabeth. "After my father's admonishment, she departed Longbourn without another word."

"That is a sight I would have liked to see for myself, Miss Elizabeth."

A laugh escaped Elizabeth's lips, though she supposed there was little of humor to be found in the situation. "Then I shall tell you what happened, though I have no power to show you."

And explain the matter she did, detailing Miss Bingley's visit and what had transpired. The further she progressed in her tale the more displeased Mr. Darcy became. Elizabeth had no doubt that when he returned to Netherfield he would have words with the woman. In the end, however, he chose to focus on another facet of the confrontation.

"It seems your father's dander was raised," said he. "Mr. Bennet has always struck me as a quiet man, perhaps one who is more liable to laugh at the world than become offended by it."

"In that, you would be correct, Mr. Darcy." Elizabeth's eyes found her father where he was watching the awkward interaction between Lord Chesterfield and Lydia. "But while Papa finds foolishness diverting, he will not suffer it when it pertains to his daughters. He will not allow us to be importuned by the unworthy. When Mr. Collins first came, my father enjoyed his absurdity. But that could not last long in the face of the man's obvious stupidity. He also has little patience for those who look down on us for any reason."

Mr. Darcy nodded. "It is good that you have such a protector, then."

Elizabeth directed a long look at him. "Do you think Lady Catherine will still present herself as a problem?"

After a moment's hesitation, Mr. Darcy shook his head. "I expect that now she has not been successful in intimidating you, she will turn all her energies on myself and perhaps Fitzwilliam's father." Mr. Darcy snorted. "She will receive little notice from him, for it is well known that the earl barely tolerates his sister and considers her a virago. Regardless, I suspect she has already been in London for several days, making his life miserable."

"How unfortunate," murmured Elizabeth. "But better one who has some measure of control over her. She was truly offensive, Mr. Darcy. I know not how you can withstand her as a relation."

A sigh escaped the man's lips and he attempted to force a smile. "She is difficult when her anger is aroused, and it is for that reason most of us attempt to avoid provoking her. She is also dictatorial and overbearing. We have all learned to simply listen to her pronouncements and ignore that which is nonsensical or intrusive.

"You must understand, Miss Elizabeth," continued Mr. Darcy, "that she is my mother's elder sister." Mr. Darcy paused, some great emotion filling him such that he could not speak. When he finally did, it was evident in his tone. "My mother was an excellent woman. She was thoughtful and quiet, but she could also be forceful when the situation demanded. She was also very close to her sister, though they were not alike at all. I have always attempted to treat Lady Catherine as my mother would wish her to be treated, so as to honor her."

Mr. Darcy shook his head. "It is unfortunate, for my aunt has become more irrational as the years pass. But this matter of her wishes with respect to my cousin and me are a wedge which is swiftly driving us apart. My mother may have discussed the matter with Lady Catherine, but she did not agree to it as Lady Catherine says, else she would have spoken to me. My father, after my mother's passing, never gave any credence to Lady Catherine's assertions, going so far on more than one occasion to accuse her of making it up from whole cloth."

Elizabeth's heart went out to this young man. "It speaks well of you to honor your mother's memory in such a fashion, Mr. Darcy. I understand the difficulty of your situation. I would not wish to make it worse."

The moment the words left her mouth, Mr. Darcy's eyes darted to hers, his manner searching. After a moment of this, he addressed her, his manner hesitant.

"I hope you understand that you are *not* making it worse, as you say. My aunt does not rule my life, nor does she dictate what I may or may not do. She sees *any* young woman as a threat and acts accordingly."

"But you must acknowledge that her displeasure would not be this spectacular if you were courting the daughter of a duke."

Mr. Darcy chuckled and shook his head. "No, in that I must suppose you are correct. It is unlikely in the extreme that I would ever court a woman in such an exalted situation, but I doubt Lady Catherine would treat her as she as treated you. Regardless, now she has seen that you will not be cowed, I doubt she will attempt to work on you. In fact, she may even, in a strange sort of way, respect you for resisting her."

"If she does, then she is a strange woman, indeed."

"*That*, my dear Miss Elizabeth, is beyond a doubt."

They laughed together, and Elizabeth caught a glimpse of the viscount out of the corner of her eye. He did not appear amused, but as Lydia and Mrs. Bennet were still commanding his attention, he was not able to make his escape.

"I hope, Miss Elizabeth, you do not suspect me of anything but honest interest."

Drawn back to Mr. Darcy by his heartfelt words, Elizabeth regarded him, wondering what she should say in response. In the end, she decided to be completely candid.

"At present, there does not seem to anything else, sir. Regardless of Lady Catherine's suspicions and Mr. Collins's fears, you have made no declarations. I certainly would not hold you to such nebulous statements as those you have made."

Mr. Darcy regarded her for a moment, and Elizabeth felt warmed by that gaze. If ever there was a man who could convey his feelings with nothing more than a look, it was Mr. Darcy. There was promise in his eyes, but also mystery. Elizabeth very much wished to solve that mystery, to understand what it was telling her.

In a deliberate motion, calculated to avoid startling her, he reached out and grasped her hand, raising it to his lips to bestow a kiss on it. Elizabeth's hand had been kissed before, both in affection or simple gallantry. But never had she felt such pure emotion, such a promise of delights to come. Her hand tingled with feelings she had never experienced but wanted to. It was all too much, and she began to feel lightheaded.

"Let there be no mistake, Miss Elizabeth," said he in a soft tone, almost too low for Elizabeth to hear, though he was by her side. "I wish to know you better. I wish for us to speak as old friends, as new lovers. I wish to know everything about you and make you aware of everything of me. I feel this will lead to more in the future, and I can hardly wait for it to come to pass. But most of all, I would know if you feel the same."

"I do," said Elizabeth. To hesitate was to risk pushing this man away. She had no power to do so, not when he spoke such exquisite words to her.

"Thank you," said he. "I look forward to it."

It seemed like the viscount had seen enough of their interactions, for he rose and approached them, his eyes fixed on Elizabeth. "Miss Elizabeth," said he, his voice slightly strained. "How good it is to see you. Perhaps we might sit together and speak? I would love to hear your observations on anything about which you might wish to speak."

At first, Elizabeth was inclined to anger for Lord Chesterfield's interruption and for his continued interference. But then she realized that he had not imposed between them, for the feelings in her heart remained. One look at Mr. Darcy told her that he was similarly affected. They shared a grin which, she had no doubt, looked rather foolish to anyone who might be watching them.

For the rest of the gentlemen's stay, Lord Chesterfield stayed close to them and dominated the conversation. Elizabeth attempted politeness, to respond to his overtures and converse as she ever had. But she thought her efforts were less than successful, for she was often lost in the depths of Mr. Darcy's eyes. She thought he was lost along with her.

There was little of conversation to be had on the return journey to Netherfield. Fitzwilliam watched Darcy with suspicion the entire way, but while he appeared several times to be working himself up to say something, he remained silent. Darcy would cheerfully bear his silence, for his mind was focused on other matters.

The first was, of course, the person of Miss Elizabeth Bennet, that glorious creature he had somehow managed to find in the hinterlands of the kingdom. Darcy had not often thought of marriage. The reason for this was simple—there had never been a woman who had impressed him enough to induce him to even consider making her an offer. But he had always known it was his duty to sire an heir for Pemberley, and while it had never seemed pressing, he had always thought he would end making a marriage of convenience, settling for a woman of fortune and pedigree to have heirs, while never experiencing the bliss of a connection of minds and hearts with a wife, such as his parents had.

He could not have credited the notion of finding such a gem in such a location as this, the daughter of a country squire, no less. He might have expected himself to sneer at her circumstances, feel disgusted because of her less than proper relations and lack of those things on which society put so much weight. He could not be happier that he had seen her for the prize she was. And she was a prize he meant to win—of that he was now certain. Fitzwilliam may act the pretender, but Darcy knew that he wished to have her because he was already half in love with her, not because of some challenge or infatuation. He anticipated the coming days with scarcely concealed eagerness.

The second matter which occupied his thoughts came to a head when they arrived at Netherfield. When Darcy exited the carriage, he immediately bounded up the stairs and entered in the front door, asking the butler where Miss Bingley and the Hursts may be found. When he had their location, he was about to turn away when the sound of his cousin's voice arrested his going.

"Darcy, is there something amiss?"

"Yes," replied Darcy, though with a shortness of manner. He had not missed his cousin's behavior at Longbourn, and he was not pleased with what he saw. He wished for nothing more than to deal with the matter at hand and then sequester himself in the library again. Though he might not have credited it even two weeks earlier, the only people living in the house at present he found tolerable were the Hursts!

When he reached the sitting-room—Fitzwilliam following, though he had sensed it was best not to speak again—Darcy found the three other members of Bingley's family present as the butler had informed him. The Hursts welcomed him as was their wont—Mrs. Hurst with a quiet word of welcome while Hurst merely grunted—but Miss Bingley regarded them as though they were a juicy haunch of pork. Or rather she regarded Fitzwilliam in such a way. After this conversation, Darcy did not intend that she would ever turn her attention on him again.

"Lord Chesterfield, Mr. Darcy," cooed the woman, the coquettish batting of her eyelashes stoking Darcy's ire. "I understand you went to Longbourn this morning. I hope it was not too dreadfully dull, though had you asked, I would have been happy to accompany you."

"You would have?" asked Darcy before Fitzwilliam could muster a response. "From what I understand, I hardly think you would have been welcome there."

Shock colored Miss Bingley's features. The Hursts appeared no less astonished.

"I do not take your meaning, sir." Miss Bingley laughed, a brittle sort of sound. "In fact, *they* should be happy to receive *me*, for it is not every day they are visited by someone who has been educated as I. The younger girls, in particular, would benefit from taking my example." Miss Bennet sneered. "Unfortunately, I am of the opinion that there is little *Eliza* could ever do to improve herself."

"And I have it on good authority that the last time you visited, you were called to order by Mr. Bennet for your pretensions to high society, and you left without a word. I would give you some advice, Miss Bingley—if you wish to be accepted in town, you should confine yourself to toadying to those who enjoy such groveling."

Darcy turned to Hurst, who was watching Miss Bingley's set down with a wide grin. "If you will excuse me for saying it, Hurst, Mrs. Hurst, your sister pretends to possess the lineage of a gentleman's daughter. Your father was a fine man, but he *was* a tradesman. For Miss Bingley to lord her supposed position over the Bennet sisters is laughable."

Almost purple with rage, Miss Bingley seemed to be casting about for something to say. Mrs. Hurst, however, only sighed.

"I do not take offense sir, as I know you do not look down on me because of my parentage."

"I assure you, I do not. You have welcomed us and treated us like honored guests, and your brother is one of the best men I have ever known. Your goodness has nothing to do with your father's profession."

"I have informed my sister of this many times," said Mrs. Hurst, shooting her sister a quelling glance. Miss Bingley was fuming, but she had the sense to hold her tongue.

"It was not for this purpose that I spoke thus," continued Darcy. "You have my apologies for bringing up such an objectionable subject. What *has* angered me, however, is your sister's attempt to use *my sister* to further her own ends and force Miss Bennet away from your brother."

Mrs. Hurst gasped, and she turned a dark look on Miss Bingley. "What did you do, Caroline?"

When Miss Bingley did not speak, Darcy did so for her. "She informed Miss Bennet that not only was your brother fickle and unable to keep his attention on a woman, but that Bingley has always had a tender regard for Georgiana, even going so far as to imply that she expected them to eventually marry."

"What?" demanded Fitzwilliam. "Are you daft, woman?"

"I merely said that Charles admires Georgiana," said Miss Bingley, a superior sniff punctuating her words. "If the Bennets took my words to mean more than was intended, it is not my fault."

"You must think us witless to believe such tripe!" exclaimed Fitzwilliam. "I think highly of Bingley, indeed. But Georgiana is naught but fifteen years of age. She will not be thinking of marriage for at least another four or five years."

"And Miss Bingley," said Darcy, "I have sure knowledge of the fact that Georgiana never gave you leave to address her by her Christian name. In the future, you will refer to her as 'Miss Darcy' when you refer to her at all.

"Let me be rightfully understood: you will never invoke my sister's name to further your petty schemes again." Darcy's eyes bored into Miss Bingley's, and though she gave a credible attempt at meeting his gaze without flinching, Darcy could see the fear in their depths. "Furthermore, I will inform you that I have long known of your ambitions with respect to *me*. Let me state here and now that they will *never* be realized. I will not ever offer for you, Miss Bingley, so you may cease to pay deference to me in the expectation I will. I hope I have made myself clear."

Miss Bingley nodded, a jerky motion of one who was truly angry. Darcy did not care. Circumstances dictated that he share the house with her for the present, for his pursuit of Miss Elizabeth required him to be in Hertfordshire. Even his friendship with Bingley might not have persuaded him to stay here otherwise, for he had reached the point of not being able to tolerate her any further. Hopefully, she would make no more overtures in his direction.

"Then I hope we may exist in respect and civility for the remainder of my stay in Hertfordshire, Miss Bingley," said Darcy. "I have no intention of chastising where it is not warranted. If you feel I have waited too long before making my sentiments known, then you have my apologies."

"I believe, Mr. Darcy," said Mrs. Hurst, "you are not the one who should apologize. Do you not agree, Caroline?"

The inference was clear. Miss Bingley, though she appeared to wish to do anything but offer an apology, opened her mouth most unwillingly.

"I apologize if I have offended in any way. I had not meant my words to be taken in such a way. The only objective I have ever had was to make you welcome in my brother's home."

"Apology accepted, Miss Bingley," said Darcy with a tight nod. She did not mean a word of it he knew, but in this instance, he could afford to be magnanimous. "Now, if you will excuse me, I shall retire until dinner."

And thus, Darcy left the room, not speaking another word. If he could emerge from this visit unscathed, he would be very well pleased. But he could not leave now. There was a beautiful woman who filled his senses, and Darcy was determined to pay her his addresses.

The expected explosion of temper occurred only moments after Mr. Darcy's departure, and only after Lord Chesterfield and her husband departed as well for the billiards room. Louisa was prepared to weather the storm of Caroline's temper, but it was only made worse by the final few words the viscount had directed Caroline's way before he left.

"Miss Bingley," said he as the sound of his cousin's boots echoed down the hall, "I must inform you that there is nothing more despicable than to use a young girl as an implement to hurt another. Even if your brother did look on my cousin with an amorous eye, that is no reason to cruelly destroy the dreams of another without thought for their feelings.

"I, also, have had the impression that you consider me a potential marriage partner during our time here. Let me disabuse you of that notion at once. You should no more expect an offer from me than you do Darcy."

Then Lord Chesterfield turned to Hurst. "Do you care for a game of billiards, Hurst?"

"Of course, my lord," replied her husband. He rose and winked at her, directing a smirk at Caroline, before exiting the sitting-room with Lord Chesterfield.

"Louisa!" hissed Caroline as soon as the door closed behind them. "I am most seriously displeased. I do not take kindly to how you required me to apologize to that odious man."

"Now he is an odious man, is he?" asked Louisa. "Has he not been the focus of all your dreams these past years?"

Caroline huffed but did not speak.

"I required you to apologize because you misbehaved. I consider the eldest Bennet sisters dear friends, and now *I* must apologize for you when I see them next."

"I have no notion why you think it necessary. They are nothing more than little adventuresses, trying to pass themselves off as gentility. When I am the wife of a viscount, you can expect no notice from me. Your betrayal will be repaid in kind."

"Even you must now own that your machinations are at an end. Lord Chesterfield's words just now must extinguish any hope which still remained."

Caroline muttered and rose, stalking from the room in high dudgeon. Louisa had not been able to hear exactly what she said, but she thought it may have been "We shall see about that." Caroline would bear watching. There was no telling what she might try now.

CHAPTER XXII

"Are you certain, Lizzy?"

"Absolutely," replied Elizabeth. "When I informed Mr. Darcy of the matter he was quite emphatic in his response. Not only has Miss Bingley misrepresented her brother's intentions and his very constancy, but he informed me that Mr. Bingley informed him of his fraternal feelings for Miss Darcy. There is no reason to concern yourself on that score."

Jane thought on the intelligence for a few moments before she attempted to make a response. "I refuse to believe your assertion that Caroline is so bad. I am certain it is all simply a misunderstanding. She must have thought her brother favored Miss Darcy. Furthermore, she has a right, knowing her brother as she does, to expect certain behaviors from him. If he behaves contrary to how she expects, then perhaps it is simply a facet of his character which she has not sketched properly."

Never before had Elizabeth felt so exasperated with her sister's propensity to look for the best in others. But Mary, who had been listening to their discussion, interjected before Elizabeth could respond.

"If you prefer to believe the best of Caroline, then so be it. But the point of this conversation is that you do not believe her assertions of Miss Darcy or the possibility of Mr. Bingley staying in London."

"You must confess that, at the very least, Mr. Darcy's understanding of his sister must be superior to Miss Bingley's."

Jane responded with a slow nod. "In that, at least, you must be correct. As to the matter of his return, I believe that will soon be decided."

"Indeed," replied Mary. "So there is no need to belabor the point."

And thus, each sister left the discussion satisfied with the result, though Elizabeth wished as she never had before that Jane would throw off this naïveté and see others for who they were. Mary seemed to see through Elizabeth's pique, for it was not long after when she approached Elizabeth and spoke to her in a quiet tone.

"You will not change her, Lizzy. Now is not the time to be angry.

"But she will be ruled by that virago if she does marry Mr. Bingley," replied Elizabeth.

"I think you overestimate Mr. Bingley's tolerance for his sister. And perhaps our Jane might yet surprise you."

"I hope so, Mary. For her sake."

The following day saw the resumption of society in Meryton after the ball held at Netherfield. Before that, however, a denizen of that same estate came to visit the Bennets, and the way she entered the sitting-room told Elizabeth that she was uncertain of the reception she would receive. Mrs. Bennet's greeting dispelled any concern she might have had

"Mrs. Hurst," said Mrs. Bennet. "How good of you to visit. We hope you have been well."

"Very well, I thank you," replied Mrs. Hurst. The light of relief lit up her eyes, and she stepped forward and greeted them all warmly. They sat at tea for some moments before she moved to the true reason for her coming.

"I understand that my sister, Caroline, visited you the day after the ball."

"She did," replied Jane for the family.

"You have my apologies for her conduct," said Mrs. Hurst. "Had I known of her intentions, I would have argued against her coming. I hope it will not affect *my* friendship with you all."

"You have proven yourself a true friend," said Elizabeth. "I will not attempt to disguise the fact that your sister made some offensive comments, and I do not appreciate her attempt to hurt Jane, but we do not hold you accountable for her actions."

Mrs. Hurst closed her eyes in mortification for a brief moment. "Then you are very good to forgive me. Caroline has always . . . well, let us simply say that she has a vaunted opinion of her own position in society, as well as an ambition that will not be quenched. I am certain I do not have to say more."

"No, Mrs. Hurst," replied Mrs. Bennet. The topic had, it seemed, unsettled Mrs. Bennet a little, for she was waving her handkerchief in distress. "It is simply best to leave it in the past where it belongs."

"I agree." Mrs. Hurst turned to Jane. "Please allow me to say that Charles has no amorous intentions toward Miss Darcy, and Mr. Darcy would not allow it if he did. We expect him to return from London tomorrow. Mr. Hurst and I will not be quitting Netherfield at present, and I expect we will be here for the remainder of the year."

"That is excellent news, Louisa," said Elizabeth, attempting to turn the conversation. "Does your family have any particular traditions you observed during Christmastide?"

"We have a few," replied Mrs. Hurst. "Is it much celebrated in Hertfordshire?"

"There are always many functions," replied Mrs. Bennet. "The Lucas family always hosts an enjoyable Christmas party, where we sing carols and share the spirit of the season. My brother and his family always join us from London as well."

"The Gardiners," said Louisa. "Yes. I have heard of them. I hope I shall be fortunate enough to be introduced to them during their stay."

"I dare say that may be arranged," replied Elizabeth.

They visited for some time, and then Mrs. Hurst went away. The Bennet sisters were happy their friendship with the woman had survived Miss Bingley's behavior.

That evening, they left Longbourn to attend a function at one of their neighbors' houses. The Robinson family, their estate situated south of Meryton, had invited several families of the neighborhood to dine, of which the Bennets were one. Thus, they entered the family carriage the following evening for the journey to their friends' estate, welcomed there with friendliness when they arrived. It was only then Elizabeth discovered that the officers had also been invited and were present.

"Denny! Sanderson!" greeted Lydia in a loud and rambunctious tone, proving that her improvement had been the result of her injury rather than any change in manners. "You must come to attend me, for I have so much with which to acquaint you!"

The younger girls were soon huddled with several other young women and several officers, including the two Lydia had greeted. Of what their conversation consisted Elizabeth could not say, but she did not suppose they were exercising any restraint. At least the detested Mr. Wickham, who was also in attendance, was not among their number. The lieutenant was, in fact, standing with several other officers with a cup in his hand. When he noticed Elizabeth watching him, he raised his cup as if in toast, a mocking sort of gesture. Elizabeth ignored him.

It was not difficult to avoid Lieutenant Wickham that evening. Given what Elizabeth had heard of the man, she thought him capable of any behavior which would stroke his vanity and suit his selfish nature. But he seemed content to keep his distance from her, and though she felt the weight of his eyes upon her more than once, Elizabeth was not about to be intimidated. In addition, while he attended that evening, it was clear he was not trusted. The Robinsons had no young daughters to protect, but Elizabeth could see Mr. Wickham was watched carefully, both by the gentlemen of the regiment and the men of the militia.

"Has Wickham been troubling you, Miss Elizabeth?"

Pulled from her contemplation of the lieutenant, Elizabeth turned to see the colonel standing nearby, his gaze shifting from Elizabeth to Mr. Wickham in turn. She had been considering Mr. Wickham, Elizabeth realized, for some time now, and her scrutiny must have drawn Colonel Forster's attention.

"No, in fact," replied Elizabeth. "He seems content to stand by his fellow officers at present. He has not approached me, and I dare say my sisters have been free of his society tonight also."

Colonel Forster directed a long look at the lieutenant himself—to which Mr. Wickham feigned ignorance—before he turned back to Elizabeth. "Wickham has made few friends in the militia, no doubt due to the intelligence provided by the gentlemen. Most of the men are wary of him, and there has been a . . . falling out between him and Denny, though it was Denny who brought him to the regiment's attention."

"Oh, I hope Denny will not suffer for introducing Mr. Wickham to the regiment," said Elizabeth. "He could hardly have known what kind of man Mr. Wickham is."

"No, you are correct there. Furthermore, theirs was a slight acquaintance. Denny might have shared some censure had Wickham been allowed to accumulate debts with the merchants. As that has been averted, there is no fault to be found with him.

"How Wickham managed to obtain the commission I do not know for he will not say. He has not the resources to purchase one for himself, however, so I know it must have been in a game of chance or by persuading another to purchase it in his stead. As he has not had the opportunity to misbehave, I can do nothing against him at present. But I wish he was not a member of my regiment—I am certain he will cause trouble in the end."

"Then I suppose we have no recourse but to be watchful," replied Elizabeth.

"Vigilance is, indeed, the key." Colonel Forster smiled and bowed. "If you have any trouble with my officer, I hope you will inform me, Miss Elizabeth. Now, if you will excuse me."

For most of the rest of the evening, Elizabeth found herself engaged in pleasant diversions with close friends she had known all her life. The thought of Charlotte once again intruded, reminding Elizabeth of her friend with a pang of regret. But she was finding that the immediacy of Charlotte's absence was fading, as was the longing for her friend.

"I will *not* forget her," determined Elizabeth to herself. "I will not forget the choice she was required to make. I *will* see my friend again."

The party was a pleasant diversion with several activities for the enjoyment of those that attended. Kitty and Lydia primarily played at cards and lottery with the officers, while the matrons gossiped and the gentlemen spoke of their estate concerns. Elizabeth drifted among several groups, at times agreeing to join in the games with the younger girls, at times giving her attention to others in attendance. Overall, it was an agreeable evening, an atmosphere of laughter and peace which allowed Elizabeth to forget about some of the objectionable events of the past several days.

But that did not mean she forgot about those happenings. In fact, the subject was never far from her mind, and at one point later in the evening, Elizabeth found herself discussing it with her dearest sisters. It came about in a discussion of members of higher society, and Elizabeth, thinking of the viscount and how he had changed, could not hold back a caustic comment.

"Perhaps he should simply find himself a mistress."

"Lizzy!" exclaimed Jane. "I cannot believe you believe *that* of Lord Chesterfield! He had never given us any cause to think him prone to such behavior."

"Perhaps you are correct," replied Elizabeth, amused all over again for Jane's belief in the goodness of others. "But . . . Well, let us simply say that Lord Chesterfield has been behaving oddly. I cannot make him out. We have heard so many stories of those in his position and some of the vices to which they descend that it seemed possible that he was trying to procure a mistress."

"But you quickly learned otherwise," observed Mary.

"It seems to me that this is something that has already occurred," said Jane, glaring at them both with suspicion.

"It has," replied Elizabeth. She had not informed Jane due to all that had happened.

For her part, Jane looked between them, her gaze demanding, prompting Elizabeth's laughter.

"I am sorry, Jane. I will tell you all. But I would not wish this to become readily known, so we should speak in softer voices."

They all agreed and the three sisters huddled close. Elizabeth explained what had happened at the ball, from her experiences with Mr. Darcy to those with Lord Chesterfield, and her subsequent understanding of why the viscount had begun to behave toward her the way he had. When she was finished speaking, Jane looked at them with wonder.

"You and Mary *have* grown much closer these past months. *I* used to be the one to hear of such happenings."

"We *have* grown much closer, indeed," replied Elizabeth. She felt all the justice of Jane's charge, and a feeling of shame stole over her. "I am sorry, Jane. You are completely correct. In my defense, I can only say that you have been occupied with Mr. Bingley's attentions of late, and I have been distracted by Lady Catherine, Miss Bingley, Mr. Collins, and everything that has occurred. Still, that is no excuse for not confiding in you."

"Do not be alarmed, Lizzy," cried Jane. "I had no intention of chastising you."

"I know you did not, dear sister," said Elizabeth, catching Jane's hand in an affectionate grasp. "But that does not mean I do not feel I have neglected you."

Jane chewed her lip, her thoughts already returning to the intelligence Elizabeth had just shared with her. "You think the gentlemen both have interest in you?"

"As strange as it may seem," replied Elizabeth, "that is exactly what I think. Mr. Darcy has all but declared himself. While the viscount has not, I have noticed his dark looks at Mr. Darcy, and he seems to be going out of his way to flatter me."

"I have no doubt of the truth of what you speak, Lizzy," said Jane.

"It should not be any surprise to anyone that you are able to draw the attention of *any* man."

"Here, here," said Mary, her tone playful, as Elizabeth blushed.

"What I wish to know, however, is what you intend to do about it."

Elizabeth frowned. "I do not know there is anything I *can* do. Lord Chesterfield will behave in whatever manner he sees fit."

"That is not what I asked, Lizzy," said Jane. "I know you are not drawn by riches or status, so the viscount's greater standing will mean nothing to you."

"No, indeed," replied Elizabeth. "In fact, I find myself annoyed by his lordship's behavior."

"And Mr. Darcy?"

That was, indeed, the question. "I can find nothing amiss in Mr. Darcy. As I told you, when he speaks to me, I can feel his genuine interest. He is not an eloquent man, but when he speaks, I find my heart responding to his overtures."

"Then your decision is made." Elizabeth turned a shocked glaze on her sister, but Jane only laughed and patted her knee. "I am not suggesting you know you want to marry Mr. Darcy at present, Lizzy, but it seems to me your choice between the two gentlemen is a simple one. In the end, we Bennet sisters have naught to offer a man but ourselves. It would be best to marry where there is true affection, where a true measure of respect exists. Given what you have told me, it seems like the viscount views you through eyes of infatuation, not true love. I would not advise you to allow his continued addresses, should he choose to offer them."

Then Jane smiled, and she rose and walked away, greeting some of their acquaintances and standing with them. Mary also shot Elizabeth an amused smile before she went away, leaving Elizabeth to her thoughts. Jane's advice was nothing she and Mary had not discussed before. But somehow Jane's wisdom at this moment meant more to Elizabeth than it would have in any other time of her life.

"Miss Elizabeth Bennet."

The sound of her name on a man's voice startled Elizabeth from her thoughts. She looked up to see the smirking countenance of Mr. Wickham looking down at her.

"It seems to me you Bennet sisters travel in packs," said Mr. Wickham as he sat nearby. "I have rarely had the opportunity to speak with any of you this evening."

"Oh?" asked Elizabeth, against her better judgment, more than a little scorn coloring her voice. "Must we be alone before you approach?

Are you fearful that if you were forced to speak with more than one of us your sensibilities might be offended?"

The man laughed at her sally, but Elizabeth could sense it was false. "No, indeed. But where women gather, laughing and talking together, a man must beware lest he is burned by the flame of their combined wit."

"I think, Mr. Wickham, that you have more with which to concern yourself than merely the wit of a family of five daughters."

"Do you, perhaps, refer to something in particular?" Mr. Wickham's eyes glittered. "Speak plainly, Miss Elizabeth, for I would not have misunderstanding fester between us, driven by vague words and innuendo."

"I assure you, Mr. Wickham, that I meant nothing more than your duties as an officer. For are they not the first concern of a military man such as yourself?"

Mr. Wickham directed a long look at her, in which Elizabeth could see him attempting to discern whether her words were spoken with sincerity. It was doubtful he believed her; he had to know that Mr. Darcy had already warned the Bennets away from him, given Mr. Bennet's warning the only time he had visited Longbourn. In fact, given what her father had said then, Elizabeth had already made an error in speaking with this young man at all.

As she was thinking to excuse herself, Mr. Wickham spoke again. "In my opinion, one of the greatest failings of our society is the tendency to speak in innuendo. Is it too much to ask to speak in language which cannot be misunderstood? Do you not think that much confusion may be avoided if we only speak clearly?"

"Perhaps you are correct," replied Elizabeth. "But then again, you have already heard someone speak in a clear fashion in language which was not, in any way, ambiguous. Have you not?"

"I wish it were so, Miss Elizabeth," replied Mr. Wickham. His manner was mournful, as if a great weight was sitting upon his shoulders. "But I have found that I have been the recipient of words spoken against me since my coming, words that are without foundation and prompted by naught but envy."

"I cannot say anything as to the veracity of what has been spoken of you, and I will not discuss that matter any further. In fact, the incident to which I refer was when my father warned you against speaking with his daughters and informed you not to return to Longbourn. Do you not remember the concise way in which he spoke *then*?"

Mr. Wickham's eyes seemed to bore through Elizabeth, but he did not respond. "And yet you have approached me tonight."

"You responded to my overtures."

"I did. And I should not have. If any apologies are required, I offer them, sir. But I will do what I should have from the beginning."

Elizabeth rose to leave, but Mr. Wickham rose with her, his countenance anything but friendly.

"You know nothing of me, Miss Elizabeth," said he, his voice nearing the snarl of a wild animal. "You should not presume to think you know everything."

"In fact, I have claimed no such knowledge," replied Elizabeth. "But I have clearly made a mistake by replying to your words."

"Miss Elizabeth, you should reconsider your faith in certain gentlemen." The man's eyes raked up and down Elizabeth's form, sending shivers down her spine. "Darcy is a proud man, one who is accustomed to obtaining what he wishes. If you are so foolish as to think you can capture him, you will not emerge unscathed in the end. Darcy has no compunction about ruining such as you. His position in society will protect him."

"You are a liar and a rake, sir," replied Elizabeth, her ire rising in response. "I have no doubt in Mr. Darcy's upright nature. It is you I do not trust."

"You should watch yourself, Miss Elizabeth. Choosing sides is a dangerous business. You never know when you might be hurt by stepping in between warring factions."

"That is enough!"

Out of reflex, Elizabeth pivoted and stepped to the side, noting her father standing, glaring at Mr. Wickham. Mr. Wickham's returning look was no less stony than Mr. Bennet's. He had a malevolence about him which was in stark contrast to his affected courtly manners. Whatever he said about himself and Mr. Darcy, Elizabeth could not imagine ever having been fooled by this man, even if they had not been warned in advance.

"It seems, Mr. Wickham," said Mr. Bennet, "that you are possessed of a short memory, for you have already forgotten the strictures I laid upon you when last we met."

Mr. Wickham's sneer prompted a tightening of Mr. Bennet's already severe brow. "Then you neglected to inform your daughters, sir. Miss Elizabeth was quick to respond to my greeting."

"Though I would not exonerate this man in any way, he is correct. I should not have responded to him, Papa."

"No, you should not have," replied Mr. Bennet. He did not even look at Elizabeth, and while she knew he was not angry with her, she knew she had disappointed him. "But your lapse notwithstanding, Mr. Wickham knew not to even address you. Thus, the greater fault lies with him."

The derision in Mr. Wickham's manner became all that much more pronounced. "Yes, it is, indeed, a grievous sin for a man to address a woman who is attending the same event. All men who commit such heinous depravity ought to be drawn and quartered at dawn!"

While Elizabeth gasped at the man's disgusting words, Mr. Bennet only smiled in response, though it was devoid of any good feeling. "I shall not bandy words with you, Mr. Wickham. I have previously informed you that you are not to speak with my daughters. That should be enough for you. I shall take this to your commanding officer if you do not comply."

"Then I shall keep my distance from your insipid progeny. As for Forster, he can do nothing. There is nothing in my conduct in Meryton to give him justification to act against me. There is nothing in your words more concerning to me than the snapping of a cowardly mongrel."

Mr. Wickham turned away then, but as he did so his gaze swept over Elizabeth, and she felt all the disquiet of having provoked the man's malice. Then he was gone. When Elizabeth turned her attention to her father, she noted that her nearest sisters were witness to the confrontation, but it was in a far enough corner of the room that it seemed to have been missed by most of the rest of the company.

"Lizzy, you are my cleverest, most capable daughter. I trust you to know your limits as I trust none of your sisters. I know you are able to protect yourself as well as any woman in England."

There was nothing of jest in Mr. Bennet's manner, nothing of the father she had always known. He was as serious as ever she had seen, and it was this which caused her to respond with the gravity he himself displayed.

"Thank you, Papa. Sometimes, however, my determination overcomes my good judgment."

"I dare say it does," replied Mr. Bennet, and this time a hint of his usual humor reappeared. "As I said, I have no doubt for your competence. But this Mr. Wickham is a completely different manner of man. I do not like the way he watches you. Please, Lizzy, for my sake—do not reply to him again, even if he should address you. I wish all you girls to stay strictly out of his way."

"I shall, Papa."

The rest of the evening, Elizabeth stayed close to Mary and Jane, and she rarely spoke to any of the officers. She often felt Mr. Wickham's eyes upon her, and his countenance seemed to suggest he knew something she did not. But he kept himself away from all Bennets, and Elizabeth was relieved. Her father was correct. Mr. Wickham was a dangerous man.

Chapter XXIII

*M*any years before, when Bennet had been a young man, there
had been another regiment of militia encamped at Meryton for
the winter. As he had been a young man at the time, he had
not truly paid much attention to the officers of the militia. He had been
acquainted with some, but his interest had been modest; his position
as heir to Longbourn had meant he had never had to think of joining
the army, and at the time he had been more interested in hunting, his
beloved books, and the society of pretty young ladies.

But that did not mean he was not cognizant of some of the goings
on when the regiment had been in residence. Most of the men had been
good sorts, though perhaps not the cream of English society, and in
many ways not the equal of the men of the regulars. But acceptable
nonetheless. But even then, there had been those who were not to be
trusted, and when the regiment had departed, there had been rumors
of unpaid debts, of young women of whom the men had taken
advantage, of debaucheries and gambling. Such stories were often
embellished in the telling, but there was enough of a grain of truth in
such tales to make a prudent man cautious.

Mr. Bennet considered himself a prudent man, though he was
aware that many would call him slothful, satirical, or uncaring. He had
often laughed at his youngest daughters and his wife, made sportive

comments of their excesses, and enjoyed their sometimes poor behavior. His was not laudable behavior, but he had often rationalized that it was the best a man, disappointed by life and stuck with a companion for whom he had little respect could do. The fact that Mrs. Bennet, in recent weeks, seemed to have calmed and returned to more of the woman he had married did not miss his attention. But still, he did not think he would have acted any differently with respect to Mr. Wickham than he had determined now, even if his wife had remained the silly creature she had been for the past decade and a half.

Thus, he made his way to Netherfield the morning after the Robinson dinner party, intent upon seeing the gentlemen he knew could exert control over the detestable Mr. Wickham. He was correct about one thing—so long as Wickham had not caused any problems in Meryton, his colonel could do nothing about him. Mr. Darcy most certainly could, and unless Bennet missed his guess, he would do something if Bennet presented the facts in the appropriate manner.

"Mr. Bennet!" greeted Mr. Bingley when Bennet was shown into the other man's study. Bennet had not expected to see the gentleman, for his intelligence suggested it would be another day before Mr. Bingley returned. "Welcome to Netherfield!"

"Mr. Bingley," replied Mr. Bennet. "I had not expected to see you, sir."

"I finished my business in a timelier manner than I had thought. Eager as I was to return to Hertfordshire, I decided to set out yesterday afternoon, and arrived just in time for dinner."

"Your enthusiasm will be marked by certain parties, I am certain."

In fact, though Bennet's words were sportive, he was pleased for Jane's sake. He knew there had been some question posed by the man's sister as to whether he would return. But Miss Bingley's actions reeked with desperation, and Bennet had never doubted the certainty of Mr. Bingley's return.

"Excellent!" exclaimed Mr. Bingley. "I intend to call on your family today if I have your approval."

"You are welcome to visit at any time, Mr. Bingley," replied Bennet. "But at present, I must ask for your assistance. I wish to speak with the viscount and Mr. Darcy. Might I trouble you to have them summoned here?"

A frown settled over Mr. Bingley's face, but he agreed readily enough. "Of course, of course. I shall see to it immediately."

He rang the bell, instructing that the two gentlemen be summoned when the butler appeared. While they waited, they exchanged some few words. Mr. Bingley was in a talkative mood that morning and waxed poetic, only avoiding mention of Bennet's eldest daughter by the barest of margins, his admiration was clear and the subject of his thoughts no less so. For Bennet's part, he had little attention for any matter other than his errand, and even being presented with Mr. Bingley's easy nature, with whom he could make sport with little effort, did not tempt him to cleverness.

When, at length, the two gentlemen entered, Bennet had no attention left to spare for Mr. Bingley, and he lost no time in advising them of the reason for his visit.

"So you see," concluded he when he had informed them of the events of the previous evening, "I am concerned by the actions of this Mr. Wickham. While the man tries to hide behind the veneer of civility, I see little but a man who wishes to cause as much havoc as he possibly can."

"It is difficult to understand how your neighbors can still include him in their invitations," said Mr. Darcy. "I have given them enough to be wary of him."

Bennet snorted. "You have told me enough to make me give pause. But the Robinsons, for example, have no daughters to protect. And some of my other neighbors either think the stories are exaggerated or that they are well able to protect their womenfolk. Either way, though most do shun Mr. Wickham, there are always a few who will court danger."

"I should have excluded him from the invitation to my ball," said Bingley, apparently distressed at his oversight. "Perhaps the gentlemen of the neighborhood have been lulled into a false sense of security because he was present then."

"You give them too much credit, Mr. Bingley," replied Bennet. "Either way, I am concerned about this man's current actions. Though he has kept away from my daughters as I demanded, I have seen him watching them on the few occasions when they have been in company. That first day at my estate, he seemed intent on wooing my youngest. Since I put a stop to that, he seems to have lost all interest in her. Now it is Lizzy on whom he seems to have fixed his attention. I will not have *any* of my girls hurt by Mr. Wickham. I have come today to ask you to take a direct hand against him. The colonel can do nothing at present, for Mr. Wickham has not done anything to warrant censure. But I am certain you gentlemen can, and I would ask you not to wait until he has made his move."

It was clear that neither gentleman was amused by this new news of Mr. Wickham's perfidy. But it was Mr. Darcy who seemed to be the most offended, and the most determined to do something concerning the matter. It was as Bennet had thought. While he was not excited to lose Elizabeth to a man who lived three days distant from Hertfordshire, Bennet was at least happy that she would be cherished as she deserved.

"You have my word, Mr. Bennet," said Darcy, confirming Bennet's suspicions about who would be likely to take decisive action. "Mr. Wickham will be brought to heel. I will not allow him to prey on your family when it is in my power to stop him."

"Thank you, Mr. Darcy," replied Bennet. The relief he felt at Mr. Darcy's agreement was enough to make his joints weak from the release of stress.

"I shall go to the colonel and speak with Wickham myself. I have the means to see to his good behavior, and I will not hesitate to use it."

They spoke for some moments about what Mr. Darcy expected to accomplish when they went to visit the colonel. Satisfied that the man was sincere in his determination, Bennet soon excused himself to return to Longbourn, confident that everything which could be done was being done.

When Darcy and Fitzwilliam arrived at the militia headquarters, they found that Wickham had already been called in to account for his misdeeds. The short ride into the town from Netherfield had been characterized by silence between the two cousins, not to mention a sense of ill-usage and bruised feelings. It was so different from anything Darcy had ever known with Fitzwilliam before—rarely had anything come between them. He supposed, with a sour grimace, that if anything was to do so, it would be a woman.

That it was the first woman Darcy had ever found who provoked his interest made the conflict between them particularly galling. Had she not responded to him, he might have quit the field and allowed his cousin to go to it. But Darcy was certain his heart had spoken to hers. She was not indifferent to him. It was because of this that Darcy would not step aside for his cousin—his happiness was at stake in a manner he did not think Fitzwilliam quite understood.

When they were shown into the colonel's office by a junior officer, it was to the sound of Forster berating the very officer they had come to threaten.

"I do not know what you were thinking when you threatened the girl in such a way, but men under my command do not behave in such a manner! I have half a mind to let you rot in the stockade."

"I was not aware that approaching a young lady and speaking with her was grounds for court-martial."

"It is when the lady's father has expressly forbidden you from speaking with his daughters! Did that patron of yours not drum good behavior and manners into your thick head?"

"All my father's—and Wickham's—efforts were for naught," said Darcy as he entered the office. "He is, unfortunately, of a vile character. I lost hope in his redemption many years ago."

The colonel turned to face them, though Wickham, standing at attention with his back to them, did not. "I suppose I should not be surprised to see you here today, Mr. Darcy, Lord Chesterfield, though I am curious as to the source of your information. I, myself, just learned of his actions this morning when one of my officers saw fit to inform me of them."

"The lady's father," replied Darcy. He stepped into the room, shaking the colonel's hand, though there was little of friendship in it. It was a facet of Wickham's character that he was prone to driving others' apart by the force of his disgusting habits. "He came to us this morning, begging us to do something about your wayward officer."

Colonel Forster grunted and turned back to Wickham, who still had not moved. "Perhaps it is just as well. It seems that little *I* say has any effect on him."

Darcy, with Fitzwilliam following, entered the room fully and stepped around Wickham, noting the man's eyes following him. His usual disgust and revulsion shone in their depths, but in behind Darcy sensed fear. Wickham had never been the bravest specimen, often fleeing at the first sign of trouble. That he had stayed in Meryton this long was a sign either of his desperation or his desire for revenge, whatever that meant.

"Well, Wickham?" said Darcy. "What have you to say for yourself?"

"Nothing to *you*," spat Wickham.

"That is your first mistake. You *do* understand that I hold power over you, do you not?"

"You know nothing. I have done nothing wrong. Shall I be flogged for speaking to a young lady at a society event?"

"I am warning you, Wickham," snarled the colonel, putting himself directly before Wickham, "if you affect the welcome of this regiment in Meryton you will pay for it. You were told directly to leave the man's daughters alone—I had it from Carter as soon as you were thrown unceremoniously from Mr. Bennet's estate."

"I was not thrown from the estate."

"Perhaps Mr. Bennet did not have his footmen deposit you by the side of the road, but he informed you never to return."

"And I have not."

"Yet you spoke with his daughter last night, and from what I have heard, some of the language you used was rife with innuendo!"

"Denny knows not of what he speaks." The sneer on Wickham's countenance spoke volumes as to his opinion of the other man. "I merely attempted to defend myself against the vile slander which has been leveled against me."

"You have not been slandered, Wickham," said Fitzwilliam. "There is no slander when the account is naught but the truth."

Wickham glared at Fitzwilliam, but in the end, he chose not to respond.

"He seems to have developed a modicum of restraint," said Darcy. "That is, indeed, a surprise. He has never possessed any such virtue in the past."

"I possess more virtues than you will allow," snarled Wickham. "Perhaps if you would give me my due, I would surprise you."

"Do not bring up that tire old grievance with the living," said Fitzwilliam. "Your signature on the contract relieves you of all claim to the living and you know it."

"But the amount I was paid for it was nothing more than a pittance. I know not how Darcy here thinks he has met the spirit of his father's will with such miserly behavior."

"Did you not agree to it, resigning all future claim to the living?"

"I knew I would receive nothing if I did not accept."

"You are a fool, Wickham. The amount I gave you was worth ten years of that living, and you squandered it in less than two."

Wickham glared at Darcy, but there was little he could say. Darcy's words were nothing more than the truth."

"Now, you will stay away from the Bennet ladies or you will pay the price."

A snort escaped Wickham's lips. "I have done nothing to warrant any reprisal in Meryton. You say I approached a young woman without her father's consent? That is not a punishable offense. If you do not believe me, you may question the shopkeepers or any of the fathers in the neighborhood. You can do nothing to me."

Darcy smiled at his one-time childhood friend, though it was void of any mirth. "That has always been the trouble with you, Wickham.

You think that the past is done and forgotten. You *are* aware that I still hold your debt receipts in both Lambton and Cambridge, are you not?"

"Of course, he has forgotten," said Fitzwilliam when Wickham's scowl deepened. "It is Wickham's custom to forget that which he does not like. He would not be Wickham if he remembered such insignificant details."

"Then I shall remind him."

Darcy stepped forward and put himself directly in front of his erstwhile friend. A stray thought entered his mind, that while Wickham had been the taller between them in their youth, now Darcy stood at least two inches taller. This disparity in height apparently did not cow Wickham, however, for he regarded Darcy, pure poison in his gaze.

"I cannot say what you are planning, but I know you well enough to know there is some scheme turning in your mind. I care not what it is. From this moment forward, you will leave the Bennet ladies strictly alone. If you so much as greet one of them while passing on the street, I will know, and I will call your debts in."

"Without proof?"

"It is easy enough for me to have the receipts sent from Pemberley. They will be here in less than a week. If I call them in, you will likely never leave Marshalsea. This is the last warning I will give."

With one final glare at Wickham and a nod at the man's commanding officer, Darcy turned and left the room. He had a letter to write to his steward, one which had best be composed as soon as possible.

George Wickham had rarely been more furious in his life. After the bastard Darcy had left, Forster had seen fit to ring a fine peal over him for a further twenty minutes. Wickham went away with the man's voice echoing in his ears, knowing that his time in Meryton was coming to a close. He needed to leave and he needed to do it quickly. The only question which remained was whether he could exact revenge on Darcy before he departed.

Fearing him to be a flight risk, Forster had decreed he was not allowed near the horse pens and was to be watched at all times. It was nothing, however, to slip his watchers and make his way to the edge of town for an important meeting. Or, rather, it was important to Wickham if he was to have vengeance, for it served little purpose otherwise.

"You are late. I was forced to wait here for more than fifteen minutes. Lady Catherine does not tolerate tardiness."

The whining of the bird-witted parson set Wickham's teeth on edge, and he came very close to telling the fool just what he thought of him. Then the image of Darcy prevented from having the lovely Miss Elizabeth entered Wickham's mind, and he managed to hold his temper.

"I had some duties which could not be delayed, Mr. Collins. I came as soon as I could."

The parson sniffed and looked around, a shiftiness in his manner which almost set Wickham to laughter. The tall beanstalk, dressed head to toe in his clerical suit could hardly think to be inconspicuous. "Let us speak and be done with this, so I may return to my rooms. The weather is not fit for standing outside."

"Very well," replied Wickham. "What says your patroness?"

"Lady Catherine demands that Mr. Darcy's interest in my cousin be ended by any means necessary."

Wickham stroked his chin, affecting deep thought. "And how does she propose we go about doing this? Both you and I have been barred from Longbourn." The parson's eyes narrowed, his countenance furious over being denied his future home. Wickham ignored his anger. "Has she any notions about how this may be accomplished?"

"It is not for Lady Catherine to condescend to consider such matters. She has commanded, and we are to obey—she cares not how we accomplish her designs."

He had expected nothing more from Lady Catherine, though her fiction of being above the fray was amusing. "As I said, it can be done. Is Lady Catherine prepared to compensate us according to the risk we will be taking? Lord Chesterfield and Mr. Darcy are not men to be crossed lightly."

A look of distaste came over Mr. Collins's features. "Our reward is the privilege of serving Lady Catherine."

"I am sure it is. But you have the benefit of a fine living and a parsonage to return to when this is over. Darcy will not appreciate my interference in this matter and will be out for blood."

Mr. Collins glared at him, suspicion alive in his gaze. "I thought you claimed a close friendship with Mr. Darcy."

"I do," replied Wickham, not missing a beat. "But it is clear he is infatuated with the chit. It will take some time before reason reasserts itself, and while he is angry, I would prefer not to be nearby."

"Then you may rest easy, for you will be compensated

254 254 254 254 Jann Rowland

accordingly."

"Compensated accordingly in Lady Catherine's words means little," said Wickham, caring little if Collins heard the sarcasm in his tone. He produced a piece of paper from his jacket pocket and handed it to the parson. "This is what I want. I will meet you again tomorrow to confirm Lady Catherine's agreement."

Mr. Collins looked at the paper and his eyes bulged. Wickham only laughed. "Remind her that it is a small price to pay to ensure her nephew is not sullied by an inferior woman.

"And Collins," continued Wickham, prompting the other man to glance up from the paper he held, "I find myself . . . eager to resign my commission and leave this place, and I must do so before long."

"Why?" was the man's blunt question.

"The reason is immaterial. You should inform Lady Catherine, however, that if she takes too long to consider my price, I will be forced to depart. She will then need to find someone else to accomplish her goals."

"Perhaps she should do so anyway. This," Mr. Collins waved at the paper in his hand, "is little more than extortion."

"I am merely aware of how valuable my services are," replied Wickham with aplomb. "I know Darcy. I know how he thinks. I know what it will take to induce him to release his infatuation with your cousin. If your patroness thinks she can find someone else who has these advantages, then she is welcome to ask *him* instead.

"I will wait until she comes to a decision, of course. But you should remind her that I will not wait long."

And Wickham turned and left, hurrying back toward headquarters. With any luck, his tails would not even know that he had given them the slip. A glance back as he strode away revealed that Collins watched him for several moments before he too turned and departed. Wickham was not concerned that Lady Catherine would not pay. She was an impatient lady, one who would leap at the chance to have her wishes carried out as expeditiously as possible. Wickham would do the deed, see Darcy's dreams extinguished, and be gone, all before the man even knew he had been assaulted. It was time Wickham left these shores, along with all that money Lady Catherine would give him for ruining the Bennet girl.

CHAPTER XXIV

*P*erhaps it would be best to simply return to Netherfield, but Darcy found he had no desire to do so. Netherfield was the last place he wished to be at that moment, and it was not only because it was the location of that viper, Miss Bingley.

So Darcy left the colonel's office, and finding that Fitzwilliam had not followed him, he took the opportunity to leave without his cousin, avoiding any unpleasantness between them. As he rode down the street and away from the town, Darcy had no thought in mind as to a destination. Though early December, the air was not chill enough to penetrate his great coat, and he thought a little exercise atop his trusty mount would not be amiss. It was some time later before he reined his blowing horse in before a manor house beside a tiny hamlet. It appeared his subconscious had a destination in mind all along.

There was little else to be done, so Darcy swung his leg over the side of his horse and patted it with affection when he was standing on the drive. A stable hand appeared from around the side of the house and greeted Darcy with deference, accepting the reins passed to him.

"Shall I stable him, sir?"

"No, I do not think I shall be here long. A little water and some oats, if it is not too much trouble."

"Of course, sir," replied the man. He knuckled his forehead and led Darcy's stallion away, while Darcy presented himself at the door. In short order, he was shown into the sitting-room where the ladies of the estate awaited him. Their greetings were all he had come to expect from this family, but Darcy found he had little patience for them. The youngest girls were giggling about something between them, and while Mrs. Bennet had proven to be more tolerable than Darcy had ever imagined, still her voice was a little shrill and her welcomes, while he appreciated them, grated on his nerves. Darcy had not the slightest notion of why his footsteps had directed him here, but he was not about to squander the opportunity which had been presented.

"Thank you for your welcome, Mrs. Bennet," said Darcy at the first opportunity. "But the day is fine and I have no doubt Miss Elizabeth has found being inside chafes at her nerves. Perhaps she—and her sisters, of course—would appreciate taking a turn around the gardens?"

"What a splendid idea, Mr. Darcy," replied Mrs. Bennet, with only a hint of the exuberance she had shown at their first meeting. "I am certain Lizzy will be vastly pleased to oblige you. As for my other daughters . . ." Mrs. Bennet frowned as she looked around the room.

"I shall not go," said Miss Lydia in a loud tone. "This blasted ankle still won't allow it."

Though the girl was far forwarder than she ought to be, in this instance Darcy was grateful for her lack of manners. Since she would not go, of course, Miss Kitty declined, as did Miss Bennet. Miss Mary, however, shared a look with Miss Elizabeth before speaking up.

"I would be happy to accompany you," said she.

Mrs. Bennet appeared like she was about to object. But she paused, looked on them all with a critical eye, before she nodded her head, though slowly. "Yes, I suppose that would be for the best. Be sure to wear your fur-lined pelisses, for it is cold."

The girls assured her they would, and they all left the room to gather their accouterments before proceeding out the front door. It seemed an unheard communication passed between the two Bennet sisters, for while Miss Elizabeth took Darcy's offered arm, Miss Mary declined, instead hanging back to look at, in Darcy's opinion, some uninteresting bit of the ivy climbing Longbourn's outer wall, before falling in several yards behind them.

Had Darcy been in any mood to consider such things, he would have commented to the effect that Longbourn's back lawn was a pleasing bit of space. It was not large and spacious, teeming with gardens, topiaries, and hedge mazes like one might have seen at Rosings or even, to a certain extent, Pemberley. But it was pleasing, with several benches scattered about the paths and several flower gardens, including one large plot full of rose bushes, which he imagined the Bennet sisters lovingly caring for during the warmth of the summer months. All this he took in with an absent sort of detachment. In reality, Darcy was struggling to find the words to say what he wished. In the end, it was Miss Elizabeth who spoke first.

"I had imagined when you first came in the room and then so precipitously lured me out of doors that you had something you wished to discuss. If you only wish to see our gardens, I invite you to return in July, for they are quite pretty at that time of the year."

Darcy made the only response he could — he chuckled, all the while marveling at the ability of this woman to put him at ease with only a light jest.

"Then I surely shall, Miss Elizabeth. It is clear they have been tended with great care, for it is easy to see the imprint of your family's love for your home on every leaf, branch, and stone which comprises Longbourn's walls."

Though she considered him for a moment, Miss Elizabeth said at length: "We *do* love our home, Mr. Darcy. But I hardly think you came here in all this state to pay such compliments to us for our home."

"In all this state?" asked Darcy, amused at her insight.

Miss Elizabeth fixed him with a long look. "It appeared you were . . . agitated when you arrived, sir. Is there something amiss?"

All levity fled Darcy's mind, and he was instantly back in the state in which he had arrived. The fact was that he did not know what he wished to say, nor even why he had sought her out. He only knew that he esteemed this woman — was in a fair way to being in love with her. He could easily see that whatever her experience with Wickham had been, she was unharmed and happy. Her resilience was one of the things he admired the most about her. But he had to know . . . What he had to know he was not certain, but the need was there regardless, pawing away at the walls of his mind with a desperation he could not ignore.

"I wish . . . I would like to . . ." Darcy paused, cursing his lead tongue for its inability to decipher what he wished to say.

Miss Elizabeth only looked at him, her amusement overflowing from her eyes. "It is clear you want something, sir. Should I guess what it is? There seems little chance of my discovering it by any other means."

"Is it your practice to jest always, Miss Bennet?" asked Darcy. "One might think it the product of an unserious mind to turn everything into a joke."

"I hope not, Mr. Darcy. But it seems as if such banter as this is much easier for your current sensibilities. Perhaps we should continue in such a fashion to lighten your mood, so this other communication loses some of its intimidation."

Darcy shook his head and chuckled. "I have nothing of which to inform you. I merely wish to ascertain my chances."

"Chances?" asked Miss Elizabeth, clearly confused. "I have not the pleasure of understanding you, sir."

Darcy stopped and turned toward her, catching the hand which had been settled in the crook of his arm in one hand. "Yes, chances. You see, Miss Bennet, I find myself in a unique position in my experience. I have never found any woman who has intrigued me as you do, and it has quite left me bereft of my wits."

"All of this you explained to me at the ball, Mr. Darcy," said Miss Elizabeth.

"Perhaps I did," replied Darcy, feeling no more assured of her regard than he had before. "But . . ." Darcy paused, struggling to find the words to say. "I have informed you that I will not see you as a prize to be fought over with my cousin. It seemed like you were receptive to my advances, but I am still unsure."

Darcy stopped and let out a heavy breath. There was nothing to be done but to put his heart on the line, for this woman was worth it. If she crushed it with her answer, at least he would know. He did not think she had it in her to be cruel.

"Miss Bennet, I know you will not trifle with a man's heart, and as such, I will bare it to you. I am not an eloquent man. At times I have been called distant and fastidious, proud and disagreeable. I am not articulate, nor am I prone to displays such as will amaze those watching us with the force of my regard for you.

"I have often found myself . . . overshadowed by my cousin, though we have long been the closest of friends. Fitzwilliam is everything I am not—he is gregarious, always knows when to make a jest or drop a compliment. I have never had that talent. But when I feel, I do so with all my heart. I have informed you of my interest in you, of my wish to know you better, as a man and a lover. But I have found myself wondering why you would take a taciturn and awkward man such as myself when you have attracted a bright, amiable man such as my cousin. I suppose . . . I hope you will tell me if I am . . . hoping in vain. There is not much of my heart left which is not yours, but I wish to guard what there is to protect it from completely shattering should you refuse me."

"I had not the slightest notion that you looked on me quite that way, sir."

It was a reflexive answer, Darcy was certain, but no less true regardless. She looked at him with wonder unfeigned, and he thought he saw the beginning of warmth appear in her countenance. And her eyes — her glorious eyes — flowed with the admiration of a woman who knew, for the first time, that she was cherished, even loved. Darcy could not help but squeeze her hand, still held in his own, and he was gratified when she returned the gesture.

"May I take that as an acceptance of my regard, Miss Elizabeth?"

"As I said before, Mr. Darcy, I have not the pleasure of understanding my feelings on this subject. But I can tell you that I am not unmoved. It is, perhaps, still early, but I know without any doubt that I feel I *can* return your regard."

"Thank you, Miss Bennet," said Darcy, his heart soaring. She was not his yet, but he now thought it more likely than ever that she would be.

"I am curious, however," said Miss Elizabeth. "Why would you think that I have an interest in your cousin?"

Darcy turned, tucked Miss Elizabeth's hand in the crook of his arm again, and began walking again, noting that as a chaperone, Miss Mary was efficient, yet not intrusive. He knew with an instinctual surety that should he cross a line she deemed improper, she would interfere with alacrity. As it was, the girl hung back and watched her sister with happiness shining in her eyes, allowing them enough privacy for their conversation. He smiled at her and nodded, letting her know he would not abuse her trust.

"In matters such as these," said Darcy, turning his attention back to Miss Elizabeth, "I have always felt myself at a disadvantage, for reasons of which I have already spoken. It seems only natural to me that a woman such as you would prefer my cousin to me."

"If one only wanted an unreserved companion, you might be correct. But a discerning woman wishes for more than a man who makes a joke about everything in life."

Darcy regarded her, noting the passion in her response. "Can you elaborate?"

"Of course," replied Miss Elizabeth. "I have always had the impression that your cousin is a good man. He is as you have stated:

amiable, open, and not appearing to give the impression of thinking himself better than anyone else for the simple reason of his elevated status.

"But whereas you speak to me as an equal, debating or bantering with no hint that you think my opinion inferior because I am a woman, your cousin, especially of late, flatters excessively." Miss Elizabeth paused and colored. When she spoke again, it was in a voice which Darcy had to strain to hear. "At Mr. Bingley's ball, I actually began to wonder if he was attempting to let me know he wished to make me an offer . . . of another kind."

She spoke the final few words in a rush, and Darcy could do naught but gape at her. "I assure you, Miss Bennet, in the strongest words possible, that Fitzwilliam had no such meaning. I beg you do not consider such a matter for another instant!"

"I understand *now*, Mr. Darcy," said Miss Elizabeth, hastening to reassure him. "I realized what he was about later that evening when I informed you of my desire to avoid being fought over by warring parties."

A sense of relief fell over Darcy, but he was still unable to fathom what she was saying. "It is still unbelievable you thought that of him."

"What would *you* think?" Her tone was defensive. "We have all heard stories of men of high station. I have always spoken with your cousin in a friendly manner, and he always responded. But for him to suddenly flatter to such an extent struck me as odd. He did not seem serious in his interest for me—he did not behave as you did. So naturally, I assumed he was considering me for *another* position."

"I can see where you might have obtained that impression, Miss Bennet," replied Darcy. Inside he was still caught in the grips of disbelief. But at the same time, a niggling thought made itself known: Fitzwilliam had finally stepped into it with his behavior. And then he felt vindicated for all the times he had informed his cousin he should restrain his impulse to flatter and tease. Perhaps Fitzwilliam would listen to him now.

"It is of little matter." Miss Elizabeth's tone was firm. "I knew that evening what his true purpose was, and to tell the truth, I do not care for it. His actions speak to frivolities, to a competition between cousins. I have enough sisters, sir, to know much of vying between siblings. I have no desire to be caught up in it."

"And *my* attentions?"

Miss Elizabeth turned a smile on him. "Now I think you may be attempting to stroke your vanity, sir." Darcy grinned at her and Miss

Elizabeth laughed. "I appreciate being spoken to as an intelligent woman, not as a man might speak to a dog performing tricks. I have rarely had such attention from anyone other than my father. I find that I like it quite well, indeed."

"It surprises me that anyone could treat you differently, Miss Elizabeth." Darcy stopped and turned to face her, His hand rose of its own volition, and he trailed a finger along one velvety cheek. "I see you as the intelligent woman you are, Miss Elizabeth. It is one of the attributes which attracted me to you. I hope I will be successful in my suit, for I believe we are well suited. To debate such topics as Milton for the rest of our lives together—could anything be closer to paradise than that?"

"We shall have to see, Mr. Darcy. But you have made a good start of it.'

"I hope, my dear Miss Elizabeth, I have made more than a start. Patience is not one of my virtues. Now that I know you are receptive, I shall proceed at a great pace."

Her voice was breathless when she replied. "Then go to it, sir."

It was with the heady feeling of a love which might yet be requited that Darcy returned to Netherfield. His senses were full of Miss Elizabeth Bennet, such that nothing affected him on the way there; neither the chill of the wind as his steed galloped along the roads, nor the thought of what awaited him when he arrived. Miss Elizabeth was receptive to his overtures—what could possibly be of greater importance than that?

When he reined his mount in front of Netherfield, he passed the care of the animal off to the groom and made his way up the stairs two at a time. He directed his footsteps toward his suite of rooms and changed his clothes to something more suitable for an evening at home. Snell, his valet, eyed him askance, clearly seeing something in his master's manner which differed from usual. Darcy chose not to illuminate him. Snell would discover it soon enough.

When Darcy had finished dressing, he sat at the escritoire in his room and dashed off a quick note to his steward at Pemberley to have the packet of Wickham's debt receipts sent posthaste to his attention at Netherfield. The letter was then given to Snell, Darcy instructing his valet to send it via express. Then Darcy considered descending to do his duty to his hosts. He gave some thought to simply staying in his rooms but decided at the last moment it would be polite to be seen in their company. In the end, he wished he had simply stayed above stairs.

The house was quiet that afternoon. Mrs. Hurst and Miss Bingley were nowhere in evidence, and Hurst was also absent. What surprised Darcy was the fact he could not find Bingley anywhere. He *did*, however, find his cousin in the sitting-room, and by Fitzwilliam's swift and unsettled pacing, his cousin had been nursing some disturbance of mind for far too long.

"You have returned," said Fitzwilliam the moment he saw Darcy. "I found it difficult to credit how you abandoned me in Meryton when we were finished dealing with Wickham—a man who, I might remind you, is a problem created by *your* family."

Fitzwilliam was spoiling for a fight, it seemed. Darcy, however, had little interest in obliging him. "You did not follow me, so I left. And Wickham might be, as you put it, my family's problem. It may have missed your attention, but *I* also dealt with that problem without assistance from you."

"I did not assist?" A snort of disdain issued from Fitzwilliam's lips. "It is just like you, Mr. high-and-mighty Darcy, to attempt to resolve every crisis by yourself, and take the credit of it, even when others are present."

"If you will explain to me what you did, I will be happy to extend the credit of it to you. By my account, I have sent for the man's debts, demanded he stay away from the Bennet sisters, and threatened to see him in prison if he did not comply. Your contributions consisted of a few pithy remarks."

Fitzwilliam's eyes blazed with affront, but he changed the subject. "For that matter, I would like to know what you think you are doing with Miss Elizabeth."

"What I think I am doing?" asked Darcy, raising an eyebrow at his cousin. "Are you, perhaps, accusing me of something underhanded?"

"I am accusing you of trying to insert yourself where you were not wanted!" snarled Fitzwilliam. "You could see that I was interested in Miss Elizabeth. But no—the Darcy of Pemberley cannot abide being bested by his cousin. He finds he must interfere with his cousin's happiness and try to steal the woman out from under his nose. It will not work, I tell you!"

The angry man in Darcy longed to throw Miss Elizabeth's words of his cousin's behavior in Fitzwilliam's face. But he would not behave in so underhanded a manner. "I am surprised to hear you state such, Fitzwilliam. By my account, you behaved toward Miss Elizabeth the same way you behave toward any other young woman. You flattered her and spoke with glib comments and amiable nothings. And since you have always behaved that way to any woman who crossed your path, I could not see anything remarkable in your behavior."

"Well, there was," replied Fitzwilliam, his tone abrupt. "If you did not see it, then perhaps you do not know me as well as you think."

"Perhaps I do not, for this is not how my closest cousin behaves."

Fitzwilliam glared at Darcy, but Darcy only returned his look with equal resolve. "Then let me be rightly understood—I intend to win Miss Elizabeth and make her my wife. Have I made myself quite clear?"

"You have."

"Then I will thank you to retire from the field."

"I shall do nothing of the sort."

Fitzwilliam's eyes narrowed in fury. "I should have known. Do you fear being bested?"

"No. I simply have a regard for Miss Elizabeth which is far above anything you can boast. I will not give her up because I know that, at least in some part, she returns that regard."

"She will marry where her best interest lies. Why would she marry a mere gentleman when someday she might be a countess?"

"You should ask her that yourself. Believe me, Fitzwilliam, I think more of Miss Elizabeth than to think she will be swayed by riches and titles. Heavens, man, listen to yourself! When have you ever subscribed to such nonsense as this? Has your elevation to the peerage addled you? Or have you simply begun to think so well of yourself now that you can claim a high position in society?"

His cousin was affronted—Darcy could tell by the silence which ensued after his last comment. Fitzwilliam was attempting to master himself, a welcome sign, as he had done little of that in recent days. He was hardly recognizable as the man Darcy had known from his earliest years.

"I am much as I ever was," said Fitzwilliam at length. "We have avoided open rivalry, but it seems like we have finally reached that state."

"*You* have reached that estate, Fitzwilliam," replied Darcy. "I am not interested in being your rival."

"Then cease importuning Miss Elizabeth!"

"I have not been importuning her. I shall not cease my efforts to woo her."

Fitzwilliam threw his hands up in the air and stalked about in his anger. "This is beyond belief! I begin to think I hardly know you."

"I find myself in the same situation."

"We should simply call Lady Catherine back to Netherfield and form the engagement between you and Anne. You and Lady Catherine seem to be destined for each other, it seems, for your temperaments are by no means unalike.

Darcy could hardly believe his ears. "You wish me to marry Anne when you have known all these years how much the very notion repulses me?"

"It *is* your duty, is it not?"

"It is no such thing, and I will thank you not to insinuate it."

"Did your mother not wish for it?"

"It matters not. I will inform you here and now, Fitzwilliam, that I will not back off in the matter of Miss Elizabeth Bennet. If you wish to attempt to woo her away from me, you are more than welcome to try. Let me warn you, however, that she will not be receptive to your overtures, as she finds something lacking in your manners."

"Oh, I do hope you are not arguing about the Bennets."

Both men whirled at the sound of the voice only to see Miss Bingley glide into the room. Mrs. Hurst trailed her, watching her sister as if she was some sort of wild animal ready to pounce. Miss Bingley just ignored her.

"Though I wonder if this incident has not informed you both what a poor influence on us the Bennets must be. Why, they are naught but an insignificant and improper family, intent upon ruining us all."

"I hardly think anyone at Longbourn possesses such intentions, Miss Bingley," replied Darcy. His tone was short, but the argument with Fitzwilliam had left him bereft of his usual control on his temper, and he had not the patience to listen to the woman's poison.

"Of course, they do," said Miss Bingley with more than a little heat. "They wish to sink their claws into two eligible men, thereby bringing themselves up to your level." Miss Bingley huffed. "Of course, they will not achieve any such elevation. They would merely drag you down to the sphere in which they inhabit."

Miss Bingley released a scornful laugh. "The thought of Mrs. Bennet moving in London society fills me with such hilarity. She would cut a swath through them, I have no doubt. She would be the most famous socialite within a week, though all would look on her with scorn and derision. Whether she would even understand it is debatable."

"I must agree that Mrs. Bennet would find it difficult moving in London society," said Darcy. Fitzwilliam shot him a triumphant look, but Darcy only ignored him. "There is a distinct lack of artifice about her, which makes mingling with those of the ton, for whom artifice is a second nature, difficult. Her manners are a little countrified, but not displeasing.

"As for the Bennet family, I will assume that you do not know them well, Miss Bingley. They are naught but country folk, but I find them estimable nonetheless."

"I agree, Mr. Darcy," said Mrs. Hurst, clearly attempting to defuse the situation. "I count the three eldest Bennet girls among my closest friends."

"I must think you are both mad, to be spouting such tripe." Miss Bingley's gimlet eyes turned to Fitzwilliam, and she simpered at him. "I am thankful that there is at least one present who agrees with me concerning the unsuitability of the Bennet family."

"I assure you, nothing could be further from the truth." Fitzwilliam darted a glance at Darcy. "In fact, I am hoping to make them *my* family. Surely my interest in Miss Elizabeth has been too marked to be misunderstood."

Miss Bingley gasped. Darcy regarded his cousin, noting the slight note of victory in his manner. If Fitzwilliam thought that Darcy would subside with nothing more than a simple declaration, he was destined to be disappointed. Mrs. Hurst seemed to sense it too, for she looked between the two men, first with disbelief at Fitzwilliam, then askance at Darcy. Darcy only shook his head—they had argued enough that day.

Into this volatile mix arrived Bingley, proving once again to Darcy that his friend was often prone to entering at the worst times. Bingley, however, was to shock them, for the ill feelings in the room were about to explode due to the news he brought.

"Good afternoon, everyone," said Bingley, his tone more than usually cheerful. "I see you are all present." Bingley glanced around. "Except for Hurst, of course. Well, no matter—I shall simply tell him later."

"Tell us what, Charles?" asked Mrs. Hurst, a hopeful tone in her voice.

"I have just come from Longbourn," replied Bingley.

"You have?" asked Darcy. "I was just there myself, but I did not see you."

"I arrived while you were walking outside with Miss Elizabeth and Miss Mary."

Before he could speak any further, Miss Bingley huffed and

complained: "As if a visit to that insignificant speck is worthy of such a pronouncement. Really, Charles, I wish you would simply stay away from Longbourn. Nothing good can come of associating with *that* family."

"Something of good *has* come of it, and you should become accustomed to associating with them, Caroline, for I have the happiest of news. I had a particular purpose in calling at Longbourn this morning. I have made Miss Jane Bennet an offer and have been accepted. We are now engaged."

"What?" screeched Miss Bingley. "Charles, how could you offer for such an unsuitable woman? You will return to Longbourn this instant and inform her you made a mistake. Then we will quit this little town forever! How I wish we had never come!"

"I shall not," said Bingley, clearly having expected this reaction from his sister. "I have asked her, as a gentleman, and been accepted. You are well aware that a man may not break off an engagement for any reason, Caroline. I love her, and I will not renege."

"Love!" spat Miss Bingley. "You would throw away our family's respectability on something as transitory as love? What are you thinking, Charles?"

"I am thinking of my own happiness and that of Miss Bennet. I care nothing for society."

But Miss Bingley was not to be silenced. She screeched, screamed, demanded, and cajoled that he break off his engagement. But Darcy was surprised by Bingley's fortitude, for he withstood his sister's rage as a rock stands against the battering of the tide. Mrs. Hurst was agitated, attempting, in turn, to calm her younger sister and congratulate her brother. Then Hurst arrived.

"Am I to understand from all this caterwauling that you have made an offer to Miss Bennet?"

"I have," replied Bingley.

This show of defiance only seemed to amuse Hurst. "You have not known the girl long, but it is clear you have been mooning after her since the first night of your acquaintance. Well done, I say!"

"Thank you, Hurst."

This, of course, only served to whip Miss Bingley up into a greater frenzy. She took no heed as to her pretensions toward higher society and the need to impress Fitzwilliam, for she demanded and yelled, such that Darcy was soon tired of her antics. He congratulated Bingley in a quiet voice and excused himself. Fitzwilliam, it seemed, had a similar objective, for he did the same. But not without a glare at Darcy.

He added a small comment to his words, however.

"Perhaps, Bingley, you should take some thought to controlling your sister. If she continues to behave in such a manner, your family will never be accepted by those of higher society."

And with that, Fitzwilliam stalked from the room, never seeing the look of affront which came over Bingley's face.

CHAPTER XXV

*T*he mood at Longbourn was jubilant. While Elizabeth had been distracted by Mr. Darcy and Lord Chesterfield, she had not imagined that the relationship between Mr. Bingley and her sister had progressed so far. Jane was quick to tease her for her inattention.

"Something quite particular must have commanded your interest, Elizabeth. You have always known of the interest a man has in me before I have known of it for myself."

"And so I have," cried Elizabeth. "But I must own that your Mr. Bingley has come to the point in a far more expeditious fashion than I had ever thought possible!"

"I suppose he has," replied Jane. "But I cannot repine my good fortune."

"You deserve it, if any of us does," said Mary. "But I must own that I find myself wondering if I am not to lose another sister before long." Mary turned a raised eyebrow on Elizabeth. "Mr. Darcy and Lizzy were quite cozy out on the back lawn. At one point, when he turned and caught up her hand, I thought he might actually propose too!"

"It is still too early for that," replied Elizabeth, though she felt the heat in her cheeks from the memory of the feelings which ha coursed through her at that moment. "I do not know him nearly well enough yet. He is much more reserved than Mr. Bingley and much more careful in his deliberations."

"Lizzy!" exclaimed Jane, her gaze falling on Elizabeth with mock affront. "Are you calling my Mr. Bingley impetuous?"

"No, indeed, dearest Jane. Though I wonder if impetuosity is not a part of his character. Mr. Darcy is anything but impetuous. He will come to the point in his own time if he decides it is a course he wishes to pursue."

"I am sure he will," replied Jane, catching Elizabeth up in a tight embrace. "And I am very happy for you, my dearest sister. You will be happy with him, I think."

Elizabeth forbore mentioning that all was as yet *not* decided.

"Now we will simply need to take thought for our dear Mary," said Jane, the teasing glint in her eye now focused on their younger sister. "Have you noticed anything about her that suggests interest in a man?"

"Please desist, Jane," pleaded Mary, though there was a rosy hue on her cheeks which suggested Jane might have stumbled on the truth. "I am content to remain unmarried for some time yet. I am not looking for a husband."

"Do not fear, Mary, my dear," said Elizabeth. "You shall not have to search yourself, for Jane and I will be happy to do it for you."

Mary fixed Elizabeth with a withering glare, but Elizabeth only laughed.

On such a joyous occasion as this, it was not a surprise that Mrs. Bennet responded with jubilation, as her lifelong goal of seeing her daughters married finally saw its first success. Elizabeth had wondered if her mother's newfound composure would survive such momentous news. It appeared the answer was a decided no.

"Oh, Jane, Jane!" cried Mrs. Bennet the moment the news was made known to her. "I am so happy! I dare say he is the handsomest man I have ever seen, and I congratulate you!" Mrs. Bennet paused and glanced at Elizabeth. "Well, I suppose Mr. Darcy is equally as handsome as Mr. Bingley. I hope you will forgive me at present, Lizzy, if I inform you that Mr. Bingley is quite my favorite at present. When Mr. Darcy finally comes to the point, I am sure he will take his turn as my favorite at that time!"

Elizabeth laughed. "I will be certain to inform him of it, Mama. I know he will be happy to occupy such a preeminent position."

"Oh, Lizzy! Again, you speak such nonsense! I am certain Mr.

Darcy does not care two figs if he is *my* favorite. However, I am certain he will be vastly pleased to be *yours*."

In all the years her mother had embarrassed her, it had never been with her teasing. Elizabeth hardly knew how to react, even as her family laughed around her.

"I believe your mother has the right of it in this instance, Lizzy," said Mr. Bennet. He stepped forward and kissed Jane on her forehead. "Congratulations, Jane. I have no doubt you will both be very happy, though I wonder how you will get on together. Every marriage needs one partner who is forceful. You and Mr. Bingley are both so complying, that it will be a wonder if any decisions are ever made."

Jane smiled in the face of her father's teasing. "I believe, Papa, that he may just surprise you."

"Perhaps he will at that." Mr. Bennet turned to Elizabeth. "Mr. Darcy, on the other hand, suffers from no lack of resolution. How long do you expect it will be before he accosts me in my library as Mr. Bingley has done today?" he grinned at both his daughters. "I would wish to get it over with, for I am not accustomed to being interrupted by every man in residence at Netherfield."

"I do not know, Papa," replied Elizabeth, feeling all the embarrassment of the situation. "Mr. Darcy is also deliberate, so it might be some time before he acts."

"Well, then I suppose we shall simply need to wait for him. But remember, Lizzy—he gives all the impression of a man besotted. I am sure you can hurry him along if you try."

Mr. Bennet winked and excused himself, leaving the womenfolk of his family to their jubilations. It was a propitious day, indeed. Hopefully, there would be more to come."

The mood at Netherfield was in no way equal to that at Longbourn. While those at Longbourn celebrated, the company at Netherfield was beset by a mass of ill feelings, suspicion and fury, the likes of which Louisa had never seen before in her life.

Dinner that evening was largely a quiet affair, and Louisa took the simple expedient of not speaking with anyone, for there were few with whom she could speak with any equanimity. Besides, she was too busy ensuring Caroline remained calm to devote much attention to what was occurring at her table. Charles was angry with Caroline for her violent reaction to news which should be happy and with Lord Chesterfield for his comments concerning Caroline—comments for which Louisa could not blame the man. Mr. Darcy and Lord

Chesterfield were at odds. Lord Chesterfield made a comment here and there about various subjects, seeming to focus on betrayal, which Mr. Darcy ignored. Only Hurst seemed unaffected. He ate with gusto, glancing about the room and chuckling from time to time. Louisa might have found it inappropriate, had she not been able to see the dark humor in the situation.

No one showed much inclination to gather in the sitting-room after dinner, and the party separated to see to their own concerns, most retiring for the night. Louisa, however, watched her youngest sibling, concerned that Caroline was contemplating something which would ruin them forever. When she took herself to her room, Louisa decided she had little choice but to confront Caroline.

When she entered her sister's sitting room, it was to the sight of Caroline pacing the floor muttering to herself. Caroline had been badly upset these past days, not only because of Charles's engagement to Miss Jane Bennet, but also because of her dawning comprehension that she was not so favored by either Mr. Darcy or Lord Chesterfield as she had thought. It was making her desperate. A desperate Caroline was not a situation to be ignored, for anxiety also made her foolhardy.

"Do you finally see it, Caroline?" demanded Louisa. Her sister ceased her pacing and turned to glare at Louisa. "Do you finally see you have no chance to elicit a proposal from either of our guests?"

"Mind your own concerns," spat Caroline.

"Your concern *are* my concerns," replied Louisa. "Especially when I fully believe you are contemplating actions which would have a detrimental effect on our family in society."

"Do you believe I am so incompetent as this?" This sneer with which Caroline beheld Louisa was truly offensive. "You have become a milksop since you married that sodden drunkard of yours, Louisa. I have always been the best of us. I am fully aware of what I am doing."

"Please stop, Caroline. Come to your senses. Lord Chesterfield will not marry you, and Mr. Darcy has all but declared himself to Miss Elizabeth. Nothing good can come of this. Hurst and I will be happy to take you back to town. I am sure there are men aplenty who will see your worth."

"I do not want a man of society!" screamed Caroline, stamping her foot in her petulant anger. "I want to be a countess. I *will* be a countess!"

Caroline waved her hand, dismissing Louisa. "Leave me be, Louisa. I shall know what to do."

There was nothing to be done, for Caroline turned and continued her pacing and muttering. She took no more notice of Louisa, though Louisa watched her for several more moments before exiting the room. Before she left, however, Louisa spoke quietly to herself, vowing: "I, also, shall know how to act, sister *dearest*."

When Louisa shared her concerns with her husband that night, he laughed, as she might have predicted. "I have wondered when Caroline would come to the point. It would be most amusing to simply allow her enough rope to hang herself.

"Hurst!" exclaimed Louisa. "I am trying to save the family from infamy! You should recall that your connection to us is such that your father would not be pleased, should scandal arise because of Caroline's imprudent actions."

But Hurst only continued to chuckle, "I did not say we should allow it to happen, only that it would be amusing to see. I suppose you must take this to Bingley and alert the housekeeper."

"What can Charles do?" fretted Louisa. "She is becoming so ungovernable that he will be forced to lock her in her room or send her to our aunt's house in Scarborough."

"Then so be it," replied Hurst. "She deserves nothing less." Hurst paused for a moment, his thoughtful expression very unlike him. "You know I do not like your sister, Louisa. I have tried not to make an issue of it, but she is rude, arrogant, treats both you and Bingley with contempt, and delusional besides. I cannot think of anything which would suit her more than to be taken down a peg or two and shown that she is not the center of everything."

"I know," replied Louisa with a heavy sigh. "I have not liked Caroline for many a year. I simply do not know how to manage her, and I am afraid of her ruining us."

"Then some action must be taken. If some way can be found to allow her to dig her own grave, I would suggest we take it. It will be easier to ship her off to the north if she is already aware she has no prospects left here."

Louisa thought about her husband's words for some time after, but no solution presented itself. How Caroline might be ruined without her family partaking in her disgrace was quite beyond Louisa's ability to fathom.

The following morning Louisa went to see her brother as soon as she could. Fortunately, Charles's mood was improved from the previous evening. He listened to her with a gravity which was not usually a part of his character, asking a few questions to clarify her words. In the end, he let out a sigh and pinched the bridge of his nose.

"Where did we go wrong, Louisa?" asked he. "How did she come to this end? She was sweet and obliging as a child. How has she become such a bitter, scheming shrew?"

"To you, she might always have been sweet," replied Louisa. "But she was never to me. She was always aware of her position as mother's favorite, and she used it to her advantage."

Charles nodded slowly. "I suppose you are correct. She only acted sweet when it suited her purpose."

"She was conniving almost as soon as she learned to walk," said Louisa. "Though I am hesitant in general to assign a bad temperament to another, in Caroline's case I think it is warranted. She has always treated us all as if we are her personal retainers, and her plans have never taken our happiness into account. She cares little for whether we are happy — only our position in society as it affects her own."

"Nature versus nurture?" asked Charles. It was a rhetorical question. "In this instance, I believe you may be correct. But our parents may share some of the blame, for they never acted to curb these tendencies of hers."

"Father was never present," replied Louisa. "You know he put his heart into the business, dreaming that you would one day be a gentleman. As for mother, she was not so different from Caroline in essentials. She merely lacked the means to make her dreams a reality."

"Caroline will not confess it, but she lacks the ability herself."

"Which is why we must control her. Even if she successfully compromises Lord Chesterfield, I doubt he will willingly marry her. Failure of such a scheme, without severe censure on our parts, will be disastrous, especially if Lord Chesterfield proves vindictive."

Charles's countenance turned stony. "Perhaps he deserves it. A shrew-like Caroline as a wife might pierce his puffed-up pride."

"Charles —"

"I know, I know," said Charles, raising his hands in surrender. "But the viscount has proved himself less amiable than I had ever thought."

"He was not incorrect about Caroline."

"No, he was not. *That* I can acknowledge. But he should not have spoken so either. Darcy has long thought ill of Caroline, yet he refrained from speaking to me of her in such a way."

"Yes, Mr. Darcy has proven to be a great friend,"

They were silent for a moment until Charles shook himself free of his dark thoughts with a visible effort. "Please speak with the housekeeper and inform her of our suspicions. I will talk to the butler and ensure he keeps a careful watch. We will need to be careful of this,

Louisa. If any word is carried out by the servants our name will be ruined."

"We will take every precaution."

When Darcy sought his friend that morning, he found Bingley in a pensive, most un-Bingley-like mood. There was something weighing on his friend's mind, quite different from what Darcy might have expected, considering his engagement to Miss Jane Bennet. He greeted Bingley, prompting a bit of his friend's previous amiability in response, before sitting down in front of the hearth in Bingley's study to share tea and a little conversation.

"I apologize for not telling you this last night, Bingley, but you have my congratulations on your engagement to Miss Bennet. She is a lovely girl; I am certain you will be happy with her."

Darcy might have expected Bingley to reply with pleasure, jubilant thanks for his well wishes, or perhaps a long monologue concerning the virtues of his new fiancée. But Bingley surprised Darcy by regarded him with no little suspicion, his brows drawn down in a scowl.

"I might have expected condemnation or at least an attempt to convince me I was making a mistake. That seems to be all the rage, recently."

"I do not know where I might have given you that impression, my friend," replied Darcy, taking care to speak with caution. "I do not believe I have said anything against the Bennets. Quite the opposite, in fact."

Though Bingley peered at him for a moment, suspicion alive in his countenance, he soon sighed and turned away. "You have my apologies, Darcy. Of course, you have not. It is simply . . ." Bingley paused for a moment, struggling with his emotions before his words came out in a rush. "After Caroline's behavior last night, I remembered all the times you have counseled me regarding marriage and my attentions to young ladies. I hope you will forgive me if I expected you to advise me that marrying Jane Bennet would do me no favors in society."

"She *is* a gentleman's daughter," replied Darcy, again speaking slowly to avoid being misunderstood. "She will not assist you in society in London, for she is an unknown there. But it is clear that is of no concern to you. No, my friend, I can do nothing other than congratulate you for finding a woman who makes you happy and possessing the fortitude to ensure she does not escape."

Bingley nodded. "Then I accept your sentiments. Thank you, my friend. I cannot tell you how much your support means to me."

"As much as your support will mean to me," replied Darcy. Though he had not thought to inform Bingley of his own designs on a Bennet sister, Darcy felt now was the right time to do so. Bingley was not so caught up in his own happiness that he missed Darcy's words.

"Oh? I will support you, of course, but I would like to know your meaning."

"Only that I have designs on my own Bennet sister." Bingley's eyes widened in surprise. "Surely you have seen the attention I have paid to Miss Elizabeth."

"I have, but I had not thought your interest so advanced." Bingley paused and then continued: "And I have also noticed that Fitzwilliam has some interest in that quarter."

"He has," replied Darcy. "But I have confirmation from the lady that she is not averse to my presence, whereas she finds Fitzwilliam too intent upon flirting and flattery."

Bingley's countenance fell again. "He does lay it on a little thick at times." Then Bingley laughed. "Then again, I suppose he is not so different from me. I would, however, prefer that he keep his opinions to himself. I am well aware of Caroline's temper. He does not need to inform me of it."

The situation demanded Darcy's response, but once again he proceeded with care, not wishing to offend his friend as Fitzwilliam had.

"His manner in stating his opinion was, of course, deplorable. But in essence, I cannot help but think he is correct. Your sister has ever had an ungovernable temperament, Bingley, and she does you no favors with her behavior."

A sigh escaped Bingley's lips, and he put his head back against the chair in which he was seated. "And her behavior is bound to raise new problems."

Darcy turned a sharp glance on his friend. "Do you speak of something particular?"

"Louisa came to speak with me this morning," confessed Bingley. "She has been concerned about Caroline for some time now and is convinced she means to make an attempt to compromise your cousin. I have no need to tell you how this would affect our standing in society if she tried and failed, and the matter was made known.

"For that matter, I wonder if we could escape censure regardless."

"Perhaps we should simply leave him to her," muttered Darcy.

Bingley regarded him with a grin, quite incongruous to the situation. "That sentiment seems to be in vogue today, Darcy. When Louisa informed me of the matter, my first thought was to leave him to his fate."

"He has been a bit troublesome lately," agreed Darcy, "but I cannot allow him to be compromised into marriage. I would not wish him the misery of such a situation, and your sister might find that there are certain drawbacks to procuring a husband in such a way."

"You flatter her," was Bingley's short reply. "Had she the status of a countess and the means to lord her position in society over all and sundry, I am certain Caroline would not allow herself to be unhappy."

"You might be correct, my friend. But I cannot betray my cousin. Every feeling revolts against it, even though in some ways he deserves it."

"Agreed," replied Bingley. "Louisa has informed the housekeeper. If she attempts anything, we will ensure she is not successful."

The two friends sat together for some time, and at length, Bingley did begin to extoll the virtues of his newly betrothed. Darcy was more than willing to simply listen to his friend. Moreover, Bingley injected more than a few comments about the goodness of her younger sister and Darcy's rapidly growing feelings for her. He was beginning to think them both the most fortunate of men.

CHAPTER XXVI

*V*iscount Anthony Fitzwilliam, Lord of Chesterfield was becoming a problem. Under normal circumstances, Elizabeth would not have thought such things about a member of the peerage. English society, after all, was taught to revere and venerate those of high status, and Elizabeth was no different from any other.

The new feelings and sensations of being loved by Mr. Darcy—for Elizabeth was certain the man was rapidly approaching that state—rendered the viscount's constant attempts to flatter her an annoyance. While she could not speak openly and ask him to desist, Elizabeth knew there would come a time when he would need to be told that she had no interest in him. That time came only the day after Mr. Darcy had visited, with his sweet and heady words of admiration.

It was almost too early to be receiving visitors, but when the youngest Bennets reported the sight of Lord Chesterfield on the drive of Longbourn, mounted on a grey stallion, Elizabeth knew that he had come for her.

"Lizzy," said her mother, speaking in a hushed and hurried manner, "what does the viscount mean by importuning you in this fashion? Are you not set on Mr. Darcy?"

A laugh threatened to burst forth, but Elizabeth checked it. "I am not *set* upon Mr. Darcy, though I do like him very well, indeed."

"It seems his lordship does not understand that fact yet."

"Oh, I think he understands it very well," muttered Elizabeth. "He simply has no intention of being bested by Mr. Darcy."

Mrs. Bennet gasped. "The gentlemen are fighting over you?"

"I do not know," said Elizabeth with a sigh. "Mr. Darcy's attentions are true. But the viscount appears to be determined to pay his addresses too. I do not know what to make of him."

The sound of someone in the hall drew the attention of them all, and Elizabeth rose in anticipation of Lord Chesterfield's entrance, as did all her sisters. Mrs. Bennet, however, directed a thoughtful glance at her Elizabeth, and the soft sound of her voice reached Elizabeth's ears: "Perhaps we may still turn him to Lydia."

"Courage, Elizabeth," said Mary, standing close by Elizabeth's side. Elizabeth felt her sister grasp her hand and squeeze it, and Elizabeth was gratified by the support she offered.

When the gentleman was led into the room and announced by Mrs. Hill, he greeted them all with his usual amiable words. But it was clear his focus was on Elizabeth as soon as he had greeted Mrs. Bennet as was proper.

"You appear positively enchanting this morning, Miss Elizabeth," said the viscount. He strode toward her and, upon reaching her, grasped her hand and bestowed a kiss upon its back.

It was all Elizabeth could do not to roll her eyes at this man. His flattery was back in full force, and he appeared to expect her to swoon at his feet when he employed it. Elizabeth considered it to be a particularly clumsy weapon, one which he wielded like a bludgeon rather than a precision tool she had always thought it would be. In this respect, he was, perhaps, not unlike Mr. Collins.

The very thought caused Elizabeth to hiccup as she attempted to hold in laughter. The viscount looked at her, puzzled by her reaction, while Mary regarded her with uncertainty. Elizabeth was saved when Mrs. Bennet asked Lord Chesterfield to take a seat and offered to send for refreshments.

"Thank you, Madam," said Lord Chesterfield, bowing his head. "As always, Longbourn's hospitality is without equal."

Mrs. Bennet frowned as he turned the weight of his continued flattery on her, but Lord Chesterfield had already turned away. "Miss Elizabeth, it seems like it has been an age since I last saw you. I trust you—all of you—have been well?"

"We have," replied Elizabeth. She kept her tone reserved,

determined to avoid giving this man any encouragement when none was warranted.

"Good! Excellent! I am glad that it has been so."

"And your party at Netherfield?" asked Elizabeth, feeling obliged to do so.

"All very well, thank you," replied the viscount. He opened his mouth to say something more, but then he decided against it at the last moment.

Tea arrived some moments later and soon all were served. They sat in this attitude speaking of inconsequential matters. Or, rather, Lord Chesterfield spoke, most of his words directed at Elizabeth, and while he allowed her to respond, he often did not seem to even hear what she said. He was a man on a mission, Elizabeth thought, unwavering in his intention to complete it, regardless of what happened or what anyone else said.

"Do you often go to London?" asked Lord Chesterfield. They had been speaking of society, the viscount relating some anecdotes of his doings in London the previous season. When he turned to her, he seemed to have some expectation of her response. He did not receive whatever he expected.

"I dare say Lizzy and I will each spend upwards of a month in London every year," interjected Jane. Elizabeth turned to look at her sister, and though Jane made no mention of it, she knew Jane was attempting to draw some of the viscount's attention away from her to give her a respite.

"Ah, yes," replied Lord Chesterfield, never pausing, even for a moment. "Your uncle, as I recall. Have you any other relations in London?"

"No, not a one," replied Elizabeth. "Our father's family consists of nothing more than distant cousins, and our mother's other sister resides in Meryton."

"And when you go to London, do you attend varied events?" Lord Chesterfield turned once again to direct his attention at Elizabeth. "I dare say you would be the brightest belle at any ball you attended."

Elizabeth was starting to feel annoyed. "We rarely attend such events in London, my lord." Lord Chesterfield's countenance fell. "I do enjoy the theater and attending exhibits. But my uncle does not possess vouchers to Almack's, and the Bennets have never had a presence in London."

"I prefer the opera," said Jane. "Lizzy, however, does not appreciate it as much."

"Oh?" asked Lord Chesterfield. "I had thought you a connoisseur of all displays of art and culture."

"The music is not much to my taste," replied Elizabeth, "though there is, of course, some that is very pretty. I must prefer chamber music to opera, which I have always found loud and grating on my nerves."

"Whereas I love the sounds of singers of true talent," said Jane. "It is one of the few subjects on which my sister and I have ever disagreed."

"My Lydia loves music too, do you not, my dear?" interjected Mrs. Bennet.

Lydia assumed the look of a hare in the sight of a fox. "Music is fine enough," replied Lydia. "But I prefer to listen to it while dancing. There is nothing so fine as dancing, and I cannot think well of anyone who does not know the steps to all the popular reels."

"A woman after my own heart," replied Lord Chesterfield with a laugh. "I, too, dearly love to dance, Miss Lydia."

His eyes had shifted back Elizabeth when he made his comment, clearly expecting her to say something in support. Elizabeth, however, said nothing, contenting herself with smiling at Lydia.

"And Lydia is quickly recovering from her mishap with Mr. Bennet's cousin," added Mrs. Bennet. "Why, when the next assembly or ball is held, I am certain she will return to her lively self."

"I cannot imagine anything else, Mrs. Bennet," said the viscount.

Though there was nothing in his tone to suggest interest, Mrs. Bennet acted as if he had just declared undying love for her youngest. "In that case, I expect you will wish to dance with her. In fact, I know of no young man who has caught her eye, so if you act quickly, you may secure an important set with her."

Lord Chesterfield gaped at Mrs. Bennet. Elizabeth watched, diverted at the way in which her family was distracting the man from her. Under normal circumstances, she might have been chagrinned at their behavior, but at present, she could only feel he deserved it.

"When the time comes, Mrs. Bennet," said Lord Chesterfield after a short delay, "I am certain I would be happy to dance with Miss Lydia."

He turned and fixed his gaze upon Elizabeth. "In fact, I believe I would be happy to dance with *all* your daughters if they will oblige me."'

"I am certain they would," replied Mrs. Bennet, frowning at what she likely considered to be an obtuse man. "They are all good girls, though I say it myself. Jane is, as you must know, betrothed to Mr.

Bingley now. I am sure she deserves the happiness which must result from being the focus of attention from such a good man."

"Yes, I believe Bingley did mention something of it." Lord Chesterfield turned what Elizabeth thought was the first genuine smile he had displayed since his arrival at Longbourn. "You have my congratulations, Miss Bennet. Bingley is, indeed, an excellent man. I am sure you will be happy with him."

Jane smiled. "Thank you, Lord Chesterfield. I am certain I shall."

But Lord Chesterfield had already turned away from her. "Miss Elizabeth, it is a beautiful day today. Shall we not take a turn about your family's back gardens?"

It was so similar to what had happened when Mr. Darcy had come to visit that Elizabeth was speechless for a moment. Was he so insensible to her lack of interest in him? Or perhaps his pride could not imagine a simple country miss such as Elizabeth rejecting him.

It was not in Elizabeth's nature to reply with rudeness, however, so she acquiesced with a few quiet words. Perhaps this would be an opportunity to inform him of her indifference without all her family looking on.

"I will go with you," said Mary. "I feel a need for a little fresh air myself."

The viscount turned to look at with her with astonishment. At the same time, Mrs. Bennet regarded the viscount, a pensive frown directed at him. "That is likely for the best, I should say. Remember to dress warmly, girls."

"I assure you, Mrs. Bennet, that you may trust your daughter on the back lawn with me. Surely Miss Mary would be more comfortable staying in your sitting-room."

"I might," owned Mary, "but the proprieties must be observed. I will not intrude, your lordship—of that you may be certain."

Mary's words silenced the viscount's objections. He still did not seem pleased, but he allowed it to pass. With their outerwear donned and footwear secured, they soon exited through the main doors and made their way around to the back of the house. As she had when Mr. Darcy had walked with Elizabeth, Mary hung back, allowing them privacy, but staying closer than she had to Elizabeth and Mr. Darcy the previous day.

"You have an excellent family, Miss Elizabeth," said the viscount as soon as they were walking the paths of the lawn. "But I appreciate this time we are able to speak together without interruption."

Elizabeth did not respond, contenting herself with a noncommittal response, and even she was not certain what she said. Lord Chesterfield frowned; it was clear he had expected a reply of more substance. What did he expect? Should she break out in a paean of praise for the way he had forced his attentions on her? Elizabeth was determined to allow him to say what he wished without her interruption. Perhaps this interview would be finished quickly.

"I *am* curious, Miss Elizabeth," said the viscount after silence had fallen between them for a few minutes. "Now that your sister is to be married, I wonder what are your plans for the future."

"At present, I do not know that I *have* any plans, Lord Chesterfield. Perhaps once Jane has settled into her new home, I shall be induced to stay with her for a time. Or I may continue at Longbourn as I have. I am in no hurry to determine my future. I am, you know, not yet one and twenty."

Lord Chesterfield fixed her with a long look. "You must have aspirations, Miss Elizabeth. Do you wish to travel, for example?"

"Seeing new places is always welcome, Lord Chesterfield," replied Elizabeth. "But my father is not in a position such as to make frequent journeys to exotic places practical."

"But you might attract a gentleman who loves you enough to show you those places."

It was no less than a blatant attempt to induce Elizabeth to confess her interest in him. Elizabeth was determined not to allow the man any unwarranted hope.

"That is possible."

It was obvious he was disappointed with her response. "Surely you wish for such a life, do you not?"

"I do, my lord. But I cannot see the future."

He changed course. "Is there anyone in your life at present who might fulfill this desire?"

"Lord Chesterfield," said Elizabeth, her tone admonishing. "I hardly think this is the trivial sort of detail which should be discussed between mere acquaintances."

"And you think we are naught but inconsequential acquaintances, Miss Elizabeth?" There was some heat in his tone, and it reeked of disappointment as if she had committed some unpardonable error. "I had thought us close friends, at the very least."

"Friends we may be. But one does not ask such a question of anything less than a family member or lover."

As soon as Elizabeth said the final word, she knew it was a mistake to do so. The heat on the viscount's gaze scorched her, and Elizabeth was left feeling breathless from the desire in his eyes.

But it seemed like the desire to possess, rather than the interest of a man for a woman. He was not a bad man, she knew, and she could not say for certain of what his feelings consisted. But she also did not feel the same warmth when he looked at her as she did when she was the subject of Mr. Darcy's intensity. Perhaps he did not realize it, but that passion she had always wished to have between herself and her husband did not exist between them.

"I would wish to be that lover, Miss Elizabeth. I wish to have you as my wife all the days of our lives, to have and hold you and no other. Have I not bared my feelings enough for you to see this?"

If his plea had been that of a man, pouring his heart out to a woman, Elizabeth might have been moved by it. Moved to pity, at the very least. But there was a haughty undertone to his words that Elizabeth did not like. She could not quite put her finger on it, but it seemed to Elizabeth that he was in disbelief that she would not fall at his feet and thank him for bestowing his attention on her. A stinging retort was poised at the tip of her tongue.

But there some something else, a longing for her regard, tinged with a hint of desperation. Seeing it forced Elizabeth to remember that this was not a bad man. He was, in actuality, a man likely as good as any she had ever met. At present he was something of a misguided one, she suspected, one which had, perhaps, been a little seduced by the elevation of his position, one who was attempting to impress a woman. She could not behave with asperity toward him. He had paid her a high compliment, after all, one which, under other circumstances, she might have given her joyous acceptance.

"Lord Chesterfield," she said, speaking in a soft and friendly tone, "I am not unaware of your feelings. I am not unaffected by the honor you have bestowed upon me. I regret to say that I am unable to accept your assurances at present."

"But you mean to accept Darcy's."

Elizabeth was unsurprised by his bitterness and determined not to be affected by it. "Again, I will not answer that question, my lord. It is a private matter, and I cannot respond at this time. Believe me when I say that I do not intend to hurt you with my words."

Many emotions seemed to pass over the viscount's face, and Elizabeth was not certain which would reign supreme once he had regained his composure. In the end, it seemed determination had won out, for he regarded her with a fierceness which almost forced her to step back.

"Then I will prove myself to you, Miss Elizabeth. I will prove my constancy, demonstrate the true nature of my regard. I have no doubt that in the end, I shall prevail."

"There is nothing over which to prevail," said Elizabeth. The frustration she felt was beginning to seep into her voice. "There is nothing to prove. You are a good man, Lord Chesterfield, but I am simply not interested in a deeper relationship."

"That will change, Miss Elizabeth—this I vow. I will show you that you can love me."

With those final words, Lord Chesterfield turned and began to walk back toward the house, moving past a surprised Mary before she could react. Elizabeth, shocked as she was by his sudden actions, hurried after him. She thought of trying to persuade him away from this mad quest for which he had set himself, but it seemed he was determined.

When they reached the front door of the house, Lord Chesterfield turned to regard her. He opened his mouth to speak, but before he could, a figure emerged from the shadows of the portico, interrupting whatever he was about to say.

"Lord Chesterfield. I would like to have a word with you if you will oblige me."

If Bennet had not been witness to the transformation of his wife in the past weeks, he might not have believed it possible. Then again, the years had altered her, and the woman he saw before him now was nothing more than his wife of old, returned to him in the most improbable circumstances.

Bennet had always known that his wife was not the most intelligent specimen. Though some of the neighborhood thought he had married her in a fit of passion, a moment of infatuation in which he was blinded by her youthful beauty and good humor, that was not precisely the truth. Yes, he had been so captivated, and it had played a part in their marriage. But the truth was that as a young woman, Mrs. Bennet had been an acceptable companion, and even after their marriage, he had found himself more than fond of her.

It was only as the years passed that she had changed, become the nervous, flighty, and loud creature he had known these past years. It had started not long after Elizabeth's birth when a chance comment from Bennet had revealed the situation with the entail. Bennet had never truly considered it to be a problem, as he had been certain he would father a son. Though Maggie had never been able to understand the reason of entails, she had understood the consequences readily enough. And as each subsequent daughter had been born with nary an heir to protect her against the hedgerows, she had become sillier and more nervous. By the time Lydia had been born and subsequent attempts to conceive another child had failed, her character appeared fixed, and her ambition was then to marry all her daughters to wealthy gentlemen in as expedient a manner as possible.

Bennet was amazed at the changes which had been wrought in her due to her eldest daughter's engagement and the prospects of other gentlemen paying attention to her younger daughters. She would never be a clever woman, but she had begun to remember what she had been before and was thinking a little before she acted, had learned to temper herself a little. Perhaps the years of their retirement might not be so onerous after all — if this transformation persisted, she might once again be an acceptable companion.

Underlining this change in her were the moments after Lizzy left for the back lawn in the company of Lord Chesterfield. Though Bennet had come to despise her intrusions into his bookroom over the years, of late he had been pleasantly surprised by her insights. Today was one such day.

"Mr. Bennet," said she, entering his study after both knocking and waiting until he answered before she opened the door. "I must ask for your assistance and your attention for Lizzy."

"For Lizzy?" asked Mr. Bennet, setting his book down on his desk. "Has your daughter got herself into some mischief?"

"No, Husband," replied Mrs. Bennet. "But it seems Lord Chesterfield is intent upon imposing himself upon her. It is time for you to inform him that he will not be allowed to have his own way."

Bennet's grave look and softly spoken "Please explain" induced her to be explicit. At the end of it all, Bennet found himself once again surprised — in the past, he was certain she would have insisted Lizzy throw aside the other man for the one at hand, especially since the newest suitor was a member of the peerage.

"You say they have gone to the back lawn?" asked Bennet.

"Yes," replied his wife. "They should be visible from your window."

Bennet nodded and rose, going to his window and looking out over the gardens. As his wife had informed him, Lizzy stood speaking with the viscount, and from their animated exchange and her stance — feet apart, back straight — Bennet thought she was attempting to hold her own against him.

"Thank you, Maggie," said Bennet. He stepped around the desk and gazed down at the woman he married, catching her hand and squeezing it while kissing her forehead. "You did well in coming to me. I will explain to his lordship what we expect of his behavior."

Maggie nodded, her face suffused with a rosy hue. Bennet had not often complimented her, a fact for which he now felt more than a little guilty. She was a good woman, and while manners were a little forceful, she wanted the best for all her daughters.

With a final squeeze, Bennet left the room, hurrying toward the door. As he stepped through it, he heard the sound of footsteps approaching around the house and, expecting that his daughter and her persistent suitor had quit the gardens, he stepped behind one of the pillars to observe them.

Lord Chesterfield came into view first, his gait that of a man perturbed, while Lizzy followed behind, her rapid footsteps attempting to match the viscount's. Mary followed Elizabeth. When they reached the edge of the entrance, Lord Chesterfield turned, his sudden movement enough to surprise Elizabeth, who stopped and met him, surprise evident in her countenance. It was time for Bennet to intervene.

"Lord Chesterfield. I would like to have a word with you if you will oblige me."

It was clear Bennet had startled his lordship with his sudden words, for he proved his military background when he whirled and confronted Bennet as if suddenly faced with an enemy. It took him a moment before he could gather himself, a moment Bennet used to excuse his daughter from any further importuning on the part of the viscount.

"Lizzy, Mary, you may go inside. Your mother and sisters are waiting for you."

The girls nodded and curtseyed before they fled into the house. When the door was closed behind them, Bennet turned back to regard the viscount. For his part, the man was shocked at the sudden disappearance of the object of his interest. But he gathered himself without ado and faced Bennet, a congenial smile coming over his countenance.

"I would be happy to speak with you, Mr. Bennet. What may I do for you?"

Bennet favored him with a slight smile. "It appears to me, Lord Chesterfield, that you have some interest in my daughter. By the same measure, I have also noticed the same interest from your cousin, Mr. Darcy."

As expected, the viscount scowled at the mention of his cousin. Bennet pressed forward. "The purpose for my request to speak to you, then, is to inform you that my Lizzy—*all* my daughters are precious to me, and I do not wish for them to be caught between warring cousins."

"I . . . I understand, Mr. Bennet," said Lord Chesterfield with a visible attempt to calm himself. "I assure you, sir, I have no intention of seeing your daughter hurt. Quite the opposite, in fact. I do not know what my cousin intends, but my intentions are entirely honorable. If, perhaps, I might beg for a courtship with her, you may be assured of her continued peace of mind."

It did not escape Bennet's attention that this man had tried, with a subtle jab, to put Bennet on his guard regarding Mr. Darcy. Bennet searched the other man's face, and he thought the viscount was not even aware he had done it. There was something happening here, something Bennet could not quite put his finger on. For some reason, Lord Chesterfield was desperate to woo Lizzy. Bennet was not about to stand for it.

"Have you proposed a courtship with Lizzy?"

"I have not yet," the viscount was forced to confess. "But if I might be so bold, I will do so forthwith, with your blessing, of course."

"At present, I think it is best to exercise prudence and refrain." The viscount's eyes bulged out, as if unable to credit that he was being refused. "I am sorry, my lord, but Lizzy appeared perturbed just now, and I do not wish her to be importuned with a proposal until she has regained her equilibrium."

The viscount attempted a smile, though it was a miserable failure. "I understand. I shall return tomorrow."

"Lord Chesterfield," said Bennet, "whether you return tomorrow, a week from now, or every day for the next month, I would wish you to know that I will not force my daughter's compliance. It is *her* decision whether to accept you, to accept Mr. Darcy, or neither."

"Do you care nothing for your daughter's happiness?"

"If I cared nothing for my daughter's happiness, she would already be beyond your reach. You *are* aware that my cousin proposed to her."

"Yes, but he is clearly unsuitable."

Bennet regarded him pointedly, and the viscount had the grace to blush. "How unsuitable do you call him? He is in possession of a valuable living, one connected to your aunt, I believe, is destined to be a gentleman himself when he inherits this estate, and would have secured my family's future in their current home."

"But he is—" Lord Chesterfield checked himself. Bennet was quite diverted when the man hesitantly completed his thought, saying: "But the man is not the most . . . intelligent specimen."

"You do not need to take care of your words with me. He is no less than a bacon-brained buffoon. But that is not the point. By society's reckoning, he is respectable and able to provide my daughter a good home, making her the wife to a gentleman someday."

"And *I* can make her a countess someday," retorted Lord Chesterfield. "I might wonder why you did not simply marry her off to your cousin, then, if he possesses all these benefits."

"Because I knew Elizabeth did not favor him." Bennet paused and grinned, which Lord Chesterfield mimicked, though he did so with reluctance. "Had Lizzy favored him, I might have questioned her sanity, but I would not have stood in her way."

"Mr. Bennet," said Lord Chesterfield, "I assure you that I am not Mr. Collins. I can give her a good home, love her as she deserves, see her take a position in society which will be the envy of many. You have no need to concern yourself with her happiness if you cede her care to me."

"I will reiterate, my lord—it is *Elizabeth's* choice. I will not force her."

"Do you not want to see your family protected?" demanded the viscount, his patience waning. "You have introduced the subject of Mr. Collins. You must know now that he will not succor your family in the event of your passing. I can secure all their futures."

Bennet restrained a sigh and forced himself not to shake his head. This man was behaving the same way many peers of his acquaintance had when Bennet attended Oxford. "That presupposes their futures need to be ensured. You know nothing of my finances nor whether I have provided for my daughters, and I will thank you not to assume or listen to every rumor you have heard. The betrothal between Mr. Bingley and my eldest also gives them some additional support."

"Bingley is in no way able to see to their care as I am," replied Lord Chesterfield. "He possesses not a fraction of the wealth of my father's earldom."

"I am certain you are correct, sir. But be that as it may, I have no intention of bartering my daughter for my family's security. I shall inform you for the last time, it is *Elizabeth's* choice. If she chooses to refuse your offer, I will support her. Do you understand?"

"I do," replied Lord Chesterfield, "though I cannot fathom what you are thinking."

"I am thinking of my daughter's happiness, my lord," replied

Bennet. "Nothing more, and nothing less. Now, if you will excuse me, I believe the time has come for you to depart."

Lord Chesterfield gave a jerky bow and turned to stalk away. Bennet watched him go, noting the stiff quickness of his stride, and he sighed. It was time to have a word with Elizabeth. Perhaps it was best to simply forbid her contact with either young man, regardless of the fuss his wife would undoubtedly raise.

CHAPTER XXVII

As Fitzwilliam rode away from the Bennet estate, he could hardly understand what he had heard there. It was unheard of in their society for a woman of Miss Elizabeth Bennet's status to refuse a man of Fitzwilliam's.

"It is almost unheard of for a man of my status to even offer for a woman of hers," said he to the air around him.

His horse whinnied in response to his frustrated words, though it did not hesitate in its steady progress toward his current place of residence. Fitzwilliam reached down with absentminded affection and patted the beast, earning a further nicker in reply. But his heart was not in the gesture, nor was his mind on his mount. The problem of Miss Elizabeth Bennet consumed his thoughts. He could think of little else.

"She is altogether far too independent," said Fitzwilliam aloud. He had a captive audience to whom he could vent his frustrations, one who would not reply with impertinence, one who would never betray him. He would use it, and perhaps he would gain some perspective.

"Then again, her independence is the trait which is, perhaps, her most alluring." Fitzwilliam paused and thought about the matter for a moment. "That and her obvious intelligence, though I will own that there are times when I wish she would show a little more respect. It is not her place to contradict me, after all. The vast majority of young ladies would not even consider it. Like they would not consider refusing me."

It was a conundrum, indeed. He *did* find Miss Elizabeth's independence to be one of her most interesting traits, but at present, it was damned inconvenient.

"Can she not understand what I can do for her?" demanded Fitzwilliam. His horse, content in its cantering pace, decided against responding. "Of course, she understands. She is an intelligent woman. Then why does she not accept my overtures with pleasure?

"And Darcy! Why can he not simply step aside as he should? And why does she seem to respond to him? *I* am the friendlier, the more amiable." Fitzwilliam snorted. "To call Darcy amiable at all is to stretch credulity beyond recognition. Darcy is a good man, but he is taciturn to the point of surliness, unapproachable, severe—she would be miserable with Darcy as a husband. Surely she would be happier with a man as open as she is herself.

"What woman would give up the opportunity to be a countess to be the wife of a mere gentleman, even if he is wealthy? I simply do not understand what she is thinking."

Fitzwilliam chewed on the matter the entire distance to Netherfield, alternately thinking about what he appreciated about Miss Elizabeth and wondering how she could be so blind as to refuse his suit. Netherfield eventually came into sight, but Fitzwilliam hardly saw it. He dismounted from his steed, entrusting it to the care of the stable hands, and went into the house, still chewing on the problem. Once he had changed with the help of his valet, he made his way back downstairs, still considering the matter.

Mr. Bennet did not bear thinking about. The man had made his position clear. If Fitzwilliam was able to persuade Miss Elizabeth, Mr. Bennet would not stand in the way. That did not prevent Fitzwilliam from thinking about how any other gentleman would leap at the chance to betroth his daughter to a viscount, whether she was willing or not. The Bennets truly were an odd family!

"What foul luck is this? The one woman I want has a father who acts as strangely as his daughter. I cannot understand the Bennets at all."

"I believe, Lord Chesterfield, that it is not for us to understand the likes of the Bennets."

Fitzwilliam started at the sound of a voice, noticing for the first time that Miss Bingley stood in the entry hall, watching him as he made his way toward the main sitting-room.

"It would be best, I believe," continued Miss Bingley, oblivious to the fact he had made no response, "to simply forget about the entire family. They can barely be called a gentle family, given the behavior of many of their members. Perhaps it would be best to simply return to town, to once again be among people whom we understand?"

Fitzwilliam regarded Miss Bingley for a moment, wondering how much of his monologue she had heard. Certainly, she had heard his comment about not understanding the Bennets. But what of the rest of it?

"It seems unlikely your brother would agree to return to London at present, considering his newly acquired status," said Fitzwilliam, choosing to push his questions to the side. Though she attempted to hide her annoyance about the matter of her brother's engagement, Fitzwilliam could see it as clearly as the bright sun on a cloudless day. "Perhaps you might induce your sister and husband to return with you to London, but if they go your brother will not have a hostess until his marriage."

Miss Bingley favored him with what she considered to be a beguiling smile. "I was not only referring to *our* return to town. I thought it might be best for us *all* to return. This society is truly not what any of us is accustomed to, and I simply believe it would do us all good if we returned to that with which we are familiar."

Ignoring for the moment her suggestion that he should quit Netherfield, Fitzwilliam replied: "The problems I previously stated will still prevent such an action, Miss Bingley. I doubt you could drag your brother away from here with a team of horses."

"Oh, I think it may be accomplished." The woman's tone was casual—too casual by half. "If someone he respected were to take him aside and persuade him it is in his best interest to return to town, I am certain Charles will be reasonable."

"I wonder at what you call reasonable," said Fitzwilliam, his tone not at all friendly. "Is it reasonable for a man to go back on his word? Should breaking an engagement, an act which is, I might add, specifically forbidden in the society in which we live, to be contemplated? It seems your definition of reasonable is different from that of most others."

"I find it eminently reasonable," said Miss Bingley, the rage he knew was coursing through her veins finally making its way into the tone of her voice. "Yes, breaking an engagement should not be contemplated, but when the family is so obviously inferior, when my brother has been tricked into offering for an unsuitable girl, I do not find bringing him to his senses and encouraging him to free himself from her grasping talons to be unreasonable at all."

"It seems to me you have a different interpretation of recent events. Your brother went to Longbourn and proposed to Miss Bennet of his own free will. There was no coercion involved. She did not attempt to compromise him. In fact, I doubt such a sweet girl as Miss Bennet could fathom making such an attempt. She is a gentleman's daughter; there is no unsuitability."

"In matters of fortune and connections, she is entirely unsuitable!" spat Miss Bingley. "Why can no one else see this?"

"I will not attempt to explain it if you do not understand. But let me inform you of a few important facts."

Fitzwilliam stepped close to the woman, looking down at her and allowing her to see the full measure of his considerable dislike for her.

"The first is that I support your brother to the fullest. He knows his own mind, and since he has decided he cannot live without Miss Bennet, it is his right to choose her.

"The second is that I have no intention to leave Netherfield at present and plan to stay for as long as your brother will have me here.

"The final item I would have you know is that I would appreciate it if you would cease to importune me concerning matters such as this. Do not presume to know what I find comfortable or acceptable regarding society or anything else. The people of this neighborhood are good, honest people, the Bennets no less than any other. I would highly appreciate it if you refrain from assuming my opinions mirror yours. I hope we understand each other."

With these final contemptuous words, Fitzwilliam stepped away from her. Though he had intended to go to the sitting-room, he changed his destination to the billiards room, knowing Miss Bingley would not follow. With any luck, the room would be empty, allowing him to take his frustrations out on the balls and billiards table. It would allow him much needed time to think.

The stinging denunciation Lord Chesterfield leveled at her sister was overheard by Louisa Hurst, and when the viscount stalked away, Louisa stayed out of sight, watching Caroline, wondering what she would do. For a moment she watched him leave, her entire being exuding affront and fury.

Then Caroline turned on her heel, her actions abrupt and her stride jerky as she marched down the hall toward the servants' area and the kitchen. Louisa had been waiting for her sister's move, knowing what havoc she was capable of unleashing.

But it would not do to be seen. When she had confirmed Caroline's destination, Louisa turned and hurried away. A few moments later, she had notified the housekeeper.

"Are the keys locked away?"

"They are, Mrs. Hurst," replied Mrs. Nichols. "The butler and I are the only ones in possession of the key to the cupboard in which they are kept."

"Good," replied Louisa. "Please watch my sister as much as you are able and inform me if she requests any keys."

Mrs. Nichols paused and spoke carefully. "What shall I do if she demands I allow her access to them?"

"She is not the mistress," replied Louisa. "She has no business with them."

Then another thought came to Louisa. The housekeeper, however, looked at her, a hint of dread in her manner, no doubt thinking of how Caroline would act should she be denied.

"If she requests it, you may provide her access to them. But I wish to know of it. I do not need to tell you that Caroline is angry and may very well do something rash." The housekeeper shook her head. "Should the worst happen, I wish to make certain all the staff are controlled and not able to witness what she does. Mr. Bingley, Mr. Hurst, and I will deal with her. I will trust in your discretion in this matter, Mrs. Nichols."

Though the staff was paid by the owner of the estate, Mrs. Nichols had been hired, in part, for her discretion. She had been in her position long enough to know when she must hold her tongue. This situation was no different.

"I understand. If Miss Bingley should ask me about the keys, I will inform you at once."

"Thank you, Mrs. Nichols. Regardless of what my sister said at times, I understand your value to this house and appreciate the efficient manner in which you see to your duties. I know my brother does likewise."

Mrs. Nichols paused again and then said: "You and your brother are quite pleasant to work for, Mrs. Hurst. The staff and I are happy to assist."

Once again, Louisa thanked her and excused herself. Caroline had, at times, been so hateful to the staff that Louisa might have expected them to spread stories regarding her with glee. Then again, some of the maids and footmen might anyway. But with Mrs. Nichols's help, perhaps that could be avoided. Louisa hoped so. She did not wish to be known as the sister of the woman who had attempted to compromise a viscount.

As soon as he entered the house, Mr. Bennet requested Elizabeth's presence in his study. She went without complaint, having suspected he would wish to speak with her about the morning's events. Elizabeth's initial shock had given away to ire at Lord Chesterfield's continual attempts to woo her in face of her clearly stated disinterest. Her father, it appeared, was in a similar state.

"This is a fine pickle in which you find yourself, is it not?"

It was typical for Mr. Bennet to alleviate uncomfortable circumstances with a jest. Elizabeth, however, was not in a mood for his flippant comments at present, a fact which her father seemed to understand at once.

"Lizzy, my dear, do not allow yourself to be cast down because of a proud man's actions. Surely looking at the matter with a little humor will not make it appear so onerous."

"That may be," replied Elizabeth, unable to keep the testy note from her voice. "But at present, I must own that I find little at which to laugh in this situation."

Mr. Bennet sighed and sat back in his chair. "You are correct, of course. I *am* concerned. For all that Lord Chesterfield came into his position only a few years ago, he behaves as if he was born to it. I would not call him haughty, precisely, but it is clear he expects to have his own way.

"And then there is Mr. Darcy. I have not missed his attention to you. Though your mother extols his virtues to the heavens, I do not like these men fighting over you as a wolf pack fights over scraps and bones."

"It is not like that, Papa."

Mr. Bennet's eyebrow rose in question. "Oh? Then you should inform me because I am much in need of reassurance. Has Mr. Darcy behaved better than his cousin?"

"He has," replied Elizabeth. Part of her wished to keep her interactions with Mr. Darcy between them alone, for it was a private, wonderful, and personal matter, one to be treasured and savored. But she knew her father, as her guardian, had the right to know of their dealings together, tasked, as he was, with her safety.

"Mr. Darcy has been nothing but a gentleman, father."

"The implication being that Lord Chesterfield has *not* been a gentleman?" asked her father, leaning forward and directing his intent gaze at Elizabeth.

"No, I would not say that. The viscount has never ventured beyond propriety. I have never felt threatened by him. I am only frustrated that he does not seem to understand that I have no interest in him."

Mr. Bennet snorted. "It is not surprising. Most men of his status are raised to believe they can have whatever they want, whenever they deign to ask for it."

A nod was Elizabeth's response. "Though when we first met him I would not have said that was a faithful portrait of his character; it seems to have become so, increasingly, of late."

"Enough of Lord Chesterfield, then. What of Mr. Darcy?"

Elizabeth considered it and chuckled. "When we first met them, Mr. Darcy presented himself as a taciturn man, and I initially thought him to be too proud to give his attention to so inferior a company as he might find here. But it was soon revealed to be nothing more than reserve, for Mr. Darcy is well able to please the company. He is intelligent and rational, and he speaks to me as an equal. When I speak to Lord Chesterfield, I experience this feeling that he is intent upon flattering me, as if he believes such behavior is the key to a woman's heart. It is as if he is competing with his cousin for my good opinion."

"That agrees with my own observation," said Mr. Bennet, nodding and rubbing his chin his in thought. He paused for a moment. "I *had* given thought to simply insist you have no contact with *either* gentleman. But given what you have told me, I do not think you would welcome that. Am I correct?"

When he first suggested he might forbid her contact with Mr. Darcy, Elizabeth felt a panic well up within her, which was only forced back down by his subsequent words. Though he appeared to be leaving the decision to her, Elizabeth sensed that her future association with Mr. Darcy was in the balance. Thus, she replied accordingly.

"I do not wish it, Papa. I could cheerfully do without the viscount's attentions. But I have begun to esteem Mr. Darcy very much. He is . . ." Elizabeth paused and directed a helpless look at her father, which prompted a grin in return. "He is, perhaps, not the kind of man I had thought would turn my head. But I am rapidly coming to the conclusion that he is the best of men, and when he speaks gently to me, I feel my heart responding. No, I would not wish to be barred from his acquaintance."

"As I suspected," replied her father. He rose from his chair and came to sit near Elizabeth, his hands upon her shoulders as he gazed directly into his eyes. "I only ask you to be certain as you can about this Mr. Darcy. I would not wish you, my daughter, to be hurt by either of these men, if they are only vying for the attention of the brightest light in the district. If you are certain, then I shall not stand in your way."

The love she felt in his words touched Elizabeth, and she felt tears well up in her eyes. A verbal response seemed impossible, so she only nodded her head. Mr. Bennet smiled at her and rose to place a kiss on her forehead. Then he returned to his seat behind the desk, and Elizabeth excused herself from his bookroom.

Though Elizabeth thought to return to her room for a little much-needed solitude, her mother appeared to have been listening for her. As soon as she exited the room, Elizabeth heard her voice, beckoning her into the sitting-room. Elizabeth thought of feigning ignorance of her mother's summons, but she knew Mrs. Bennet would only come looking for her in her room. It was best to simply respond so that she might escape all that much sooner.

"Well, what did your father say?" demanded Mrs. Bennet when she caught sight of Elizabeth. All her sisters were present, Mary and Jane looking at her with concern, while Kitty and Lydia spoke softly together, sending her what they thought were surreptitious looks. Elizabeth contented herself with ignoring them.

"He only wished to ask me about Lord Chesterfield," replied Elizabeth.

Mrs. Bennet huffed. "And well he should. While Lord Chesterfield presented himself to be a man who was everything amiable and good when he first came, I must own that I now have some reservations about his character. I thought to match him with Lydia, but now I am not certain I could withstand seeing my daughter with a man of his ilk."

Surprised did not even begin to describe Elizabeth's reaction to her mother's words. Mrs. Bennet had never so much as spoken against any man of wealth before—at least not until after they had proven their indifference to her daughters. It was sometimes difficult to remember that her mother had changed much these past months.

"Oh, do not look at me in such a way, Lizzy," said Mrs. Bennet in a testy tone. "I am well able to see when a man is not behaving as he should. It is clear Mr. Darcy is the better man between the two cousins, even if he is reserved." Mrs. Bennet turned a warm smile on her eldest. "Of course, our Jane is quite reserved herself, so I do not know that we can label the trait as a poor one."

Jane blushed but did not say anything. By her side, Mary seemed a little displeased.

"I do not think the viscount is a bad man, Mama."

"No, I suspect you are correct," replied Mrs. Bennet, nodding at her middle daughter slowly. "But I do not know *what* to make of him. His behavior has deteriorated the longer he has been here, and I find myself quite confused about *who* he truly is."

"With that, I cannot argue," replied Mary. Her voice was quiet and introspective, but then again, Mary often was, even with the progress she had made these past months.

"Regardless," continued Mrs. Bennet, turning her attention back to Elizabeth, "I do declare that it is best that you avoid Lord Chesterfield as much as possible and focus on Mr. Darcy. I am certain he is quite taken by you. Should you only expend a little effort to inform him of your regard, there is every indication that he will make you an offer."

Mrs. Bennet sighed, a dreamy expression appearing on her countenance. "Two daughters married, and to such good men. What an excellent thought to consider! You will both be happy with such good men, I am absolutely certain, and we shall be saved from the tyranny of the odious Mr. Collins."

The sisters all exchanged looks, and they smiled, though attempting to hide them from Mrs. Bennet. *This* was much more like the Mrs. Bennet they all knew, though a tempered version to be certain. In this instance, however, Elizabeth thought her mother was correct. Jane could not be anything other than happy with Mr. Bingley, and Elizabeth's opinion that she would live a blissful existence with Mr. Darcy was growing daily.

Such silliness again threatened to produce a laugh. Life would provide hardships aplenty, and no one could be in a state of ecstasy at all times. But finding the right man to provide assistance and return that aid throughout the course of her life would be a boon which could not be discounted. And suddenly Elizabeth anticipated his coming again very much, very much, indeed.

"I believe Elizabeth is caught up in thoughts of her beau," said Lydia *sotto voce*.

"Of course, she is!" replied Kitty, her response suffused with her typical giggles. "Who would not wish to be the object of that man's desire?"

"Who, indeed?" asked Elizabeth, intending to turn her sisters' teasing back on them. "Perhaps if you both behave yourselves, you may find a man who is determined to make love to you too."

Lydia, however, only ignored her. "I am not certain *I* would wish to be the object of Mr. Darcy's affection. Though he carries on charmingly with Lizzy, I believe he might be too stuffy for me, and I would not wish a husband to forever be spouting poetry to me."

"Trust me, Lydia, it is not a hardship at all to be the recipient of a man's attempts at wooing you with poetry."

"Perhaps," replied Lydia, her tone noncommittal. "Of course, it does not at all hurt that he is as handsome a man as any of us have ever seen."

The sisters exchanged glances, and they all laughed. Even Mrs. Bennet joined in the merriment. Elizabeth, though she saw the humor in Lydia's words, contented herself with a few chuckles and a glare at them all.

"He is even more handsome than Mr. Wickham, who we all know has as good of face and feature as anyone else."

"Lydia!" scolded Elizabeth, ignoring the embarrassment which Lydia's words provoked. "After all we have heard of Mr. Wickham, how can you speak of him in such a manner?"

"I do not care three figs for Mr. Wickham," countered Lydia. "I only speak the truth. Can you say that Mr. Wickham is not handsome, almost as much so as Mr. Darcy?"

"I dare say he possesses a pleasant countenance, my dear," said Mrs. Bennet. "But his fairness of face and ability to charm is undone by his vicious character. It renders a pleasing countenance so much less appealing."

"I agree, Mama," said Elizabeth, feeling as if her mother was surprising her at every turn of late. "Beauty fades with age, Lydia. I would prefer to marry a good man, rather than a pretty one."

"What a funny way you have of referring to Mr. Wickham!" exclaimed Kitty. "Pretty, indeed."

"I expect he thinks that much of himself," said Elizabeth. "Given how he attempts to make love to us all."

"Well, I think I can have both," said Lydia. "Once my foot heals and I can dance with gentlemen again." Lydia shook the offending appendage—which had improved enough to allow her to walk without much of a limp.

"It seems like Lizzy will be the next one to be engaged," said Mary, winking at Elizabeth. "The way Mr. Darcy was carrying on yesterday, I am sure he means to propose soon."

At Mary's words, there was a chorus of feminine laughter, and a plethora of teasing comments directed at Elizabeth. But she was happy to receive them and parry them in her turn. Never had she felt closer to her sisters, even the youngest, who often tried her patience.

CHAPTER XXVIII

*I*t was the day after Fitzwilliam's visit that Darcy made his way back to Longbourn in Bingley's company. The previous day, after attending Bingley in his study, Darcy had planned to visit Longbourn again. But an urgent letter from his steward had prevented his going, and he had spent the rest of the morning drafting a response. By the time he had completed that unavoidable task, he could not justify imposing himself upon them. In a certain way, he almost envied Fitzwilliam, for his father was still alive and managing the family estates.

Darcy pushed those feelings to the side. The pang he felt for his father's absence when he thought of such matters once again hit him. *That* was the true reason he would wish for his father's presence, not for any wish to avoid the responsibility of Pemberley.

Fitzwilliam had been in a foul mood that evening, after having disappeared somewhere the previous morning while Darcy was engaged with Bingley. Darcy was content to leave the man alone, as he had found his ill humors and pride difficult to endure the past days. When they had been in each other's company that morning, little was said by either. Darcy and Bingley had excused themselves to depart, and Fitzwilliam had watched Darcy go, his gaze accusing. He had almost expected Fitzwilliam to follow them, to insist on visiting the Bennets himself. He did not, and Darcy was grateful for it.

When the gentlemen presented themselves at the door to Longbourn that morning, they were admitted readily enough. But there was something different about the atmosphere of the estate. For one, the estate's mistress watched him, betraying nothing, but somehow expectant. Darcy could not quite understand her. The two youngest were not present that morning, and while the three elder sisters greeted him pleasantly enough—though Miss Bennet, understandably, had eyes only for Bingley—he was still assailed by that feeling of being watched. Or perhaps it was as if they were judging him. The only one who seemed unaffected by whatever had come over them was Miss Elizabeth, who appeared as happy to see him as he was to see her.

Contrary to what he might have expected, when Darcy greeted the ladies and was welcomed by them, he was largely left to the sole company of Miss Elizabeth. Miss Bennet and Bingley were soon seated together, heads in close proximity as they spoke in soft tones to each other, while Miss Mary took herself to another room, and soon the sounds of a pianoforte reached them. Mrs. Bennet remained, but she only watched over her charges, a fashion magazine, which Darcy noted she rarely even looked at, held loosely in her hands.

"Did something . . . happen, Miss Elizabeth?" asked Darcy when they were seated together and afforded relative privacy.

Miss Elizabeth's responding gaze gave nothing away. "Why do you say that?"

"A feeling, I suppose." Darcy paused and thought on the matter. "It seems that as I entered this morning I was carefully watched in a manner I have not noticed before. There appears to be an atmosphere, almost like . . ."

"Like what?" prompted Miss Elizabeth.

"Expectation? Wariness? In truth, I am not certain. I did not feel unwelcome when I entered, but it seemed like everyone held their breath." Darcy laughed ruefully. "I do not imagine that Bingley often provokes such a reaction when *he* comes."

Miss Elizabeth laughed, pulling Darcy along with her. A trickle of relief entered his mind, for if she was able to express her mirth in his presence, he could not be the reason this change he detected. Or could he?

"Perhaps we are a little wary, sir," replied Miss Elizabeth. "There have been many changes in the neighborhood of late, and we have learned of some less than estimable characters which have come into our midst. And then . . ."

Perplexed as he was by her words, Darcy smiled at her and urged her to continue. She did, but not without hesitating first.

"I am afraid to speak openly, sir. I do not wish to speak ill of anyone of your acquaintance."

"You know I will not judge you for it," said Darcy. Inside he was considering what she had said, and a moment's thought later, he could only think of two she could possibly be speaking of. Unless, of course, Miss Bingley had come t̶o̶ ̶a̶n̶n̶o̶y̶ them yet again. Darcy did not think so—that woman would stay far from Longbourn, given the circumstances of her last visit.

"Your cousin visited yesterday."

Darcy had to strain to hear her words, and when he understood their import, it was all he could do to avoid scowling. What the blazes had Fitzwilliam been doing now?

"And his coming is cause for consternation?"

"It is when he refuses to believe that I have no interest in him."

Her words were spoken in a tone which was more heated than what she usually used. Darcy was relieved to hear about her lack of interest in his cousin, but at the same point, he felt her annoyance for him for continuing to importune her.

"What has Fitzwilliam done now?" asked Darcy, feeling the unfamiliar annoyance with Fitzwilliam welling up within him again.

Miss Elizabeth proceeded to explain the happenings of the previous day, and the picture she painted was not a pleasing one. Darcy did not know what had happened to his cousin, but it seemed like Fitzwilliam was becoming the privileged noble he had always despised. His vow to prove himself to Miss Elizabeth, Darcy dismissed with nary a thought. The only way he could do so was to behave properly and cease to importune where he was not wanted.

The other part of Darcy was heartened. It was true that her disinterest in Fitzwilliam did not necessarily mean she wished to receive a proposal from Darcy himself, but it was certainly a good sign. Her words, her actions, all the little hints a woman displays when interested in a man told Darcy she was receptive to his overtures. But he was a man in love who still fretted about whether the woman of his affections would accept him.

Suddenly Darcy wished to know, and he thought this was an opportunity to not only be certain of her feelings but also provide her with protection from his cousin. He had long passed the point of admiration and interest, and he thought he loved this amazing young country miss. They would be unassailable together. Darcy very much wished to finalize their relationship.

"I am curious, though, Mr. Darcy," said Miss Elizabeth, breaking through Darcy's thoughts.

"I will answer if I am able."

"Your uncle, the earl. Should he become aware of his heir's interest in me, would he not disapprove? The Bennets have no connection to the nobility. I would not have thought his lordship would settle for anything less than a peer's daughter."

Darcy's heart almost skipped a beat at her mention of Fitzwilliam's father, but he tamped it down quickly. It was a legitimate question to ask. Darcy wondered when he had become this nervous—it was not usually in his nature to over analyze to such an extent. Then again, he had never had his happiness bound in the person of a single young woman.

"My uncle is quite liberal-minded," replied Darcy. "Perhaps he might pause should Fitzwilliam choose you as a bride, but I think in the end he would put his son's happiness first." Darcy paused and chuckled. "My uncle often complains that he has more alliances with objectionable people than he can remember. Perhaps you would be a breath of fresh air to him."

"Then I am sorry to disappoint him," replied Miss Elizabeth. "I know you are close to your cousin, sir, but I have always felt that he did not speak to me as a man speaking to a woman he esteems."

"Oh?" asked Darcy, trying to understand her. "In what way?"

"His constant flattery," said Miss Elizabeth, her frustration appearing in her voice, "By contrast, when you first came, he was friendly and did not stoop to inconsequential flattery."

"Fitzwilliam often flatters," replied Darcy without thinking. "He is easy in society, and it seems to come as second nature to him."

"Then I wonder if he is serious enough. When *you* speak to me, I feel like you are speaking of subjects of substance, not just meaningless chatter. I feel like my opinion is valued and respected."

"Anyone must respect your opinions, Miss Elizabeth. It is clear from speaking with you that you are intelligent. What you say is colored by rational thought, not the whims of the moment."

"I should hope not, and I thank you for it, sir." Miss Elizabeth smiled. "Then there you have it. My father spoke with your cousin yesterday and informed him it would be my choice whether to accept or refuse any overtures. I believe he went away unhappy, little comprehending why I would not just fall at his feet in thanks for being blessed with the favor of his attention."

"I can hardly fathom what has become of him," replied Darcy with a shaken head. "He has always been an excellent man. His fascination with you does not seem to me to be indicative of a true regard. You are unlike any other woman he has ever encountered. Perhaps it was my actions which led to his desire to best me. When we were younger, he was a younger son, and I was the heir of a large estate."

"You think he envied you?"

"It is possible, but I do not think so. It seems more likely to me that he has acquired this notion that he should have what he wants, and if we both wish it, I must give way to him."

"That is silly, Mr. Darcy," said Miss Elizabeth her tone chiding.

"I do not disagree."

"There is perhaps a way to ensure he does not bother you any longer," said Darcy, after thinking about it for a moment. "Unfortunately, I could never betray my cousin in such a way, so I must simply trust in my own efforts to win you."

"What way is that, Mr. Darcy?" asked Miss Elizabeth, her eyes alight with curiosity.

"It may be best if I did not say, but as it concerns you, I will tell you." Darcy hazarded a glance at Bingley and noticed that he was far too engrossed in his conversation with Miss Bennet to hear them. Nevertheless, he spoke in a softer tone. "Netherfield, Miss Bennet, is a difficult place at present. I am sure you know how difficult Miss Bingley can be?"

When Miss Elizabeth nodded with a grimace, Darcy continued: "When Bingley returned with the news of his engagement to your sister, Miss Bingley did not take it well. Saying this is akin to stating Napoleon is mildly ambitious. I do not wish to dwell on it, but let us simply say she waxed long and eloquent about all the reasons her brother could not possibly marry your sister."

"I am not surprised," was all Miss Elizabeth said, though it was clear to Darcy she was clinging to her temper.

"After we had experienced enough of her tirade, Fitzwilliam and I departed, but not before Fitzwilliam made a rude comment to Bingley about his sister. Bingley, of course, took offense. Miss Bingley is angry and determined to capture Fitzwilliam, I have been annoyed with my cousin and he with me, and we have had little peace since the ball. Furthermore, it seems that Miss Bingley is determined to capture Fitzwilliam by any means necessary."

Miss Elizabeth gasped. "She means to compromise him?"

"Her sister believes so," replied Darcy. "So you see, it is a difficult situation. If she tries and fails, the Bingleys' reputation suffers. Her presence is already a strain on our friendship, and Bingley has had to contend with a difficult sister when this should be a happy time."

At that moment, Miss Elizabeth proved herself to be an excellent woman. She thought about the matter for several moments, chewing on her bottom lip as she did so. Darcy watched her with a fond smile, for as a habit, it was endearing. And alluring, he was forced to own, though he controlled himself with an iron will.

"As tempting as it may be, your cousin does not deserve to be forced into marriage in such a way."

Darcy laughed. "I can only agree. I will own, however, that both Bingley and I thought initially to leave him to his devices with her — or at least that he *deserved* that fate. You are clearly a much better person for not coming to that conclusion."

"I never said I did not consider it, Mr. Darcy," said Miss Elizabeth, her eyebrow arched mischievously. "I only took some time to formulate my reply before speaking."

They laughed together at her admission. "Then perhaps you are just as fallible as we are, Miss Elizabeth. But I still must say that even taking time to think about it before saying the first thing to cross your mind is admirable."

"By all means, Mr. Darcy," replied Miss Elizabeth. "Make my feeble attempts to avoid saying something I ought not into virtues. I am quite delighted by it." She then sobered and looked up at him. "I hope your cousin is taking precautions against Miss Bingley's schemes."

"My cousin knows nothing of our suspicions," replied Darcy. Miss Elizabeth's countenance darkened with confusion, but Darcy hastened to say: "I believe the bulk of the plans to thwart Miss Bingley's attempt is being borne by Mrs. Hurst. She is the one who reported it to her brother, and they both believe — and I concur — that it would be best if she is prevented without Fitzwilliam's knowledge. Their reputations are at stake, after all."

Miss Elizabeth nodded slowly. "I suppose you are correct."

"I also must own that as no one at Netherfield is very happy with my cousin at present, none of us wish to risk his further misbehavior by bringing it to his attention."

"Your choice of words suggests that you will not leave him in ignorance forever."

Darcy agreed. "I may inform him eventually. Miss Bennet, you must understand that my cousin of the past few weeks is not the man I have known all my life. If I can use this to remind him of himself, I shall do it. Though I find myself vexed with him, I wish my cousin returned to me."

"I understand, sir. If Jane were behaving in such a way, I believe I would feel the same."

"There is another matter which has arisen recently. I do not know if you are aware, but your father visited Netherfield the last time you saw Wickham."

Miss Elizabeth frowned. "I was not aware."

Darcy nodded—he had suspected as much. "I have sent for the debt receipts I hold, and I intend to use them to ensure Wickham is no longer a problem."

"You will call them in?"

"When I first heard of his continued malfeasance, I had thought of holding them over his head to force his good behavior. Further reflection has convinced me that I have allowed him to carry on hurting other people longer than I should have. I will see him in prison to pay for his misdeeds."

Miss Elizabeth looked at him, her gaze seeming to see through to his innermost thoughts. "Will you do this on my account, Mr. Darcy?"

It was a fair question, and Darcy could not help but admire her all over again. "I have given some thought to this matter as well, Miss Elizabeth. I will own that my initial determination was motivated, in no small part, to protect you. But I now see where I have erred, and I wish to correct my mistake."

Darcy paused and considered the matter, then directed an abashed look at her. "When we were children, Wickham and I played together, as you know. I considered him a friend. Though I have known what he is for many years, I realize now that part of me did not wish to lose hope that he was beyond redemption. He was my father's favorite, Miss Elizabeth, and condemning him to a life in prison seemed a betrayal of my father."

"You father might still love him as his mentor," replied Miss Elizabeth. "But he would not like the man he has become."

"Again, you see clearly." Darcy shook his head. "And you saw this in a matter of weeks, while I have struggled with it for years."

"But I do not have an emotional attachment to the situation, Mr. Darcy. That must cloud your thinking."

"That is true. But your perspicacity still amazes me. You are like no other lady I have ever met."

The rosy blush on Miss Elizabeth' cheeks told Darcy she was not unaffected. Now was the time, he decided.

"Miss Elizabeth," began he in a soft voice, reaching out to grasp one of her hands in his own, "I feel . . . I feel a close connection to you. As I said, I have never met anyone who affects me as you do. I find I am captivated by your poise and charm, entranced by your intelligence and wit, and helpless before your beauty and goodness."

"Then I must think you blind, sir," said Miss Elizabeth Her cheeks were so stained with red he might have thought she had just come in from a cold day. "Jane is the beauty of the family."

Of its own accord, Darcy's finger reached out to stroke her jaw. Her eyes darted up to meet his, and Darcy could almost feel himself falling into them, as if diving into the warmth of their clear, brown depths. She leaned into his hand, and Darcy, mindful of propriety, stroked her cheek once more before allowing his hand to fall.

"I beg to differ, Miss Elizabeth," said he, his voice rough-sounding to his own ears. "Your sister is, indeed, very pretty. But I have never seen a more beautiful sight before me than I do now. You have bewitched me, and I have no hope if you do not consent to a courtship with me."

"Only a courtship?" asked she, her laughter bubbling up and caressing him like the wind on a spring day. "My sister received a proposal, and all I receive is a request for a courtship?"

Darcy grinned back at her. "Bingley is more impetuous than I am myself. I am more measured and rational."

"Ah, but love is anything but rational."

"Miss Elizabeth, are you attempting to elicit a proposal from me?"

His raised eyebrow caused another laugh. "No, Mr. Darcy. A courtship would be wonderful."

Then all was right in his world. Indeed, Darcy could imagine many days of happiness ahead with this wonderful creature at his side.

Since Bennet had spoken with Mr. Darcy's cousin only the previous day, he thought it prudent to speak with Mr. Darcy as well, and his wife alerting him to the man's presence provided that opportunity. The same warning Bennet had given Darcy's cousin would need to be imparted to the gentleman himself.

That Mr. Darcy might seek him out first, Bennet had never considered. When the man sat in front of him, regarding him with his usual gravity, Bennet wondered what had happened to precipitate his request for an audience. Surely he could not be so precipitous as to request this for the usual reason a young man accosted a lady's father!

"Mr. Bennet," began Mr. Darcy when they had exchanged the usual pleasantries, "I have asked to see you this morning because I have requested a courtship from your daughter, Miss Elizabeth, and she has accepted me. I come begging for your permission and blessing."

It was a pretty speech, indeed. Bennet did not think Mr. Darcy often assumed such a humble demeanor. But Bennet could hardly think of *that*—he was shocked that the man had moved so quickly, and even more so that Lizzy had accepted. Did she already esteem him that much?"

"I apologize for not answering immediately, Mr. Darcy, but you have surprised me exceedingly."

Mr. Darcy regarded him with impassive attention. "Surely my interest in your daughter was not ambiguous."

"No, Mr. Darcy, they were not." Mr. Bennet sighed. "But given the difficulty which has persisted for my Lizzy with your cousin, I am surprised you have acted so quickly." Bennet paused and fixed Mr. Darcy with a stern glare. "Or perhaps it is not. With your cousin competing with you for Elizabeth's attention, I suppose it makes sense you would ask for her hand first."

"No, Mr. Bennet, I did not apply for the courtship in order to obtain it before Fitzwilliam could. I do understand why you might think that, but I assure you that I offered for your daughter for no other reason than because I have come to esteem her."

The man was calm and apparently able to hold his temper. Good, thought Bennet. He would need his wits about him to keep up with Elizabeth.

"And Elizabeth accepted?" asked Bennet, though he knew it was rhetorical at that point.

"She did."

"Then I give you both my permission and blessing. I believe you will be good for Lizzy, as you are a man who can match her in wit and understanding. Yet I suspect you will not attempt to stifle that intelligence which defines her character.

"But I will tell you what I told your cousin, sir," added Bennet. "It is Lizzy's choice and hers alone whether to accept you or not, and I do not consider a courtship to be binding. If she decides in the end that she does not wish to marry you, I will support her decision."

"I understand," replied Mr. Darcy. "I do not consider myself engaged to her. I will do everything in my power to induce her to accept my hand when I offer it. She is too great a prize to consider anything else.

"Very well," replied Bennet with a nod. The young man was saying all the right things. The question was, would he follow through when the matter came to a head? Only time would tell.

Fitzwilliam very nearly got up and followed Darcy and Bingley, joining them on their visit to Longbourn. In the end, however, he decided against it, though he could not quite understand the reason himself. Giving Darcy unfettered access to Miss Elizabeth seemed akin to a disaster. But when he considered going along with them, the memory of Miss Elizabeth's face as she informed him she did not wish for a closer connection with him entered his mind, and he was taken aback by it again. If she was so disinclined, why would he impose himself on her?

It was a matter Fitzwilliam could not quite understand—why she would refuse him, yet accept Darcy when his position was so clearly inferior to Fitzwilliam's own. A small voice inside his head added a question to the cacophony of voices fighting for supremacy in his mind—why was it so important that he win her anyway?

This last question became more and more prevalent in Fitzwilliam's mind the longer the day dragged on, but Fitzwilliam did his best to ignore it. There was little to occupy himself. Bingley and Darcy were both, of course, gone to Longbourn. The only other gentleman resident of the estate was Hurst, but even if Fitzwilliam enjoyed his company at times, he was often an inadequate companion. Today was not the best of times, for he was sleeping off an excess of drink from the previous night.

Finally, in desperation, Fitzwilliam had his horse saddled and rode into Meryton, seeking relief from his tumultuous thoughts. Perhaps a little time perusing Meryton's shops would allow him to finally bring his wayward thoughts under control. At the very least, it was better than brooding in his room or pacing the sitting-room, waiting for Bingley and Darcy to return.

As was typical for an early afternoon, the streets of the small town were abustle with those going about their business. Here and there, the more elaborate dress of a gentlewoman stood out against the drab clothing of the lower classes. But he did not see anyone he knew, which suited Fitzwilliam well. He spent some time in the bookshop, but he was not Darcy and could not spend hours there. Soon he was engaged in wandering up and down the main street, peering in through dusty shop windows at the merchandise inside. It was while he was thus engaged that he was interrupted by the sound of a detested voice.

"I never thought to see you slumming in a small market down, Fitzwilliam."

Fitzwilliam straightened and turned to face the smirking visage of Wickham. "You do not have the right to address me in such an informal way, Wickham. You will address me as 'Lord Chesterfield' if you wish to keep your freedom."

"Of course, my lord," said Wickham, dropping into a mocking bow. "You have my apologies for neglecting to show you the proper respect." Wickham paused and peered about. "I suppose Darcy is somewhere nearby? It is rare that you not in each other's company when you are in the same neighborhood."

A pang for the strained state of his friendship with his cousin ripped through Fitzwilliam's heart, but he pushed it aside. "Darcy is at Longbourn, I believe. I had no business there, so I did not impose upon them."

"Why would you need a matter of business as an excuse to visit a neighbor? Has business replaced good manners?"

Fitzwilliam fixed Wickham with a level look. "Why this interest in my doings, Wickham? What is it to you if I call on the Bennets?"

"It is nothing at all."

"Then why speak of it?"

The shrug with which Wickham responded was casual and entirely false. What the man's purpose was, Fitzwilliam could not quite determine. But Fitzwilliam was certain he had some reason for accosting him in the streets, and knowing Wickham, it could not be good.

"To be honest, I had thought you had some particular reason for going to Longbourn. Or have my eyes deceived me?"

"When have you ever been honest?"

Wickham's eyes flashed. "Is it not odd that much of what you have heard of me has come from Darcy? To the best of my knowledge, you and I have never had any reason to quarrel."

Fitzwilliam snorted. "Are you trying to inform me that Darcy has misrepresented you in some way?"

"I know not precisely what Darcy has told you, so I cannot say one way or another. But it does strike me as strange that while you and I have never had any disputes between us, you assume that I have always been in the wrong. The one common factor here is Darcy."

"And you did not take three thousand pounds in exchange for giving up the living? You are not a degenerate wastrel, some of which I have seen for myself? You did not leave debts behind at every place in which you have ever stayed, ruining the livelihoods of good and honest men for nothing more than your own selfish desires? Are you not that kind of man?"

"I do not wish to rehash old matters—"

"I do," replied Fitzwilliam. "If you claim that you are not the man Darcy has represented you to be, then you must be accusing Darcy of falsehood. Tell me at once, Wickham—have you not engaged in all these activities and more?"

"It matters little what I say. I am not an angel. I have never claimed to be. But my behavior has not been as bad as Darcy claims."

"Then explain how he has misrepresented you."

Wickham fixed him with a stony look. "There is little to be gained, for you are already set against me. Consider this, however: while you slum in Meryton, looking through shop windows at merchandise in which you have no interest, Darcy is at Longbourn making love to the woman you want as your own. He has always behaved in this manner, for he has always assumed that whatever he wants is his by right. The question is, what will you do about it?"

Leaving those final words echoing in his ears, Wickham turned and walked away, leaving Fitzwilliam to think. Was what the man said the truth?

But the moment passed, and Fitzwilliam's eyes found Wickham as he walked away, glaring at him. Wickham was nothing more than a snake, his forked tongue spewing lies wherever he went. Though Fitzwilliam had Darcy's word about the manner in which he had lived his life to a large extent, he had actually seen some of the debt receipts, had seen the contract which exchanged the money for Wickham's claim on the living. For the other matters, while Fitzwilliam had not as much experience with Wickham as Darcy had, he had seen enough to know that Wickham was not a good man.

But the voice in the back of his head whispered to him, repeating what Wickham had said about Darcy and the Bennets, and his ire from the previous day began to rise again, bringing with it the bitterness of being rejected by the woman he wanted. She had chosen Darcy, and Fitzwilliam still had no notion of why.

Still chewing on his thoughts, Fitzwilliam turned and made his way to the end of town where he had tied his horse's reins to a post. The matter still churned within his mind, though Wickham had largely been forgotten. As such, it did not occur to Fitzwilliam to wonder how Wickham knew of his dealings with the Bennet family and, in particular, Miss Elizabeth.

Chapter XXIX

$\mathcal{F}$itzwilliam was nothing less than an idiot. But he was a useful one. When he had left the barracks, Wickham had had no notion of seeing the man in Meryton and approaching him had been the impulse of a moment. Wickham did not know whether his gambit had any real effect, but it would at least add to the man's confusion. At present, Wickham had more important matters to consider.

As he had known they would, the men assigned to watch him were less diligent after a few days of nothing happening. This worked to Wickham's advantage, for when the time came to depart, he would find it easier to give them the slip and make his retreat. But before he could do so, he had business to finish, business which would end being very profitable, both for his purse, and in . . . other benefits. It was truly unfortunate he was forced to deal with a fool and a termagant to get what he wanted.

Collins was waiting for him as usual, taking care not to be seen. As well he should — Darcy and Mr. Bennet would not be pleased to learn the parson was still in the area. He was as foppish as ever, his lank, greasy hair plastered against his head, as if he was sweating, even in the middle of winter. What an odd creature he was. But his stupidity worked to Wickham's advantage, for it was nothing to mislead him in any way Wickham chose.

"We need to make our move soon, Collins," said Wickham without preamble. "It is nearing the time for me to depart from Meryton. If Lady Catherine wishes my assistance, she had best make her decision now."

"Lady Catherine is not to be dictated to by the likes of you," replied Collins with an arrogant sniff. "It is a privilege to assist her in whatever matter she requires of us."

"You are her parson, are you not?"

Collins puffed himself up with pride. "I am. Lady Catherine chose *me* among many candidates for the position. I am her most trusted advisor."

Wickham almost laughed in the man's face. The only reason Lady Catherine had chosen such a toadying worm as Collins was because she surrounded herself by those who would never dream of disagreeing with her.

"But you have a home, a roof over your head, and a steady income. I am willing to help Lady Catherine obtain that which she desires, but I cannot live on her ladyship's good will alone. If she wishes my help, she will meet by price."

"You should be happy to serve!"

"Altruism is well and good, but a man needs to make his way in the world."

A sniff of disdain met Wickham's words. "You have no need to worry. Lady Catherine had agreed to pay you what you want."

"Excellent," exulted Wickham. He had known all along how it would be. Darcy and Pemberley were far too great a prize for Lady Catherine to refuse to pay him, though it had taken longer to persuade her than Wickham might have thought. Now it was done, and they could move on with their plans.

"Then we will proceed as soon as is practicable. When we are finished with them, no one of any reputation will marry Miss Elizabeth, and Darcy will go crawling to Lady Catherine for permission to marry her daughter."

An unpleasant smile of glee was Collins's response. "I shall inform Lady Catherine."

"A piece of advice, Collins." The parson turned and directed a questioning glance at Wickham. "Please ensure Lady Catherine understands that she needs to leave this matter strictly to us. No word of our agreement should make it back to those at Netherfield, else all will be ruined."

316 *ᨏ Jann Rowland

"I will tell her," replied the parson, and then he was gone.

Wickham then left himself, knowing he would only have so long before he was missed. The sweet scent of revenge was filling his nostrils. He could hardly wait.

That night the event for which they had all been waiting took place.

"We are to be brothers, my friend!" said an irrepressible Bingley, raising his glass in a toast. "It is not in the manner which Caroline always wished, but I am quite happy whether she appreciates the irony or not."

"We shall be indeed," said Darcy, raising his glass to his friend before sipping from it. "Though I have nothing but a courtship at present, I am confident in my eventual success. I cannot but feel we are the luckiest men alive."

"Here, here! I will own, however, that I am surprised you decided to pursue Miss Elizabeth. She is everything lovely and more than a match for you, I dare say, but I had thought your fastidious nature might get the better of you."

"It very nearly did," said Darcy, thinking about his conversations with Fitzwilliam soon after they had arrived. Though his annoyance with his cousin had not dissipated in the slightest, he knew he owed much to Fitzwilliam for setting him straight. Darcy might have dismissed the notion of an alliance with Miss Elizabeth out of hand, had Fitzwilliam not opened his eyes.

"Was it merely my imagination," asked Bingley, pulling Darcy from his thoughts, "or did Fitzwilliam look on you with less heat tonight?"

"I noticed the same," said Darcy. "It may just be my imagination, but he appeared more pensive than anything."

"'It has been hard, I suppose. I hope you do not lose your closeness because of this. It would be a shame, considering how close you have always been."

"Indeed," replied Darcy, though he could hardly hear his own words.

"Do you know where he went after dinner?"

Darcy looked up. "The billiards room, I assume. I think Hurst joined him."

"He has been wearing out the balls on the billiards table these past days," replied Bingley. "I have never seen him play so much."

"Nor have I. But it keeps him occupied. I have not the stomach for his poor mood or his injured silences."

"I understand, my friend."

They sat speaking in a desultory fashion for some time, though both were more engaged in their own thoughts than in exchanging words. When they had been there for some time, Darcy began to give thought to retiring to his room for the night. His thoughts were interrupted by an urgent knocking on the door.

When Bingley gave permission to enter, his eldest sister hurried into the room. Her distress was evident for them both to see."

"Charles, you must come now!"

Bingley paled and shared a glance with Darcy, who knew they were both thinking the same thing.

"Please, Charles, we must hurry!"

"Mrs. Hurst," said Darcy, rising to speak to the distressed woman. "You can trust in my secrecy. Your brother has already shared your suspicions with me. Has your sister made her move?"

Though Mrs. Hurst regarded him with shock, she soon gathered her wits and nodded. "The housekeeper reported to me this afternoon that Caroline had requested keys for various chambers. Her maid has just informed me that she was dismissed for the evening and instructed to go to Lord Chesterfield's room after the viscount retired for the evening, no doubt to catch them *in flagrante*. As his lordship's man has been dismissed for the night, I have no doubt she is making the attempt even as we speak."

The dismissal of his valet was a legacy of Fitzwilliam's time in the army. He maintained he was well able to remove his own clothes, and as such, his valet usually did not attend him until the morning. Miss Bingley had obviously become aware of this fact and was now using it to her advantage.

"It is good Miss Bingley's maid is not nearly as loyal as Miss Bingley believes," commented Darcy.

Bingley snorted. "Loyalty has nothing to do with it. I bribed her. Let us go and put an end to Caroline's scheming."

Darcy shot a look at his friend, noting the grimness of Bingley's countenance. This matter had the potential of ruining him forever, and perhaps ending his own engagement. Darcy was heartened to see his friend act with the decisiveness he knew was warranted in this situation.

They left Bingley's study and quickly made their way back to the entrance hall and the stairs to the second floor. As they passed the billiards room, they stopped and listened to the clacking of the balls for a moment, confirming that Fitzwilliam was still there, before proceeding above stairs. In a moment, they were standing in front of the door to Fitzwilliam's suite of rooms.

"I will lead," said Bingley, and he opened the door, not waiting for an answer. The room inside was lit with a selection of candles, and a small fire crackled in the fireplace, warming the room for when its inhabitant would return to prepare for the evening. Bingley ignored all this, moving to the door to the bedroom.

When Bingley opened the door, Darcy noted that the room within was dark, with nary a candle lit, nor a fire in the hearth. As Bingley entered, the light of the candle he held spilled into the room, illuminating it in a dim light, and chasing the shadows to the corners of the room. There, in the bed, on the far wall, lay Miss Bingley, her seductive smile of triumph changing to a gasp of mortified surprise.

"Charles!" shrieked she. "What are you doing here?"

"I might ask the same thing of you, Caroline," snapped Bingley. "Unless my memory is deficient, I do not think this is your room."

For once, Miss Bingley had no reply to her brother's implacable question; Darcy thought it was the first time he had ever seen the woman at a loss for words. The longer Bingley stood and stared at her the more uncomfortable she became, her jaw working with no sound emerging and the light of panic shining in her eyes.

"Let us get you to your own room, Caroline," said Mrs. Hurst. "I think it is time we spoke about your future."

"Yes, it is," growled Bingley. As Mrs. Hurst helped her sister from the bed, and into the robe she had thrown with careless disinterest over a nearby chair, Charles, so furious now that he was stalking in front of the door with disgust, turned on her again. "This is the end, Caroline. I will no longer be responsible for you. I will arrange for you to go stay with Aunt Amelia. Perhaps she will have some success in reforming your character, for I certainly have not."

Miss Bingley gasped. "You cannot send me to the hinterlands of the kingdom! I will not tolerate it!"

"You will do what you are told, *dearest sister!*" Miss Bingley gasped at the disgust dripping from Charles's tone, and Darcy himself was surprised to hear it. "I still control your dowry until you are five and twenty and as of this moment I am revoking your allowance. I will not have you in my house accosting my guests, spewing your vile slander on my neighbors, or attempting to compromise a viscount who is staying with me.

"How could you, Caroline?" yelled Bingley. "Do you care nothing for the credit of our family? You, who have always been so keen to climb society's ladder. Your actions might have seen us banished from society forever!"

Miss Bingley found a little of her spirit. "I am not the one who offered for an unsuitable country adventuress!"

"At least I offered for her, rather than resorting to compromising her!" Bingley glared at his sister, who returned it in full measure. "You have become a stranger, Caroline, though I will own that I never truly knew you. I have no faith in your ability to treat my future wife with the respect she deserves, and as such, I have no choice but to banish you from my home forever. The only place you can go is to Aunt Amelia."

"I will live with Louisa," snapped Miss Bennet. "She will not betray me as you have done."

"No, Caroline," said Mrs. Hurst. "I will not allow it, and even if I was amenable, Hurst would not be. We have had enough of your airs and your ill humors and your cutting remarks. And we do not wish to support someone who could behave in so dreadful a manner."

The look with which Miss Bingley regarded her siblings was filled with horror. But at that moment, they were all interrupted by the sound of a voice none of them wished to hear.

"What is the meaning of this?"

Hurst truly was not a bad companion at times, Fitzwilliam decided. The two men had spent the evening in the billiards room, but as the night had deepened, so had their consumption of the fine brandy Bingley kept in the room. When they finally quit it for their beds, Fitzwilliam felt himself to be pleasantly half-sprung. For once, however, Hurst was not completely foxed, though he was in much the same state as Fitzwilliam.

When they entered the corridor above stairs, however, both noticed a commotion in one of the rooms, and it was with a start that Fitzwilliam realized it was *his* rooms. A quick step took him to the door and he passed through it, noting that there were several figures in the door of his bedchamber.

"What is the meaning of this?" demanded he, stepping forward, only wobbling a little because of his state.

At once, four sets of eyes found Fitzwilliam's: Darcy and Bingley turned and regarded him without emotion, while Mrs. Hurst squeaked and jumped in sudden fright, fixing wild eyes upon him. The fourth person in the room, Miss Bingley, clad in nothing but a nightgown and robe, eyed him with what could only be called cunning.

"Oh, Lord Chesterfield!" cried Miss Bingley. "I was waiting here for you when these *people* interfered. Our assignation cannot proceed as planned. But now it seems to be a propitious time to announce our happy news to our relations."

The implications of Miss Bingley's speech hit Fitzwilliam like a carriage careening through the streets of London. He felt the blood run from his face at the thought of being tied to this harpy for the rest of his life.

"I have no notion of what you are speaking, Madam," declared Fitzwilliam. The cruel smile ran away from Miss Bingley's face. "I was never a party to an assignation, and I deny any 'happy news,' as you put it. I would not offer for you if you were the only woman alive!"

Shock settled over Miss Bingley's face, and Fitzwilliam idly wondered if the woman thought her schemes would be successful merely because she planned them. What conceit this woman possessed!

"B-but, your l-lordship," attempted she, stuttering over her words. "Surely you will not betray me in this fashion. Just because our family has not discovered it ere now, does not mean we have not come together since your coming to Netherfield."

"Do not be ridiculous, Miss Bingley," snapped Darcy. Fitzwilliam regarded his cousin with surprise, but Darcy only glared at the woman, his gaze filled with pitiless loathing. "Until Fitzwilliam came to Netherfield, you were fixed upon *me*. Will you now attempt to lie about *our* relationship?"

"That is enough," said Bingley, speaking in a firmer tone than Fitzwilliam could ever remember him using. "There was no assignation with Lord Chesterfield, and there never was anything between you and Darcy, much though you wished it had been different. It is time to return to your room, Caroline. As soon as I can manage it, you are for the north and Aunt Amelia."

The woman squawked and protested, but soon Bingley had herded her from the room in the company of his elder sister. As Fitzwilliam watched them go, he noted that Hurst had followed them into the room. He stood watching them leave, his face lightened with a truly unpleasant smile of satisfaction. When he noted Fitzwilliam watching him, Hurst laughed and shook his head.

"Well, my lord, it seems you have managed to avoid the headsman's axe at present. You should be especially grateful—my sister-in-law possesses a singular ability to make a man miserable. I should know, for she has intruded upon my marriage since we left the church. Actually being married to Caroline would have been infinitely worse."

"You knew what she intended?"

Hurst shrugged. "It was not difficult to guess, even if my wife had not spoken to me of her suspicions."

Struggling, as if his head was encased in molasses, Fitzwilliam turned a glance on Darcy. Fitzwilliam scowled at his cousin.

"I suppose you were aware of this too?"

"I was," replied Darcy, his tone short. "If you had been paying attention, you would have noticed it yourself, for Miss Bingley was entirely transparent."

"Then why was I not told?"

"Because it was Bingley's intention to deal with the issue and ensure you never knew about it." Darcy turned his gaze upon Hurst. "Did you lead Fitzwilliam back here of a purpose, so that he would be aware of it?"

"I did not know it was to happen tonight," replied Hurst, his tone entirely insouciant. "But it has occurred to me that an event of this nature might induce a little humility in your manner, Chesterfield. You have always been a good man with whom to associate. I hope this haughty behavior in which you have indulged of late does not mark a change in your character.

"Well, well, I believe it is time to retire. I wish you a good night."

Then Hurst turned and departed, leaving a befuddled Fitzwilliam staring after him. Haughty behavior? Fitzwilliam had not the foggiest notion of what the man referred to.

Darcy watched his cousin as Fitzwilliam stared after Hurst's departing form. Though he wished to return to his own room, Darcy waited, for there were a few choice words he wished to direct at his cousin. But when Fitzwilliam made no indication of even remembering that Darcy was in the room, he spoke up himself.

"It is my hope as well."

Fitzwilliam blinked and turned to Darcy, a frown settling over his countenance. "None of you are speaking sense this evening." He paused and when he spoke again, it was clear his words were more grudging than sincere. "I suppose I must thank you for your assistance with respect to Miss Bingley. I do wonder, however, why you simply did not take the opportunity to remove me as a threat. Without my presence, you would have the field all to yourself."

Darcy knew exactly to what his cousin was referring, and his ire exploded into a white-hot flame of anger. "Perhaps I should have just left you to your fate. Given how you have behaved of late, I declare, you and Miss Bingley deserve each other."

The shocked expression with which Fitzwilliam regarded him touched a dark chord of amusement in Darcy, and he fixed his cousin with a cold smile. "But I am not one to behave in such a manner, regardless of how you deserve it.

"And Fitzwilliam," said Darcy, passing by his cousin toward the door, "I do not need you out of the way. The field does not exist."

"What?" demanded Fitzwilliam.

"Oh, yes," replied Darcy. "Did you not know? I requested a courtship from Miss Elizabeth today, and she accepted. We now have her father's blessing. So you see, I have no fear of your attempts to woo her. Contrary to what you might believe, I never did. If I continue to treat her with respect and show my regard for her, that courtship will become an engagement before long."

The shock in Fitzwilliam's countenance quickly turned to anger. "A courtship is not tantamount to an engagement."

"And well I know it. Mr. Bennet informed me himself that he would not force his daughter in this matter. It will remain her decision. Then again, you already knew that, did you not? Mr. Bennet informed me he told you the same thing only yesterday."

Fitzwilliam had the grace to appear a little shamefaced, but this was soon swallowed up in his continuing fury. "I cannot believe you, Darcy. I had not thought you would act in this way, to steal away a woman I wished to make my own."

"Listen to yourself, Fitzwilliam!" exclaimed Darcy, his patience with his cousin exhausted. "Your words stink strongly of possessiveness. Do you think Miss Elizabeth wishes to be dominated?

"You know, she has informed me of your actions herself. Do you know how disgusted she has been with your behavior of late?"

"What? She has always enjoyed my company!"

"She did before you began to behave as a true member of the nobility. Did you think you deserved her simply because you outrank me? Your opinions are shocking. You have always disdained the airs of the nobility, but now you behave worse than any of them."

Rendered speechless by Darcy's charges, Fitzwilliam did not seem capable of mustering a response. But Darcy was not finished.

"Yes, she enjoyed your company when we first came, for you spoke to her, friendly and open as if her opinion was valued. But as I began to fall in love with her, you began to compete with me, flattering her, making her feel as if you were interested in her only because *I* was.

"Do you know that at Bingley's ball she actually thought you meant to make her an offer of *carte-blanche*?"

Fitzwilliam gasped. "I would never do such a thing!"

"I know that," spat Darcy. "I informed her of it myself. But by then she had already worked out the reason for your changed behavior for herself. And if you think about it, her fears were justified. You, yourself have spoken harshly of members of your set, of their dissolute ways, gaming, wenching, keeping mistresses, of their excesses and immorality. When you suddenly began to flatter her, what else was she to think?"

"She should have thought I was interested in her as a potential wife!"

It was clear Fitzwilliam was determined to defend himself. Darcy was not about to allow him.

"Members of the nobility do not marry country misses, Fitzwilliam. It happens but rarely. She had not known you long enough to be confident of her understanding of you. Such a sudden turnabout cast aspersions on your character, and rightfully so!"

It was clear Fitzwilliam had no response to Darcy's words. There was no defense, after all. He had been behaving the same as that which he hated. A little humility would do him no harm.

"I do not wish to argue with you, Fitzwilliam," said Darcy. "I will leave you to your thoughts. At the very least, I think you owe Miss Elizabeth an apology, especially since I fully intend to make her my wife. She will be family someday—do not forget it."

As Darcy was departing from the room, the sound of his cousin's voice arrested his leaving. "Surely you do not think I was contemplating offering such a disgusting position to her."

"No, I did not," replied Darcy. "But I know you better than she does. Or at least I thought I did."

Then Darcy left without a backward glance.

CHAPTER XXX

✦❦✦

An invitation to spend the day at Netherfield arrived the day after Elizabeth's courtship became official, and the Bennet sisters cheerfully accepted it. Elizabeth was interested to note that the invitation had included them all, even the two youngest. But then again, the writing on the note was in Louisa's hand, which meant that Miss Bingley had no say in it.

Kitty, who had been showing signs of ennui, as her usual companion was unable to indulge in the activities they often pursued, was eager to be gone from Longbourn, even if the activity was not one she would usually favor. Lydia complained about it, as one might have expected, but she did not see fit to refuse the invitation.

"Of course, you will all go," said Mrs. Bennet when the news had been imparted to her. "It is very kind of Mrs. Hurst to request that you all attend, and I am certain she means to further your friendships."

Elizabeth shared a glance with Jane and Mary, and the three hid smiles behind their hands. Louisa was, indeed, a good friend. But Elizabeth was certain she had no particular desire to forward Elizabeth's connection with Mr. Darcy.

"Mary, you will need to attend your sisters," continued Mrs. Bennet, regarding them all, seeming a little pensive. Her gaze found

Kitty and Lydia where they were sitting together speaking quietly. "I do not suppose our youngest girls can be counted on to provide proper chaperonage."

"Mrs. Hurst will surely agree to assist," said Mary.

Mrs. Bennet brightened. "You are correct, of course. Please give Mrs. Hurst my regards."

Her words, Elizabeth understood, meant they should request Louisa's assistance. Elizabeth had no intention of doing so, and she knew that Mary did not either. Louisa was an intelligent woman—she would surely understand the need herself.

They entered the carriage the following morning and made their way to the neighboring estate. On their arrival, they were welcomed there by those in residence. Or most of them were present—Miss Bingley was nowhere to be seen.

Furthermore, Elizabeth noted the earnest inspection of her person by Lord Chesterfield, and she wondered at it. In the past days and weeks, he could be counted on to greet her and attempt to dominate her conversation as soon as he saw her. But at present, he did nothing but watch, an undefinable quality in depths of his eyes. Elizabeth could not quite make him out.

"Please, come to the pianoforte with me," said Mrs. Hurst as soon as the greetings had been completed. "I would like to play some duets with you if you will oblige me."

Mary and Elizabeth both agreed readily, though Elizabeth was more interested in speaking with the man who was now courting her. She turned her gaze to him as Louisa pulled her away, and she noted his smile, his nod indicating they would speak later. Soon Elizabeth and Mary were huddled around the instrument with Louisa, and they began to play, though there was as much laughter as music. Mr. Darcy was standing with Mr. Bingley and Jane speaking, while Lord Chesterfield entertained the two youngest Bennets. That did not, Elizabeth noted, prevent him from continuing his scrutiny of her.

In time, the three ladies quit the pianoforte and gathered with the rest of the company. Tea was sent for and arrived with some of the cook's fine cakes, and the company sat down to partake. It was a merry party, Elizabeth noted, even more so because Miss Bingley was not present to spew her insults or kill the mood with her ill humor. But Elizabeth still felt the woman's absence was odd, and even more odd was how none of the company had spoken of her. Knowing what Mr. Darcy had said about her, she determined to ask him at the first opportunity.

326 🌿 Jann Rowland

"I can sense your curiosity, Miss Elizabeth," said Mr. Darcy. It was some time after they had arrived, and it was the first opportunity they had managed to speak privately together. The viscount was, as ever, watching them, while speaking with Mr. Hurst, but he still made no move to join them. Mrs. Hurst had taken Elizabeth's younger sisters to another side of the room where they were discussing London fashion, unless Elizabeth missed her guess, and Mr. Bingley was speaking quietly with Jane.

"Then it appears I have failed, Mr. Darcy," said Elizabeth, injecting a mournful quality in her voice. "A young lady being courted by a man hopes to maintain an air of mystery about her to keep her suitor interested. If you have seen through me this easily, it must mean I am not nearly so successful as I would have hoped."

Mr. Darcy chuckled. "Perhaps I am coming to know you well. From a man's perspective, it is best to come to know your partner, so a decision may be made about whether to make an offer."

"You do not know?" demanded Elizabeth, regarding the man with mock affront. "My failure is complete, it seems. I had hoped to make you wild with desire, force you to struggle to restrain yourself from throwing me over your horse and carrying me off to Gretna Green."

"Miss Elizabeth," said Mr. Darcy, leaning close to her and speaking in a husky voice, "there is no need to tempt me further, for I would do just that with little provocation. You must have mercy on your poor, besotted suitor!"

His tone of voice told Elizabeth that he was not completely teasing, as did the fire in his eyes. Feeling rather proud of herself, Elizabeth showed him a contrite expression. "You have my apologies, sir. Even though I must revel in my success."

Catching one of her hands in his own, Mr. Darcy brought it to her lips and left a lingering kiss on its back. "You are uniformly charming, my dear. But I do ask you to have mercy on me. I am like putty in your hands.

"I believe, however, I was about to answer your unspoken questions. You have noted something different today, have you not?"

"I have," confessed Elizabeth. "Miss Bingley is not present, which leads me to suspect something might have happened. And your cousin has not approached me."

She saw his eyes dart to where Fitzwilliam was still speaking with Mr. Hurst. Then he once again returned his attention to Elizabeth.

"You are correct on all fronts. Miss Bingley did, indeed, make her attempt last night. She was thwarted by her brother and sister, but they were not, unfortunately, able to keep the incident from Fitzwilliam's attention."

"Hence Miss Bingley's absence."

"Bingley has decreed that she is to go to his aunt in Scarborough, and he refuses to support her any longer. He received word just this morning that his aunt was prepared to receive her. You will likely not be surprised to hear that he has considered this course for several days and sent word to his aunt when he first heard of Mrs. Hurst's concerns. She is to depart tomorrow for the north."

Elizabeth sighed. "It is unfortunate, but understandable." Her eyes found Jane, where she was speaking closely with Mr. Bingley and, unless Elizabeth missed her guess, was hearing the same communication as Elizabeth was receiving from Mr. Darcy. "I must own that I am relieved for Jane's sake. Jane is such a . . . trusting soul. She believes in the inherent goodness of those about her. I shudder at the ways which Miss Bingley might mislead her if she had Jane's trust."

"It has been coming for some time. Bingley has long been frustrated with his sister's actions. Though in the past they have been directed toward *me*, attempting the compromise of a peer is a matter he cannot ignore."

"What was Lord Chesterfield's reaction?" asked Elizabeth.

"Bewilderment, if you can believe it." At Elizabeth's questioning glance, Mr. Darcy shook his head. "He was so caught up in his rivalry with me and his fascination with you that her plotting completely escaped his attention. I will own that I directed a few . . . choice comments in his direction last night."

"Oh, Mr. Darcy."

Still holding her hand, Mr. Darcy began to caress the back of it with his thumb, his ministrations somehow soothing. Elizabeth wondered if he should not be soothing him instead, given his troubles with his cousin.

"Fitzwilliam needed to hear what I had to say," said Mr. Darcy. "I informed him where I thought his behavior was deficient and exactly what I thought of it. He was shocked—in fact, I believe he was not even aware of how his manners had changed."

"I hope you will not lose your closeness with your cousin because of this."

The tender smile Mr. Darcy directed at her threatened to turn Elizabeth's insides to jelly. He raised her hand once more to his lips, lingering there before lowering it again. Elizabeth noticed that he did not release her.

"I believe our former closeness may be restored, but it is now up to Fitzwilliam. If he can release this fascination with you and regain his old joviality, I believe all will be well. He spent most of the day yesterday in his chambers. I hope his ponderings have borne fruit. I do not know why he felt compelled to compete with me for your hand, but I will not have this competition continue any longer."

Mr. Darcy directed a level look at her, and Elizabeth felt her lips curling upward in response. "I know it is naught but a courtship at present, Miss Elizabeth, but I consider myself engaged to you, even though I have not made an offer. I will do my utmost to convince you I am a good risk to take, and as such, I believe it is only a matter of time. Fitzwilliam needs to accept this."

"Then I hope, for your sake, he does," replied Elizabeth. "And if you mean to convince me, then you had best begin. I should warn you: I am reputed to have a stubborn, ungovernable temperament. I may be difficult to persuade."

Mr. Darcy raised her hand to his lips again. "I would have it no other way, Miss Elizabeth."

"Mr. Wickham! Mr. Wickham!"

Wickham cursed and ducked in behind a building when he heard the wild tones of the parson's voice calling out his name. What did the fool think he was doing? Wickham had an interest in keeping his acquaintance with the man quiet until they struck.

When Mr. Collins followed him, Wickham rounded on him. "Silence, Collins! Do you wish the entire town to know of our association?"

"What care I for such secrets, now of all times?" The fool was so distressed he was wringing his hands. Not for the first time, Wickham wished he had been given a little more to work with in a confederate. Collins was useless. The man did not even breathe unless instructed to do so by Lady Catherine, and his ideas concerning how they might deal with the situation were laughable.

"What has changed?" demanded Wickham, feeling he was close to simply planting a facer on the man and leaving him behind as a bad investment.

"Oh, it is a disaster! I know not what Lady Catherine will say? She will be so angry, her sensitive feelings injured to death by the news that I bear!"

"Mr. Collins!" yelled Wickham, grabbing the parson by his

shoulders and shaking him. "What has happened to put you in this state?"

The parson focused on him, though his eyes were still wild enough that Wickham could see the whites. "I heard in town this morning that Mr. Darcy has offered courtship to my cousin and been accepted!"

"Is that all?" asked Wickham. Inside he was filled with glee. Darcy had actually asked for a courtship from a country miss! The irony was delicious, given how the fastidious man had spurned ladies as high as the daughters of dukes.

And this would make Wickham's revenge that much sweeter, indeed! If the sanctimonious bastard truly possessed feelings for her in that cold, shriveled heart of his, taking her away from him and making her unmarriageable would hurt him that much more.

And then such thoughts caused Wickham's outlook to shift. Perhaps there was another way which would not require him to leave the place of his birth. For if Darcy was disappointed in love, made to be miserable, perhaps Wickham could swoop in and relieve him of his sister and her dowry while he was distracted. He had wished to do it earlier that year, but Darcy had not hired his confederate as Georgiana's companion, and Wickham's schemes had gone unfulfilled.

"Whatever shall we do, Mr. Wickham?" whined Mr. Collins.

Wickham turned back to Collins, noting with disgust that the man was on the verge of falling apart. For a moment, Wickham thought of severing their agreement, but he restrained himself. He could still relieve Lady Catherine of her money, even if he now had his eye on greater possibilities. Besides, the parson may be of some use.

"Calm yourself, Collins," said Wickham in as soothing a tone as he could muster. "This changes nothing."

"Changes nothing?" cried Mr. Collins. It was very nearly a shriek. "How can you say such a thing? It is in every way disastrous!"

"No, it is not," said Wickham. "Darcy may still be detached from her."

A maniacal gleam entered Mr. Collins's eyes. "Yes! That is it! I must go to Netherfield now!"

"Do not be a fool, Collins! Darcy will throw you out on your ear, should you importune him concerning such a matter. And you will ruin all of our plans."

"I shall not speak with Mr. Darcy," said Mr. Collins, casting his gaze about. "The Bennet sisters are at Netherfield today—I saw them passing through Meryton this morning in the Bennet carriage. It took the Netherfield road."

"Foolish man!" roared Wickham. "Did they see you?"

"Of course not! I hid myself. But now that I know what is to be done, I shall not hesitate. Lady Catherine is depending on me, and I shall not fail her!"

With that, Collins turned and sped out of the alley, Wickham close on his heels.

"Do not be a fool!" called Wickham after him, but short of resorting to that facer Wickham had contemplated earlier, there was no stopping the man. He hauled himself up on the horse he had been using to travel to Meryton, and the beast began to lumber away, Collins swaying on its back like a sack of grain.

Cursing the silly man, Wickham looked about for his own means to go to Netherfield. The time for secrecy had passed, it seemed. He needed to make his move before Collins ruined everything.

Fitzwilliam was beginning to feel like a fool for not seeing what existed between Darcy and Miss Elizabeth, and having it pointed out by a man he had not, perhaps, treated as he should did not make the situation any better. But so it was, and there were times, he knew, when a man must accept his share of the blame and do his best to make amends.

When the Bennet sisters arrived that morning at Netherfield, Fitzwilliam felt the urge to approach Miss Elizabeth as he usually did. The thoughts which had been coursing through his head since he learned of Miss Bingley's attempt caused him to hesitate, and instead of imposing on her, he sat back to watch, nominally listening to Hurst as the man spoke about inconsequential matters.

He watched as they spoke, knowing that Darcy was likely informing Miss Elizabeth of Miss Bingley's attempt, an uncomfortable feeling of how *he* might be portrayed in such a tale running up his spine. He forced the feeling down, knowing that Darcy was unscrupulously fair and would not make him out to be worse than he was to Miss Elizabeth.

I have injured myself in her eyes quite well enough on my own, thought he, feeling the moroseness of the situation.

They continued to speak, and when they laughed, he felt his spirits rise, and when Miss Elizabeth sighed, he felt them fall. When Darcy took her hand and kissed it, and then continued to hold it, Fitzwilliam noted his posture and knew that had he been allowed, Darcy would have held her in his arms like the precious jewel she was.

"I believe this is more difficult for you than it needs to be."

Surprised, Fitzwilliam turned, his gaze falling on Bingley. A look about the room revealed that Miss Bennet had joined Mrs. Hurst and her sisters, as had Hurst himself. While he could not determine what the man was saying, he was speaking to the assorted Bennet sisters, and Fitzwilliam noted more than one laughing in response. Wonders never ceased—Fitzwilliam had never considered Hurst to be the kind of man who could induce young women to laughter.

"Perhaps it has been," said Fitzwilliam after a moment, realizing he had yet made no response to Bingley's words. "But I . . ."

In the end, finding the words to say was more difficult than Fitzwilliam had ever imagined they would be. Rare was the time when he had been so afflicted. Words had always come easily to him. Perhaps at times, they had come too easily.

While he was thinking, Bingley remained silent, for which Fitzwilliam was grateful. They were much alike, Fitzwilliam thought. With Bingley's recent maturation, perhaps they were much more alike than they had been before. Fitzwilliam had always considered himself to be superior to the other man, with his infatuation for every pretty young lady he met and his, at times, lack of direction in life. But that was all changing.

"I hope you do not think my interest in Miss Bennet was not genuine."

Bingley raised an eyebrow, an action reminiscent of Darcy. "I never thought anything else."

Fitzwilliam suppressed a sigh of relief, suspecting that Darcy had never told Bingley of Miss Elizabeth's suspicions at the ball. Fitzwilliam still could not fathom how she had thought such a thing, but he was thankful no one else had been informed.

"It seems, however, that I have not gone about it the best way."

"Perhaps not," said Bingley. "The true question is, what will you do about it now?"

"I am not certain."

"Then allow me to give you some advice. It seems to me that you and Darcy have always been closer than brothers. If I am not very much mistaken, I think you were closer to Darcy than you were to your own brother."

"You are not mistaken," said Fitzwilliam. The good times they had often shared flashed before his eyes. Even the early part of their visit to Netherfield had been marked by their continued affection and association.

"Then you would be a fool to throw that away."

Fitzwilliam turned and fixed Bingley with a wry smile. "Even over a woman? I thought the one thing which might cause us to come to blows was an interest in the same woman."

"It appears you were correct." Bingley's reply was equally dry. "But I think if you look at them, you will note that there is no longer any rivalry. Darcy has Miss Elizabeth in the palm of his hand—or perhaps it is more accurate to say that *she* has *him*. Either way, I doubt anything can come between them."

"At this point, I would not even wish to try," replied Fitzwilliam. He surprised himself by meaning it—Miss Elizabeth was a fascinating creature and had the situation been different, he thought she would have made an excellent wife and countess. But he no longer burned to make her his.

"I . . . wonder if Darcy will be so forgiving," said Fitzwilliam. "He does not forgive easily." Fitzwilliam laughed, though he felt no mirth. "He has always claimed that when his good opinion is lost, it cannot be regained."

"There is only one way to discover it. I doubt Darcy feels that way about you and your friendship. And he is not so fearsome as he seems."

With those final words and a genuine smile, Bingley rose and walked away, joining the group on the far side of the room. Fitzwilliam continued to watch Darcy and his lady for several moments before he rose and joined them. He would never have thought that Bingley would dispense such excellent advice.

When they had been at Netherfield for some time, Elizabeth suggested they all go walk in the back gardens. Though it was getting late in the year, the drive to the estate that morning had informed Elizabeth that the weather was mild, with a hint of warmth in the air, more than enough for a hardy soul, as she considered herself, to brave the elements and breathe the fresh, crisp air. Of course, not everyone was so eager as Elizabeth was herself.

"Oh, Lizzy!" exclaimed Lydia.

By her side, Kitty only smirked. "Trust Lizzy to wish to walk in the dead of winter. I declare not even a blizzard would deter her."

"There is no blizzard, Kitty," said Elizabeth. "It is warm and clear, and we may not receive such an opportunity to walk out of doors again this year."

"Well, I have no intention of walking out," declared Lydia. "My injured ankle will not allow for it, regardless."

The rest of the company looked on Lydia with amusement; her ankle was well healed, though it was true she had best not tax it yet. She had taken to using the injury as a crutch, to be used whenever she did not wish to do something.

"For my part, a walk sounds like an excellent thought," said Bingley. "I would be happy to oblige you." He turned a casual eye on Jane. "Will you do me the honor of walking with me, Miss Bennet?"

"Of course, sir," replied Jane.

Mary soon indicated her agreement to the plan, and when the viscount and Mr. Darcy also agreed, their party was set.

"I shall stay and keep Kitty and Lydia company," said Mrs. Hurst, as she looked on the rest of them with amusement. It was little surprise to any of them that Mr. Hurst also voiced his preference for staying indoors, though according to Mr. Darcy the man was a great hunter.

They made their way to the vestibule to retrieve their coats and gloves, and soon they were out in the gardens, breathing the fresh air, so clean in the early December beauty. Elizabeth looked about, noting the branches of the trees, bare of their summer bounty and how the flower bushes had been tended, preparing them for the coming spring which was still months away. The air was too warm for the branches to be coated with frost, for the morning sun had burned off any which had accumulated the previous night. But there was still a cold and stark beauty to be seen and in which Elizabeth reveled.

They had just exited the house and were breaking into several groups when Lord Chesterfield approached and addressed Mr. Darcy. "Darcy, a word if you will?"

Mr. Darcy weighed his cousin's demeanor for a few moments before agreeing, saying a quick word of apology to Elizabeth.

"I shall be well with Mary for company, Mr. Darcy. Go speak to your cousin."

With a nod, Mr. Darcy fell back and they began to speak, though Elizabeth noted that it primarily consisted of Lord Chesterfield speaking and Mr. Darcy listening. Hoping that the cousins were on the road to mending their differences, Elizabeth chose a path and began walking, Mary at her side.

"Lord Chesterfield seems . . . pensive this morning," said Mary.

"He does," agreed Elizabeth, glancing back at the gentlemen. "His behavior has been different from what I have ever seen from him. In the beginning, he was friendly and loquacious, then he became a flatterer. This reflective viscount is completely different."

"It is unsurprising," said Mary. "I do not know the full extent of what happened, but it seems as if he has had his eyes opened. I do not doubt it has been a humbling experience."

Elizabeth regarded her sister, though she suspected that Mary had descended into her own thoughts to the extent that she did not even notice Elizabeth's scrutiny. For a moment she considered informing Mary of the events Mr. Darcy had related to her. In the end, however, she decided against it. They had been told to her in confidence. The viscount deserved to at least maintain a little of his dignity.

How long they wandered the paths of the back gardens Elizabeth could not say, and she had quite lost track of where Mr. Bingley and Jane had gone. Mr. Darcy and his cousin were also out of sight.

"May we go in, Elizabeth?" asked Mary after some minutes. "I believe I am beginning to become a little chilled."

"Of course, Mary. You do not need to ask."

They turned and began to make their way back to the house when they were confronted by an obviously irate Miss Caroline Bingley.

"You!" spat the woman. "I was correct—you *are* here. Well, you can go back to that hovel you call a home and never darken our door again."

Elizabeth looked at the woman with some pity. She was proud and disagreeable, and she possessed the haughtiest streak Elizabeth had ever seen. Miss Bingley was learning that she was not so high and mighty as she thought, and it made her bitter. Elizabeth had little desire to argue with her.

"If you will excuse us, Miss Bingley."

"No! I will *not* excuse you. You have turned my brother and sister away from me, and you have the audacity to beg my pardon." Miss Bingley stooped close to Elizabeth, and Elizabeth could smell sherry on her tongue—it seemed the woman had been drowning her sorrows. "If you think to attempt to trap the viscount, you should reconsider. He would never offer for a penniless little baggage like you."

"My sister has no interest in his lordship," said Mary in response. Elizabeth looked at her, surprised by Mary's manner—she seemed to be affecting Miss Bingley's haughty tones. "Do you not know that she is already being courted by Mr. Darcy? What kind of daft woman are you?"

"Mr. Darcy cannot be courting you!" exclaimed a new voice. "I will not allow it!"

CHAPTER XXXI

The voice belonged to none other than Mr. Collins, as he hurried toward them, thunderous fury showing in his jerky stride and ferocious glare. Shocked at the man's appearance and wondering from where he had come, Elizabeth took an involuntary step back. This proved to be a mistake.

Soon the parson had reached them, and he loomed over Elizabeth, blazing affront radiating from his very being. By his side, Miss Bingley, who stood several inches taller than Elizabeth, joined him, though her look was astonished, enhanced by more than a little fear. They had her boxed in. For a moment, she wondered if they were somehow confederates.

Then reason reasserted itself—Miss Bingley felt nothing but contempt for Mr. Collins, as evidenced by the scowl she directed at him. Her expression shifted to satisfied malevolence and then shock when he began to speak.

"This cannot be, Cousin! Not only is Mr. Darcy already engaged to his cousin, that excellent flower of English nobility, Miss Anne de Bourgh, but men as prominent as Mr. Darcy do not offer for the likes of you."

Avoiding an argument with Miss Bingley was one thing. Elizabeth was not about to be cowed by her father's foolish cousin.

"Perhaps you should take your objections to Mr. Darcy. It was *he* who offered courtship to *me*, after all. I could do naught but accept or reject it."

"Then reject it you must, for there is no way you can justify marrying a man of his eminence! No! It is in every way unfathomable!"

Finally, Miss Bingley found her tongue again. "Of what do you speak, you stupid man? Mr. Darcy would *never* offer for the likes of *this* . . . strumpet! He might be amused by her or wish her for his mistress, but even then, he would tire of her quickly."

"I know not, Miss Bingley," said Mr. Collins, sniffing with disdain. "But I assure you it is being talked of in Meryton."

"It must be a lie! It must!" Miss Bingley turned her wild eyes on Elizabeth. "*You* could not have elicited a proposal from Mr. Darcy. Not when I have tried for more than three years. It is in every way impossible!"

Mr. Collins turned to her, aghast at what he was hearing. "Is Mr. Darcy surrounded by sirens, all intent upon seducing him away from his rightful bride? Are you not sensible of your own good, Madam?"

"Silence, fool!" exclaimed Miss Bingley. "If you do not recall, it is this girl you came to berate. It is not *I* who has tempted your stupid patroness's nephew away from his duty."

Elizabeth listened to the two argue and a hint of fear found its way into her heart. They had hemmed her in between them, and Mary was frantically watching the scene, wondering what to do. Elizabeth wondered where Mr. Darcy was.

And then a sense of resolve came over her. She would not count on Mr. Darcy to rescue her, for she was fully capable of dealing with these objectionable persons herself.

First, to extricate her from her vulnerable position. She ducked to the side, to make her away around Miss Bingley, thinking her to be the lesser of the threats. Mr. Collins noticed her attempt, and he moved to stop her.

"You shall not escape so easily!"

Elizabeth hurried to avoid him, and as Mr. Collins attempted to follow her, he collided heavily with Miss Bingley. Still enraged, he reached out for her, further tangling himself with Miss Bennet. A cry issued from her mouth and Collins, with a look of complete shock on his homely face, went down in a heap, pulled a startled Miss Bingley down with him. The sound of fabric ripping filled the air. And then they were not alone.

"What is the meaning of this?"

It was Mr. Darcy, and he was hurrying toward them with his cousin following close behind. From another direction, Mr. Bingley appeared with Jane by his side. The two parties approached as Mr. Collins tried to free himself from Miss Bingley, but the more he tried to rise, the greater difficult he was having. All the while, Miss Bingley was crying at him, and beating him about the head with her hands.

"Get off me, you stupid wretch. Get away from me!"

Mr. Bingley stopped as he realized what had happened, and he regarded the two on the ground, shock pouring from him. As Elizabeth was watching him, she noted the exact moment when his countenance transformed from surprise to humor, and he appeared like he was stifling laughter.

"Come now, Collins," said he. "It is time to get up. Your little liaison with my sister is over."

Mr. Bingley approached the two and grasped Mr. Collins's shoulders, with Darcy assisting. Soon they had heaved the parson up off Miss Bingley's person, allowing the woman herself to rise. There was a large tear in the woman's dress, down near the hem, and as she stood, a long length of lace and fabric trailed on the ground. Miss Bingley's poisonous glare at Mr. Collins revealed the woman was unaware of the disarray of her dress.

"A thousand apologies, Mr. Bingley," Mr. Collins was finally able to say. "I do not know what happened. I am very much in your debt for your assistance."

"I am sure you are," replied Mr. Bingley. "Now, if you and Caroline will control your passion, we shall see you married before long. We would not wish scandal to erupt from this little incident, now, would we?"

Mr. Collins goggled at Mr. Bingley, unable to understand what he was saying. Miss Bingley was suffering under no such affliction.

"Charles!" screeched she. "What are you saying? I am not marrying Mr. Collins!"

"Of course, you are, my dear," replied Mr. Bingley, though his endearment toward his sister was brittle enough for them all to hear. "Mr. Collins has compromised you quite thoroughly. I am afraid there is no other alternative."

"Of course, there is another alternative! The alternative is that I will not marry this sorry excuse for a man!"

"Loath though I am to agree with your termagant of a sister," said Mr. Collins, sweeping Miss Bingley with a disdainful glare, "I must concur. I cannot marry her."

"Were you not just lying on the ground on top of her, sir?" demanded Mr. Bingley.

"I was, but—"

"Then the matter is clear. You have quite compromised her and ruined her reputation. It is the duty of a gentleman to restore that which he has taken, repair that which he has sullied. In our society, sir, that means you must marry her."

"Charles, do not be foolish!" exclaimed Miss Bingley, at the same time Mr. Collins cried: "I will not marry her."

Mr. Bingley chose to ignore his sister and instead focused on the parson. "Then if you will not meet your responsibilities, I shall be forced to call you out." Mr. Collins turned deathly pale. "And let me warn you, *sir*, that I am not only an excellent marksman, but I am more than skilled enough with the blade to turn you into a pincushion."

"He is right about his skill with a pistol," said Fitzwilliam, his tone almost clinical. "I have seen him shoot enough birds to know that shooting you would be no challenge at all."

If possible, Mr. Collins turned even whiter.

"And I can attest to his skill with the blade," added Mr. Darcy. "He is able to take two out of five points from me, and I am generally judged to be among the most skilled at our club."

Though Mr. Darcy's tone was equally disinterested as his cousin's, Elizabeth could sense the laughter he was trying to suppress. In that instant, the situation struck her as hilarious, though she managed to stifle the laughter which was welling up in her breast.

"It matters not what you do to this *worm*," spat Miss Bingley into the argument, "for I shall not marry him."

"And I say you will!" intoned Mr. Bingley. Elizabeth had never seen the man appearing so implacable.

"You cannot make me!"

"In fact, I can." Mr. Bingley smile was unpleasant. "What do you think Aunt Amelia will say to this little indiscretion, Caroline? You know her views of morality. I dare say she will refuse to shelter you when it becomes known to her. And since I control your dowry until you are five and twenty, how will you live until then?"

Miss Bingley's eyes narrowed. "You would not dare."

"I would," said Mr. Bingley's quiet response. "You have been on the prowl for a husband ever since you entered society, but you have always set your sights too high. If you marry Collins here, you will eventually be the mistress of an estate. Is that not something to anticipate? You have brought it upon yourself with your behavior."

Brother and sister glared at each other, neither giving an inch. In the end, it was Miss Bingley who looked away first, though Elizabeth did not think she had yet accepted her fate.

"Good," said Mr. Bingley. "Now, let us return to the house where we can discuss the particulars."

Whatever else he was intending to say remained unsaid, for at that moment Elizabeth felt an arm snake around her midsection, pulling her tight against a hard, male body. She gave a little squeak, which was muffled by another hand covering her mouth. In her ear, she heard the sibilant hiss of a man's voice.

"Well, little Lizzy. It seems that there will be more than one compromise here today."

Then everything seemed to happen so slowly that Elizabeth could see it unfold with precise clarity. As Mr. Darcy was turning in response to hearing the noise she made, Mary was already gazing wide-eyed and frightened at her. Mr. Wickham's hand, which had been tightly covering her mouth shifted down to the top of her dress. In an instant of clarity, she knew he intended to rend the fabric asunder.

A feeling of panic came over her and she did the only thing she could — she lashed out with her hands and feet, unwilling to allow this man to take her without a fight. Mr. Wickham cursed in her ear, but then her hand impacted something solid and the curse turned into a gasp. His hold on her loosened ever so slightly and Elizabeth, knowing she had one chance for freedom, twisted with all her might and slipped from Mr. Wickham's grasp.

She spun away from him, and Mr. Wickham, losing her support, crumpled to one knee, one hand placed on the ground, while the other cupped the area around his groin. On his countenance was a look so murderous that Elizabeth thought he would surely kill her, should he only lay his hands upon her.

But then Mr. Darcy was there, hauling Mr. Wickham to his feet, and by his side, his cousin appeared, his large frame towering over the shorter Mr. Wickham, his hands capturing Mr. Wickham's arms and holding them tightly behind his back. Between the two men, they held Mr. Wickham, and none of his struggles had any succeeded in freeing himself.

"You have pushed me beyond the point of any reason, Wickham," said Mr. Darcy, his tone the snarl of a mad dog. "I will finish you forever, as I should have done many years ago."

Mr. Wickham attempted to glare at his captor, but he was not able to swing his head around much. From the direction of the house, they all heard a shout, and within moments, Mr. Hurst had arrived, a pair of brawny footmen trailing behind him.

"Take charge of the lieutenant," snapped he.

The footmen obeyed, and soon they had taken the place of Mr. Darcy and Lord Chesterfield. If anything, they were rougher with the man, tightening their grip when he struggled, causing him to gasp with pain.

"Thank you, Hurst," said Darcy, still glaring at Mr. Wickham.

"Louisa saw what was happening from the sitting-room window," replied Mr. Hurst.

Elizabeth had forgotten the sitting-room was situated at the back of the house.

"Lock him in the cellar," said Mr. Bingley to the two footmen. "He can cool his heels there until we are ready to hand him back over to the regiment."

"Now, let us not be hasty," said Mr. Wickham, seeming to understand for the first time that he was in a difficult position. "I believe the established mode, as Mr. Bingley has so diligently pointed out, is for the man who compromised the woman to marry her. I will gladly do my duty with respect to Miss Elizabeth."

"Do not make me laugh, Wickham!" said Lord Chesterfield, the scorn in his voice battering at Wickham and causing him to turn paler than he was. "There was no compromise. Miss Elizabeth was effectively able to protect herself from you."

"She practically unmanned you," added Mr. Darcy.

Elizabeth blushed, but Mr. Wickham only scowled. "I held her in my arms, Darcy, which is more than I expect you have ever done. When the town hears of her disgrace, she will be ruined unless she marries me."

"If she is required to marry anyone, it shall not be *you*. I will not allow you to sully her, Wickham, and I doubt Mr. Bennet will permit it either."

Mr. Darcy nodded to the footmen who proceeded to haul Mr. Wickham away, Mr. Hurst trailing along behind them. Mary came to Elizabeth's side to ensure she was well, but Elizabeth was feeling more incensed with the libertine than afraid.

"Do not concern yourself for me, Mary," said Elizabeth, though she showed her sister smile in thanks.

But the drama had not yet ended.

"Why is *she* not required to marry when she is compromised, and *I* am?" demanded Miss Bingley.

"Be silent, Caroline!" hissed Mr. Bingley. "The situation is completely different.

"Now, you will go to your room and stay there—I do not give you permission to leave it. You had best accustom yourself to your situation, for it will not change. You will marry Mr. Collins. After that, I shall wash my hands of you!"

Mr. Collins squawked something, but he too was herded toward the house by Mr. Bingley, with Lord Chesterfield assisting. As they were leaving, Elizabeth heard Mr. Bingley address him. "Come now, Collins. It will not be so bad. My sister *does* have some virtues which will suit you well, indeed. Her twenty-thousand-pound dowry, to begin with."

Then they were gone, leaving the three sisters together with Mr. Darcy.

"Miss Elizabeth, you are not harmed?"

Elizabeth managed a smile, though she felt no pleasure in these events. "I am. I was able to escape from him before he could do anything to me."

"I am happy to hear it. Come, let us return to the house. We should send word to your father of these happenings and interrogate Mr. Collins." Mr. Darcy grimaced. "I see my aunt's hand in this. With Mr. Collins still in the neighborhood, I have no doubt Lady Catherine is also nearby."

Mary gasped. "Surely she would not descend to such malicious behavior!"

"I am beginning to believe my aunt capable of anything, Miss Mary," replied Mr. Darcy. "Regardless, let us go into the house."

And Elizabeth, her hand tucked into the crook of his arm, allowed herself to be led away. She was beginning to feel the fatigue of the events of the day and wished to sit and rest.

Inside the house, another drama was playing itself out. Miss Bingley, it seemed, had not quite believed her brother when informed that she was to marry Mr. Collins. For his part, the parson was gazing at them all, his manner defined by injured silence and dark looks. At least he seemed accepting, which Darcy did not suppose was a true sacrifice on his part. Other than the clear drawbacks of obtaining Miss Bingley for a wife, the woman did possess a dowry of twenty-thousand pounds, as Bingley had pointed out. No doubt Mr. Collins would accept the woman as a wife for that reason alone.

"I do not know what has come over you, Charles," hissed Miss Bingley when Darcy, with the Bennet sisters in tow, reached the house. She wrenched her arm from his grasp and directed a glare at him which was pure poison. "But I shall not marry that toad of a man."

Mr. Collins's mouth tightened, and his glare intensified, but Miss Bingley did not notice. She would not have cared even if she had, Darcy was certain.

"Yes, in fact, you shall," replied Bingley, implacability radiating from his very being.

"I shall not. I am of age and you cannot make me. I will not agree to it, even if you drag me to the church, and I most certainly shall not sign the register. Then where will you be?"

"Listen to me, Caroline," said Bingley, looming over the woman and forcing her to shrink back. "I was not bluffing when I said you would not have a home if you do not marry Mr. Collins. I will turn you out this very night with not a penny to your name if that is what you wish. Then in another year when you have turned five and twenty, if you have survived, you may come and claim your dowry. By then, I am certain your marriageability will be ruined, but at least you will have the necessary means to create your own establishment. You should choose now, for my patience is waning."

"You would not dare!" Though the woman projected confidence, it was clear she was filled with fear.

"I assure you I will. I am not the same man who yielded to your ill humors over the years due to a desire for peace in my home. You will obey me in this instance, or you will suffer the consequences."

Try as she might, Miss Bingley could muster no response. After watching her for a few moments, Bingley nodded his head once.

"Good." He beckoned to a nearby footman. "Please see Miss Bingley to her room. She is not to emerge from it for the rest of the day. I will ensure you are relieved from your post later this evening."

The footman nodded and approached Bingley's sister. She watched Bingley, shock warring with fury and disbelief. In the end, his stony countenance must have told her that pleading her case with him was fruitless.

"I hate you, Charles!" snarled she. "Our father would be disgusted with you."

"I believe, Caroline, that he would abhor what you have become."

Then the woman was led away by the waiting footman. The reprieve did not last long.

"I will, of course, fulfill my duty to your sister, Mr. Bingley," intoned Mr. Collins, reminding them all that he was present. "Though I declare there is no need, for there was no intention to compromise or in any way harm her reputation, I shall abide by your strictures."

"That is a *great* comfort, Mr. Collins," said Bingley. The only person in the room who did not understand the irony oozing from Bingley's tone appeared to be the parson himself.

"But I must plead with you, Mr. Darcy," said Collins, turning to Darcy, "to cease this madness. My cousin could never be a proper wife to you. She is far too independent, too outspoken, too common to sully the illustrious line of the Darcys of Pemberley. Surely you must see this."

"Mr. Collins," said Darcy, and the parson jumped at the dangerous note in his tone. "If you do not cease speaking of this matter which has, after all, no connection to you, it is unlikely you will live long enough to meet your bride at the altar."

The parson opened his mouth to respond again, but Darcy would not allow it. "Enough, Mr. Collins! I will call you out if you say another word."

"I think Mr. Collins should come with us to the sitting-room," interjected Fitzwilliam. His words may just have saved the parson's life. "There are some questions we need to ask him. I, for one, am curious to hear his answers."

"Of-of course, my l-lord," stammered Mr. Collins, clearly frightened out of his wits.

Fitzwilliam stepped forward and grasped his elbow, propelling him into the sitting-room. Bingley, along with Miss Bennet and Miss Mary, followed along behind. Darcy hesitated, however, and turned to regard Miss Elizabeth, inspecting her for any harm. She appeared to have passed through her ordeal none the worse for wear, though Darcy knew she had received a fright.

"Are you well, Miss Elizabeth?" asked he.

"I am, Mr. Darcy." Miss Elizabeth glared at Mr. Collins's retreating back with disdain. "It would take more than those villains to frighten me."

"I am happy to hear it."

He trailed a finger along the line of her jaw and even dared to lean forward and kiss her forehead. Miss Elizabeth's sigh of pleasure told Darcy she welcomed his ministrations.

Perhaps there was a way to speed things along. He would need to think on it and address the matter at a later time. For now, it was time to discover the exact influence his aunt had had on the day's events.

CHAPTER XXXII

"First, we should dispatch a letter to your father, informing him of these events." Mr. Bingley, who had addressed the Bennet sisters, looked kindly on Elizabeth. "I am certain he will wish to extract his own pound of flesh from those responsible and will not appreciate our denying him that opportunity."

"I shall write to Papa," said Mary, earning thanks from Elizabeth.

They entered the sitting-room, and Mr. Bingley showed Mary to a desk along the outer wall on which some paper and ink rested, where

Mary sat down to compose her note. As soon as Elizabeth entered the room, she was accosted by Kitty and Lydia, followed at a discrete distance by Louisa. They crowded around her, alternately inspecting and embracing her, seeking to assure themselves she was well.

"It was I who saw Mr. Collins approaching you out the window," said Kitty in a louder voice than Elizabeth thought necessary.

"Yes, but I informed Mr. Hurst, who went to your rescue," added Lydia.

"Then you have both done me a great service," said Elizabeth, smiling at her two younger sisters. They were exuberant and even wild at times, but at heart, they were good girls. "I thank you both."

"I hope you are well, Elizabeth," added Louisa.

"I am," replied Elizabeth. "Though villainy appears to exist all about me, I have never yet allowed my courage to be intimidated."

Mrs. Hurst laughed, even as Lydia exclaimed: "That is our Lizzy!"

"Come," said Mrs. Hurst, drawing them into the room nearer the fire. "At the very least you must be chilled. Come warm yourself by the fire. I have sent for tea."

With gratitude for the other woman's friendship, Elizabeth allowed herself to be led to the couches situated in front of the roaring fire. The love of family and friends filled her, and she sat, her youngest sisters on either side, reveling in the warmth of friendship she felt from everyone around her. They sat there for some time, Kitty and Lydia chattering, asking questions of Elizabeth about the confrontation which had just taken place. Elizabeth thought they were calming their own worries more than Elizabeth herself.

"Miss Elizabeth."

The voice startled her, and Elizabeth looked up with reflexive surprise to see Lord Chesterfield standing in front of her.

"If you are agreeable, I have a few matters of which I would like to speak with you. Will you do me the honor?"

Over the man's shoulder, Elizabeth could see Mr. Darcy watching them, concern written upon his brow.

"Of course, Lord Chesterfield," replied Elizabeth. "I am at your disposal." Elizabeth turned to her sisters. "Will you allow us a little privacy for the moment?"

Though reluctant, her sisters assented, allowing Mrs. Hurst to lead them away. The viscount sat beside Elizabeth on the sofa, though at a respectable distance, keeping his back erect and his manner serious. When he looked on her, Elizabeth once again felt the return of the old Lord Chesterfield she had known when she had first come, though his manner now was more beseeching than jovial.

"Thank you, Miss Elizabeth. "I have come to tender my apologies for my behavior. I behaved in a manner which was not befitting of the standards for which I strive, and I am heartily sorry for it. I hope you can extend the balm of forgiveness to me."

"Of course, I can," replied Elizabeth. "It is all forgotten. I hope we can continue to be friends and that your relationship with your cousin will be restored."

The viscount darted a look at his cousin, who was speaking with Mr. Bingley, though he was keeping a watchful eye on Elizabeth and Lord Chesterfield.

"I believe we have begun the process already. I am grateful for

Darcy's forbearance. I have always considered him the best of men."

Though this last was said in a tone of introspection, the viscount soon shook it off and focused again on Elizabeth. "Furthermore, I wish you to know . . ." Elizabeth was surprised and amused to see a hint of a blush staining the cheeks of such a large and prepossessed man as Lord Chesterfield. But he shook it off and proceeded, seeming determined to finish his thought. "I hope you do not believe I was attempting to offer you . . . such a disgusting situation, Miss Elizabeth. Though Darcy has opened my eyes to how it might have seemed to you, the thought never crossed my mind, and I would not ever contemplate such a thing. I know I have given you little reason to esteem my character, but I am not so depraved as that."

"I will own that I wondered at first," replied Elizabeth. "But I quickly understood the reason for your behavior."

"That you could even think it suggests that my behavior was poor."

"I think it is as much an overactive imagination, my lord," replied Elizabeth. "But regardless, let us forget about the past. In whatever measure my forgiveness is required, I offer it without reservation."

"Thank you."

It was a mark of what had passed between them that Darcy had felt trepidation at seeing his cousin approach Miss Elizabeth. Even Fitzwilliam's apology to Darcy himself, offered when they had spoken together upon leaving the house that morning, had not assuaged Darcy's concerns. Bingley's short recitation of his own conversation with Fitzwilliam had eased them somewhat, but Darcy did not breath easily until Fitzwilliam rose and took his leave of Miss Elizabeth.

"I suppose the first matter to consider is Mr. Collins," said Bingley, interrupting Darcy's thoughts.

The parson, who had been sitting quietly on an out of the way chair, likely hoping he would not be noticed, blanched when he heard his name. Darcy turned his attention to Collins, and Fitzwilliam, who had joined them, also regarded the man. Mr. Collins did not seem to know what to do or how to act. He was a man to be pitied, Darcy decided. Lady Catherine was a woman who had cowed men of more bravery than Mr. Collins, and the situation was made worse by his near worship of Lady Catherine, and the fact that he likely felt himself beholden to her.

"Agreed," said Darcy, moving to confront the parson. Mr. Collins blanched, and his gaze found the floor. He refused to look up.

"Well, Mr. Collins? What do you have to say for yourself?"

"I . . . Well . . . That is to say . . ." The man produced a handkerchief from his pocket and began to mop his face. "What do you wish me to tell you, Mr. Darcy?"

Given his stuttering, Darcy was surprised he was able to say that much without stumbling. Mr. Collins was petrified.

"Let us begin with Lady Catherine. Since you are still in the neighborhood, am I correct to suppose that Lady Catherine is also nearby?"

Though it clashed with Mr. Collins's loyalty to Lady Catherine, his fear of the gentlemen confronting him overwhelmed it. "She is."

"And where is she at present?"

"She has . . . has taken rooms at the Rose and Crown in Stevenage."

Darcy regarded the quivering man in front of him. "I am certain I already know what her purpose was. But tell me in your own words what she hoped to accomplish."

The parson still would not meet Darcy's eyes. "To ensure none of the Bennet sisters succeeded in capturing either you or Lord Chesterfield."

"As I thought," replied Darcy with a terse nod. "But before we continue, Mr. Collins, let me make one thing very clear, so you do not feel you must raise it again. There has been nothing improper. Miss Elizabeth has not coerced me. I have asked her for an honorable courtship because *I* wish to have her as a wife, not because of anything underhanded."

A hurried and frenetic nod was Mr. Collins's response.

"Now that has been clarified, I should think you would not need to raise the subject of your objections again. Are we quite clear, Mr. Collins?"

"Y-yes, Mr. Darcy," stuttered the man, and his nodding increased its pace.

"Good. Now, of what have your actions consisted since Lady Catherine assigned this task to you?"

Mr. Collins heaved a deep breath. "M-Mr. Darcy, surely you must see that anything I say will put me at odds with my patroness. How can I continue to serve her if she is angry with me?"

"I think, Mr. Collins," interjected Fitzwilliam, "you had best concern yourself with pleasing *us*. We are far more fearsome than Lady Catherine could ever be.

"And we have the means to ensure you are defrocked and thrown from the ranks of the clergy." Mr. Collins's eyes widened, and he began to shake his head, but Darcy had by now had enough of the stupid man. "Your conduct in this matter has been appalling, sir. I am certain your bishop would not be happy should he learn of it, to say nothing of what the archbishop would say."

A gasp escaped Mr. Collins's lips. Fitzwilliam only gazed at him without pity. "Yes, Mr. Collins, my family is well acquainted with the archbishop."

"You should also remember that once a living has been given, it may not be rescinded. Lady Catherine does, perhaps, have the means to make your life difficult, but she has not the ability to revoke the living. Only your superiors removing you from your office can do so."

Mr. Collins slumped in his chair, defeated. "Lady Catherine decreed that Miss Elizabeth was to be removed from any possibility of tempting you to propose to her by whatever means possible."

"Did you mean to compromise her, Mr. Collins?" demanded Darcy. The parson looked up in shock at the venom in Darcy's voice and then quickly looked down again. "Or did you mean to abduct her?

"What was your game, man?"

Mr. Collins jumped. "I had no such intentions, I swear!"

"Then what was your game?"

Shaking, and barely making himself understood, Mr. Collins began to speak. "When I was still at Longbourn, Mr. Wickham and I agreed to distract Miss Elizabeth and Miss Lydia from you and your cousin?"

"Wickham?" demanded Darcy. "How do you know Wickham?"

"We became known to each other during the first visit the officers paid to Longbourn. There I learned of his connection to you."

"And you listened to him?"

A spark of spirit came out in Mr. Collins's response. "He confessed to his wrongdoings and informed me that he was trying to make amends. He told me that his friendship with you, though strained, was still strong."

Fitzwilliam shook his head, and Darcy was no less disgusted with what he was hearing. "Then he misled you, sir. Wickham has no conscience, no morals, and I have not associated with him in years. I would have been happy to never lay eyes on him again."

Shock radiated from Mr. Collins, but at Darcy's stern look, he began to speak again. "Mr. Wickham was forbidden from dancing with the Bennet sisters, but I attempted to continue to induce them to see reason and leave you and your cousin alone."

"Hence your proposal."

Darcy looked up to see that Miss Elizabeth had joined them. He directed a look askance at her, but she only shook her head with impatience. She had as much right to hear Collins's account as any of them.

"Yes," was Mr. Collins's simple reply. "When we were both banned from Longbourn, I introduced Mr. Wickham to Lady Catherine, though she already knew of him. I served as the liaison between them. Mr. Wickham demanded a large sum of money from Lady Catherine for his assistance, and while Lady Catherine initially balked, eventually she agreed."

"How much and what was Wickham's plan?"

"His ultimate plan, I do not know," replied Mr. Collins. "He would not share the details. He only said I was to assist."

"Given what happened in the gardens, it is clear Wickham meant to compromise Miss Elizabeth at best. I shudder to think of what might have happened had she fallen into his power."

"And how much was she to pay him?"

"Five thousand pounds."

"So Lady Catherine would ruin a young woman's life to promote her schemes." Darcy's anger burned with a white-hot flame. "Damnation, man, did you not see what was happening? Or were you filled with the need for revenge because Miss Elizabeth rejected your proposal?"

"Lady Catherine is my patroness!" protested Mr. Collins. "She commands and I must obey!"

"Your trouble, Mr. Collins," said Miss Elizabeth, composed despite what she had heard of their intentions for her, "is that you do not think for yourself. Do you wish to always be at the beck and call of another? Could you live with yourself if your actions abetted in another being hurt, even if you did nothing against that person yourself?"

Mr. Collins had nothing to say to that. His eyes went wide, however, though Darcy was not certain if it was at the suggestion he should disobey his patroness or because Miss Elizabeth's words had struck a chord in the fog of his mind.

"It is clear that Collins, though he has behaved despicably, is not the true villain in this drama." Fitzwilliam met Darcy's eyes and he nodded. "We will confront Lady Catherine and send her back to Rosings with her tail between her legs. But my father will wish to know of this. I doubt he will be kind to Lady Catherine."

"And well he should not," growled Darcy. He turned his attention back to Collins. "Do you have anything else to tell us?"

Mr. Collins shook his head, but then he paused as something occurred to him. He hesitated, but seeing the looks they directed at him, he evidently decided that remaining silent was not in his best interests.

"Mr. Wickham was working with Miss Bingley to obtain information about Miss Elizabeth and your doings with her."

"Of course!" said Fitzwilliam. "Wickham knew Darcy was paying attention to Miss Elizabeth, and even goaded me about it."

Unsure of what referred to, Darcy said: "When was this?"

"The day you went to Longbourn to offer courtship to Miss Elizabeth," replied Fitzwilliam. He colored a little, likely remembering what had happened between them, but he pushed his embarrassment aside. "I went to Meryton as I was at loose ends with nothing to do. Wickham approached me and we exchanged words. I did not consider it at the time, but he knew much of what was happening. I am certain he was attempting to drive a wedge between us."

"They became acquainted at the ball," interjected Mrs. Hurst. "Caroline saw him on the side of the dance floor and wondered what he was about. Later I saw them speaking together."

"Do you know how information was exchanged or what they planned?" asked Darcy of Mr. Collins.

The parson shook his head. "I apologize, Mr. Darcy, but Mr. Wickham did not share it with me."

"Then we shall ask Caroline," said Bingley.

"Is there any reason to?" asked Fitzwilliam. "Your sister will be married to Collins, and Wickham will soon be in prison. It does not signify whether they actually planned some mischief or if there was simply an exchange of information."

"It matters to me!" cried Mr. Collins. "How am I to know if there was nothing more than you said? If their connection was more . . . Well . . ."

"I do not believe you need to concern yourself on that score, Collins," said Darcy, understanding the thrust of his concerns. "Miss Bingley has been focused on making a match with a man of society. She would never have dallied with a mere militia officer."

Darcy's opinion was seconded by Bingley. Collins nodded, though he did not seem convinced. Fortunately, he refrained from speaking again, particularly as Darcy scowled at him, seeming to sense that he was in for a verbal lashing. "Your actions disgust me, Collins. That the three of you could conspire against a woman who had never done you any harm infuriates me. I would stop at nothing to see you thrown from the church in disgrace if ruining your prospects would not cause my friend hardship.

"Though I will not act against you, I will let you know here and now that you will never importune Miss Elizabeth, or any of the Bennet family again, and your wife is under the same stricture. If I find out either of you have so much as glared at any of them from across the room, I will ruin you forever. Have I made myself clear?"

"Y-yes, M-Mr. Darcy." The parson jumped to his feet and began bowing hastily, repeatedly.

"Good. Now sit quietly until we are ready to go to Stevenage to confront my contemptible aunt."

Mr. Collins did as he was told with nary a comment concerning his patroness. It was just as well he did not—Darcy might have strangled the man had he made another sound.

When Mr. Bennet arrived soon after, his concern for his second daughter was evident. He went to her and grasped her hands, looking into her eyes and asking after her wellbeing. As was her custom, Miss Elizabeth protested she was well, and it was the resilience of his daughter, as much as anything, that settled Mr. Bennet's concerns.

After hearing the tale Mr. Collins had related, Mr. Bennet contented himself with a disdainful glare and a few choice comments for his cousin before he ignored him.

"Are we for Stevenage to confront Lady Catherine, then?"

"Yes, Mr. Bennet," replied Darcy. "I have a great desire to speak to my aunt and call her to account for her actions. You are, of course, welcome to accompany us."

"Believe me, Mr. Darcy, I would not miss it."

It was determined that Bingley would escort the Bennet ladies back to Longbourn while Hurst and his wife would remain at Netherfield to watch after their sister and ensure her good behavior. Thus, after seeing the ladies to the Darcy carriage, Darcy, in the company of Fitzwilliam, Mr. Bennet, and the detestable Collins, entered Fitzwilliam's conveyance for the journey to Stevenage.

The Rose and Crown was a stately building, the finest inn in Stevenage, though Darcy suspected her ladyship would find it less than adequate. Above the door was a brightly painted sign proclaiming the name of the establishment, with a crimson rose hovering above an elaborate golden coronet. The carriage stopped in front of the building, allowing the men to descend, and they made their way into the inn. There, seated on a bench, as if she owned the place, was Lady Catherine.

The lady's eyes narrowed at the sight of her two nephews in the company of her parson, not to mention the presence of Mr. Bennet. But the lady was not slow of thought. She peered at them, an imperious smile coming over her face, and then proceeded to ignore Mr. Bennet.

"So, have you finally come to your senses? I knew it would be this way. Your breeding would never allow you to forever consort with those who are so clearly unsuitable."

"Mr. Collins," said Darcy, bringing the parson to him amid several bows and exclamations of attention. "I assume this inn has a private dining room."

"It does, Mr. Darcy. Lady Catherine has used them every night, for it is not prudent for a lady of her —"

"Yes, yes, Mr. Collins," snapped Darcy, bringing Mr. Collins's mouth shut with an audible clack of his teeth. "Go to the innkeeper and secure one for our use. I do not think it wise to speak of our business where everyone in Stevenage may overhear."

Mr. Collins dropped several more bows before scurrying off to do as he was bid. Lady Catherine glared at Darcy, but she did not object. Anyone could have seen that Darcy was displeased, and his companion's countenances were no less stony. She maintained her haughty demeanor as she rose to follow them to the private room which was quickly obtained by the parson.

"Let me say something before we begin," said Mr. Bennet, forestalling any discussion once they had entered the parlor. His implacable glare settled on Lady Catherine, who did not even deign to notice him. "You, Lady Catherine de Bourgh, are a foul and loathsome woman."

Lady Catherine's nostrils flared, and she turned on Mr. Bennet, flames rising in her eyes. But Mr. Bennet was not about to be deterred from making his sentiments known. "What kind of woman sets a man the likes of Wickham on a woman she does not know for the purpose of harming her? You disgust me. Were it not for your nephews, of whom I think highly, I would insist the only place fit for you is Bedlam."

Though incensed, Lady Catherine did not reply to Mr. Bennet. "Do you both mean to sit there and allow this . . . *man* to speak of me in such a fashion?"

"I happen to agree with him," replied Fitzwilliam.

"If it were my choice, I *would* see you in Bedlam," added Darcy. "Can you deny anything Mr. Bennet said? Can you refute what we have learned from your foolish parson?"

Lady Catherine sniffed and turned away. Darcy was not about to allow it.

"Well?" the woman flinched at his raised voice. "What have you to say for yourself?"

"It appears I was correct," said Lady Catherine, sniffing in disdain. "You have lost your head for a country minx. And you are no better, Fitzwilliam, for I have heard you were vying with Darcy for the little adventuress. Is she in heat, to be provoking you both to leave your senses and chase after her like rutting dogs?"

"I have never struck a woman before," snarled Mr. Bennet, "but I am tempted to at this very minute. Do not say one more word about my daughter, or I will not be responsible for my actions!"

Again, Lady Catherine turned her haughty indifference on Mr. Bennet, before turning away to address Darcy. "It matters little what this man says. Your own opinion is also irrelevant. I have discovered information which will secure your compliance."

"Oh?" asked Darcy. "And what might that be?"

"Mr. Wickham has informed me of his attempt to elope with your sister last summer. If you do not do as I demand, I will publish Georgiana's disgrace to all."

"You would attempt to ruin my sister for your own selfish designs?" demanded Darcy.

"I only act to defend you from yourself!" said Lady Catherine with some heat.

"Then you are a fool," interrupted Fitzwilliam. "Believing anything Wickham says is a path fraught with peril. There was never any attempt to elope with Georgiana. Her companion, Mrs. Annesley, is a diligent guardian. Wickham played you for a fool."

Lady Catherine's eyes widened, and she attempted to deny it. "He informed me of the matter in full! He gave me facts, locations, and details which could not be contrived." Lady Catherine's eyes narrowed. "You are attempting to deceive me by claiming it did not happen. But I know the truth."

"And did you take the time to corroborate Wickham's story?" asked Darcy. "Where was this attempt supposed to have taken place?"

"Why would I corroborate it when he shared the facts of the matter with me?" At Darcy's glare, the woman gave in. "It was in Ramsgate. He informed me how he met her there seemingly by chance, and how he made love to her, eventually eliciting an agreement to elope to Gretna Green."

"Then why did he not?"

"He informed me that you thwarted him at the last moment."

"How convenient," murmured Fitzwilliam.

"And where was her companion while Wickham was perpetrating his nefarious schemes?" asked Darcy.

"Her companion was his confederate," replied Lady Catherine, her voice exuding smugness. "You see, Darcy, I not only have the details, I am also not afraid to use them to compel you to do as I command."

Darcy was unable to believe what he was hearing. He had always known Lady Catherine to be insistent upon having her own way. But for her to descend to such a betrayal was more than he could fathom.

"Am I to assume that Wickham made this story out of whole cloth?" asked Mr. Bennet. Darcy could only nod. "Then I revise my opinion, sir—your aunt should be consigned to Bedlam as soon as may be. She is clearly beyond any hope of amendment."

Darcy could not disagree, and he was certain Fitzwilliam was caught in the same snare of disbelief. Even Mr. Collins, who would never hear anything against his patroness, was looking at her, unable to fathom what he was hearing.

For Lady Catherine's part, she only directed a withering glare at Mr. Bennet. "Your opinion, Mr. Bennet, is neither needed nor wanted. You may leave directly, as your presence is not necessary. You should be grateful that you have emerged from this situation with your daughter intact. You should look for husbands for your daughters at your level of society—perhaps a tenant farmer will do?"

While Darcy might have expected Mr. Bennet to respond with angry words, instead he only regarded Lady Catherine, sardonic amusement evident in his condescending smile. The lady did not miss it, but she decided to ignore it.

"Now that you know how it shall be, Darcy, we shall plan your wedding immediately. A spring wedding in Kent would be a lovely affair."

"You will not be planning any wedding," rasped Darcy, as angry as he had ever been in his life. "In fact, I am considering adding my voice to Mr. Bennet's regarding your suitability to be housed in an asylum."

"Darcy—"

"Be silent, Madam!" Darcy rose and bent over, putting his face only inches from hers, daring her to say another word. She fell silent, though Darcy thought it was due to the shock of being contradicted rather than being cowed by his anger.

"As I informed you before, Lady Catherine, listening to Wickham spew his vitriol is fraught with peril. Rarely does the truth pass his lips. In this instance, he has deceived you, for Georgiana was in *my* company all summer. Furthermore, I have several witnesses who will corroborate my assertion that she was with me at my family's lodge in the lake country. Among their number are not only Fitzwilliam but your own brother. Do you not recall the invitation I extended to you and Anne to join us?" Darcy snorted with contempt. "You refused, informing us that Anne was too delicate to travel so far."

Shocked, Lady Catherine's gaze darted to Fitzwilliam. He sat with his arms crossed, glaring at Lady Catherine as if she was something foul. Then he slowly nodded his head.

"Furthermore, it is beyond vile to threaten your own niece — the daughter of your dearly departed sister — with derision and infamy to further your own selfish designs.

"Finally, I might wonder why, after you thought you possessed the means necessary to ensure my compliance, you still set your attack dog on Miss Elizabeth. Should you not simply have called me here and told me of your *information*, demanding that I bow to your will? Why attempt to ruin Miss Elizabeth at all?"

"Because the little adventuress deserved to be punished for her temerity," said Lady Catherine, speaking without thinking. The woman had never known when it was best to simply stay silent.

"You may now consider all congress between the Darcys and the de Bourghs hereby severed," rasped Darcy. It was all he could do to restrain himself from laying hands on the woman and administering a more physical form of vengeance. "I will not associate with a woman who can consider such actions. You may be assured that if you contact me again, your letters will be returned unopened. If you should choose to show yourself at any of my properties, you will be barred entrance. Do not come to Pemberley, and do not attempt entrance to my London home, for I will take great pleasure in throwing you from my house where all society can see your shame."

"Darcy!" exclaimed Lady Catherine, shocked.

Darcy only glared at the woman and rose, quitting the room with a few long strides. He cared not what Fitzwilliam said to her, or if the earl ever heard of her shameful actions. For Darcy, he was through with the woman. He would never call her aunt again.

"Darcy!"

Whirling and glaring at the owner of the voice, Darcy noted his cousin, Anne, approaching him at a hurried pace. Darcy scowled at her; he did not wish to endure his cousin at present, not when the anger against his aunt was filling him with the need to break something. He spun on his heel and walked out of the inn, knowing as he did so that Anne would follow.

"Darcy! Why will you not speak to me?"

Having attained the courtyard outside the inn, Darcy spun on his heel, causing Anne to jerk back in sudden fright.

"Because I can tolerate no more of your foolishness. It ends now!"

"Of what foolishness do you speak?"

With a growl, Darcy began to pace the driveway, throwing his hands up in the air with frustration. "This matter of your mother's desire to see us wed. The lengths to which she will go astound and horrify me."

"I do not understand," said Anne, though her lower lip jutted out in a pout. "Mama only said Miss Bennet would be made to see reason."

"Your mother is a liar and a madwoman," spat Darcy.

Anne's eyes widened. "I cannot understand you."

"And I will not explain it. If you wish to understand, speak to that virago you call a mother. *If* she can be trusted to speak the truth."

"Darcy," said Anne, "have we not always been destined to wed? Your mother and mine agreed to it while we are young. For what possible reason do you resist?"

"Why should you do everything your mother says?" asked Darcy. "Has she complete control over your life? Do you think she even cares about your wishes? Of course, she does not! She merely commands and you obey.

"My advice to you, Anne, is to seek a way to win your freedom from your mother, for I shall never marry you. Perhaps Uncle Hugh would be willing to help, but I have severed my connection with your mother. I will never see her again.

"Now, if you will excuse me."

With only a trace of a bow, Darcy turned on his heel and marched away. He made his way to the carriage and stepped inside, determined to wait in its confines of the rest of the party. He did not wish anyone to witness his agitation. He hoped that the rest of the company would return quickly, for Darcy wished to return to Longbourn to see for himself that Miss Elizabeth was well.

Chapter XXXIII

"You have well and truly done it this time, Caroline."

"How dare you speak to me in such a way! You insipid, worthless excuse of a woman!"

"She speaks to you in such a way because you deserve it."

Hurst stepping into the room caused Caroline to step back and blanch in surprise. Louisa knew it was likely fruitless to confront her sister in this matter, but she had felt it necessary to make one last attempt. After she was married to Collins, Louisa felt it likely she would see her sister but little, and though the thought was not onerous, some vestige of sibling affection won its way past her absolute disgust for Caroline and urged her to try to talk sense into her.

"You will keep a civil tongue in your head, Caroline," continued Hurst. "I will not allow you to continue to treat your sister as you have all these years."

"Perhaps you should return below stairs and marinate yourself in your brandy," snarled Caroline. "It *is* what you do best, is it not?"

More chilling for Caroline than had Hurst lost his temper was the fact that he only fixed her with a cold smile. "Putting you over my knee *is* an option, Caroline. Please, continue to insult us. I would enjoy administering the punishment you so richly deserve. Your father should have done so many years ago!"

"You both disgust me," said Caroline, ignoring Hurst's words. "I have been working all these years to increase our standing and bring respectability to our family's name, and you have all ruined it! I could have been the wife of a viscount and later, an earl! It would have been instant respectability for the Bingley name!"

"You are a fool, Caroline," said Louisa. "Nothing but infamy would have followed, even had you been successful. Do you not think rumors would have existed, even if it had been hushed up? The gossips of society would have spoken of it without cessation. The daughters of tradesmen do not marry future earls."

"And Chesterfield would never have married you, even if you had been successful," added Hurst. "He would have refused and I—and your brother—would not have insisted."

"Of course, I would have married him! It would have been a perfect match."

Louisa exchanged a look with her husband. There was no reaching Caroline, for she was convinced she was in the right. It was pointless to even make the attempt.

"I hope you are happy with your parson, Caroline," said Louisa. "I hope even more that the marriage is concluded quickly and that you are taken away to your new home without delay, for I cannot even bear to look at you."

Then Louisa departed from the room, through the door her husband opened for her. A scream of pure rage issued from Caroline's throat and the sound of glass shattering impacted the door through which they had just passed. Caroline's maid, Louisa dismissed with a kind word, and when the woman indicated that she wished to leave Caroline's employ, Louisa assented, informing her that she would receive her pay and a letter of recommendation. When she departed, it was clear to see how relieved she was.

"You will not see Caroline again, Louisa," said Hurst when they were alone. "I will not allow her to hurt you."

"I have no intention of going to her again." Louisa felt weary, as if she had been awake for a month without sleep. "She is dead to me, and you should have no doubt she feels the same way."

Louisa allowed herself to be drawn into her husband's embrace, enjoying the feeling of the strength of his arms about her.

"I hope she stops before she breaks all her things," said Louisa after a moment of silence.

"She may break everything she owns," replied Hurst. "It is nothing to me." He paused and seemed to consider it. "In fact, I believe I will encourage your brother to take whatever damage she causes out of her dowry. It is only fitting she should pay the price for her lack of control."

Though it was not a matter to provoke amusement, Louisa could not help but laugh. Trust Hurst to see things clearly.

The mood in the carriage was subdued, which was just as well for Darcy, for he had no desire to speak of the woman he would not refer to as "aunt" again. The other gentlemen returned to the carriage some fifteen minutes after Darcy had quit the room, and soon thereafter Collins joined them.

"Mr. Collins is to stay in Meryton while waiting for his nuptials," said Fitzwilliam. For his part, Mr. Collins said nothing, contenting himself with a wide-eyed stare at the other gentlemen. "As for Lady Catherine," continued Fitzwilliam, "she will return to Kent at once. I believe I have put the fear of God into her, for though she continued to bluster and snap, she was eager to quit this place." Fitzwilliam grinned, an unpleasant one, to be certain. "She can expect a visit from my father. He will not be happy to hear of her actions."

Darcy grunted and the subject was dropped, for he had no desire to speak of it. The other gentlemen all appeared content with their own thoughts as well, for even between Mr. Bennet and Fitzwilliam there was little conversation.

When they arrived back at Netherfield, they found Bingley waiting for them there, having already seen the Bennet sisters back to Longbourn. He greeted them, none of his usual joviality evident in his manner.

"I believe we must get down to business, Mr. Collins," said Bingley, his tone uncharacteristically firm. "Given what occurred this morning, it would be best if you were to marry my sister as soon as possible. The best way to accomplish this is for you to go to town and obtain a common license."

The other gentlemen were watching Mr. Collins, their sternness seeming to weigh down on him. His licked his lips, displaying his nervousness before he responded: "While I am certain your sister is a beautiful woman with a fine dowry, she seems . . . set against the match."

Hurst, who was also present, snorted at the man's understatement. Collins, though he frowned, ignored him.

"Perhaps it would be best if we did not force her in this matter? I have no desire to live with a woman with whom I will be perpetually at odds."

"You should have thought of that before you accosted Miss Elizabeth in the gardens and thoroughly compromised my sister." Bingley was implacable, and Collins wilted in the face of it. "Another thing you may wish to consider, Collins: one day you may be master of Longbourn and resident of this neighborhood. People have long memories—if you do not marry her, those who live here will remember that, and you may have some difficulty being accepted when you come."

A slow nod was Mr. Collins's response. When he replied, he was the Collins of old again.

"Of course, Mr. Bingley. I shall do my duty, of course, and marry your excellent sister. I am certain we shall have a most felicitous life together. Uh . . . Once she . . . accustoms herself to her situation, of course."

"I am certain you will, Mr. Collins," replied Bingley.

In fact, Darcy thought there were few things less likely than the Collinses experiencing felicity in marriage, but in the end, Darcy decided it did not concern him. As long as they were both removed from his life forever, he cared not what they did.

"Bingley," said Fitzwilliam, "as you noted, it would be best if your sister and Collins were to go before the parson in as expeditious a manner as possible. To that end, I would like to offer my services. I am required to go to London, as my father will wish to hear of his sister's behavior in person, rather than through the post. Since I am bound for town anyway, I will take Mr. Collins with me so that he may obtain the required license."

Fitzwilliam turned and eyed Mr. Collins, who seemed uncertain whether he was about to be castigated once again. "There is also the matter of the marriage settlement. Might I assume, Collins, that you have no solicitor to prepare the documents?"

"Umm . . . No, my lord. I have no such relationship."

"Then I will also arrange for him to meet with my family solicitor," said Fitzwilliam with a nod. "There should be no impediment to arranging these matters in an expeditious manner. Then we may return, likely by early next week." Fitzwilliam turned to Bingley. "You can book Longbourn chapel for a wedding, and we can consider the matter completed."

With a nod and a perceptible sense of relief Bingley nodded.

"Thank you, Fitzwilliam. Your assistance would be much appreciated. I was not looking forward to being required to leave for town at present to assist Collins."

"I knew that, Bingley," said Fitzwilliam, slapping the other man on the back. "You have a reason to stay in Meryton, and since I can assist Mr. Collins, I see no reason for you to leave as well." Fitzwilliam turned to Mr. Collins. "Come, Collins. I will inform my valet of our departure. Once I am prepared, we shall depart."

Though clearly not quite understanding Fitzwilliam's seeming friendliness, he allowed himself to be led from the room. Darcy put them from his mind and turned to Mr. Bennet.

"Mr. Bennet, might I have a word?"

The Bennet patriarch eyed him for a moment before he assented. Bingley, understanding that Darcy wished to speak in private, nodded at Hurst. "We will begin to make arrangements for Caroline's forthcoming marriage."

Darcy acknowledged his friend's statement and waited until he left the room to address Mr. Bennet.

"I know this may seem precipitous, Mr. Bennet, but I believe it may be best to expedite my courtship with your daughter to protect her reputation."

The subject Darcy had raised was clearly no surprise to Mr. Bennet. "Is that your wish, or is it truly a matter of protecting Elizabeth?"

"I believe it is nothing more than prudent," replied Darcy, though he was a little embarrassed that Mr. Bennet had seen through him. "Yes, I wish to have your daughter for a wife—that much is true. But I am concerned that word of what happened this morning will be disseminated throughout the neighborhood. Furthermore, I worry that Lady Catherine may still have some villainy in mind."

"You left before your cousin's final words to your aunt. I doubt she will cause any more trouble. I consider myself a good judge of others, and while your aunt attempted to portray unconcern and strength, in reality, I suspect she is fearful about what her brother might do."

"That may be the case," conceded Darcy. "But given the lengths to which she was willing to go, I believe it would be best to ensure she can do nothing. And this does not even cover the possibility of rumors in town."

Mr. Bennet watched him for several more moments before he shrugged and then followed it with a grin. "You take no compassion on *me*, Mr. Darcy. Elizabeth is my favorite daughter, and though I will own that her younger sisters have improved of late, they still are *not* my Lizzy. I will miss her companionship very much, indeed.

"However, I can see the sense in your suggestion, so I will allow it. But you must convince Lizzy it is the best course of action, for she has a mind of her own, as you well know. I have no doubt she will claim there is no need to hurry things along."

"I suspect you are correct, sir," replied Darcy.

"Do not be cast down, young man," replied Mr. Bennet, his joviality entirely inappropriate, in Darcy's opinion. "Consider it a trial run. If you marry my Lizzy, you will be required to deal with her. Trust me: you will need all the practice you can obtain."

Darcy showed Mr. Bennet a slow smile. "I am quite looking forward to it, sir. I would have it no other way."

In the aftermath of what had happened that morning, Elizabeth found herself feeling a little annoyed at her sisters. Though she appreciated the concern they were showing for her, their attempts to reassure themselves of her wellbeing were grating on her nerves. In fact, she had been far too angry with Mr. Wickham's actions — not to mention those of Miss Bingley and Mr. Collins — to feel any fear for her situation. It was a relief to arrive back at Longbourn and return to her room for a few short moments to compose herself and escape their smothering.

It was no surprise that her respite in her room did not last long, for she knew her mother would wish to hear an account of what happened from her own lips. Elizabeth responded to the summons as a dutiful daughter, and when her mother asked, she explained the incident from her perspective, taking care to assure Mrs. Bennet she was well and had suffered no ill effects. Elizabeth also refrained from saying anything concerning Miss Bingley's compromise attempt — her mother and two youngest sisters retained enough of their love of gossip that such a story would be all over Meryton, should she share it with them — and intimated that Miss Bingley was made angry because of Elizabeth's courtship with Mr. Darcy.

Mrs. Bennet listened without reply until Elizabeth's tale had run its course, and then she sighed. "We have been beset by such odious people of late that I can scarcely comprehend it. At least Mr. Collins and Miss Bingley will soon be out of our lives."

"And do not forget about Mr. Wickham," said Lydia. "Mr. Darcy has pledged to see him in prison, which is exactly where he belongs."

With a nod, Mrs. Bennet said: "I dare say he does, Lydia my dear. But there is one matter which vexes me about this affair. To think that

Miss Bingley, of all people, will one day take my place as mistress of this estate! After her villainy, she is being rewarded, rather than punished. I can scarce take it in!"

"But, Mother," said Elizabeth, "you have not considered the fact that to become the mistress of Longbourn, she must be married to Mr. Collins. I dare say *that* is as much of a punishment as anything we may design."

A slow smile spread across Mrs. Bennet's face. "Yes, I suppose you are correct, Lizzy. In fact, the more I think about it, the more I realize that Mr. Collins and Miss Bingley are made for each other. They are both so odious in own their ways that they shall make each other quite miserable, I am sure.

"But what of Mr. Darcy and your courtship? He has not decided to throw you over because of the actions of his former friend, has he?"

"Given how Mr. Darcy looks at our Lizzy, do *you* think he would?" asked Jane.

Elizabeth looked at her sister, promising retribution for her tease. For Mrs. Bennet's part, she only seemed to consider the matter for a moment before she replied with a slow nod.

"Yes, that is quite true, I suppose. Mr. Darcy does show all the signs of a man in love."

"He does," replied Jane. "In fact, I will be very much surprised if he does not come to you offering to marry you sooner to protect your reputation."

"But my reputation is not threatened," protested Elizabeth.

"You are correct," exclaimed Mrs. Bennet, eyes wide at the thought. "It is *exactly* what a man like Mr. Darcy would do." Mrs. Bennet was suddenly once again the nervous and excitable woman Elizabeth had known all her life. "Oh, I shall go distracted! Two daughters engaged! How shall I ever bear the happiness?"

Elizabeth and Jane shared a look and shook their heads. Whatever improvements had been made to Mrs. Bennet's demeanor of late, it was clear she was still the same woman she had ever been.

When Mr. Bennet returned later that afternoon, it was with Mr. Darcy, and as Elizabeth had thought about what Jane had said in the intervening hours, she found she was not surprised to see him. The gentlemen came into the sitting-room, where they explained what had happened with Lady Catherine, and the ladies responded with the appropriate exclamations, words of disgust for her behavior, and hopes that she would not continue to ▓▓▓▓ them.

While Mr. Bennet bore most of the burden of communication, Mr.

Darcy sat quietly, answering questions when necessary. Much of his attention was on Elizabeth, and she felt the warmth of his earnest gaze covering her like a blanket. As the conversation wound down, he turned to her to speak for the first time.

"Miss Elizabeth, might I have a moment of your time in private? The weather is still fine—perhaps we could go out to the back gardens."

Now certain that Jane had been entirely correct, Elizabeth assented, and with the ever-dependable Mary in tow, they soon departed the house. Elizabeth did not miss the significant look which her father bestowed on the man who was courting her, further firming her understanding of what was about to happen.

When they were walking behind the house, Mr. Darcy lost no time in making his communication, as he stopped and turned to face her.

"Miss Elizabeth, as the most intelligent woman of my acquaintance, I am certain you have seen something unusual in my manner, and I have no doubt you already expect what I am about to ask you. I also understand you to be an independent sort of woman. Thus, I ask you to hear my entreaty and consider it carefully. I would not importune you unless I believed it for the best."

"Very well, Mr. Darcy," replied Elizabeth. "You may speak, and I will give your words careful consideration."

Mr. Darcy smiled and nodded. "Miss Elizabeth, I know that we have not been courting long. But given the events of this morning, I cannot help but think that you could be affected, through no fault of your own, by the actions of those who, after all, possess not a hint of your goodness. As such, I feel it proper to make you an offer of marriage. I esteem you very highly, and I believe this would be the best course for your continued happiness."

As proposals went, it was not objectionable—not like Mr. Collins's had been. But it was also not the romantic declaration of undying love that a young woman of Elizabeth's temperament had always hoped to receive. Though she would never be unkind to this man, she opened her mouth to refuse him in hopes that his eloquence could be rediscovered later, when she noticed him shifting his feet while he waited for her answer.

Mr. Darcy was nervous! As nervous as ever a man was. Elizabeth was shocked. He was as confident a man as she had ever seen, and yet he was acting like a schoolboy. Of course, it was not every day that a man proposed to a woman. Elizabeth decided that a little gentle teasing might be in order.

"I doubt Mr. Wickham's actions will affect me to any great extent, Mr. Darcy," replied she, affecting complete nonchalance. "I was able to escape from him very quickly, and no one was in the garden watching us."

"But we were easily visible from the house. You never know if a maid was watching through a window."

"Hmm . . . Perhaps not. But I am also confident of the esteem in which the people of Meryton hold me. They would see the situation for what it was and would not punish me for the actions of another. Your testimony of Mr. Wickham's character will further exonerate me."

"I understand your faith in the people of your neighborhood," said Mr. Darcy, his manner grave. "But many a person has had such faith, only to have it destroyed. The whispers of a few can have a detrimental effect on one in our society."

"That may be the case, sir, but I do not think it is likely."

Elizabeth made a show of considering the man, and Mr. Darcy was wise enough to remain silent while she thought.

"I do not know, Mr. Darcy," said she at length. "I do not believe rumor and innuendo will be a problem. It is also possible I might receive a better offer. A viscount, for example, might find himself violently in love with me. It would not do to be hasty."

While Mr. Darcy appeared shocked at first, he was soon grinning at her. Elizabeth returned it with an impudence she did not think he often encountered.

"You are teasing me," said he.

"To an extent, Mr. Darcy," said Elizabeth. She was feeling a little giddy, which was making her flippant. "You should have known, given what you know of my character."

"'To an extent?'" echoed Mr. Darcy. "Can you please explain?"

"Of course. You see, I am an impressionable and romantic young woman. I have always thought the proposal I would accept would be one which filled all my hopes of romance and, furthermore, informed me of the full extent of the man's love for me and desperate need to have me. No matter what is being said about me by my neighbors, I do not think an ill-advised attack by a libertine on my person is enough to induce me into matrimony. I wish to be loved and respected. I do not wish to be a duty."

"You think I consider you a duty?"

"I cannot say," replied Elizabeth. "But one might think likely, considering your presence here and what happened earlier today."

Elizabeth arched an eyebrow at him. "Do you care to disprove my theory?"

It seemed it was always the way with this woman—just when Darcy thought his love could grow any greater, she proved him incorrect. Nothing discouraged her, nothing intimidated her, and no matter what happened in her life, she bounced back with a resilience he had rarely seen in anyone.

And she was correct. Nervous that she was so independent that she would refuse to marry him, Darcy had gone about his proposal all wrong. He should have asked with confidence and poise, rather than as a child fearful of being denied a treat. She deserved nothing less than his complete devotion and his boldness. And Darcy was determined to give it to her.

"Miss Elizabeth," said he, reaching down to take her hand in his own. "If you wish to have my devotion, then my devotion you shall have."

She cocked her head to the side. "Your devotion? Your devotion because I demanded to be treated like a heroine in a novel?"

Darcy could not help but laugh. "No, Miss Elizabeth. My devotion to you because I simply can be no other way."

"Well, that is a start, Mr. Darcy. But I think I need to be further convinced."

"And so you shall be. In reality, Miss Elizabeth, I *do* believe that an engagement between us would be prudent. Gossip has a way of spreading with uncontrollable ferocity, much like a brush fire burning out of control in a field. But when I said that I wished you to agree to marry me, I was only speaking part of the truth.

"The truth is that the events of this morning are nothing more than a convenient excuse to speed the process."

Miss Elizabeth's eyebrow rose at his statement. "I am nothing more than a 'convenient excuse?'"

"No, Miss Elizabeth," said Darcy with a chuckle. "You are much more than a convenient excuse. You are a jewel of a woman, poised, confident, playful, beautiful, and intelligent, and I am a better man for having been admitted to your presence. You are more than I had ever hoped to find in a wife and, in fact, one I had lost hope of finding.

"I love you, Miss Elizabeth Bennet, more than I thought I could ever love a woman. You are my other half. I would be eternally grateful if you would consent to be my wife, to come away with me, to live and grow with me, until the end of our days. The matter of the townsfolk's gossip is irrelevant—we may have as long or as short a period of engagement as you wish. I only wish for the privilege of being known as your betrothed, the comfort of knowing I shall eventually have you in my life forever, and the pleasure of introducing you to all as my future wife.

"Will you do me the honor?"

His words moved her, for Darcy could see a happy tear appearing at the corner of her eye.

"Of course, I will, Mr. Darcy," replied Elizabeth.

She stepped forward and rested her head on his shoulder, allowing Darcy to put his arms around her, heedless of her sister's watchful presence. Darcy looked over Miss Elizabeth's head to where her sister was watching them, and while he might have wondered if Miss Mary would disapprove of their actions, she only regarded them with a happy smile. Then, with a wink, she turned around—quite deliberately—and looked in the opposite direction.

"Your sister appears to approve, Miss Elizabeth."

With a sudden jerk of movement, Miss Elizabeth pulled away and looked around at her sister with alarm. When she saw that Miss Mary was looking in the opposite direction, however, she grinned.

"She has grown much these past months. I am fortunate to have such devoted sisters."

"As am I. I cannot wait to introduce you to Georgiana. She will love you as much as I do, I am certain."

Miss Elizabeth turned to regard him. "Do you intend to stay in Meryton for the Christmas season?"

"I do. I will not be parted from you."

A rosy hue spread over her fair cheeks, but she gathered herself. "Then you should bring her to Netherfield. I would be happy to make her acquaintance."

"Then I shall, if only to please you. Now, if you do not mind, I believe I should have a word with your father."

"Then let us go into the house, for I am certain my mother would be interested to hear of these developments."

And so, arm in arm, they went to inform her family of the news. A feeling of contentment such as Darcy had never felt settled over him. He would have her in his life forever. There could be no joy so great.

CHAPTER XXXIV

*I*n the months and years to come, the Darcys prospered in health and happiness. The gossip Darcy had feared did not erupt into scandal, though there were a few choice observations made in Elizabeth's hearing from time to time. The fact that she was already known to being courted by Mr. Darcy and the announcement of the engagement, which they delayed for more than two weeks, did much to quell what little was said of the affair.

Darcy and Elizabeth, though each wished to meet at the altar in a speedy fashion, exercised patience, finally marrying in April, about a month after the Bingleys were joined in matrimony. They enjoyed the season of their courtship, Darcy being required to leave only once for about a week to prepare the marriage settlement. For the rest of that time they laughed and talked, growing in the knowledge of the other and the love they possessed, which lasted for all the days of their lives.

While Darcy and Elizabeth were happy in their lives, not everyone in their tale could be said to experience the same felicity. As Mr. Bingley had designed, his sister was married to Mr. Collins only six days after he had compromised her, returning to Hertfordshire with the marriage articles completed with Fitzwilliam in tow. Fitzwilliam, though he affected a joviality, was eager to remove himself from the parson's company.

"The man is a born sycophant," said he when Darcy asked about his time in London. "It is not only Lady Catherine—he latches on to anyone he deems higher than he in society and treats them with the same reverence as Lady Catherine."

"He never did that with me," said Darcy.

His cousin grinned at him. "That is because he was set upon preventing Miss Elizabeth's growing attachment to you. Once I had him in London, he treated me, and especially my father, with an even more exaggerated deference. Father was ready to throw him out and ordered him to cease his toadying more than once. But it is in his blood.

"I dare say that should Miss Bingley take the trouble, she will find herself ruling him with very little effort."

"But she is not above him in society. Quite the contrary, little though she wishes to own to it."

"No, but he also instinctively searches out those who are more intelligent than he is."

"He should have no difficulty there," muttered Darcy.

"I do not disagree," replied Fitzwilliam, still grinning widely.

The wedding proceeded without a hitch. The only problem was the unwillingness of the bride to be married to a man she could not respect, and actively disdained. It took all of Bingley's newfound resolve to induce her to say the proper words and sign the register.

"I almost thought she would refuse to do it," said he after returning from Longbourn church. "Even after saying her wedding vows, she hesitated before signing. I made absolutely certain that she did not sign a spurious name, as you can imagine."

Though Fitzwilliam had attended to stand up with Mr. Collins, Darcy had refused, not wishing to see the odious parson again. Or the new Mrs. Collins, for that matter.

"In the end, she glanced at me, and it was my implacability which eventually forced her to sign. I am glad to be rid of her. I hope she and Mr. Collins find some felicity together, though I am not hopeful of it."

Whether the new Mr. and Mrs. Collins *did* find some measure of felicity shall be left to the reader's imagination. It is true that for the first five years of their marriage, the Collinses did not produce any children, their first being born when Mrs. Collins was almost thirty. A second child followed three years later, the two being the total of the Collins's efforts—such as they were—to reproduce.

"I thought Collins was about to fall over from apoplexy," reported Fitzwilliam, later that year when he visited the Darcys. "Miss Deborah

370 `%` Jann Rowland

Collins is quite the little cherub, and it is easy to see that Mrs. Collins dotes on her, but Mr. Collins was frantic for a son. I shall not sport with your intelligence and attempt to inform you that the arrival of Miss Frances Collins did not send him into a tizzy."

"Another girl," said Elizabeth, delighted that Mr. Collins, for all his pomposity and affected superiority, still had not produced an heir. "I would feel pity for him, except for the fact that he does not deserve it. I *do* pity those two girls, however. With Mrs. Caroline Collins for a mother, I do not doubt they shall be just like her in temperament."

"The elder already is," said the viscount. "The younger will be corrupted soon enough."

The Darcys were in company with the Collins but rarely over the years, and even more infrequent were the words which passed between them. Several years after the birth of his younger daughter, and with the possibility of more children growing remote by the years, Mr. Collins and Mr. Bennet came to an agreement to end the entail. But it was only with Mr. Collins's written promise that the estate would not be broken up and would be left to his eldest daughter. Thus, Mr. Collins had his security, though Elizabeth had no hope he would actually manage Longbourn well enough to leave it solvent for his daughter.

Lady Catherine, on the other hand, cut all ties with Mr. Collins, and though she could not force him from the living, she no longer showed him the favor she once had, blaming his incompetence for the failure of her dreams. The earl did descend on Rosings like an avenging angel, and though he did not see her in Bedlam as was threatened, he made it very clear that any more trouble from her would result in her being a resident of that hated institution. The lady remained ever after a bitter woman, one who railed against fate and the younger generation. She rarely left Rosings, however, so those who had a grievance against her were at least comforted in that her mischief was ended.

Her daughter, remarkably, threw off her mother's shackles, following Darcy's advice, making something of her life. Though she was ever frail and unhealthy, she would remove to London that season, partaking in the delights society had to offer with her aunt, the countess's, help. Miss de Bourgh never did marry and passed Rosings down to the Darcys' second son in her will, but her life was filled with much more joy than it had been previously.

Mr. Wickham, unfortunately, was to spend the better part of a decade incarcerated in Marshalsea. With no hope of ever paying off the large debts he had amassed, his pleas to Darcy to forgive his debts were frequent, but Darcy, having thrown off the memory of his father's affection for the man, remained adamant that he pay for the misery he had caused, troubles that he had brought upon himself. Eventually, however, he decided to relent, though not in a matter Mr. Wickham had expected or desired.

"I assume Mr. Wickham was not pleased with your decision?" asked Elizabeth when Darcy returned from his objectionable errand.

"That is a fool's wager, my love," replied Darcy. "He expected, of course, to simply be released." Darcy paused. "Of course, given the fights he has engaged in while in prison, and the effects of whatever drink he could procure and the scarcity of the food he has been eating have rendered him a changed man. He will never charm anyone with two teeth missing."

"Then I hope he will eventually come to an understanding of where he has gone wrong in life. But I am quite happy he will do it in the penal colony, rather than in England."

As for the rest of their family, while all did not always go smoothly, the Bennets, Darcys, and Bingleys generally were happy in their lives in the ensuing years. The youngest Bennets both married—Kitty to a man possessing a small estate, and Lydia to an officer of the regulars. Louisa Hurst, free of her younger sister, was finally able to welcome children into her life. She remained ever after a close friend of Mrs. Darcy and Mrs. Bingley. Hurst became somewhat less dependent on his vices, though they never truly left him. And the Bennets lived after the departure of their daughters in pleasant harmony. Mr. Bennet was even known to say, on occasion, that he missed the noise of having five daughters in the house.

But there are two others whose fates took a curious turn, one which none of the players of the drama might have expected.

The first was Mary Bennet. Beloved of her eldest sisters, Mary chiefly lived with Elizabeth and Jane after their marriages. Though she loved the new Bingley estate, purchased about a year after the Bingley marriage and situated only thirty miles from the Darcy estate at Pemberley, it was Pemberley that she favored, meaning she was more often with Elizabeth than Jane. It was during one of these visits that an announcement was made that shocked them all.

"You are engaged to Lord Chesterfield?" asked Elizabeth, bewildered by her sister's announcement. "What can you mean by it, Mary?"

Her husband snorted. "I am surprised *you* did not see the growing felicity between them. It has been evident ever since Fitzwilliam came to stay with us last month."

The viscount, who was by now completely reconciled with his cousin, only grinned at Elizabeth, not feeling the need to respond. Later, after the matter had been explained to Elizabeth, she managed to get Mary alone, intending to assure herself of her sister's happiness.

"I *am* happy," said Mary when Elizabeth asked. "You know my expectations in marriage have ever been more modest than yours. But I am certain with my future husband I can rival that blissful estate in which you dwell with Mr. Darcy."

"I am happy for you, Mary. But I am concerned."

"I know you are, Lizzy. But you may release those concerns. Though I might have worried that I was being used as a surrogate for you, I am assured that is not the case. He has confessed to me that he was infatuated with you—he never felt true love. His love, in this case, is reserved for me."

Thus comforted, Elizabeth witnessed her sister wedding a man more prominent in society than any of them, knowing that while Mary might never be a leading light in society, she would hold her own. The Fitzwilliams, by all accounts, were happy in marriage, eventually producing progeny of their own. And one of the Bennet sisters became a countess, and mother to a future earl, though it was not the sister any of them might have thought.

Finally, after several years of being separated from her dearest friend Charlotte Lucas, Elizabeth heard that her friend's employment had ended, and as Elizabeth had newly become a mother herself, Elizabeth wrote to Charlotte, inviting her to Pemberley to become little Victoria Darcy's governess. Originally, she had wanted Charlotte to simply live with them as a guest, but she knew—correctly—that Charlotte would see that as charity and would not wish to impose.

But Elizabeth had another design in mind, for the parson of Kympton was a man of about five and thirty, and a bachelor. Elizabeth had long thought he would be perfect for the practical Charlotte. In this, she was correct, for, within a few months of arriving, Charlotte was released from Elizabeth's employ with her blessing and married to her parson. In this, Elizabeth was happy that she had been able to assist her friend in finding her calling in life.

As for the Darcys, they were blessed with three girls and two boys, all of whom trod the pathway of life, encouraged by their parents to follow their dreams. The Darcys lived to a great age, and of them it was said that no couple was closer or more loving, even after the first bloom of love and the heady days of courtship were behind them. It was said of them that if any couple was destined to be together through this life and the next, it was the Darcys.

The End

"I might have known," spat Philip. "Of course, my jackal of a brother would run home, intent upon stealing *my* birthright from me!"

Bennet's eyes widened in shock at the vitriol in his brother's voice. But before Bennet could even think of responding, Philip continued, saying: "You may as well return to Portsmouth or from wherever you came. I am not Esau to your Jacob, Brother. You shall not take what is rightfully mine!"

The words did not make Bennet's confusion any less. His relationship with his brother had deteriorated over the years, particularly during their joint time at Cambridge together, when Philip—two years ahead of Bennet—had been more interested in carousing and gambling than in using his time to study. But Bennet had never thought their connection had weakened to this degree.

"I am unaware of the charges you lay at my door, Philip," said Bennet as he walked into the room.

"I hardly believe that to be the case," replied Philip.

"You may believe what you wish. Our father requested my presence and I have come. I am certainly not here to steal anything."

"No, you are not!" exclaimed Philip. There was an edge of desperation in his tone which Bennet detected, and he could not help but wonder what made his brother fear such a thing. "Go! Leave at once and return to your life, *soldier*." The final word was spoken with contempt. "We have no need of you here."

"*I* called your brother here," said Mr. Bennet, rising again to confront his eldest son. "I am still the master of Longbourn, and you had best remember it, Philip.

Philip made to speak, but Mr. Bennet cut him off. "No! I will not hear another word of it. You will not speak of your brother in such a way, and you will not minimize the damage you have done to this family."

"Damage?" demanded Bennet. The icy claws of worry had begun to grip his heart with his father's words. "What has my brother done?"

"It is none of your concern!" said Philip in a shrill cry.

"Enough!" thundered Mr. Bennet. He turned to Bennet and said: "He has accumulated enough debts of honor and that of poor investment that I fear for our solvency!"

"Father! Send my brother away and allow us to handle this between us. *He* will be of no assistance."

"And you think you have? What is possibly going through your mind, boy?" Mr. Bennet leaned forward and his hands gripped the desk so tightly that Bennet wondered that he had not left grooves in its surface from the pressure exerted by his fingers. "For years I have put up with your wild ways, paid your debts and smoothed matters with other landowners when you trifled with their daughters. And this is how you repay me? Your association with Baron Godwin may cost us our home!"

"I can negotiate with him! I can make him see reason! I will make it all right again, I swear it."

"How can you make *this* right again?" cried Mr. Bennet, his hand fumbling for a folded piece of paper on his desk, which he brandished in front of Philip's eyes. "The man is demanding immediate payment, threatening to bring suit against us if we do not pay him immediately. Is this what you call your vaunted skill in negotiations?"

"Baron Godwin?" said Bennet, stepping into the fray. "Philip, do not tell me you fell in with that . . . man. He is well known in London for gaming and wenching, for business ventures of questionable legality and an unacceptable level of risk."

Philip only waved Bennet's statement aside. "There was nothing illegal about it, not that you would understand, Henry. It was a business arrangement between two gentlemen, and one which had the potential to pay off handsomely."

"And just what was this business arrangement?" demanded Bennet.

"It is none of your concern. Suffice it to say that I am well able to handle my own affairs and deal with the likes of Baron Godwin. You need not concern yourself, for I shall arrange for him to withdraw his letter."

"It has *not* paid off handsomely!" exclaimed Mr. Bennet. "In fact, this *investment* which you presumed to make without consulting me has been further complicated by your further imprudent action of wagering the entire amount of the investment with him and then losing it!"

"It was a good wager," said Philip. "It was only the cruelest of luck which prevented me from winning and cancelling the debt entirely."

"It was nothing less than stupidity!" roared Mr. Bennet. "The debt you owed before was ruinous—*this* is nothing less than catastrophic! Given how you have drained the family coffers over the years, can you not fathom the fact that there is nothing left to pay this?"

"How bad has this become?" asked Bennet, aghast at what he was hearing.

"I warn you, Henry," snarled Philip. "Stay out of this! Be gone!"

"*I* asked your brother to come and I will dismiss him if necessary!" Mr. Bennet then turned to Bennet. "If we cannot put this man off, we might lose the estate."

Bennet's eyes widened and he turned on his brother. "How could you have been so stupid? Have you no care for our family's honor, for the wellbeing of your mother and sister? I cannot imagine how you have grown so selfish."

"This can all be repaired!" Philip's voice was shrill by this time. "I can deal with Baron Godwin!"

"Philip," said Mr. Bennet, his tone shaking with the effort of suppressing his anger, "this letter threatens legal action unless we pay the man thousands of pounds — money, which I might add, we do not possess! You are attempting to make light of the situation as you *always* do. How do you expect me to continue to overlook your imprudent and dissipative ways without consequence? Is there no extent to this recklessness in your character?"

"It seems you must live with it, Father," said Philip. His tone was offhand, but there existed in it a hint of smugness. It was clear that his father noted it too, for his jaw clenched in his anger. Bennet was scarcely less angry himself.

"I am the heir, and one day all of Longbourn will be mine." He turned an acid look on Bennet, one which spoke of all his contempt. Why his brother had come to hate him, Bennet could not quite understand. Bennet had never coveted his position as heir, as he had been taught what his life would be from his earliest memories.

"I will, therefore, act as I see fit to improve its standing. This is a minor setback, and one which may be overcome, given the correct information."

"You think that, do you?" His father's rasping voice caught Philip's attention from his own delusions, and for the first time since Bennet had entered the room, he thought Philip was actually listening to his father's words. "I must remind you yet again, Philip — *I* am the head of the family and master of the estate and *I* make the decisions which concern us all. No business arrangement or agreement with another may be entered into without *my* approval, and I certainly would not approve of any dealings which would involve the likes of Baron Godwin."

"It is too late father, for I have already entered into the agreement in your stead." Philip's tone was flippant, and Bennet could see his father's ever-growing fury. It was a match for Bennet's own. "You need not concern yourself. On the morrow, I shall ride to London and resolve this with Baron Godwin. It will all be resolved to your satisfaction. There is no need to worry."

"In fact, *you* will not be speaking with Godwin, or anyone else on my behalf." It was the implacable will in his father's voice which once again drew Philip's attention, and he gaped at his father. Mr. Bennet had so often excused Philip's indiscretions or attempted to explain them away, that Bennet was feeling more than a little surprised himself.

"It might be too late to disengage ourselves from Godwin, though I will not know until I see this contract of which he speaks. But I may certainly act with respect to *you*, and by god I will. I should have acted years ago, when it became apparent you listened to nothing I said!"

"What can you do?" asked Philip, his tone daring his father to take the situation any further. "*I* am your heir. I have been trying to tell you, Father—we must work together to resolve this. Godwin is a hard man, but he is not unreasonable. He will smell any blood in the water. We *must* present a united front before him."

"Are you forgetting that I have another son who may inherit?"

The quietly spoken words seemed to reverberate throughout the room, penetrating them all and infusing them with a premonition of where this argument would end. Later, Bennet would acknowledge he had known where it must end as soon as he had entered the room—indeed, it was clear as soon as he had received the letter. At that moment, however, he was shocked with his father's words—as shocked as Philip was. But Philip quickly overcame his shock, as it exploded in anger.

"You would not dare." The words were flinty with a quiet undertone of menace. "I am your heir. What can Henry possibly do for Longbourn? He has been playing at being a soldier this past year—surely you cannot rely on him to save Longbourn."

"If you are not aware, then you are a fool," rasped Mr. Bennet. "I have both the legal authority and duty to this family to disown you if you cannot be controlled. This situation is beyond ruinous, and I am left to wish that I had possessed the fortitude to disown you years ago when you proved ungovernable."

Philip's eyes narrowed and he glared at his father. Bennet, who had always known that Philip possessed a volatile temper, moved closer to prevent any attack he might make.

"Do you know that your actions have caused the dwindling of our family fortune until there is almost nothing left? For years I have fooled myself that I could reach you and amend your behavior." Mr. Bennet laughed a hoarse, almost manic laugh. "More the fool was I, it seems. But you were my favorite and I indulged you, always taken in by your promises to change, to take your responsibilities with the seriousness you should. I believed your lies, even as our family coffers were drained by your imprudence and thoughtless actions.

"No more. No more, I say!"

The two combatants leaned across the desk, staring at each other, but while Mr. Bennet's breast heaved with the emotion of the moment, Philip was entirely lacking in passion, his cold gaze resting on his father with the pitiless force of a blacksmith's hammer striking an anvil.

"So you mean to make *him* your heir?" Philip sneered. "He will not receive much. If I do not deal with Godwin, I doubt anything will be left of Longbourn, though perhaps he will allow you to occupy one of the tenant farms."

"Longbourn is not entailed, Philip, though at times I wish it was. Had it been so, I would have been forced to act before so that the estate would remain intact. At the very least, the terms of an entailment would have allowed me to shift the responsibility for the debts off my shoulders and onto yours, as the estate could not have been sold."

Philip's eyes widened in astonishment. "You would have done that to me? You would have allowed me to rot in debtors' prison?"

"I would have had no choice, boy," growled Mr. Bennet. "Can you not see that?

"But as there is no entailment, I have no choice but to deal with Godwin. As for who will inherit whatever is left, since there is no entailment, I may leave it to your sister as well. But Henry will inherit after me. I only hope we are able to save your sister's dowry."

"Let me treat with Godwin, Father," said Philip. "I am certain I can induce him to see sense."

"You are a foolish child, Philip," snapped Mr. Bennet. "You have no idea how men of Godwin's ilk do business. He has no interest in your pleas. No one will deal with the man except for young fools such as you who are far too naïve to see through his lies. His concern is receiving the money you foolishly agreed to invest with him, and he does not care who is ruined as a result. If you step foot in his house, he will do naught but laugh at you while he commands his men to see you to the door."

"He would never do that to me."

"Then I suggest you throw yourself on his mercy, for I am done with you. I am finished attempting to make your mistakes right. I wish I had possessed the strength to do this many months ago."

"Is that your final word?"

"Get out, Philip. Do not return."

**COMING IN 2018 FROM
ONE GOOD SONNET PUBLISHING**

http://onegoodsonnet.com/

FOR READERS WHO LIKED
WHAT COMES BETWEEN COUSINS

Chaos Comes to Kent

Mr. Collins invites his cousin to stay at his parsonage and the Bennets go to Kent and are introduced to an amiable Lady Catherine de Bourgh. When Mr. Darcy and his cousin, Colonel Fitzwilliam, visit Lady Catherine at the same time, they each begin to focus on a Bennet sister, prodded by well-meaning relations, but spurred on by their own feelings.

Out of Obscurity

Amid the miraculous events of a lost soul returning home, dark forces conspire against a young woman, for her loss was not an accident. A man is moved to action by a boon long denied, determined to avoid being cheated by Miss Elizabeth Bennet again.

In the Wilds of Derbyshire

Elizabeth Bennet goes to her uncle's estate in Derbyshire after Jane's marriage to Mr. Bingley, feeling there is nothing left for her in Meryton. She quickly becomes close to her young cousin and uncle, though her aunt seems to hold a grudge against her. She also meets the handsome Mr. Fitzwilliam Darcy, and she realizes that she can still have everything she has ever wished to have.

Netherfield's Secret

Elizabeth soon determines her brother's friend, Fitzwilliam Darcy, suffers from an excess of pride. It is a shock when the man reveals himself to be in love with her. But even that revelation is not as surprising as the secret Netherfield has borne witness to. Netherfield's secret shatters Elizabeth's perception of herself and the world around her, and Mr. Darcy is the only one capable of picking up the pieces.

The Angel of Longbourn

When Elizabeth Bennet finds Fitzwilliam Darcy unconscious and suffering from a serious illness, the Bennets quickly return him to their house, where they care for him like he is one of their own. Mr. Darcy soon forms an attachment with the young woman he comes to view as his personal angel. But the course of true love cannot proceed smoothly, for others have an interest in Darcy for their own selfish reasons…

The Companion

A sudden tragedy during Elizabeth's visit to Kent leaves her directly in Lady Catherine de Bourgh's sights. With Elizabeth's help, a woman long-oppressed has begun to spread her wings. What comes after is a whirlwind of events in which Elizabeth discovers that her carefully held opinions are not infallible. Furthermore, a certain gentleman of her acquaintance might be the key to Elizabeth's happiness.

For more details, visit

http://www.onegoodsonnet.com/genres/pride-and-prejudice-variations

ALSO BY ONE GOOD SONNET PUBLISHING

THE SMOTHERED ROSE TRILOGY

BOOK 1: THORNY

In this retelling of "Beauty and the Beast," a spoiled boy who is forced to watch over a flock of sheep finds himself more interested in catching the eye of a girl with lovely ground-trailing tresses than he is in protecting his charges. But when he cries "wolf" twice, a determined fairy decides to teach him a lesson once and for all.

BOOK 2: UNSOILED

When Elle finds herself practically enslaved by her stepmother, she scarcely has time to even clean the soot off her hands before she collapses in exhaustion. So when Thorny tries to convince her to go on a quest and leave her identity as Cinderbella behind her, she consents. Little does she know that she will face challenges such as a determined huntsman, hungry dwarves, and powerful curses . . . .

BOOK 3: ROSEBLOOD

Both Elle and Thorny are unhappy with the way their lives are going, and the revelations they have had about each other have only served to drive them apart. What is a mother to do? Reunite them, of course. Unfortunately, things are not quite so simple when a magical lettuce called "rapunzel" is involved.

If you're a fan of thieves with a heart of gold, then you don't want to Miss . . .

THE PRINCES AND THE PEAS
A TALE OF ROBIN HOOD

A NOVEL OF THIEVES, ROYALTY, AND IRREPRESSIBLE LEGUMES

BY LELIA EYE

An infamous thief faces his greatest challenge yet when he is pitted against forty-nine princes and the queen of a kingdom with an unnatural obsession with legumes. Sleeping on top of a pea hidden beneath a pile of mattresses? Easy. Faking a singing contest? He could do that in his sleep. But stealing something precious out from under "Old Maid" Marian's nose . . . now that is a challenge that even the great Robin Hood might not be able to surmount.

When Robin Hood comes up with a scheme that involves disguising himself as a prince and participating in a series of contests for a queen's hand, his Merry Men provide him their support. Unfortunately, however, Prince John attends the contests with the Sheriff of Nottingham in tow, and as all of the Merry Men know, Robin Hood's pride will never let him remain inconspicuous. From sneaking peas onto his neighbors' plates to tweaking the noses of prideful men like the queen's chamberlain, Robin Hood is certain to make an impression on everyone attending the contests. But whether he can escape from the kingdom of Clorinda with his prize in hand before his true identity comes to light is another matter entirely.

About the Author

Jann Rowland is a Canadian, born and bred. Other than a two-year span in which he lived in Japan, he has been a resident of the Great White North his entire life, though he professes to still hate the winters.

Though Jann did not start writing until his mid-twenties, writing has grown from a hobby to an all-consuming passion. His interests as a child were almost exclusively centered on the exotic fantasy worlds of Tolkien and Eddings, among a host of others. As an adult, his interests have grown to include historical fiction and romance, with a particular focus on the works of Jane Austen.

When Jann is not writing, he enjoys rooting for his favorite sports teams. He is also a master musician (in his own mind) who enjoys playing piano and singing as well as moonlighting as the choir director in his church's congregation.

Jann lives in Alberta with his wife of more than twenty years, two grown sons, and one young daughter. He is convinced that whatever hair he has left will be entirely gone by the time his little girl hits her teenage years. Sadly, though he has told his daughter repeatedly that she is not allowed to grow up, she continues to ignore him.

Website: http://onegoodsonnet.com/
Facebook: https://facebook.com/OneGoodSonnetPublishing/
Twitter: @OneGoodSonnet
Mailing List: http://eepurl.com/bol2p9

CPSIA information can be obtained
at www.ICGtesting.com
Printed in the USA
LVHW01s0314190318
570313LV00019B/633/P

9 781987 929775